PEACH

Published by Fish Out of Water Books
Ann Arbor, MI, USA

www.fowbooks.com

Song lyrics courtesy of Pete Yorn (front matter) and Charles
Baker (throughout).

ISBN: 978-1-947886-02-5.

Library of Congress Control Number: 2018956421.

Pop culture · coming of age · culture shock · going against
the grain · adversity · triumph · extraordinary lives · ordinary
lives

non-fiction - creative non-fiction - realistic fiction

Michigan via Manchester, England.

We are all fish out of water.

Cover design by J. Caleb Clark, www.jcalebdesign.com.

For further information, visit www.fowbooks.com.

PEACH

Wayne Barton

in this world
are we just
strangers
when we fail
to makE
A
connection

Prologue

Sometimes I wonder whether I have felt everything I'm ever going to feel, and, whether, from here on out, I'm not going to feel anything new; just lesser versions of what I already felt once before. There is a perpetual numbness, which hangs like a melancholy cloud.

Right now, I feel like I know everything, and yet I look back and think of how I was a year ago, and I balk at the naivety of that individual. And I wonder if it means, in fact, that not only do I *not* know everything, but, indeed, that I know *nothing* at all. I suppose this should feel liberating. Then again, I doubt I'm the only person to have an epiphany in that barely conscious state we find ourselves in after long flights; and as soon as it appears, despite the best of intentions to grab hold of the lightning, it goes again.

As we circled to land at Idaho Falls Regional Airport, I noticed how small the airport was. It was possibly the smallest I'd ever seen, something I couldn't quite correlate with my expectation of America, even if it certainly fit my perception of a small town place.

In his most recent email, Hal had written to tell me he would pick me up. I had thought of offering to get a cab, but then he would have probably offered to pay, so I decided against it.

Once I collected my suitcase I continued through arrivals. Hal wasn't there, but I wasn't overly concerned. I walked outside and the first thing that struck me was how warm it was for a September day. I was about to go back in and get a bottle of water when, suddenly a friendly voice boomed from behind me. "Freddie!" I turned and there was Hal, larger than life, and looking quite humorous in his Hawaiian garb. It was quite a departure from his attire at the black tie event where I'd met him. His smile was infectious.

"Hey, Hal... how are you doing?" I asked, shaking his hand. His grip was firm but his skin had an aged relaxation to it; a softness which belied his size. The bones in his hand still gave the handshake a strong grip.

"I'm not bad, not bad... here, let me help you with that," he almost insisted on dragging my suitcase before I kept a firm grip on it.

"Don't be silly, I've got it, thanks."

After we got in the car and made small talk about my travels, and the weather, Hal surprised me.

"So, I've been listening to a lot of music lately," he said.

"Oh yeah?"

"Yeah, your stuff."

"And the verdict?"

"It's good. You're a good songwriter. You know what you're doing. Hey, listen, you wanna take the short way or the long way?"

"What's the difference?"

Hal looked at me as if I was an idiot.

"... aside from the distance, I mean."

He smiled.

"Well, the long way is more picturesque."

"Hal, you're the boss," I replied.

"Hell, you're right. I am the boss. Let's go the long way. You tell me if you get tired."

I was worn with jetlag, but I had the adrenalin which comes after such a journey. I figured I could let it do its own inevitable damage.

"So, we'll head west on 26 past 93. It's a nice drive. I'll leave the sightseeing to you."

They were just numbers. I assumed they were the route numbers, but I hadn't done any studying of what I might find in Idaho, and I didn't know much about the place.

"We're approaching what's known as the Craters of the Moon," Hal said after we'd been driving for a while. "You ever heard of it?"

"I think so," I lied, trying to sound informed. "But I really can't quite remember."

"It's a crazy place. You should come up here sometime. You can walk... hell, some people even camp out here. It's..."

Hal stopped talking, as if waiting for something.

To our left were miles of wasteland, shrub and desert, and to our right, hills and valleys. They were in the distance but as the path of the highway continued, it met some of the hills on the curve. Then, the landscape of the wasteland appeared to dissipate, and in its place was a hard, dark rock surface which seemed out of place.

Hal slowed, but didn't stop.

"Let me know if you wanna get out."

"I'm good... why, what is that?" I enquired.

"Lava. The lava fields."

"Really?"

"Can't say I know too much. Don't really pay much attention to all of that stuff, but it's a neat place to walk around. While you're in town you gotta check it out."

I couldn't tell too much from the driver's side that would make it particularly distinctive against what I would consider to be wasteland. Then again, the windows in Hal's car looked like they needed a good wash.

"You can walk on the lava?"

"There are plenty of trails. Hey, you wanna get out?"

"No, no, it's fine. But yeah, I'll come up one day."

"Yeah, if you like that sorta stuff, it's really... really something, you know?"

"So, Hal, erm... tell me, what are you looking to do?" I responded, changing the subject.

"Whad'ya mean?"

"With the songs. What's your aim?"

He went to say something and then coughed quite hard,

spluttering so violently that I thought he'd either let go of the wheel or we might have an accident by veering off the road.

"Gotcha," he replied once he'd composed himself. "Let's talk business later, once we've gotten you settled in, okay?"

"Okay, sounds good."

"Let's listen to something though," he said, pausing, as if something came to mind, before adding, "I was sorry to hear about Eddy."

It hadn't even been two months since Eddy's death. When it happened, Eddy was everybody's property; everybody's friend. He was, after all, the kind of rock star who would be in the news for the most insignificant of things. Like his hair turning grey. After his sudden passing, the grief belonged to an entire nation. I knew it also belonged to his family. I was somewhere in-between. I had been a part of his return from relative obscurity. Eleven consecutive top twenty singles had reaffirmed his place as a national treasure, and not just a novelty seventies act coming back on the scene. Three sold-out tours had confirmed his modern popularity. And then he was *gone*. Just like that. Even after his death, he was in the newspapers, with a bitter legal battle over his estate threatening to break out. I was relieved to have been leaving that behind. Hal had caught me off guard, reminding me I had a personal reason to grieve. I had been his colleague—well, I had written songs for him—but I had also been his friend.

"Thank you," I replied, touched by Hal's thoughtfulness.

"Sudden, by all accounts."

"Yeah... yeah, it was."

Hal put on a CD, which, after two or three songs, appeared to be a compilation of various artists I'd worked with in the past. I found myself cringing a little as he hummed along and occasionally banged the steering wheel to join in with the drums.

I'd always written for personal release until it actually paid, and then, somewhere along the way—and I'm not sure when, exactly—the fact it was a job had taken over. That, and, after meeting Ailie, for a while I didn't even *feel* like writing. But the funny thing was, when I eventually had to again, I found that I actually enjoyed the songs I was now creating, some on my own, some with Ailie, because they weren't about Kaia, or some one or two-month fling that had gone horribly wrong. They were more about the melody than the words, but it was that pleasant sound which I enjoyed, the creation of it and the listening to it afterwards. Of course, Hal was listening to the earliest material I'd written for The Cause, with a couple of those songs covered by other artists, and he was singing along to them. Most of those songs had existed for years and generally been the material I'd played at those dark and dingy pubs in the usually unwelcoming corners of the U.K.. *Oh God*, I thought. *What if he wants me to write like this?* I found myself panicking about my own material. Did I have enough songs left from that time that I haven't already used? Could I get back to that place? I tried to consider that I was a lot older now, no longer restrained by the clutch of a young heartbreak, but, I was suffering from a new pain and that might well manifest itself in new material. Panic over. Although, the idea of using it as creative motivation when I was still feeling the aftershock of everything seemed like I was cheapening the experience. I'd used my grief over Eddy as an excuse to reconnect with Kaia—the first love, the first broken heart—after a chance encounter. Ailie, the love of my life and the person responsible for my success, had walked away from me. And now I was running away from it all.

At my stopover at Gatwick, I couldn't help but overhear a conversation between two people at a table near me. They were arguing about influential bands in recent times and one of them was The Cause.

I smiled as I listened.

"Looking for a Way Out, man," one of them said. "That's the song of a generation."

I smiled, and almost shrunk into myself with self-consciousness as he began to hum the melody and sing the chorus.

"Lookin' for a way out, way out, way out... tryin' to find an answer."

"And what about that bassline?"

I remembered exactly where Ailie and I were when we hashed that bassline out; the room, the weather, what I was drinking. The mind is a funny thing. Something about long-haul travel makes you prone to reflection. My immediate reaction was to turn my phone on and call Ailie, but as I pulled it out of my pocket, I remembered. I even thought about texting Kaia to tell her but, no, it was more of something I needed to share with Ailie. Or wanted to. It brought the shock of the last few weeks home to me, even, the last few years, remembering walking with her and telling her of where I saw myself in the future. Before I'd known it, she had become so much a part of my future that she was at least equally as responsible for everything good in my life that had happened. And probably more. And, given the fact that those benefits would last with me for a long time to come, she had also had a huge impact on my life going forward. It evoked a bittersweet feeling that stayed with me until it was time to get on board the plane to take the first leg of my journey to New York.

I don't know what I was expecting when it came to Hal's house, but I found myself surprised when he slowed down and turned into a plot of land a couple of miles after we passed a sign for Bliss, Idaho: Population 299. There was a long driveway decorated by tall trees, which seemed strange, as there had barely been any along the highway itself. We hadn't passed any towns, shopping areas or malls and this house was right alongside the highway. I was a little confused when Hal appeared to confirm that this was in fact our destination by turning off the car and exiting.

The house was grand enough. Two story, and regal looking, but somewhat unloved. The grass wasn't overgrown but wasn't freshly mown; the exterior of the house looked like it needed more than just a lick of paint. There was an exterior garage which was large enough to fill the rest of the land by that side of the house up to the tree formation which I assumed formed the perimeter of the property. To the right of the house there was open land, and only the road in the distance gave me any indication at all where the border of Hal's property must end on that side. It was vast enough, alright, and I don't know if I expected more, or less. The guy was still a millionaire, easily, I reckoned.

As we went inside I noticed that the house itself seemed stuck in time. Not exactly in a state of disrepair, but the garish colours of the patterned furniture struck against the bold oak cabinets had a distinct 1970's feel. It was probably cool enough to be retro, though my impression was that it hadn't changed from that era.

"Your room is the... in fact, don't worry, I'll show you," said Hal, starting to climb the staircase.

I had anticipated I would be put up—the question had never come up—although I did half expect it to be a hotel. No worries, I liked the idea of spending time out here. The charm of the place had immediately grown on me and I was quite excited about starting work.

Hal led me to an impressively spacious room overlooking the back of the property.

"Why don't I give you a few minutes to freshen up, son," he said. "Would you like a drink?"

"Err... yeah. Water, please." I didn't want to be too much of a burden.

I put down my suitcase and guitar case and surveyed the room; it was pale blue, fairly neutral, probably not in keeping with the rest of the house but the kind of room you knew was specifically for guests. Maybe it had always been this way? I looked out of the window and the back yard was as large as I expected it might be, bordered by a fence about two hundred yards back. And then fields, and fields, and in the distance, hills.

I sat, and then laid on the bed. Hal surely wouldn't mind if I took ten or fifteen minutes. I turned my phone on. I expected it to be out of service—in fact, part of me was somewhat hoping that would be the case. I had barely given thought to Ailie or Kaia since landing. Well, if I had, those thoughts were mulling away like a subplot in my mind. No, this had been refreshing, and I had taken it all in. If my phone had connection issues, then that was too bad. I'd just have to make do.

However, it worked fine, having connected to a local network. I placed it on the bedside table, as I waited for it to load up, and laid back on the bed.

Beep beep, beep beep, beep beep. It sounded as though a dozen text messages were coming through. *Great.* I'll deal with them in time, I told myself, as I closed my eyes.

I must have been out for a while. I woke with that unfamiliarity in a darkened room and took a few seconds to get my bearings. Oh, how embarrassing, I thought. I checked my phone for the time. 8:26 p.m. It's only been a couple of hours, I guess. Nine text messages. Well, I had been travelling for around a day. There were a couple from my family, hoping I'd got there safely, and I scanned the others, nothing from Ailie. Six, however, from Kaia.

"Safe travels, text me when you land."
"Hope u got there okay."
"Hey, babe, u get there okay?"
"Guessing no connection. Text me. Miss u x."
"You okay?"
"Hope you're ok x."

"Hey," I began my reply. *"Arrived safely. Was about a day travelling. Very tired. Will text tomorrow x."*

I went downstairs a little tentatively and into the lounge where Hal was watching TV. As he noticed me, he reached for the remote control to turn down the volume. I entered the room and noted with humour how this large modern television dominated one corner of this room where it almost looked out of place.

"Hey there, son," he said.

"I'm so sorry, Hal. I put my head down and... I must have been more exhausted than I thought."

"No problem. Don't worry about it."

Hal stood—making the sort of groan which indicated he'd been sat in that position for a long time—and made his way out of the room.

"Make yourself comfortable," he said.

I sat on the sofa next to the one where he had been sitting. I looked around the room and saw pictures of family, all old pictures, and Hal looked much younger in them. Frozen in time was a pretty apt description, I thought.

"I've upgraded you," Hal said on re-entering the room and handed me a small translucent tumbler with a brown liquid, probably a brandy or a whisky. The glass was worn, but clearly cared for, as if it had been in that house a hundred years.

"Thank you," I said. "I really am sorry. Like I say, I think the flight took more out of me than I realised."

"Don't worry about that. I wasn't expecting to get down to work right away."

It did feel as if, being here, I was constantly on the clock. I felt the expectation to work, even now, closing in at 9:00 p.m. on the day I'd landed.

"We can..."

"Nah. Don't worry 'bout it. Take your time. How long does it take to write a song?" Hal asked, rhetorically.

Ok, pressure off then, I thought.

"About that," I replied. "What will work best for you? I have a bunch of old songs. You were listening to some there in the car earlier, and, there are a few I wrote from around that time."

"What am I paying you for?"

"To work with... for us to work with each other," I stumbled, wondering if it was some kind of trick question.

"Exactly. So don't worry 'bout it now. We can try a bunch of ideas."

"Okay, sure. Whatever you want."

We both took a drink. It was fairly awkward. That was how I felt, anyway. Hal, of course, was as comfortable as he could be.

"How much of my music have you heard?" he asked.

Well, I was in luck there, as I'd taken an iPod to listen to his back catalogue on the plane. The only problem was although I'd done my research, all of the names of the most popular songs had clean vanished from my mind. The only thing I remembered was the name of a record, "Even When I'm Wrong," which I particularly remembered enjoying on the flight from New York to Minneapolis.

"Even When I'm Wrong! I love that record," I replied, confidently. "It's got that late Johnny Cash sound. I don't know. Maybe it's because it's one of your most recent bits of work, and I found myself connecting with it because I was imagining how your voice would work with the songs I had. But I did love it."

"Oh, man, I hate that shit," Hal responded. "It's awful."

"No, I like it, honestly," I laughed, awkwardly, not knowing what else to say. Bang went my idea of producing something similar.

"It's like I don't even recognise that person," he continued. "I'm old enough and ugly enough to know that, you know... you listen to yourself and it sounds different to what was in your head. But there were fourteen years between that record and the one before it. And I sound like an old man. It spoke to me in a different way."

I didn't know how to respond. I had been excited enough about the project. I'd enjoyed working with Eddy so much that the opportunity to write songs for this hardened and experienced American crooner was something I was enthusiastic about. But the very thing I wanted to do was what he was against. I appreciated that he had identified me as someone worthy of working with, but I couldn't turn back the hands of time.

"I know you're not a miracle worker," Hal replied, as if reading my mind. "But I thought Eddy sounded younger. Younger than I'd thought when listening to it the first time. I was surprised."

Okay, well, that was something. Perhaps it was simply the songs.

"We can work on that," I insisted. "So... tell me what is your favourite record of yours?"

That broke the ice and got the conversation flowing. Hal's preference was clearly his earlier efforts, particularly his first two releases, *You Might Need Me Someday* and *Mayday*. As he spoke about them, it became increasingly clear that his fondness was more to do with that particular time in his life. His introduction to celebrity, being spotted and trailed by paparazzi, meeting the girl who would become his wife. There was a great enthusiasm in his eyes; he was alive. He loved all of that lifestyle, or at least, seemed to revel in remembering the early days. I tried to connect with that in my own tenuous way, as is human nature. As he talked so warmly and fondly of Betty, his former partner, I thought of Ailie, especially as he begun to attribute his success to her.

"I know exactly what you mean," I said. "I mean, I wasn't in the same league as you, but when I was with my partner, I really felt as if I was... I don't know how to really describe it. I was like the *me* I always thought I should be."

"That's love for you, my friend. It makes you better. It makes you *want* to be better.'

"Yeah, you're right. It really did."

"Hope you don't mind me asking, but it sounds like you're speaking in past tense. Don't tell me you were so crazy as to throw her away? She was beau... you kids looked good together," he said.

"Yeah... sadly. We broke up. Just... I don't know why. It just went horribly wrong very quickly," I replied, trying my best to summarise the situation and failing miserably.

Hal looked at me curiously then, as if trying to ask me a question without saying a word. I wasn't familiar enough with that look yet to understand what it meant. Was he figuring me out? Was he asking me if it was my fault, if either of us had been unfaithful, if it had been about money? I couldn't tell.

"Don't worry, kid. I ain't gonna grill you too much tonight," he finally said with a smile. "You need to call home? You can use my phone if you like."

"No, it's okay, thanks. I've got this," I replied, holding my mobile phone. "It's really late there now. Well, early morning, actually."

"Yeah that's right. Well, it's a little past my bedtime here, too. Been a long day," he said.

As we both prepared to go up to bed, I thanked Hal again for picking me up at the airport and told him that I looked forward to working with him.

I came around very early, having stirred during the night. I was fully awake from just after 6:00 a.m. and finally decided I could stay in bed no longer just before seven. I was careful and quiet in the bathroom and downstairs, helping myself to a bottle of water from the fridge (after a moment's hesitation thinking of how cheeky it might be to do so) and then went out of the back door to see the land from ground level. It fit the cliché of a remote country farm house and I smiled at the thought. There was a wooden decking skirted around the back of the house with two chairs and a bench on it, and then the steps going down into the garden. I sat on the steps and observed my new surroundings. There was a deceptive breeze coming from the cloudless sky to let me know it was going to be a warm day.

I loved it.

I thought it was probably best to call home before the day begun and so tried to call my mother. She was unavailable, so I left a voice message telling her I was okay, and that I'd text or email later.

I thought about texting Ailie, but I hadn't heard anything from her, and so I felt it was probably appropriate to give Kaia a call.

"Hey," she sounded surprised when answering.

"Hey... you free to talk?"

"I'm at work, but just about to go on lunch."

"Oh, don't worry—don't let me keep you."

"'No, please, it's fine. How is everything? You get there safe?"

"Yeah... it's great here. Hal's really nice. He's the guy I'm working with. It's a really nice place, from what I've seen of it. Hey, sorry I didn't text much. I was totally knackered."

"It's okay. I did worry a bit. So what are you doing today?"

"Working, I think. Getting right on it."

"Will you be able to video call me a bit later. Maybe six or seven hours?"

"I don't know. I can try. I might be busy. No idea what the schedule is, really. Might be best if I text you. Don't hold your plans for me."

"Okay, Freddie. So... is everything alright?"

"Yeah, everything's really good."

"No, I mean with you and me."

"Yeah, yeah, course. Everything's good. Don't worry about that. How's work?"

"Yeah, it's okay... it's work, you know. Okay well, text me or call me later, okay. Call me if you can."

"Yeah, okay. Have a nice day, Kaia."

"You too, Freddie."

It was a little more awkward than necessary. I had suspended thoughts of that growing relationship and bond, it wasn't something I was obligated to fill my time with. I had work to do.

I guess talking on the phone or my movement must have disturbed Hal because after I ended the call with Kaia, he came out on to the porch with his dressing robe on and a drink in his hand.

"Mornin', son," he said.

"Good morning. Really sorry if I woke you up," I replied, "And, sorry, I... erm, took a bottle of water. I'll replace it."

"Don't be crazy, son. It's fine. I get up early myself."

"Yeah, me too normally. I think today was probably the jet lag though."

"Yeah, it'll do that," Hal replied, sitting down.

"It's so nice out here."

"I guess so."

"You don't like it?"

"Sure I do! I live here, don't I? I mean... it's familiar. Anyway, what did you want to do today?"

"I guess we can just get on to working. If you want."

"Well, I've got to go grocery shopping. Might be a good idea to get... I had no idea what you want, you see, what you eat. Thought it too impersonal to ask. And I know you must be hungry. I was lying awake last night thinking I didn't offer you anything to eat. Sorry, I can't even remember the last time I had a house guest, so you're just gonna need to holler if you need anything. Or if you're hungry, just take whatever you want. You're very welcome here, my friend. I'm just a little rusty."

"Yeah, I'm getting there," I admitted.

"Well... see, I don't really cook for myself. I go out. So I don't have anything in to really offer. There's a few of those fast food places you can get a breakfast. One has a drive thru, it's on the way to the grocery store. Then after that we can have an early lunch. I know a nice place."

"Yeah that sounds good," I replied, as if I was going to be anything other than agreeable.

It still took us close to two hours to get ready, Hal first politely waiting for me to take a shower and my hesitating, not knowing he was waiting. Once we were ready to leave, I was ravenous and so pleased when we pulled up to the drive-thru for something to eat. I was surprised by how close the restaurant was—it couldn't have been more than a mile; I figured I could easily have walked there, eaten and come back in the time it took us to get up and leave the house.

Then we went food shopping and my eyes were bigger than my stomach, buying all the unusual candies and confectionary that we couldn't get in England. Hal gave my basket a couple of disapproving glances, directing me toward the aisles with healthier food. Once I'd got a healthy balance and stock I made my way to the checkout. I didn't get too much to carry as I figured I could always walk here for exercise. I also wanted to get there and pay without going through the inevitable awkwardness of Hal offering to pay. Sure enough, as I stood beyond the checkouts waiting with my bags, Hal said to me he would have been happy to pay as I was his guest.

"Well, brunch is definitely on me," he insisted.

We drove a little while longer—far enough to say if I were to walk there from Hal's, it would be an effort, particularly if it was hot—until we came to a row of stores. The sand coloured small building blocks were dominated by door height blackened windows on all the stores, making it virtually impossible to see inside or distinguish the nature of what each store provided.

"Ramon's," "Hill's," "DFT,"—none of these names gave any indication as to their business, but there was no real secret about the one we headed into, "Murphy's Bar and Grill." It seemed a tad too early to be drinking.

"They got the best sandwiches in town here, son," Hal enthused as we walked inside. "Where you wanna sit?"

I surveyed the venue and decided maybe a booth would be best.

"You sure? Not the bar?"

"Sure. We can if you want?"

"Yeah, come on."

We sat there for a little while before the bartender came over.

"What can I get you?"

"Isn't Louise in today?"

"Yeah, she's just running a little late."

"Ok... um..." Hal looked at me. "You wanna beer?"

"No, thanks, not yet. It's a bit hot out. Just a coke with a lot of ice."

"You got it," said the barman.

"I'll take a coffee, please," Hal decided. "Can we grab a couple of menus too?"

"Sure."

Before I'd even had a chance to open my menu, Hal was giving me the benefit of his advice.

"You gotta get the Philly cheesesteak. It's the best one this side of the East Coast."

"Yeah, sure. Looks like that's what I'm having!" I laughed to the barman.

"Same for me," replied Hal.

We made small talk, while the food was being prepared. I asked if it was usually this warm at this time of year, if this was a popular bar, that kind of thing. Hal was polite with his answers but seemed distracted, a feeling confirmed when his whole demeanour appeared to change when a woman, whom I presumed was the Louise he had spoken of, arrived.

"Hey! Sorry. You know. Brooke will be Brooke," she said to the barman, whose name I had yet to pick up.

Hal was looking across at her, almost itching to get her attention.

"Oh, hello you! You're in bright and early," she duly welcomed him. "And this must be your British friend. Freddie, right?"

As she came over she leaned over the bar for a friendly kiss, and then did the same to Hal.

"Yeah, he arrived last night and has been sleeping ever since," Hal laughed, nudging me with his shoulder.

"That's about right. Pleased to meet you," I said.

"Likewise. So... you're gonna be working with Hal?"

"Yeah. I'm honoured."

"As you should be. Hal is... he's quite the guy. A real character in this town."

I couldn't quite tell if Hal was cultivating or embarrassed by the praise, but he seemed to be loving the attention.

"Come now, Lou, you're the glue of this community," he replied.

"What he means," Louise turned to me, "is that I have a generous discount policy with my favourites."

"Pays to be nice!" I said to Hal.

"Yessir. It certainly does."

"This is a nice place. Bliss is apt," I added, trying to be complimentary to people who seemed proud of where they were from.

"Well, technically you're in Gooding. Bliss is barely more than a neighbourhood," Louise replied.

There was the shout from the kitchen that the food was ready, and Louise brought our sandwiches over to us.

"So, what you gentlemen doing today? Writing the next number one hit?"

"That's what I'm paying him for. This guy's a big deal in England you know."

"I don't know about that," I laughed, embarrassed.

"He worked with Eddy Crowe," Hal continued.

"Is that so?" Louise sounded impressed.

"Yeah... I was pretty lucky to get hold of him!" Hal added.

I gathered he was joking, so didn't really consider whether or not he was being disingenuous.

"No, seriously, Hal is legendary. Everyone knows him in England," I said, a little disingenuously myself, but at least with the right intention. "I'm sure he'll make my songs sound better than they really are."

"What's that?" asked Louise, caught in an obviously pensive moment. "He who speaks without modesty, will find it difficult to make his words good."

Hal raised his eyebrows at me in a look I took to mean "She told you so."

"Same goes for you, too," she added, whipping Hal's hand with a bar towel.

"This is good," I said, referring to the sandwich.

"Yeah, so... I don't know, I was thinking of taking the kid up to Shoshone Falls. Or to see the lava fields," said Hal.

Louise said we should go the falls since it was such a nice day. As I had never heard of Shoshone Falls before, Louise explained how it was a waterfall higher than the Niagara Falls and seemed quite proud and defensive of it in the way that local people tend to be. I liked that. In fact, Idaho seemed to be turning out to be just what I needed.

even when I'm wrong

I saw you yesterday
  you didn't look the same
your eyes were filled with pain - was that me?

  The road is winding
    don't talk so kindly
  I'm not worth it
    I can't be
        but
will you need me when I'm old
hold me when I'm cold
love me when I'm right
      even when I'm wrong -

If our time has come & gone
  then your were still the one
and I'll keep holding on
            That's just me

Our roads are winding
  don't walk so blindly
  I'm not perfect
        i can't be . . .

1

We didn't see the falls or go to the lava fields. Maybe it was partly down to my enthusiasm about Hal's reputation as a performer, so that the man himself was motivated to do something to live up to it, or maybe for some other reason altogether, he decided he wanted to go back to the house and start work.

When we arrived back at the house, he led me down into his basement where he had assembled a rehearsal space. It looked as if all of the equipment and instruments were brand new.

"This is pretty cool. How long have you had all of this?" I asked.

"When you said you would come over... I went out and got some new stuff last week. I figured we wouldn't need much more than this."

He was right. There were two acoustic guitars, one electric guitar, a drum set, and a piano. I couldn't really play drums, but I guessed Hal would know someone. He'd also purchased an eight-track recorder, which was fairly basic but would do the job in terms of laying down demo tracks.

"So... why don't you show me what you got?"

I went to fetch my notebook which contained notes for the songs I'd intended to present to Hal.

"I think I'd like to work with you and see what we come up with, but I'll play you a few of mine that I think would work really well," I said upon my return.

I performed two or three of my songs for Hal. It must have been a pretty poor performance, as I was anxious to finish and hear what he thought of them. He nodded and smiled in a couple of places, but mostly he held an attentive but otherwise emotionless gaze.

"Okay," he said, once I'd finished. "Hmm."

"What do you think?" I said, anxious for a response.

"Yeah, could possibly work."

So after he'd learned how the songs went and practiced them a couple of times, we recorded a couple of performances to see how they would sound. There was a moment of surrealism as I let what was transpiring consciously invade my thoughts. *Holy shit, I was jamming with Hal Granger!* People would pay serious money to listen to this guy so close up, and here I was, working with him. People would give their right arm for this opportunity. What a privilege. I hoped being aware and appreciative would never leave me. I guessed that feeling that way in the moment was appreciation enough.

After we'd finished recording—and we must have spent a good four hours in there working—Hal said he was going to go and see what he could fix for dinner, saying we could always go to Lou's again. I guessed by that, he meant Murphy's.

I spent a little while longer in the basement, listening back to each song. It was work, sure, in the truest sense of the word, but it was pure indulgence listening back to these creations. Whenever I recorded my own versions of these songs, they would never quite sound as I had intended. There was always something missing. I was not the performer the inner me desperately wanted to be. Regardless of that, I had this ownership over the songs I had written and this interpretation of how they should sound. Hal just blew me away with how he seemed to get the point of the lyrics. His intonation and inflection in certain parts of the songs, provided an essentially unquantifiable improvement. I loved it. I had never been more sure of anything being successful than those fledgling recordings.

As I returned to the kitchen, I wasn't really surprised to see that Hal wasn't cooking after all. Instead, there was a bottle of beer waiting for me on the table, along with a pizza flyer.

"I thought we might get some more work done. So how about we order in some food?"

I wasn't going to disagree.

Time got away from us and we finally called it a day well after midnight. I had hit the wall shortly after eating, but was so enthusiastic that I kept going. As the evening wore on, we began to write together, only verses, melodies, and fragments of songs, but more than enough to get excited about.

As we said our goodnights, Hal told me that he'd leave me to do some editing, as he had things to do the following morning. He'd be back in the afternoon and we could carry on working then, or he'd be happy to take me out somewhere.

So, the next morning, I took advantage and caught up on my sleep, finally rising around 9:30 a.m., and feeling a little guilty with it. Sure enough, Hal was gone. Breakfast, then, was leftover pizza. And I couldn't resist going back down and listening to the songs again. I found myself working to expand some of the fragments of songs we had worked on together. It wasn't as much fun alone, so I thought I'd leave it and wait until Hal retuned.

I was growing a little restless, so left Hal a note, to let him know that I would be in town, and set off on a walk.

It was the first time I'd truly had time to gather my thoughts, and as I walked along the side of the quiet country road, carefully noting the lack of sidewalk, I thought more of the people back home and the situations I'd left behind. I didn't know if I was hoping that distance could somehow provide me with a greater clarity, but now, actively trying to confront those thoughts, I realised that they were as confusing as ever. This only confirmed to me that I was right to get away and that I wasn't quite yet ready to deal with everything.

My strongest pull was still to Ailie; a desire to talk to her and tell her what was happening; to share the excitement of my experiences over the last day. Really, that would have been a conversation for the *old* me and the *old* Ailie. That was one thing I'd have to get used to. Or, was the fact that my thoughts constantly seemed to return to Ailie something I would simply have to live with? Would I have to admit to myself that she was the one for me, face up to it, and try to win her back?

That was the way I was leaning, but it would mean total honesty. Total honesty would mean sharing the events of the days before I went away, after she left. Total honesty would mean facing up to my own truth. Total honesty would not facilitate the repair of our relationship. What was wrong with me? Why couldn't I have had some discipline, some restraint, for just a few days?

And Kaia.

I didn't even want to check my phone, because I knew that, waiting there, would be a message I would feel the need to respond to. A phone call I would be obligated to make. But what would I say? Would it be wise to make a decision from this place, where I had a distinct lack of clarity? I was hesitant to do that for all the reasons, and selfishness that got me here in the first place. What was the right thing to do? Our reconnection hadn't struck me as the universally accepted fate that I had once thought it would be. But was that to do with the guilt? Even if guilt had something to do with it, more strongly than that, it was a fear of being alone. There was a despondence in that; reuniting with Kaia once represented a closure, a natural conclusion to the torture which had been suffered in the meantime. But that wasn't the reality, and it strongly unsettled me to consider that my judgement on a matter so fundamental to my happiness in life was not right. But then, if that was so, if my judgement wasn't always right, then perhaps I ought to wait it out, amd not make any rash decisions. I was already in an emotionally difficult place, and once I had jumped some hurdles, who is to say I wouldn't start feeling like being with Kaia was the right thing? Did I really want to run the risk of losing her again in this period of ultimate indecision?

So, in the hesitancy, I felt it still better to keep quiet, not to do, or say anything I may later regret. I had already done that enough.

I wandered around the small town, though the stores didn't really have much in the way of appeal. I felt like a lemming, inevitably drawn to Murphy's, due to its familiarity. More importantly, the distraction that conversation promised to provide was something that would be very welcome.

On this early Saturday afternoon, there were already quite a few patrons in the bar, watching American football on the big-screen TVs. Thankfully there was an open seat at the bar I was able to squeeze into.

Louise recognised me.

"Hey! Freddie! No Hal?"

"No, he's busy this morning. Or afternoon, I mean."

"Beer? Tall or short?"

"Yeah, a short one, please."

Louise poured the beer and handed it to me. As I reached toward my pocket for my wallet, she quickly looked around to make sure nobody else saw and shook her head, putting her hand on mine. I liked this place.

It was warming to see what Hal meant in action; the way Louise riffed with the regulars and the way they seemed to love her. Eventually, the bar began to empty as the games ended, aside from a few—like me—who were sticking around. I was on my third beer when I decided that it would be my last. I didn't want to take too much of an advantage and leave a bad impression for when Hal next came in.

Once it was quieter, Louise came over and stood at my end of the bar.

"So, it's really good of you to come all the way from England for Hal, y'know."

"No, not at all. Hal is amazing. And I hate to sound all clinical, but work is work. I don't often get the opportunity to travel to places as great as this," I replied.

Louise seemed surprised.

"As great as this? Honey, I love this town, but you obviously need to get out more!"

"No, not at all," I protested, "it's great here. There are so many things I want to see. The falls and the lava fields... I can't wait to explore when I get the chance."

Just then, we were interrupted by the door opening and Louise's eyes being distracted.

"Hey, hun! Come over here. I got someone to introduce to you. Freddie—this is my daughter, Brooke... Brooke, this is Freddie. He's working with Hal and he's here from England."

My immediate reaction when I turned toward Brooke was that she seemed far too young to be Louise's daughter. Not in any unkind way; simply, an immediate, honest conclusion. Brooke couldn't have been out of her teens and I'd figured Louise to be in her early fifties. Maybe she was careworn? Maybe I ought to stop jumping to conclusions?! Brooke also looked like she'd walked right off the page of a high-end fashion magazine. I couldn't tell if she was trying too hard to be cool or not hard enough, with her platinum blonde hair up in a twisted bandana and denim ensemble, like some kind of modern, country Barbie.

"Hey," said Brooke, extending her free hand—the other held a bunch of bags. "Nice to meet you."

"You too," I replied.

"Hal's the coolest, ain't he?"

"Yeah, he's really great."

"So, what you been buying?" inquired Louise, prompting something of a fashion show from Brooke, displaying the various garments she'd bought.

Brooke and Louise attempted to keep me engaged in the conversation, talking about clothes shops back in England and asking if teenage daughters did the same, spending all of their parents' money. I was able to confirm this was, indeed, a universal thing.

"Freddie was talking about going to the lava fields. Or the waterfalls. Did you wanna go with him, show him around?" Louise asked Brooke.

I felt an awkward insecurity. I was at the age where it felt like there was a generational fracture between me and Brooke; she, from the era of selfies and me, still only in my mid-twenties and yet still wondering whether social media was a positive or negative thing for mankind. Worse, I felt like a burden.

"Sure, no problem," Brooke responded immediately, breaking my train of thought. "Where do you wanna go?"

"I don't know. You choose. Whichever is easiest. And only if it's no bother. Honestly, I'm sure you've got better things to do."

"No, it'll be fun. So when do you wanna go? Now?"

"Oh, no!" I insisted. "Not now. I've got to get back. Hal will... I was... we're working on some new songs. Probably should be back there now. Don't want to cross the boss."

"How 'bout tomorrow, then?"

"Um... yeah, sure. When's best?"

"I can pick you up at Hal's. How about, say, eleven?"

"Yeah, okay... thanks. Sounds good."

I had grown rather too comfortable in the seat I was in and had to make a bit of a groan to get off of it. I thanked Louise for her generosity and hospitality, and she simply told me to send her love to Hal.

"See you tomorrow then," Brooke said.

"Great! Yeah... thank you. I look forward to it," I replied, before leaving.

When I arrived back at Hal's, I noticed that his car was back in the driveway. At first, I didn't know whether or not to knock on the front door. I did, but received no response, so I gently pushed on the door. It swung open. Only then did I realise I had the keys anyway, so surely, I could have walked in without any of the fuss and procrastination.

"Hi! Hal! I'm back," I called out, to no response. Hal wasn't in the living room, nor the kitchen. I eventually found him out on the back porch, looking as if he was waiting for the sun to set.

"Hey," I said, walking out toward him.

"Hey, kid! Good day?"

"I was actually just at Murphy's. Louise sends her love."

"Mm-hmm."

"Yeah, and her daughter... Brooke?"—I mentioned with that quizzical intonation—"she's offered to take me to see the waterfalls tomorrow... if that's okay?"

"Yeah, sure. No worries. We got time."

"So, I was thinking," I said. "How do you think it went last night. Are you happy with how we're working?"

"Yeah... sure. It's all good, right?"

"Yeah, but you have to be enjoying it. If something isn't

working, we can change it."

"Nah, I'm good," Hal replied, noncholantly.

"I have to say, Hal, I've listened back to some of the stuff. I love it! It sounds brilliant. I mean, not my involvement, but... even as a demo, it has that earthy, lo-fi quality to it. I almost don't want to polish it."

"That good, eh, kid?" Hal sounded vaguely impressed, but also slightly distracted.

"Yeah... I..." I began to feel as though I was imposing. "I'm going to take a shower, if that's okay? And then we can do a little more work?"

"Maybe not tonight, son. It's Saturday night. We can get back to it tomorrow."

After I'd showered and changed, I went back downstairs only to discover that Hal had left the house again.

I went into the kitchen where I saw a note. "Gone to Lou's."

I thought of going back there, but decided against it. I'm sure that nobody would have minded, but there wasn't an invitation on the note. I didn't want to encroach on Hal's personal time. I was still trying to distinguish what was work and what was pleasure, a line blurred by the fact I was staying with Hal.

Instead, I went to the basement and got one of the guitars to play out on the porch. If I couldn't find inspiration there, where would I? Instantly I found myself humming something new which I was into. The melody was strong and the ideas I had for lyrics could have formed a thousand verses; whenever I had a good idea, it was like that, until I'd written the first two lines, and then the field would narrow, and the creative options would suddenly become far more limited. I wasn't ready to part with the creativity just yet, and so I just played, and played, without writing anything down.

My phone rang.

Kaia.

I looked. It must be two in the morning, at least, back home.

"Hey... Kaia... you okay?"

"Yeah, fine... was just thinking about you... wanted to hear your voice."

"Are you drunk?" I thought I'd better prepare for that kind of conversation on a Saturday night.

"No... no, I haven't been out... just... can't sleep."

"Oh... okay."

"Freddie. Why aren't you messaging me? Or calling?"

"I'm sorry. I'm just... I'm still getting used to this. You know, when you're at work, I'm asleep, when I'm working, that's when you have your free time and when I'm chilling out, you're asleep. Usually."

"Have you been working today?"

"No, but... not really... you know."

"No... actually, I don't."

"Don't be like that, Kaia. Please. You know I've been going through some stuff... it's not easy. We're good. I just don't need any of the..."

"Any of the what, exactly?"

"What I mean is, don't be sad. If you think I'm not thinking about you, I am. I'm always thinking about you."

"Really?"

"Yeah, really."

"Okay... well that... that makes me feel better. It's just that it's really hard being away from you."

"I don't mean to sound uncaring, but, you know, it's not easy for me either. But I need to be in a good place. I can't be feeling negative. Things are good. I'll try to call and text more. Promise."

"Okay. So... what's it like out there?"

"It's really good... you know... you go places on holiday and imagine living there. It's like that. But I suppose I'm used to that feeling. Or I used to be."

"What do you mean?"

It dawned on me that my nomadic side had only really been born after Kaia and I went our separate ways. I had travelled around so much, so often, and grown so comfortable in my own skin—not to say I was always at ease with who I was, but, I grew to tolerate my own company. It was a conversation I'd really only ever had with Ailie and made me realise there was so much that Kaia didn't know about me. Not that I was concealing anything, and not even a white lie kind of mistruth, simply, the various facets of growing as an adult that do not immediately come to mind.

"I don't know how to explain it. It's just nice here," I settled on. I guess she was probably happy for a deep and meaningful conversation. I wasn't averse to it, but that topic was one I associated so strongly with Ailie that I was at least trying to be fair to Kaia and dedicate my thoughts and conversations to her. That was the problem. There were few topics which wouldn't make my mind drift back to Ailie. It left for a limited stream of conversation.

"So anyway... what have you been up to?" I asked.

"Me? Oh, nothing much, really. I feel like I'm just waiting for you to come back."

"Well don't do that... that's just wasting time."

"You are coming back to me, aren't you?" Kaia asked.

"I always do, don't I?"

"Well, it's not wasted then, right?"

Normally these conversations would have meant the world to me. In any other circumstance, a beautiful girl telling you she was putting her life on hold because she was waiting for you would be seen as romantic. Exactly what any guy would want to hear. But I felt frustrated, agitated. Yet what could I say? If I showed any amount of agitation, Kaia would question it, which, in turn would lead to further agitation. I was still internally contending the merit of unnecessarily rocking the boat.

My only path, it seemed, was to go along with what she was saying. And of course, before too long, it all did get really deep.

"I honestly didn't realise that I'd miss you so much," she explained with a candid openness I had never heard from her. It was the kind of thing I used to wish she'd say back when we were together. "It just hurts so bad. I'm crying all the time."

"Why, Kaia? Don't be sad."

"No, but you're way out there... and it's just... after spending so much time with you those last few days."

There was a pause in the conversation, slightly awkward, but one I saw as a convenient point to make a break.

"You sound really tired, Kaia. You'd better get some sleep."

"Yeah. Okay. Will you promise to text me tomorrow?"

"Yeah, I promise."

We said our goodnights, and I continued to play guitar for a while. It couldn't have been ten minutes before my phone beeped.

"Sorry... but I'm too scared to say it in case you don't say it, or don't feel the same. I feel like I've fallen for you again. I can't stop thinking about you. x"

I did smile. It was a pleasant thing to read and I think that not having the pressure of instantly responding allowed me to rationalise what I was really feeling. It wasn't awkward. I didn't feel guilty. It was nice. I didn't know where I was at in terms of how I should respond, but I was hovering my fingers over the empty reply panel when Kaia texted again.

"You don't have to say it back. Night x"

And then, immediately after.

"PS. Text me tomorrow x"

Hal came out on to the porch.

"Heard you playing out here," he said.

"Hey, Hal. How are you? I was just... you know."

"I'm good. You coulda taken some time off, you know."

"Yeah, but I'll be doing that tomorrow. We've got a masterpiece to create. It's not going to create itself," I joked, adding, "I feel like I'm taking a bit of a liberty. We've barely done any real work and I've been here three days now."

Hal went back inside and brought out two beers.

"You know as well as I do that you can't rush these things. Not in any kind of rush, are you kid?"

"No. I'm happy to stay as long as you need me around. You know, within reason. Don't want to outstay my welcome."

"You're very welcome here," Hal replied.

He seemed pensive again. Distracted.

"Is everything okay? I mean... I know it's not really my place, but you seem a little distant."

"Yeah, it's just this," he said, raising his bottle before taking a drink from it. "A few of these gets you to thinking."

"Yeah," I replied.

There was an easy silence. It felt as if Hal were about to open up to me. I liked that. Any development in our relationship would hopefully translate and manifest itself in our work.

"So, you were on the phone, when I came back?" Hal finally said.

"Yeah."

"To your ex?" Hal looked at me with a mischievous grin.

"No... actually... Oh God, it's a long story."

I decided to tell Hal everything. I went right back to the beginning, explaining how Ailie had changed my life in so many ways. About meeting her, how we had moved in together so quickly. How we fell for each other, how she believed in me. How swiftly things moved. I didn't even get to the breakdown when Hal asked me why we hadn't got married.

"I thought about it so many times... you know, asking her," I said. "But Ailie... she's the kind of girl that I imagined would feel restricted by that. I think she liked the freeing aspect of not being legally bound to another. Or, at least that's what I thought at the time."

"How would you have proposed?"

I think Hal missed the point.

"I hadn't gotten that far. I needed to visualise her saying yes before I actually thought through a plan."

"Ah. People love a good story."

"Romantic gestures are so cliché though, don't you think?"

"Who said anything about a gesture? I said story. I think all they want... is a story to tell. *How did you get engaged? Well... that's a funny story.* You know, that kind of thing."

"I don't think there was ever a time she would have said yes."

"You don't *think*?" Hal replied. "But you don't *know*."

"What about you? How did you propose to Betty? I'm guessing that there has to be some sort of story there?"

Hal's reaction wasn't immediate. He took some time to think about it and I found that strange. Surely the memory of something so significant would be fresh, particularly as he was the one who had brought up the subject. Or maybe he was thinking about a diplomatic way to say he didn't want to talk about it anymore.

Finally, he answered.

"We were in Toronto one Christmas. The snow was awful. I mean, *really* awful. We couldn't get anywhere. Planes were cancelled for days. So we were stuck in this hotel. I mean, they loved it. I was in town to play a show and this was when, you know, people wanted to know me."

I tried to interject with a sycophantic comment, but Hal continued to talk, a little louder.

"So I was there. And Betty was with me of course. I remember saying something about how we might be stuck there forever. And she said to me, 'You know honey, if that were the case, I couldn't be happier.' And so I asked her, right there and then. I mean, I didn't have a ring. But it was about *knowing* in the moment. What would you rather... have it all planned out, or just happen like that, in the moment?"

"That sounds nice. I take it she said yes."

"Oh yeah," he nodded. "And she loved the story. She loved the little addition, that I didn't have the ring. She loved it. That became the punchline."

"Sounds like she was a funny lady."

"Yeah, she was. She was," Hal sighed. And, then, trying to turn it back around, "I still can't believe you never asked. So, what the hell went wrong?"

"To be perfectly honest, Hal, I still don't really know. Still trying to figure that one out," I replied.

"Well... this is a good place to think. As good as any," Hal said.

"Yeah... I don't know if it's about thinking. I've done plenty of that. I just... you know, I think it's about being honest with myself. I made some bad mistakes. Choices."

"Oh, yeah... tell me about it."

He was ribbing me like we were two high school kids.

"Yeah, I think you can tell where this is going."

"So who was on the phone? The one you have or the one you let go?"

"I didn't let her go. She left. But yeah, the other."

"You let her go. Man, I had you down as a smart kid."

I found myself stung, defensive. It was irrational. Hal was a star, a big name, and my host. Yet in that moment he had personally insulted me. I considered my response.

"I don't think it was to do with intelligence... you know, after Eddy died, I kinda... I don't know, I made some pretty stupid choices," I said, using grief as my excuse again.

"Does it feel any better when you use that line?" Hal asked, instantly reading between the lines.

"I don't know if it's a line, I think it's probably the truth," I insisted.

"Yeah, you're probably right," Hal said. "But you know, I thought you made a sweet couple. What about this other girl? Was it worth it?"

"Well, I'm still trying to work that one out. I mean, we were together... I had a relationship with her a long time ago. My first broken heart. It's weird going back there," I said.

Hal looked sympathetic.

"Your first love? That's a tough one. But you know... maybe in doing what you did, it was your way of telling yourself something," he said.

"Yeah... but you know, I think you're right. I made a bad choice. I think it was more down to me than this love of my life reappearing," I admitted. "I wasn't happy."

We sat in silence for a while. I felt a strange relief, a relief that I had openly admitted and taken responsibility for the breakdown of my relationship with Ailie. It wasn't anything she had done. And it wasn't Kaia. It was all me.

"And you know... now I think about it, I do wonder whether we're only meant to be with one person. There are millions of people in the world and it's a place that is getting ever smaller."

Perhaps I was simply spewing words out now that I was apparently comfortable with admitting fault. Maybe it was part of the moving on process. I remembered something I'd read about emotional pain only lasting for around ten minutes, and the rest of it being procrastination. Dwelling. It was psychosomatic. Consciously addressing that thought, I compared it to my current situation, and sure enough, there was no pain in the gut, no actual real misery other than the misery I was inflicting on myself. A revelation such as this should have been liberating, but instead, it only served to make me feel more guilty. How dare I feel emotionally prepared to move on from a relationship, one which was more significant than any I'd ever had, in such a short space of time? How much of this was even true? Surely my new surroundings had more to do with it.

"You know," Hal said, standing up, "the hardest lies to live with are the ones we tell ourselves. And when we actually start to believe them... well, at that point, there's no hope."

He put his hand on my shoulder.

"There's hope for you, son."

Hal had breakfast waiting for me the next morning. It wasn't much—toast and fruit—but it was an effort I hadn't expected him to make. And, because he didn't go to that sort of effort even for himself, I realy appreciated it.

There were the lingering reminders of a woman's touch, those subtle provocations in matters of courtesy which remained; clearly, apparently, stirring into life after some time spent living alone.

"If you don't mind me asking, Hal," I started, hesitantly, "when... I mean... how long have you been widowed?"

Hal hesitated.

"Well, son, it will be forty-five years this year," he eventually replied.

I found it difficult to comprehend that he had been living this way, as alone as this, for longer than I'd been alive.

"Have you had relationships since? I mean, have you always lived here?"

"Yeah, this was our house. Well, it was Betty's house, really. I never married again. I couldn't bring myself to do it. You know, we never had a day of sadness. Never had a day of sadness with that woman. I didn't really believe in that 'one person for everyone' until I met her. And I never really thought about it until she was gone. I mean, you say it, but, you don't know... She was the love of my life, and nobody came close. I thought about moving on a few times, but that would mean..."

He trailed off.

I thought about the house. The way it was. I knew what he meant. I guess an outsider would have thought that was sad' heartbreaking, even. This man was so bereft that to anyone caring enough to ask, they would reasonably believe that he was simply stuck in his grief and unable to move on. They would say it wasn't healthy. But I knew Hal to be quite happy, able to have routine conversations, say things that were powerfully profound and helpful to me. He made sane decisions. If he was content to do so, then whose business was it how he processed everything?

"Do you think... don't take this the wrong way. Do you think you might ever wake up tomorrow and feel differently?" I suggested.

"Maybe. Who knows? But I don't think so. I don't shut it out. I just... know where I am. You know, when she died, I remember that day... being so broken by it. And people just kept on. The world kept moving. Everything felt colder afterwards. But you know... it's one of those things we learn in life. It comes to us all. The end. And people do carry on."

I thought of Hal, not much older than I was, losing his wife so young. I guessed it would have had to have been an accident, or illness, but I didn't really want to pry any further, particularly when he tried to change the subject.

"Brooke will be here soon. She's a good kid. Talks a lot," he said. "But those waterfalls... yeah... you gotta take those in. They're really something."

I could sense that Hal was not really concentrating, and was almost paying me lip service, dwelling on these things that I'd forced him to think about.

"While I'm gone, have a listen back to the songs we worked on," I suggested, hoping the distraction might prove helpful. "Then we can maybe do something with them later on?"

"Yeah, okay. That's a good idea. I'll do that."

I went to shower and get dressed, and by the time I'd done so, Brooke had already arrived and was waiting for me downstairs. I could hear her talking to Hal on the porch outside the kitchen. She was saying that he needed to get a hobby and was throwing suggestions at him. Trainspotting. Power walking. Knitting. Hal was almost spitting feathers, but as I stood watching the back and forth in the kitchen, I smiled fondly. Brooke was running rings around him in much the same way as a granddaughter would.

"Hey," I interrupted, much to Hal's relief.

"Mornin'!" Brooke greeted me. "You ready to go?"

"Yeah, all good."

Brooke gave Hal a hug and a kiss and spritely moved past me, leading me outside to her car.

"It's mom's, not mine," she said as we got in, as if she had to excuse the age of it. "I'm saving up. Not sure what I want yet. Something new."

God, I remember those days, where the idea and pursuit of a big purchase seemed like the only thing that mattered.

"So... working with Hal... is it fun?" she asked.

"Yeah. Well, we haven't done much yet, but you know..."

"Mom said you worked with The Cause. And you wrote all their best songs."

"I don't know about that," I laughed, awkwardly. "But, yeah, I did work with them, on their first album."

"That one was their best... so, yeah, I guess you're a big deal. *Mr. Big Deal from England... ridin' in ma car*!" she said in a playful voice. It embarrassed me a little. "No, really. I liked their first record. So take that as a compliment. I found out some stuff about you online. You don't have a Wikipedia page though. Hey, that's weird, sat here talking to someone I looked up online. I'm not a stalker or anything. I'm just curious. I figure a stalker wouldn't tell you if they looked you up, though, right?"

Hal was right. She could talk.

"It'll probably be a little busy up there. It's a nice day. Families. Tourists," she said, looking at me with that last word, with a faux-evil tone in her voice.

There was a beep of a phone. I thought it was mine as we both reached for our phones. It wasn't mine. She sighed and slammed her phone back down.

"Boys," she said. "No offence."

"None taken. I know the feeling. Relationships, huh?"

"Oh yeah? Tell me about it," she replied, asking, rather than making the rhetorical question. "I could use the distraction."

"Me? Well... it's complicated."

I didn't know where to begin. Though, with this sudden wave of externalising my thoughts and emotions with people I didn't know well, I wasn't going to hold back. Besides, I was discovering that talking out loud and being more open was helping me. I was finding wisdom in the words of strangers.

"It's funny, I was talking to Hal about it last night and he made me realise a few things... so I was..."

I let myself trail off, wondering how best to articulate it.

"Go on," Brooke encouraged me.

"Well... I've been in this relationship for a long time. And someone I was close to... well, someone we were both close to, died," I started. "And she was really there for me. She really was. She was so good. But I pulled away. I didn't accept her support. And so, she gave me distance. I didn't reconnect. I didn't ever reach out. I didn't say I was wrong. Or that I was sorry. There was a time between us where I know I could have easily fixed it and I simply never did. I just let her sort of... go. And then I met an ex and sort of... well, it turned messy. And so she left me."

"Is that it?"

"Sort of, in a nutshell."

"Tell me about her."

"Ailie?" I asked.

"Oh my god!" Brooke looked at me excitedly. "No way! You were with Ailie McIntyre?"

"Yeah," I laughed, curiously. I hadn't really thought about our relationship in terms of Ailie being successful and much more well-known than me.

"I knew that she did something... that she was connected with The Cause, but I never... Wow! You rock!" she smiled, before realising. "Oh, yeah... sorry!"

"You're okay," I replied. "Don't worry about it. I know I was lucky. And also an idiot. But Ailie... yeah, she's really amazing."

"How did you guys meet?"

"I was doing a gig at her parent's pub. And she was the barmaid there. We just hit it off immediately, really. She has this way of thinking, like, lateral thinking. But the way she says things makes it seem like the most obvious thing. I don't know, it's hard to think of an example. But she really pushed me. I was just writing my own songs and travelling around the U.K."

"That must have been nice. I'd love to go to London," Brooke interrupted.

"Yeah, everyone says that."

"Go on... about Ailie," Brooke said, casually. I looked at her and didn't doubt her interest, although she was keeping an eye on the road, as if we were lost.

"Are we on the right road?" I asked.

"Yeah, we're fine. Just don't want to miss this turn. Go on."

"Okay, well, she was the one who contacted The Cause and set that whole thing up. So you could say I have Ailie to thank for everything that's good in my life."

"Wow, you really were stupid, then," laughed Brooke.

"Yeah, cheers for rubbing that in. But, you know, we've only been broken up for a few weeks. And I've sort of been in denial about why... blaming the death, my grief... but I knew what I was doing. So maybe I... I mean, I still love her, I still have strong feelings for her. But we can't be *in* love, can we, because she's sort of moved on. And if I truly felt the way I used to, could I really have let her go? Maybe it was for the best, I dunno," I concluded.

"Don't you think that maybe she got just as much out of being with you as the other way around?"

"No, I don't think I'd say that."

"Well, she was a barmaid when you met. And now she's a famous songwriter. And she's got a Wikipedia page," Brooke joked.

"She was always going to end up as someone special. She's unstoppable. I just... I think I was simply along for the ride," I said.

"Nah. I don't buy it. I mean, she's not here, is she? But you are. You got something going for you. I get it. That lost soul, 'dare-you-to-love-me/'be my muse' kind of thing. Girls go for that."

I laughed.

"What?"

"Nothing, it's just... it's funny that you're giving me this pep talk. What are you, like, eighteen?"

"Twenty, actually. And so what? How old do you have to be to say something positive. To *be* positive."

"No. Fair enough. I get your point. Thanks, then, I guess."

"I wish I had that kind of drive, though," Brooke admitted. "I don't know what I'm doing. Or where I'm going. Or even what I want."

"You can do anything you want."

"Hmm, that's what everyone seems to tell me."

Brooke turned the radio up as a song she liked came on, and sang along to it. It was a nice distraction from the conversation.

Once the song was over, she turned the radio back down.

"So, what did Hal say that left such an impression?" she asked.

"I'm sorry?"

"You said that Hal made you realise a few things?"

"Well, he said, basically, don't lie to myself. So it feels good to just admit that I... well, I did nothing... and in doing so, lost the best thing I've ever had. I guess there's a lesson in there somewhere."

"Or, you know..." Brooke started. "No, don't worry."

"What? Go on."

"'It's not really my place to say. But you know, just an idea... do you think that when people talk about soulmates and relationships that are meant to be, that sometimes, it must be equally true to say that those relationships *can* exist but that they don't *have* to be soulmates, they don't *have* to have eternal love... that there can be relationships that are meant to be, for a certain period of time, and then those relationships end. And people move on. It doesn't necessarily mean it has to be a bad thing."

"Yeah, I know what you mean. That makes sense."

"So, like, your perception, your sadness, is more about an acknowledgement of that particular time in your life ending. But conversely, why not be happy and celebrate that time. Say a big *fuck you* to the sadness and negativity."

Brooke had more of a point than I think she realised. Or at least, I was able to connect with it on a deeper level. I felt bad for initially dismissing her as a *Barbie*.

"I did have another problem," I said, feeling more talkative now that the dam had broken.

"Go for it."

"So, before I came out here I got involved with an ex who I hadn't seen in years. She was my first love. I was still raw over Ailie but... I went with it. I think she sees it as pretty serious but... you know... I don't know."

"*You know... I don't know,*" she mimicked and laughed. "First of all, props to you, gettin' all the girls. Secondly, well, how do you feel about her?"

"This is the thing. *I don't know.* I know that I associate her with the end of my relationship with Ailie and that was a bad thing, but that certainly wasn't her fault... but I still don't know if what I feel for her is the real thing I felt when I was originally with her. I hoped the distance would help put it into perspective, but it hasn't. But I don't want to throw anything away because, well, I lost her once, and I'm not sure I want to lose her again."

"Why don't you wait until you get home? Because it might be that when you see her, you'll know," Brooke suggested.

"Yeah, maybe... I'm just... I get a bit anxious thinking about it, you know, if I'm leading her on, I just want to be honest with her," I said. "I feel like I'm being selfish or manipulative and that's what got me into this mess in the first place. I'm not a dick, normally. But I feel like I have been."

"What's honesty?"

"What do you mean?"

"You said that you want to be honest. Is your honesty that you feel you're being selfish, and manipulative?"

I thought about it.

"And does that mean you do want to be with her, or that you don't?" she asked, reading my silence.

"That, I really don't know."

"Well in that case, it's just your shit to figure out isn't it? I don't mean that in a... what I mean is, it's just shit that life throws at you and you have to work through. And you don't need to share that with anyone, you just work through it on your own. And then when you're ready... you know."

I looked over at Brooke.

"You remind me of Ailie a bit. She said a lot of smart stuff and I couldn't imagine where she had picked up that kind of insight."

"Well thank you very much," Brooke replied, sarcastically.

"Although admittedly that might be because it's what I want to hear!" I added.

I thought again of what Hal had said, about lying to myself, and understood that it had some truth. But now, the concept of a relationship—having been amazing for what it represented in its moment—simply reaching its natural conclusion, did make some sense to me. It was amazing to me that two strangers could be so on the money with personal issues, and then I thought to myself that really, these sorts of issues were fairly universal.

I smiled to myself. "You know," I thought, "I should just choose to be happy."

How could I be bitter about Ailie's decision to walk away when I had basically laid out the red carpet for her? How could I be upset about anything when I had given away that right by entering into an emotional attachment with someone else? My commitment wasn't what it should have been, and, as sad as that was, it was a truth I needed to face. It was unusual in the fact that I had only really experienced sadness in breakups when I had been the one who had been dumped, and, technically, that had been the case in this instance, though my honest participation in it had ended some time prior.

We arrived at Shoshone Falls and went up to the public viewing area. It was breathtaking. The waterfalls were huge, and the air was the freshest I'd ever breathed.

"This is amazing," I said to Brooke. "Honestly, I've never seen anything quite like it."

I was mesmerised. I hadn't really known what to expect. I had seen pictures of Niagara Falls, but had to agree with what Louise had said about Shoshone Falls being even more impressive. Maybe that's just because I was seeing them for the first time, but the formation of the rocks and the way the streams and lakes all came together was really quite a sight.

"You picked the wrong time of year," said Brooke. "In April and May, it's way more spectacular. A lot more water flows when the snow melts, and the mist that comes up is really refreshing. You can feel it up here."

The main waterfalls were supported by five smaller ones behind them. Brooke explained that one was named the Bridesmaid, for what reason she didn't know, but she used to think it was because some unlucky-in-love girl had sacrificed herself. It seemed as if she still believed it, too, although it did seem a fanciful tale.

As a stranger, unfamiliar with local tales and myths, I simply admired the falls for what they were, even if Brooke was suggesting they were hardly at their most impressive. I failed to see how they could be any more spectacular. The relentless drive of the water on the steep fall and the thought that it had been that way for thousands of years—according to Brooke, since the last Ice Age— caused me to picture myself by comparison, and how insignificant my trials and tribulations were. Even if they weren't, how many people must have stood here, whiling away the minutes and hours, pondering their own individual dilemmas.

"Coming here with someone who hasn't seen it before... you know, that you think it's all amazing and everything, and I'm like... you know, whatever, I see it all the time," laughed Brooke.

"Surely a view like this... nobody can take it for granted," I contended.

"You'd be surprised."

She sat on the steps, staring at her phone.

"You okay? Is it my turn to give the advice?"

"No, it's not me... it's a friend, she's just having a bit of a problem."

"Oh, right, so I opened up my heart and soul for nothing," I laughed.

"Not at all. You got some great advice. Trust me, it's been a while since I've been with anyone, and the more I know about relationships, the less I wanna be in one."

"It's probably a healthy position to view it from. For a while, anyway."

"Works for me. I'm just having fun, you know. So many of my girlfriends hook up with guys and... you know, you never see them again. I haven't dated since Josh Fallon in high school. I'll be the last girl standing."

I laughed.

We sat there for a while longer, Brooke giving me the opportunity to say when. I was quite content to remain staring at the mighty falls. Somehow, trivialising—or, rather, *contextualising*— my problems was proving to be therapeutic. I had arrived at a place where, for the first time in months, I didn't feel bound by the weight of the bad choices I had made.

During the ride back to Hal's, the conversation was a little more difficult to start. I didn't know if it was just my tendency to act in this manner, but it always seemed like the drive back from anywhere was infinitely quieter than it was going. I'd enjoyed the views on the drive on each occasion I'd taken it, but now, on the fourth time on this stretch, my eyes were unstoppably drawn to other, more mundane things. There was a book on the passenger dashboard that I kept looking at; a small journal or address book, I figured, but the patterns on the front cover of it kept my eyes busy. I didn't think I was being particularly nosy, but Brooke obviously noticed, and answered a question I didn't ask, or didn't even think of asking.

"You can take a look if you'd like."

"Oh... no, that's okay," I replied, embarrassed.

"Really, it's okay. But you might think it's... oh, I don't know. So about a year ago... actually, it's probably longer, maybe eighteen months. That was probably right around that time anyway. My friend Maria, well she's really smart. She went away to college and she had this big going away party. They called it a *cacharpaya*, which, basically means, going away party. I don't know why it stuck with me, but I was like... wow, you have a word for that? I learned a lot of Spanish that day."

"So, that's your big book of Spanish phrases?" I interjected, relieved I hadn't been staring at Brooke's personal diary.

"No... well, kinda. *I* wasn't going to go away anywhere. I couldn't leave Mom. But Maria and I said we'd write each other. I said I'd try and find new... well, you know, what *really* fascinated me was that there are not only words like *cacharpaya*, like, simpler ways of saying things, there are words out there in other languages which describe things that in English are just... either too difficult to articulate. Or too long to shorten."

"Wow, that sounds fascinating," I said.

"Are you being sarcastic?"

"No, not at all. It really does."

"Good," she smiled. "Because I find it very interesting."

There was an awkward moment or two where I didn't know

what to say. I didn't want to reassert that I didn't find it boring, because that would have been protesting too much.

"Go on, test me," she said, directing her eyes to the book. "Find some words in there and I'll see if I can remember what they mean."

I picked the book up and flicked through it. It was written neatly, with bright blue ink for the words and their origin country, and purple ink to explain their meaning. The book was almost full.

"Even though Maria and I never talk now, it was still fun to learn. That's me. I have like, a ton of useless shit in my head, like, literally, nothing of use."

I found one word which caught my eye because of the spelling. "*Famn. Fam. n*," I said, pronouncing the "n" separately.

"Which country?"

"Swedish. Sweden."

"*Famn*. Wow. I don't know. Tell me."

"You're not very good at this."

"Tell me!"

"The space between two arms; in my arms."

"Oh yeah," she said, suddenly remembering. "Like in a hug. I like that, I don't know why, because you'd never use it. I just like that there's a word for the feeling. So, go on. Next."

"Forelsket."

"Also Swedish?"

"No, but close."

"Norwegian?"

"Yep."

"Forel...?"

"Forelsket."

"Hmm... something to do with love. Is it like limerence?"

"What's limerence?"

"Limerence is English!" she laughed, as if I ought to have known every single word in the English language. "Limerence is like the infatuation stage of love. When you got it bad."

"The euphoric act, and or feeling of, falling in love," I read.

"Close enough. It's all connected. In Spanish you would say, *Te quiero.* which is that ballpark between *like* and *love.* I love all of those words. They're so... warm. Go on, another."

I deliberately looked for one that wasn't Scandinavian or connected to matters of the heart. It took a while. Brooke wasn't wrong, she really did seem to like those sorts of words. Nonetheless, I found it interesting, and pretty revealing.

"Sunao," I said, pronouncing it "Sun how."

"Japanese... submissive," she replied, immediately.

"Impressive."

"It's a positive term."

"What do you mean?"

"Well, submissive is generally... if you say someone is submissive, then it feels like it's a negative thing to say, right?"

"Yeah, I guess so."

"But *sunao* is saying it in a *positive* way. I think that it's like... agreeable, easy. You know."

"Yeah, but we have words for that," I replied.

Brooke smiled and nodded her head as if I'd caught her with a good one. I closed the book and put it back on the dashboard.

When we arrived back at Hal's, Brooke didn't come in. Hal opened the curtain and waved. Brooke waved back. I thanked Brooke. I was grateful for the day and experience, and Brooke's generosity in taking the time to show me around. She said it was fine, any time, and keyed her number into my phone.

I went inside, excited to hear what Hal was now thinking of the work we'd done so far.

2

three years earlier

It happened again. I'd travelled so many hours, this time to get even further away.

No, wait—in reality, the truth of the matter was that the chances of being hired anywhere within my local area were growing increasingly slim, every time and every place I performed. I was ostensibly a dirt-cheap karaoke guy looking for residency and showing willingness to travel, but when every night invariably ended with me and my guitar hogging the stage, the landlords were, unsurprisingly, reluctant to hire me again.

It was a strong enough plan to get a little money to live, pay for my rent back home, and to travel. I had seen so many beautiful pockets of the country that I was beginning to take it all for granted. This time, I had deliberately scouted somewhere close enough to the beach up in Scotland. Somewhere close enough to the northernmost point. I settled on Aberdeen, as Cove Bay sounded exotic, as if it could have been on the California coastline.

I turned up at The Anchor in the early afternoon and couldn't help thinking that the landlord and I had lied to each other. I had travelled under the impression that this was a chain of local pubs and felt that I would simply be on the blacklist after that evening when they realised I wasn't the next coastal maverick on the microphone. Landlords like routine and they like familiar. They aren't interested in indulging the casual daydreams of a wannabe rockstar. They had no interest in hearing me play *my* songs. They didn't care what I had to say. I knew how they felt, most days.

When I went inside, it was even more dour than I had imagined. And I thought the word dour was possibly the most apt word I could use to describe this place. Inside were a couple of locals—old-timers, who looked as if they had one hand glued to their pint glass and the other to the bar. They looked more like the kind of people who were racing to death on their barstools, the sort you imagine would see suicide as the easy way out, rather than the type who would want to belt out some of Neil Diamond's classics.

Startlingly out of place in this generationally-forgotten watering hole was a strikingly beautiful, pale-skinned young girl— the kind you instantly assume to be demure—behind the bar.

"Hi... I'm here for the, erm, karaoke," I said with an awkward smile.

"Room four," she replied, handing me a set of keys.

The evening didn't bring any surprises. The lounge was fuller, as you would expect of a coastal bar on a Friday evening, but it was hardly heaving. The clientele was largely as I had anticipated. On surveying the crowd and considering that I was hardly likely to be hired again come what may, I decided to just break straight into the routine, disregarding the karaoke machine completely and instead just going straight for the guitar.

I played a couple of covers until I realised I could have been reciting some hell-fury scripture and they wouldn't have noticed, so, decided to simply take advantage of the absolute ignorance and pointlessness of my existence in this setting and indulge myself in playing my own songs.

No sleep when you lose a day,
No voice when you lose your say,
No save when it falls away for you.
I'm saying what I mean,
but I don't think it's coming out the right way,
No save when it falls away from me.
Save me now, we're slowing down
We were running blind, but I don't mind.

It was a release. *My* release, for those moments.

The reaction to "my" songs was a smattering of disinterested applause. I didn't expect anything else. I didn't want anything else.

I finished playing and took a while to consider how I was feeling. *Okay.* I was used to dealing with extremes, that after emotionally pouring myself out in a few of these songs, that meant nothing to anyone other than me, that I felt like I should be closer to an edge than I was.

This was often the case.

Almost as if on autopilot, I ordered a pint with a whisky chaser. I considered that thought about staying somewhere long enough that you become part of it, and instantly disregarded it, though, then, challenged myself to think more carefully. Well, yes, maybe. I didn't have to share these stories to be more aware of my own. Maybe we were all at the end of our respective lines. Solitude, I had learned, was wonderful for magnifying melodrama.

I sat at my own small table, staring at my drink, and then my phone, wondering who I could text, if I ought to contact anyone. My mother or father, to let them know it went okay. I hadn't been hounded out yet, anyway. Or Clare. Or Alice, even. Probably one of those. I thought I'd take until the end of my drink to decide, but as I was finishing, the barmaid came up to my table.

"Another?"

"Um... yeah, please, go on... no whisky this time, though."

She duly brought my drink to the table.

"Mind if I join you?"

"Sure. No problem," I started. "Sure you haven't got some place better to be?"

"Would someone my age be here if they weren't forced to be?" the barmaid responded.

I didn't need to extend an invitation. When she returned with her own drink, I offered a toast.

"Here's to purgatory."

I felt that was the most profound thing I could offer.

"Ailie, by the way," she replied. "And it's not really purgatory. My parents own it."

I smiled in acknowledgement but didn't know how much else I could offer. I wasn't a great ice breaker.

"I like your songs," she said.

"They're not, really... well, I'm not..." I admitted.

"You're good. You have a talent. I can tell," Ailie insisted.

"We don't know each other," I smiled.

"Yeah, but I can tell. You're good," she repeated.

It was sincere enough. I could believe.

"Thanks," I said, biting my tongue on that second between accepting a compliment and being so grandiose as to declare how brilliant I felt I really was.

Ailie smiled. My cue for conversation.

"So, are these your days?" I asked, "Serving the hopefuls and the hopeless?"

"Yeah, most days. Probably."

"Well, in that case I don't know if I feel more sorry for you, or for me, being here and thinking it's an advancement in *my* life."

"I think I'd rather spend my Friday night alone if all you want to do is dwell in misery," Ailie replied.

It seemed a remote place. Of course, I couldn't tell how close she was to a dear friend, or someone more, but I knew I was at least a couple of hundred miles away from anyone who cared about me enough to engage in conversation. I had enough time to be alone.

"So, what do you do?" I asked.

"How do you mean?"

"When you're not working here?"

"Come on," she replied, grabbing her drink and standing up. I followed her outside.

There was a narrow road in front of the bar which separated the property from the onset of a pebble dash beach. I could imagine that in the dead of night it would have looked quite fearful, but illuminated by the lights of the pub and the intermittent glare and spin of the beam from a nearby lighthouse on the shore, there was a tremendous beauty. I followed as Ailie walked across the road and across the pebbles until she reached a hill of pebbles, steep enough to not be affected by the night tide. She must have been here thousands of times before.

We sat, listening to the social noise of the pub collide with the waves on the stone shore. The sun had long gone down. It was September after all. But I could imagine being out here in May or June when the days are long.

"This is yours then? This is pretty cool."

"No, I don't come out here often. Not like this. You take what's in front of you for granted."

Yeah, I thought. That was a pretty heavy comment. My instant reaction was to think, *at least she had something to take for granted*; and then, I realised how heavy those words hung in my own mind. I did have plenty of things *I* was taking for granted. But the things I wanted were things I thought others took for granted. At this moment in my life I was beginning to accept things which proved me wrong. In fact, I embraced it. Because change had to be a good thing.

"I don't know," she said, in that way that friends often impulsively return to an earlier point in the conversation. Normally you know where they're going because you're familiar with them enough to be aware of that.

"I don't know," she repeated, "because sometimes I think of this place and wonder whether it's the place I'll end up in forever... do I need anymore?"

"Well, it's certainly nice."

"I don't mean like that," she responded. "I mean, I have things I want to do. I do want to be something and make something of my life. But if I end up back here and I'm here, now, anyway..."

"It's not the destination, it's the journey..." I tried to profoundly offer. "That's what they say."

"That's easy for you to say. This is part of your journey."

I didn't want to interrupt again, for fear of misinterpreting the point she was attempting to make.

"This place seems like it's stuck in time," she eventually said.

"There is a certain charm to that, though," I replied.

"Yeah, of course, when you're passing through."

I think I was beginning to understand what she meant. I liked the scenery, but how long could I remain without feeling suffocated? Even acknowledging that it could present those difficulties made me feel some of the claustrophobia.

"So, tell me about you," she said. "Why are you all the way up here?"

"Well, I go where the work is."

"Even so... I mean..."

I knew what she meant.

"I guess I'm just passing through."

It felt like the right thing to say.

Whether it was due to her intoxication or my simply being new, and maybe different to the local lads, when I turned to look for her response, I noticed that Ailie was hesitantly leaning in to kiss me.

Of course, my own response was to go along with it.

After acknowledging my willingness to participate, Ailie locked eyes with me and drew me in for a more intense kiss. I was stung by a sudden tension that I hadn't yet acknowledged as even existing between us.

She stood up and waited for me to rise, holding and leading me by the hand, as we walked back across the beach towards The Anchor, and around the side entrance, up to room four. She was in control, with every movement.

"Are you sure?" I asked—momentarily, I was surprised, as if I were really asking myself the question.

Ailie didn't stay. She heard someone—I presumed to be her father—calling her name. She dressed quickly and got ready to leave.

"See you tomorrow," she hurriedly said, leaving me on the bed with a soft kiss on the cheek.

I was exhausted—from the travel, the long day, and the energy I'd just exerted—but now, with this most brief of encounters in my mind, I found myself revisiting the things Ailie had said, connecting with them in a stronger way now we had been so intimate. I felt some sort of moral obligation to understand her path and her feelings. I had every intention of doing just that, at least, until I drifted off, unable to remain awake any longer.

The pebbled beach and shore looked magnificent in the dawn light. I felt a stronger awareness the following morning and I had Ailie to thank for that—not because of our tryst, but, those moments and our company together meant that I hadn't filled too many hours drinking myself to oblivion. And now, with a fresh head and clear mind, I really was able to appreciate the beauty of the North Sea. What that beauty was, well, I was never sure I could even articulate it to myself. It just felt free.

She must be mad, getting tired of this, I thought. That in itself was curious. Did I just entertain the notion of spending more time here? What exactly was I thinking? I shouldn't get too carried away. There was bound to be an awkward conversation to follow.

Sure enough, it wasn't too long before I was approached on the beach by Ailie. I knew it was her, though I didn't turn to look. The sound of the approaching footsteps on the pebbles, slowing, then that presence of another person behind you.

"Morning." She sounded as if she was in a pleasant mood.

"Good morning."

"I, erm... brought you a sandwich. I was going to ask if you wanted a full breakfast, but I didn't want to bring a plate out, you ken?" she said.

"Ken?"

"Know."

"Oh! Thank you." I graciously accepted. I was hungry.

Ailie was here and prepared for conversation and I had precious little time to prepare, or to think of what I could say to her as I ate. I hoped that she would start, so I deliberately slowed my chewing.

"So when do you plan to leave?" she finally asked. It took me by surprise.

"Well, err... I have an open ticket. But I know there's a couple of trains today," I replied, between mouthfuls.

"Well if you wanted you could always stay here. We do have a band on Saturday nights, but you could open for them. Could give you your room and meals at least."

My first thought was to wonder if that meant she wanted me around. Well, of course she must, or she wouldn't have offered.

"Yeah... yeah, okay. That sounds great," I said.

Only then did I embrace that awkwardness of really looking at her for the first time, so I could smile, a smile to show I was grateful for her offer.

There was some awkwardness. But I also felt an attraction now, which had obviously developed as I procrastinated over-night. I wondered if she would kiss me again and so I waited— she had made the move last night after all. Eventually she simply asked if I was finished with my plate, which I confirmed, and then she took it from me and rose.

"I'll get ready and come back out. If you want, that is?" she said.

"Yeah... sure. I've got nothing else to do."

I immediately realised how bad that sounded as soon as the words left my mouth.

She was gone a while. Long enough for me to wonder if I ought to get back and freshen up again myself—I loved sitting by the sea but would always forget how it would make my hair feel gritty and salty; its length was already difficult enough to manage—not for any reason other than being sat out there so long, as long as it took for her to return, would now look as if I were waiting for her. Of course, I was, but that wasn't the point.

Now, with adrenalin and nervous energy flowing through my veins, I was unable to sit still. I stood and walked further along the pebble beach, mindful of how far I was walking, so as not to disappear from sight. I noted a couple of large boulders that were easily big enough to sit on near the end of the beach, where the hills started, so I figured that I could sit there and observe the scenery of the village behind me.

I did so, and I could see from a distance, Ailie had already returned, and was walking towards me.

"You trying to get away from me?" she laughed when she was close enough to speak without raising her voice. I got the impression that shouting wasn't her style.

"Just fancied the walk."

I hadn't yet scaled the rock to sit on it and as Ailie got closer I had a moment of apprehension, wondering what the right move would be. She made it. Her hand moved towards me and as it caught my attention, she moved her head towards mine and kissed me.

"Did you want to stay here for a while?" she asked.

"No... I was just... yeah, walking. We can walk back."

"No, come on. I'll show you some nice views."

We walked around the beach, observing the sights, with Ailie taking pride in one surprising ascent—it didn't feel like we had climbed that high, so it took me back to see how steep the hill was, looking down to the sea.

"So what do you want to do? With your music?"Ailie inquired.

"I really don't know at this point. I appreciate what you said, but I'm not really any good," I insisted.

"Get away," she responded, "So you are."

"Well, thanks, but I don't really... It's not what I want. I had... well, I'm quite sure you don't want my life story."

"Yes, I do."

I looked at Ailie. She smiled and squeezed my hand.

And just like that I felt the words tumbling out of my mouth. How I felt I was just using what I could think of to justify a nomadic lifestyle, roaming around scenic and idyllic spots to absorb some life experience. It at least made me feel like I was doing something with my time to get over broken hearts and bad relationships. I paused, wondering if such a topic was appropriate.

"Every artist is a tortured soul," she laughed. "Think of how many songs and poems are inspired, daily around the world, by heartbreak."

"And I thought I was the only one," I laughed.

"Mine are worse," she said. "At least you have the confidence to get up and play."

"You write?"

"Yeah, I write. But, now, mine really *are* bad. That's how come I know the difference."

"I'm sure they're not."

"Well, all I know is that they're not ready for public consumption."

"Well, I'm not the public! If I can do it."

"That's the difference between us!"

Ailie briskly changed the subject. "Anyway. If it's not what you want. What do you want?"

"I don't know. I figured that if I just kept on, soon enough, I would find out."

"Sounds like a plan."

"I don't know if that's true. More like the opposite."

The silence felt palpable.

"So you've recently broken up with someone?" I asked.

"No, not exactly."

"Well, what exactly?"

"We haven't exactly broken up."

"What?!" I pulled away.

"No. Wait. Let me explain. He's been cheating on me. I know. But I... It's weird. We haven't been together very long. I won't... I can't be with him. But I am waiting for him to be honest."

"That sounds weird. Why don't you just end it?"

"Because... well. You don't want my life story."

"Go on."

"We had this big argument and he ended up... well, he hit me. It's not a great relationship," she laughed awkwardly. "But I was going to... I was so angry with him. I was going to steal his car and... I don't know, set it on fire or something. I hadn't thought that far ahead. So I sneaked into his house and I caught him with this girl... he didn't see me... I just ran away quickly."

"So why not just end it?"

"I can't, because if he knows that I know then he'll know I broke in. His mam's a bitch and she's a cop."

"Sounds like a real mess."

"Uh-huh... and you know... I thought... it's good for my pain," she said.

"What? That makes *no* sense."

"I'm over that now. Now it's just like a scab. I'm surprised he hasn't taken the hint. It's actually quite fun in a perverse way," she said.

It was a lot to take in.

"Don't worry, I'm not a pyro or anything like that," she tried to reassure me. "After I saw him with the girl I sort of went cold. It was like this person I'd known for years and been with for about five months was not the person I was seeing. Does that make any sense?"

"Well it makes perfect sense, obviously."

"I mean, like, he... I think I had this perception in my head of our relationship. And as soon as he hit me, it opened my eyes. It was like all of the love I felt had transformed into a different emotion. If anything I felt stupid, because I'd believed he was someone he wasn't. I actually feel a bit guilty because I should tell her. But, hey, guess I'm the bitch now!"

"Yeah, you cheated on him too," I laughed.

More silence. But more comfortable, this time.

"So you're quite impulsive, then," I said after a while.

"I guess so," she replied. "Funny how you do the things that seem natural to you, and then, when someone else notices it, it becomes an attribute. Part of your personality. Whereas before, you just did it."

"I never thought of it like that. I guess it's true though."

"Hmm... like... it's weird. How the label of one attribute is supposed to mean that you don't feel the opposite. The world is so small and so big, and we have all of these different emotions and things we can experience, and, yet, we allow ourselves to be categorised. Or told that we can only process one thing at a time."

"Yeah, you mean like, you can't be happy and sad at the same time."

"Right. That's the base point of it, I think. The real fundamental point. Because you can be, really, if you think about it."

"I've never really heard anyone put it like that. You're really quite smart," I said. "It's... I don't know... it's really aware. I guess feeling like that is liberating."

"And suffocating," she replied. "When you live in a place like this then all there is to do is *think*."

With every passing second, I was finding myself becoming increasingly attracted to Ailie. Every time she spoke, it was as if she was unwittingly luring me in; her intelligence, or, at least, her explanation of things I hadn't even cared to give thought to before, somehow making her appear even more captivating. And, without even realising it, I felt completely emotionally connected to her. Drawn to feel sympathy by what she had been through, and attracted by her ability to bounce through it to become this effervescent light that sat beside me.

I was hooked, I knew that already. I could feel it. I was compelled equally by what I knew about her and what I didn't. What else was going on in her mind? It was an unpredictability that was irresistible. It was also intimidating. While she was speaking so eloquently my mind was hammering *IlikeyouIlikeyouIlikeyou* in the most childish way possible, and I froze, scared to say anything that might make me look foolish or frighten her away.

"So, now that you've seen a bit more of this place, do you still think it has its charms?" Ailie asked.

It was only then I realised how far we'd walked and that we were almost back on the pebbled beach.

"Well yeah, *some* of it definitely does," I tried to flirt.

"*Apart* from my obviously captivating company, that is."

"Yeah, I guess, when you've grown up in a city, you appreciate that which is untouched," I said.

"Wow, well you passed the first test," she joked. "Now you just have to live here a year and if it doesn't feel like a hundred, you're sure to fit right in."

"You're joking, but it does appeal. My idea of a perfect life is some small town in America, like the Wild West or something, with sandy trails."

"Sounds nice. A world away from here though."

"Literally, yeah. But, I don't know. It's probably different, but in my mind at least, my idea of that is one of *community*. And people getting on."

"But that's people, not the place. Tell me, honestly, then what?"

"I don't know. I hadn't thought of it like there was a *then what*. I guess I thought I'd simply enjoy life."

"But what's the goal, at the end of it all?"

"Well... that was it... until you shattered my dreams!"

"I'm just trying to get to know you. For all I know, I might well be pregnant with your child."

Wow.

It was probably inappropriate, but I couldn't help but burst out laughing. Ailie did too. She was proving to be quite the expert of manipulating a conversation where she was already two steps ahead. I considered the thought of her coyly trapping visitors and strangers in her web and running conversational rings around them. The shockingness of her statement, delivered so blasé, gave me cause to consider how well I knew her. Not very, not at all, she could have led me on quite a fanciful dance. She could be a pathological liar for all I knew, although my gut feeling was that she was honest. I barely knew her, that much was true, but I always considered my first impressions to be fairly accurate. It seemed to be as if the only relationship she was completely at ease with was her relationship with the truth and her power was in that.

I wanted to have some of that, too. I wanted her relationship with the truth, but the first step of that would be dealing with how my own currently stood. I was honest, to an extent. But I had so much that was unresolved, it was better to just leave it where it was and instead allow myself to be captured within the spell that Ailie was casting.

And it seemed as if she was feeling the same way. At the gig that evening, I played my own material. The pub crowd was a little larger than it had been the previous night, but I was playing to an audience of one. Later on, I absorbed Ailie's enthusiasm about my supposed talent a little more. I knew she liked me. She wasn't the kind of person who said it; she was so articulate, yet preferred her actions to speak louder.

Still, I have no real way to explain how and why, a day later, Ailie was sitting next to me on the train as we made our way back to where I lived, in Alderley Edge, a village south of Manchester.

I can't explain what was going on within me that permitted her to take over my life so swiftly. But, as she was teaching me, sometimes some things are best left unexplained.

Ailie quickly had a lot of stuff worked out. I wasn't going to support two people on the wage of, essentially, a travelling busker. I could barely support myself. Not that she was going to freeload from me, she insisted, but that quickly became meaningless, anyway.

One night out, we went to see a local band. I enjoyed it, they had a good sound—but it transpired they were more interested in me. Unbeknownst to me, Ailie had been very proactive, getting in touch with local bands and asking them if they needed any help with songwriting and arranging. I had never thought of that before, but this particular band—The Cause—seemed taken by my material. We stayed with them until the early hours of the following morning, talking about plans, and could barely wait to get into a rehearsal space.

Ailie had reasoned that my lack of confidence in my own ability would dissipate once I saw the enthusiasm in others, and that did work to an extent; but this new avenue, of hearing one of my creations being played by someone else, and my subsequent, unexpected enjoyment of it, seemed like it would present opportunities I had never even dreamed of.

They offered to pay me, and I thought that was a good idea, but Ailie, being far more on the ball, said she would try and get more attention. The band enjoyed a swift popularity spike, with Ailie giving me all of the credit and saying it was down to my writing. I don't know how much of that was true, but in less than a month, The Cause were being played on local radio stations and there was a big buzz online, too. Such a buzz that two fairly well-renowned record labels were offering contracts. By holding out, Ailie was able to negotiate a royalty split for me. I was effectively treated as a fifth member of the band, and that worked for me. When it came to recording their debut promotional EP, I was given a lot of creative input into the sound. I'd be lying if I said it was anything massively groundbreaking or innovative, but the melody and the sound were well received. I was still surprised that people were genuinely interested in my songs.

When it came to our agreement, I panicked at the speed by which everything had happened. Whether I was concerned about any negative feedback, or whether it was in fact an act of grandiosity or arrogance, I don't know, but I decided that I would insist on being recognised under a ghost name— "Stuart." Why? Well, the first thing that came to mind was Stuart Sutcliffe, "the fifth Beatle." It must have been grandeur, then, but in the weeks that followed, I was relieved to have retained my anonymity. I still felt unsettled by the speed in which it all happened, even though I was enjoying the ride. And there was a pretty big part of me that thought I might like to make it on my own some day, and that this would be a perfect litmus test to see if people actually liked my songs.

The first EP—*Exit*—received a lot of attention, and anticipation for their debut LP similarly reached fever pitch. The guys in the band were all perfectly willing to give credit where they felt it was due, but I had grown quite excited by seeing this all explode, where I could feel a part of it and dip my toes in whenever I felt like it.

Ailie was suitably proud. Within three months, she had turned my life completely around. It made me feel tremendously passive and lazy by comparison, the way that she had seized control of my life and made things happen in a way I could never have dreamed.

The advance on the deals for the EP and LP paid for our rent for nine months and we were able to fully concentrate on getting the material right. Ailie had assumed the role of unofficial spokesperson and manager for the band, and she too had a few of her own songs included in the mix when it came time to choose the list that would comprise the debut album. Ailie was in control, making most of the decisions and, seemingly, able to handle it all with consummate ease. I, on the other hand, struggled to deal with the attention the band was receiving. It was all overwhelmingly positive, yet it was all happening so quickly that I felt unable to fully appreciate or embrace it. With Ailie's role already commonly known, we agreed that if the time came, she would be "Stuart." She even drafted an agreement which essentially laid out the truth and stated that she wouldn't try and rip me off. That was unnecessary in my eyes—I was so deeply infatuated I couldn't consider any form of deception was even possible—but her calculated way of doing business almost led me to believe that she had planned all of this from the very first moment she had laid eyes on me.

I said as much to her on the day we signed the contract for the Cause's first album, *Effect*. The band had gone out to celebrate, but we went to a quiet bar to have a celebratory glass of champagne and then home. We had to be up early because the next day we were due to go and visit a new house that Ailie wanted us to rent.

"I can't believe how much has happened in such a short space of time," I said.

"Yeah, I know. It's crazy," Ailie agreed.

"It almost feels too incredible for this to be coincidence—how much my life has changed since I met you. I didn't have any direction."

"You just needed someone to believe in you, Freddie, that's all," Ailie replied.

I didn't know how much of that was necessarily true, yet how could I disagree? Ailie herself would probably have challenged my description of my life situation as having improved, rather than changed, even if it was for the better, but she was certainly right to take the credit for it, if that was indeed what she was doing. She probably wasn't. She was giving *me* that power back in what she said.

We moved into the new home. It was in a neighbouring village with a sprawling back garden overlooking some wonderful countryside in the Peak District. Our neighbours were older; old enough to not have any real interest in our career, or in anything we did outside of what might directly affect them. Ailie had identified this house as the perfect place for us to live, fulfilling my wish of a secluded, idyllic lifestyle.

Effect was released and surpassed everyone's expectations. The strangest thing ever was driving from our house to the local supermarket and hearing my song on the radio. We pulled over to let that moment sink it. We ignored all speculation about how the record was selling and waited to listen to the radio that Sunday. We knew it would chart and had a feeling that it would be top 20, but when the presenter got to ten and we hadn't been mentioned, we presumed we had just missed out. When it was announced that we were in at number five, the rush of excitement was almost un-fathomable.

We opened a bottle of champagne that evening, too. It seemed like we didn't stop drinking the stuff over the next year. Two of the singles made it in to the top five, the second of which—*Mirrors*—was one of my own songs, the first, a song Ailie and I had written together soon after we knew that the band had an interest in using my songs.

We remained mostly anonymous, although to those in the industry, Ailie and I became a much sought-after commodity. Our label took great pride in "discovering" us and, being flavour of the month, an opportunity came up to write songs for the as-yet-unknown winner of a television talent show for budding singers. Morally, I was against it. I didn't like the way that youngsters were being exploited, and, in a way, I was also against the whole concept, and the way in which it made things difficult for modern musicians who had *real* talent. For a little while, I confused myself with inclusion in that category, but, in truth, I was far from a real musician. Most of the time, I felt as though I was simply moonlighting, and that I would eventually be found out as someone barely able to play the piano and guitar. To some people in the industry, I was renowned for my composition skills, without really having any. Regardless, I considered shows of that nature a roadblock for those who found the "biz" difficult enough to break into as it was.

But what did I know? As soon as I saw the contract and saw how much money we stood to make, well, my principles suddenly seemed to evaporate. Strange, that. I did put up protestations and deliberations in private. With Ailie, I pondered how much of a difference it would make either way. As ever, I listened to her, and she made sense. What was my responsibility? To whom did I owe my loyalty? Life has to be filled with some selfish pursuits, and we ought to consider the validity of the stands we choose to make. I had obligations which did not concern the health of the music industry, and was my moral point strong enough to be worthwhile or even worth sacrificing my public anonymity? Valid enough reasons for maintaining what could be described as a dignified silence, although, I couldn't help feeling they were simply bad excuses—a feeling that was soon forgotten after the first two royalty statements came in. Professionally—or, to be more apt, personally—I found some justification when we were asked to write arrangements to Shakespeare's work for a series of live plays that were being shown on national television. That, to me, provided a cultural antidote.

For the next eighteen months, we enjoyed an incredible lifestyle, attending events where we would walk in—and out—as unknowns, yet leave with more invitations and contacts than we knew what to do with, both socially and professionally. It was hard to keep track of it all, and so I simply gave up, allowing Ailie to organise our diary. I enjoyed that for a long time, going to these gatherings, meeting socialites and somebodies, and receiving a great deal of commendation for our work.

Our label received requests from the management of several very well-known musicians who were keen for us to write for them, and I was able to perceive that as the payoff for the sacrifice I felt I had made. In the meetings to secure agreements, it became clear that our anonymity would no longer be guaranteed, due to the profile of one particular singer we'd be working with.

Eddy Crowe, now in his early seventies, had been phenomenally successful, and universally loved, in the early 1980s. In recent years, however, his star had fallen, and he was now derided as an act wheeled out for those "Evening With" specials on television, or for tours at working men's clubs, where he would essentially perform cover songs as a glorified karaoke singer. Eddy's management was keen for a new, original record, to capitalise on what they felt to be a renaissance of "old timers" releasing new material. Ailie and I were still hot property, and, hence, became the chosen ones to write Eddy's big comeback record.

Our meetings were quite an experience. Eddy was one of those household names who I had not paid much notice to beforehand, but now, faced with the real prospect of working with him, Ailie and I were nervous and excited. When we arrived for our meeting in central London, we were like two kids on their first day at a new job. We were in the meeting room for about twenty-five minutes before Eddy showed up, rail thin, to the point where I didn't know if I was more concerned about his health, or curious about how he generated the tremendous lung capacity for which he was renowned. Eddy's managers were happy with our request to remain anonymous, but the man himself was almost insistent and oblivious to the point that it was our preference to remain that way.

"You can't let me take the credit for what these beautiful kids are doing," he insisted. "I want their names big and bold, beside mine."

As gracious as he was, I got the impression that Eddy didn't really know anything about us. It was all a very demonstrative procedure, the process we go through before acknowledging the star and giving him top billing. Not that I had a problem with that, and indeed, I quite enjoyed the bravado and the generosity, even if it was ultimately a facade. After checking his Wikipedia page, I discovered that Eddy had released close to thirty albums—so to him, we were just two more people he'd be working with, even though to us, it would represent, undoubtedly, the most high-profile act we had worked with.

In the couple of years I'd been with Ailie, I had learned one thing to be true. Take a firm hold of the opportunities life presents and make the most of them. I did that with Eddy. Ailie had been professionally aggressive and had often repeated the importance of looking after number one. I think she did that to make sure I wasn't being naive. It was her way of providing me with a tougher shell.

I felt as strongly as ever about maintaining my privacy. That's not to say that I had evolved in any way, shape, or form. I had not embraced, nor entertained, any notion of addressing the potential anxiety I would feel—which was now tucked away in a safe place and needn't be revisited. Instead, I took full hold of this experience, constantly liaising with Eddy and his manager, eventually turning it into my personal project. Ailie was happy to see me so enthusiastic, and saw it as an opportunity to step back and work on her own too, taking on her own clients.

I would contact Eddy and use anything as an excuse to meet up and jam—which would, essentially, be me playing him a song, coercing him into giving some feedback and making changes, however minor, and crediting him as the co-writer. I loved it. As far as I was concerned, I was now working with the great Eddy Crowe, a real badge of honour and sense of accomplishment in my life.

As for the songs, well, they were pretty good. I had been working with Ailie on songs for so long, but I still had a veritable trove of songs to call upon that I had written in the years before I knew her and, buoyed by that confidence which had been instilled when Ailie had said I was "good," I introduced some of those into my work with Eddy. From that moment it became a project of the most ultimate indulgence.

Eddy had been a pop act at his most famous, but his voice was now slower, deeper, gravelled by time, alcohol, and cigarettes. The distinction in his voice gave me a powerful confidence in the potency of the songs. Sung by me, the lyrics felt pretentious and naive. Yet sung by Eddy, each line carried such an emotional punch, it felt as if it were being delivered by a heavyweight boxer. Before the record went to mastering, I was so excited with our demo version, that I kept a copy for myself. To me, it felt like the *truest* version, and I knew it would feel more intimate and serve as a stronger, more evocative keepsake for the time we spent together.

Without doubt, I had developed a subtle arrogance about the success enjoyed by Ailie and I. She enjoyed that side of me, and there's no doubt that she was mostly responsible for it. But even I was surprised when Eddy's album, *The Fight We Lose*, went to number one. It was described as a masterful return, touted as quite possibly his best ever work—all manner of superlatives that I had not really prepared for or even privately entertained as a consequence of our work together. There was a genuine surprise that, at the age of seventy-four, Eddy Crowe could put out such a record.

Our conversations during the final stages of our work together had revolved around the credit Eddy wished to give me—credit that I was reluctant to take. By the end, I had even convinced myself that I was behaving the way I was for purely selfless reasons—I wanted to see Eddy have this big hurrah, long after the supposed twilight of his career, and I had come to terms with the ramifications of that, thanks, of course, to another of Ailie's insightful observations.

"I just feel selfish... like I'm *allowing* someone as brilliant as Eddy to take the credit. It almost feels like I'm being condescending, like I am *letting* him take the credit because I don't want it," I admitted at a time I was going through some inner turmoil over the thought.

"What does it matter?" Ailie had said to me. "The other things I can understand, but what does this matter? You're doing something nice, what does it matter if you are doing it to be nice or for any other reason? Who are you justifying it to?"

Now, when I saw Eddy on TV talk shows, I was genuinely keen to see him be acknowledged with the credit and for him to accept it. This was a man who had justified the tag of stardom for so long and for as long as I'd known him, had humbly shrugged off any compliment I had given him.

In truth, I had grown sycophantic, partly to compensate for my prior lack of knowledge of what he had achieved, but I knew that in my heart I was genuinely delighted to see Eddy receive the praise. And I was not in the least frustrated when he accepted it. He had credited me enough in private and now, as a showman, he was out there accepting all that was lavished upon him. It was brilliant and exciting to observe. Eddy had returned to the top of the tree, and I felt that I was there alongside him.

looking out over sunset
    is this the start or the end? you have
All the words that you need to
Use when its time to pretend

lost in the summer of my life
    already caught on the slide - ~~I~~ I know
what you say when you own it - and you
know what it means to be blind -

you say - every day is a landslide but
that not what you told me last night - I
still dont know the difference between your truth
& your lies

It's a war and you know that you're losing
    It's more than the mercy you're used to
Is this the end of the start or the start of the end?

See me
    See my eyes -
look through me - like you used to
one more time

lost in the summer of my life, you say
every day is a landslide
    It's a war and you know that you're losing this time -

3

When I got inside, I saw that Hal was sitting at his kitchen table.

"Grab yourself a beer," he said.

"Thanks," I accepted and sat down across from him. "So, what did you think?"

He looked at me cautiously.

"What? What is it? You don't... don't you like the songs?" I asked.

Hal slid a small piece of paper across to me.

It was a cheque, with a figure on it. There was an extra zero on top of the fee he'd agreed to pay me.

"What's this?"

"For your trouble."

"I don't understand..."

"I'm sorry, son. I just don't think this is gonna work out. I've changed my mind. I can't get in tune with it. I've listened to the songs and... it's me, but it doesn't sound like me."

"Really?" I protested. "I love them. I know that there'd be a market for it."

"I was doing this mainly for me."

I didn't know what to say.

"Please, Hal. Think about it," I said. I panicked, almost to my own surprise. "I've been writing some new songs. Some while I've been out here. I'll play a few of them."

"I really don't think it's worth it, son. Not now," Hal replied, solemnly.

"What do you mean, not now?"

"Well... I guess my heart's just not in it. Once that's gone, I usually just walk away."

"Well, don't. Please. Everyone has moments of doubt."

"I can't go back to what I was, though, Freddie," he insisted. "Every day, I move further away from that. You're a great songwriter, but you don't have a magic wand to make me young again. To get that jazz back in my voice. And if I am not going to enjoy it, then why do I want to do it?"

"Okay... I get that. But, just give me a chance. Hear what I've been working on, and then we can talk."

He looked at me sympathetically.

"Okay... hell, why not. It's only time."

"Right... well, give me an hour, and let's go down to the basement."

I went to the bedroom and flicked through my notepad; then turned on my laptop and scrolled through documents with lyrics and songs. I remembered a band I'd been in and written the songs for and I'd never used any of those songs anywhere else, so pulled a couple of them out and decided to play them.

Down in the basement, I deliberated over how I ought to play the songs, and so I did it laboured, slower. I hadn't really considered what I ought to do in terms of material. Should I have chosen what I felt was my best material, or, should I have gone for songs that were meant to be slower, that suited that stronger and travelled, weary voice? It dawned on me that my best chance was with the latter, but I had chosen a variety of songs and it didn't work out. I could tell as I was playing that Hal was lacking in interest and simply going through the routine out of politeness.

He'd already made his mind up.

I stopped playing midway through one of the songs, and Hal stood up, walked over to me, put his large hand on my shoulder and then on my head, in an apologetic manner, and then, turned around and walked slowly up the stairs.

I was nervous and confused. I didn't know what to expect. What was I going to do now? Where was I going to go? All of these selfish thoughts ran through my head. Was it worth trying to convince Hal to carry on?

I remained in the basement by myself for a while. I would pick the guitar up, play a little, and then put it back down again. I did that for a few times, lost, before deciding to face up to facts and venture upstairs.

Hal was out on the porch.

I walked out and sat on the steps.

After a couple of minutes of silence, Hal, staring into space, and without looking at me, spoke.

"I'm dying, son. They told me I got months. Maybe even only weeks."

"What? Seriously? When...?"

I struggled to comprehend the enormity of his words.

"They said it could be months. But they meant weeks, I know that."

"What?"

"Cancer. Pancreatic. I thought it was something I ate but then... I just thought I had stomach ache a lot."

"So, is there..."

"Nothing," Hal interrupted.

An uneasy, tremendously sad silence followed.

"That's why, son..." Hal continued, taking a pause to have a sip of whisky, "... that's why I don't want to waste time on things I don't wanna do. It's nothing personal."

"But if you knew that you weren't interested, then why have us go through all that?" I asked, my curiosity getting the better of me—although as soon as the words left my mouth I regretted the insensitivity.

"Because, son..." he replied. "Creation is medicine."

I paused, before adding, "All the more reason then."

"Not for me. For you."

I was caught off guard again.

"I really don't know what to say, Hal. I'm so sorry."

"I've lived a good life. Don't be sorry. I didn't know if I should say, you know, because of Eddy and all... at least I know when. That was one crumb of comfort I got with Betty. We got a goodbye."

I wondered if I could be so reasonable, so logical, faced with the same situation. Maybe I would? Who knows? Maybe I was doing myself a disservice. Now, at an age still relatively young, I had much left that I felt I should do, even if I wasn't completely sure of what. But Hal had fought his way to a ripe old age with a life of accomplishment behind him. Just like Eddy. And, like Eddy, Hal had the means and the money to do anything he wanted in his later years. Those introspective moments where we doubt whether our life has been a fulfilled one, well, I guess Hal would have them, but he did at least acknowledge he'd led a good life.

"Betty had cancer too," Hal said. "They told her that she had weeks. She... she was way stronger than they reckoned. She took that son of a bitch all the way and you know what, she was still fighting a year on. Sometimes I just wanted her to give up. But she kept saying, one more day, Hal, one more day..."

Hal trailed off. He looked lost in thought.

"Betty... she wrote me forty letters," he said after a brief silence. "I asked her to write things for me, so I could feel that she was still with me... you know, after she was gone. She said that she wanted me to move on and that she was worried that doing something like that would simply upset me or hold me back. She agreed to write five, then ten, and then I convinced her to do the rest. Because she had time. In her last days she found the strength to write me the last few. At that point, I wanted her to rest, but by then she was insistent, and she somehow managed to find the strength to do it."

"Have you read them?" I asked.

"I'd open them on my birthdays. She was wrong, you know. It didn't hold me back. It upset me, of course, sometimes. I would read them and... I'd cry, you know. But they were the best gifts. Every year on my birthday, I'd have a new conversation with her. She'd say something that she never had said to me before. Then when twenty-five had passed... twenty-five years... I would make those letters last for days. I'd open one on my birthday and read a new page each day. When I opened the thirtieth, I treated it like a milestone, reading it all in one day. It was such a treat... even though within the letters she was now writing with the assumption that I would have moved on with my life. I didn't know if I felt like I was letting her down by staying loyal to her... but then, when the next year came around, I couldn't do it. I couldn't open the next one. I had ten letters left. Ten more conversations to have with my wife. How often do you really talk to someone? Or take that for granted? So I stopped. I haven't opened one since. I'd only have a few left now."

He paused, but I was unable to fill the silence.

"Now, I think about how foolish I was. Because I was merely trying to cheat time. And time always wins. Part of me wants to go and read them all now. I resent myself a little. That I didn't carry on reading, when she had gone to such an effort to provide that comfort..."

Hal trailed off again, and I could hear his voice beginning to waver.

I stood, and walked over towards Hal, wanting to console him. But as I moved towards him, he raised his hand in that dismissive way.

"It's okay, son. I'd rather be alone. I just need a bit of time alone, if you don't mind."

"Yeah... of course. Let me know if you need anything."

I went inside and up to my bedroom and lay on the bed. My whole body was throbbing. As I lay still, I could hear Hal start to cry, and fail to control himself. He didn't need to.

I couldn't bear to listen, and I was so emotional after Hal's stories and revelations that I had to go for a long walk. When I was sure I was alone, I cried myself. I thought about how preciously he valued those words, those conversations with Betty. I don't know if I could reconcile the gravity of that with anything in my own life, because I couldn't really comprehend that deep of a loss, and having to live with it for so many years. The insignificance of the work we were doing revealed itself in its true form by comparison.

Before I knew it, I'd reached the town. I looked at my phone. 10:21 p.m. Too late to call home. But Murphy's was still open. I went inside. Louise was there, putting the stools and chairs on the tables.

"Hey, hun," she said, brightly.

I stared at her, unable to provide any response. I wondered what I must have looked like. Lost. Distant. Empty.

"You okay, Freddie?"

"Yeah... yeah, I'm fine. Sorry, it's just been a long day."

"We're getting ready to close up, but hey, you need a drink? You kind of look like you could do with one."

"Yeah... please, that would be great, if it's not too much trouble."

While Louise was behind the bar, I thought of how much I ought to say, and how much I shouldn't. From what I could tell, Hal and Louise were close. Surely she already knew? If not, I didn't want to be the one to break the news.

Louise returned with two whiskies and a bottle of beer. She took one whisky for herself and pushed the other drinks toward me.

"Thought I'd let you decide."

"Thanks."

"Surely Brooke wasn't that difficult?" she joked.

"No... no, she was great. It was fun," I said.

"Then what? Hal? Hope he's not being too grumpy. He can get that way, sometimes, you know. Years of living alone. We try and pull him out of it, but you just... you just live with it, don't you?'

"No... no, he's fine."

"Oh... look, I don't wanna pry. But a problem shared..."

"You guys are really friendly. Brooke has... she was really helpful. I have a few girl problems, that's all."

"You mean she was interfering?"

"No, not at all. It's fine. Honestly. Brooke was really helpful, actually. It's... it's just that Hal has decided he doesn't want to work with me anymore."

I thought that a part admission of the truth could deflect the inevitable path of the conversation.

"Oh, honey, no! Now why would he do that?"

"Well," I sighed, "I think it's just... he thought he was going to be able to do something... it's hard to explain. I think he just wanted to see if he could sound like he used to. Or feel some kind of enthusiasm... or acceptance of the inevitable change. And, he just... he's just not feeling it. I guess, really, it's straightforward, and you know... no messing about, he just said it, it's not going to work."

"That's Hal."

"Yeah, I'm learning."

"Damn. So what you gonna do?"

"You know, I haven't thought about it yet. I guess, go home. I might go travelling. But I don't know what to do with the visa, so I'd have to look into that... I mean, after seeing the Falls, it has whet my appetite to see more."

"That'd be a shame."

"Yeah, but... you know, just passing through."

After saying it, I realised the familiarity of that phrase. It suddenly felt as if all I was ever doing was passing through.

We finished our drinks. Louise offered to give me a ride home, but I felt like I could do with the walk. When I got back to Hal's, I walked around the back to the porch to see if he was still out. He wasn't.

I sat alone on the porch until 1:00 a.m.—going in to help myself to another beer, for no other reason than to let the clock turn to 8:00 a.m. in the U.K., a time I felt acceptable to call. I went to call Kaia, but paused, feeling that, given the circumstances, Ailie wouldn't mind me calling her. All I had to do was tell her what I was going through. I deliberated for a few moments before another drink of beer gave me the Dutch courage, or stupidity, to make the call.

Ailie didn't answer.

I immediately regretted my action and felt like such an idiot for taking the risk.

The phone rang. It was Ailie.

I almost didn't answer from panic. Now I didn't know what I was going to say.

But I did answer.

"Hi, Ailie."

"Hello, Freddie. You called?"

"Yeah, sorry. I know it's early..."

"Where are you? I thought you were in America?"

"Yeah, I am. I'm still out here."

"It must be really late."

"Yeah, one in the morning."

"So why... sorry, I don't mean to sound rude, but why are you calling?"

"I just wanted to talk."

"What about?"

She sounded irritated. She didn't have time for this. To indulge me. Maybe once, but not now.

"Sorry... it's okay. It's nothing. I'll go," I said.

"No, it's fine."

The coldness in her voice hurt. I knew that she wasn't being unsympathetic to my situation; she didn't know it. Any of what I was thinking. She would be sympathetic if she did because she would remember Eddy. But she sounded cold, simply because I was ringing out of the blue, unannounced, and seemingly with no purpose.

What had I expected? Could I really have expected her to be pleased to hear from me?

"Is something wrong?"

"No... I just... I don't know."

"What?"

Again, that annoyance, frustration in her voice.

"I just..." I sighed, "I, erm... I went to these waterfalls today. Shoshone Falls. You should really see them if you ever get the chance..."

"Is that it? Is that why you called me?"

"No, it's... well, this place is really nice. And I think you'd really like it. Can you remember me telling you about wanting to live in one of those American towns? This is like that."

There was a brief silence.

"Okay, well thanks Freddie. I'm pleased it all worked out so well for you. Sounds like you got all you ever wanted."

Ailie's tone and words felt like daggers.

"I was just ringing to say thank you. For everything," I replied, trying to be nice.

"Are you actually taking the piss?"

"No... no. Look, I think I'd better go..."

I didn't even have time to complete my sentence, because Ailie hung up.

Yeah, I wouldn't be doing *that* again.

I sent a text simply saying *sorry*, but she didn't respond.

I let the thoughts swirl around my head for a little while before calling Kaia, hoping for something more positive to end the day on.

She answered right away.

"Hey, you okay?" she asked.

"Yeah... good, thanks. Sorry I didn't call or text earlier. Or, I guess, yesterday."

"That's okay. You're calling now. I was just about to leave for work."

"Oh, sorry..."

"No, you're alright. I've got a few minutes. Sure you're okay? You sound kind of down."

"Yeah, I'm fine. It's been a long day," I started, realising the stark difference in my lack of willingness to accept sympathy from Ailie and the way I was determined to get it from Kaia. I told her about Hal, and how I was feeling the strain of it all so soon after Eddy. Kaia could sympathise; not in the close and powerfully personal way that Ailie had, but, insomuch as she had been present and seen me at my lowest.

Kaia did her best to cheer me up, but the conversation was brief, and before long she was gone. For once, I found myself wishing that the conversation had gone on longer.

I lay awake, thinking of our call, of how I had previously resisted Kaia for whatever reason, whatever guilt I was feeling. But now, she was connecting with me. She was providing comfort and, in all actuality, she had been my crutch since Eddy had passed away. I felt like I had to give her credit for her persistence although, really, maybe I was over-compensating, because of the guilt I felt for having pushed Ailie away when she was doing the same. Whatever the reason, I felt comfort, and drifted off to sleep thinking of Kaia.

I was awakened by the noise of conversation and it took me a few seconds to remember where I was. I checked my phone to see it was already after 9:00 a.m. I listened closely but couldn't make out the voices, until they moved out on to the back porch. Now I could tell that it was Hal and Louise, although I couldn't hear what they were saying. I looked out over the back and saw them walking around the garden. Holding hands. Then Louise, wiping her eyes and putting her head on Hal's shoulder. Hal, standing awkwardly, before embracing her in a hug. It was hard to witness to such a sad moment.

I went downstairs, into the kitchen, before getting a bottle of water and walking out onto the porch, where I noticed Brooke. Her eyes were red and patchy from crying.

"Hey," I said. "I guess you've heard, then?"

Brooke nodded, as another tear rolled down her cheek.

I stood there, feeling like a stranger imposing on the raw grief of these very close people.

"I wanna get out of here," she finally said. "Wanna come?"

"Yeah, sure. Where?"

"Doesn't matter. Anywhere."

We drove, in silence, along a familiar road, the road I'd arrived into town on with Hal. We drove past Shoshone Falls. After a while, we slowed down, and Brooke pulled up at a layby.

Brooke got out and I took that as my cue to do the same.

"There's a trail along here," she said, solemnly.

We walked across the barren landscape for what was probably about a mile, but what seemed like twenty in the heat, walking toward a tree with roots that were so large that you could sit on them. It became clear that was our destination and Brooke half-sat, half-laid back on the tree and one of its off-shoots.

A sign stated "Craters of the Moon." I could see why the area was so named. The sparse greenery was completely out of place and the tree was the only thing that distinguished the landscape from pictures I had seen of the surface of the moon or Mars. It was a complete contrast to how I'd felt looking at the waterfalls. There was a profound isolation, which merely served to heighten our sombre mood. The heat was stifling and only this tiny piece of cover provided any respite.

"You can walk if you want. I just wanna sit here for a while," Brooke said.

I felt that was more of a prompt than a suggestion, and so I decided I would walk along this uncertain ground over to one of what I perceived to be the craters, to see what they looked like. The ground was unsteady, with the crusted lava remnants acting just as rocks, and, for a few seconds, I had that irrational, but somewhat logical, concern that it might still burn my feet. As I reached the crater—which, to all intents and purposes, was a small embankment—I noticed cracks in the earth; crevices not large enough to fall down, but wide enough to at least make you think that you needed to be careful with your step. I climbed the bank and turned back to see Brooke by the tree. She was further away than I would have thought. I raised my hand to wave, and she did the same.

I sat atop the bank and surveyed the area. It had its own power; different to the falls, but a strong power all of its own, nonetheless. Barren, desolate. All of these descriptions that convey emptiness; emptiness as a simple matter of fact and emptiness as an emotion. Of course, acting as the latter, it is a wholly negative thing to feel, and there was the natural impulse to attach the emotion to the place, making it the perfect environment in which to wallow in times like these. The derivation of how that came to be fascinated me at this moment.

Yes, it was desolate.

Yes, it was a negative thing to consider that nothing of value could grow here. But consider nature, the ultimate emotionless force it is, not discriminating against anything, just *being*. It just happened this way. It was effectively neutral if it was anything.

I tried to take something positive from it. It was providing a place for introspection. And while dwelling is altogether not healthy, sometimes, it is necessary. There could hardly be a more fitting or worthwhile setting for that as this and it certainly seemed as if Brooke was familiar enough with the area. I looked over at her and observed the tree, powerfully thriving against the bleak backdrop. Wasn't that strikingly beautiful? That it had broken through, against all odds, grown, flourished, and persevered. Even here, where nothing could reasonably grow, something had. In a strange, but calming, sort of way, I felt as if I were one with the lava fields. I had a lot in common with it. One catastrophic event had caused such a profoundly destabilising effect on my own equilibrium. I, like the ground I walked on, was cracked. I was changed. I was searching for an answer.

Looking over at Brooke, I began to think about Hal. Try as I might to find any positives in these austere circumstances, the inevitability in this case was one from which no positives could be gleaned. Observing Brooke, all alone, I was compelled to walk back over to the tree and sit with her.

It felt strange to observe the change in her, from the previous day. But then, I knew all about how losing someone close can change you.

"There are other trails. I can take you on those some other time. If you want," she said. "I just thought, today... I don't really wanna be around people."

"No," I understood. "I like this though. It's real."

"You know what really pisses me off?" Brooke started.

"No, go on."

"Do you know how long I've wanted Mom and Hal to get together?"

"Really?" I was quite surprised.

"Don't say you haven't noticed."

"What?"

"She's completely in love with him," Brooke said, in a way that implied her incredulity that I had apparently—but sincerely—been oblivious to it. "Like, head over heels. Smitten. For years and years. As long as I've been aware of emotions and feelings."

She stood up, indicating that she was done with the silent introspection, and turned to walk to the car.

I followed.

"So why does that annoy you?"

"Because she knew nothing was going to happen. Hal's a slave to his dead wife. And now the punchline is that he will die and Mom is going to be a widow to someone who never loved her back."

I thought about that statement.

"His wife died when they were young," Brooke explained.

"I know," I replied. "He's told me all about Betty."

"I don't mean to sound uncaring. I think it's sweet. But she's my Mom, y'know."

"What happened to your Dad?" I asked, before quickly adding, "you don't have to tell me. Just..."

"Yeah, well, I never knew him. He took off with Mom's sister when I was two. They all ran the bar together."

"Wow... I'm surprised she kept at it."

"Yeah, she's a strong lady. Stubborn as they come... to a fault," she lingered over the last few words.

I had considered it romantic in a tragic way that Hal had remained loyal to his wife. But then, if I was oblivious to something that was so obvious, maybe it stood to reason that Hal could be too. I could understand Brooke's point of view. How long is long enough to grieve? At which point does the guilt stop? And now this situation really was tragic. Having procrastinated for so long about two relationships in the past few weeks—and, really, years before that—I appreciated that I had at least had a time, a moment in our lives, however brief or however long, with people I considered that I loved. At the time, it felt like it would last forever, and I hoped it would. Now, alone, and in comparison to what both Louise and Hal were going through, I felt thankful for those moments, instead of thinking about what it meant to love just one. It was a strange set of circumstances to bring it about, but I suddenly felt more free, no longer bound by this worry which had dogged me for years and years. Like the tree, something positive had been born on this wasteland.

It seemed as if it would be another silent car journey until I decided to break the quiet.

"I know I don't know you," I started. "But this thing with Hal... I know it is going to be so hard. You're different today to how you were yesterday, and that's natural... but don't let it become something that defines you. Just, say no. Be you. There is going to be a lot of sadness coming. But you need to... to be the person that everyone around you loves. Don't lose yourself."

"I don't know. I don't know if I can be strong enough," she admitted. "I'm not Mom."

"You're more resilient than you think," I replied.

Brooke opened up more on the way home. It had promised to be a silent ride until I started playing with the book of foreign words. She told me how she had grown frustrated many times over recent years and confronted her mother about what she was doing pining for Hal. She had set up blind dates to try and turn her head; she'd done that in the bar in front of Hal to show Louise that he wouldn't get jealous; that she could have a life with a partner. She was also angry with Hal, although, she kept trying to reassure me that these moments were fleeting, and she felt bad for having them. She kept asking if that made her a bad person.

I wondered whether Brooke's outlook on love and relationships had been unhealthily influenced by this example of unrequited love, to which she had been exposed for so long. And yet I could tell, from admittedly the little I felt I knew of her, that there was a part of her that romanticised love in the way that most people did. I felt some obligation to try and balance her point of view.

"Don't be angry at your Mom," I said. "I've only recently got to know you all, and I can already tell that she is strong and wise. But I think we're all just children when it comes to love. And if it's as obvious as you say it is, then surely Hal must know."

"She does everything for him, so I don't know how he can't." Brooke replied. "She cooks for him, cleans for him, does his grocery shopping when he's not feeling well. Talks to him. Hears him talk about Betty. I've been here the whole time. No other woman has done that. No other woman could have done what she has done."

Brooke sighed, perhaps only now realising the magnitude of what Louise had coped with in her life.

"Yeah, she's pretty strong," she said after a while, as we closed in on Hal's property and turned into the driveway.

As Brooke cut the car's engine, there was an almost ominous silence. Neither of us wanted to leave the car. I sighed. I wondered how we would find Hal and Louise inside, how things might be different. And my thoughts also turned to my immediate future. If I felt like I was imposing before, then I certainly was now. Plus, I felt terrible, taking money from a dying man for work I had not done. That was an understatement. But that could wait, a least for a little while.

As we entered the house, we could hear lively conversation and raucous laughter. We walked over toward the living room, where we saw Louise and Hal surrounded by numerous open boxes of photographs and. Brooke looked at me with hopeful, smiling eyes, and I smiled too, even though there was an overwhelming sadness that weighed like an anchor on this house now.

Photographs were strewn all over the living room floor.

Hal was telling Louise of a time he was playing at a club, before he met Betty. We walked in seemingly in the midst of this tale, one that Louise had probably already heard numerous times. He had faced heckling from old-timers about why he wasn't fighting in Vietnam, and it had turned into a free-for-all as he argued back with them, refusing to back down. It all came to a head when a chair was thrown on stage. Hal had not managed to avoid it and was proud of showing off the bump on his leg, pulling up his trouser to show it. It was faint, after all these years, but then, he knew his own body.

"A million people died. I wasn't gonna be one of them, my Daddy told me that," he laughed and sat back, before, bouncing back like a spring to say with wide eyes and enthusiasm, "Oh, did I ever tell you about that time we were in Colorado?!"

In unison, Louise and Brooke both yelled, "Yes!"—almost in plea for that particular story to never be repeated, and as they laughed, I couldn't help but laugh along, though I had no clue what they were talking about.

The laughter died down when Louise and Brooke left. I had a shower and prepared myself for the inevitably difficult conversation that was to follow.

As I entered the kitchen, Hal was sitting at the table, dressed up for an evening out.

"I thought we'd go to Murphy's, for dinner," he said.

"Obviously," I laughed. "Look, Hal, I... we do need to talk."

I sat down at the table across from him.

"You know, now that we're not going to be working together anymore, there's really no point me being here."

Hal looked at me.

"Yeah. I get it. I don't blame you. You don't want to share a house with a dying man."

"No! No. That's not it at all," I honestly protested. "It's just that there is literally no purpose for me to be here."

"I paid you, didn't I?" Hal said, petulantly, in a sense I took to be joking.

"Yeah... well... about that. I can't take your money."

"Look Freddie. You came out here to work. You were good enough to do that without a contract. I broke our agreement and so you deserve to be paid. And I'm paying you. You're not going to take a dying man to court, are you?"

"Of course not. But you paid me way too much. I don't want to be paid if I'm not doing any work."

Neither of us were going to back down, and I got the sense

that he admired or appreciated my stubbornness on the point.

"Well, you're not going anywhere tonight. And you can't leave without saying goodbye to Louise and Brooke."

4

It was open mic night at Murphy's, with several local acts and budding musicians there to take part. We had arrived just after it started and were still able to find a good seat at the bar. I got the sense that a seat was always reserved for Hal. Not any one seat in particular, but every time we'd been in, there was always at least one spare at the bar, no matter how busy.

Louise greeted us with drinks before we'd even ordered, acting as if nothing had happened the day before. It was business as usual.

After a couple of classic songs had been murdered by cover acts, Louise took it upon herself to go to the mic and make a request for some original acts. As she did, she was receiving whistles and cat-calls. I was surprised to see Hal joining in with the whistling. Louise took it all in good humour.

She walked from the small stage—if you could call it that; it was essentially a raised platform with a black backdrop and a mic stand—and for ages, it seemed as if no-one was going to get up. So, the general hubbub of conversation continued, and it was only when I noticed that Hal had been gone—supposedly in the bathroom—for too long that I turned around and noticed he was now making his way toward the stage. As he approached the microphone, the whooping and hollering almost reached fever pitch.

"Calm yourselves down, will ya," Hal said through the mic. The furore died down as the sense of anticipation grew.

"Shit, you think I'm going to sing?" he laughed. "No, I ain't gonna... but I did pay for a very prestigious act to be here tonight."

A sense of dread swept over me.

"Nobody knows this kid, but he's responsible for every good song you hear on the radio or TV. Ladies and gentleman, put your hands together for, all the way from England, Mr. Freddie Ward."

Hal pointed right at me, and of course, in an instant, all eyes were on me. I had no choice. It suddenly occurred to me that the last time I had played in front of a public audience, was the night after I had met Ailie. I could barely believe that it had been that long. Sure, I'd played in front of people, but never in front of a public crowd of any size.

I took one of the guitars from the side of the stage—it seemed that the bar supplied some instruments too for those coming without—and passed Hal, who raised his eyebrows and smiled at me.

As I looked out, with the stage light beaming to obscure some of the faces in the bar, I felt a sudden rush of apprehension. A certain vulnerability. In the time between now and the last time I'd been in this position, many of the songs I had written had been played publicly, to thousands, in front of thousands, so, many of the emotions that I had poured out were now the possession of everyone else, too. I began to wonder whether anyone here— thousands of miles from my home—had even heard of anything I had done.

"Hi," I said, to a small ripple of applause. "I don't suppose any of you have heard of a band called The Cause? Or Eddy Crowe?" A few people clapped and cheered at the reference to both acts, and I felt somewhat reassured. I decided, then, to play one of the songs I'd done with Eddy.

"This is a song called *Rosie*," I announced, to an unexpected but apparently familiar reception.

I enjoyed it so much that I ended up playing a couple more, not really wanting to outstay my welcome, and eager to leave with a good impression. I had in fact tried to leave the stage after two songs, but was convinced to remain, and so I played an arrangement of a song—*Dominoes*—that I had come up with while strumming around on Hal's back porch. This new song seemed to go down well, and as I returned to the bar, I received a number of high-fives and pats on the back. I seemed almost as popular as Hal.

And, sat next to Hal, I felt like a big deal. I'd gone from originally thinking that he was trying to embarrass me, to appreciating the wonderful gesture. Several of the patrons approached to ask if I had really written those songs, who else I'd worked with, and was I in town to work with Hal? I pushed those questions on to Hal, hoping that seeing some keenness from his public would convince him to change his mind. He just laughed it off and said that he couldn't talk business, or that I charged way too much and wouldn't work with a bum like him.

Hal was in his element and obviously getting worse for wear, but I wasn't about to tell him what he could and could not do. I could tell that Louise was concerned. From time to time, she would glance over at me, with those eyes that said, *keep an eye on him*. I think that toward the end of the evening, she got to fixing his whisky and coke's whisky-free, but I noted that she never told us to leave. Hal was never rude or belligerent, but he had clearly passed the point of self-control, and I got the impression that, with closing time nearing, Louise would rather have him where she could see him.

Maybe there was something to what Brooke had told me. Or maybe I was simply reading too much into it *because* of what she had said?

My suspicion, on one score at least, was proven to be justified when Louise insisted on driving us home. When we arrived at the house, she took control of Hal, although she needed my help in getting him up the stairs. I watched from the hallway as she helped him into bed and then tenderly sat beside him. I don't think she was aware that I was still watching.

"Oh, Hal," she sighed. "What is this life? What is this life?"

As she leaned in to kiss his forehead, I turned away, and moved toward my bedroom. I didn't need to see any more. I changed for bed and went downstairs to get some water. Again, the night was quite warm, so I went out on the back porch and sat on the bench, to realign my thoughts.

Before too long I was joined by Louise.

"You don't mind, do you?" she asked, as I turned to her, to see that she was lighting a cigarette.

"No, not at all," I replied.

"I don't normally, but it's been a long day."

We shared a comfortable silence.

"I don't quite know how to leave," I admitted after a couple of minutes. "I mean, I know I should, but I just feel like I'm in some kind of limbo. I tried to talk about it tonight but Hal just wanted to go out and... you know, you just don't..."

"Yeah, I know."

A longer silence followed.

"You okay?" I asked.

"Yeah," she hesitated. "I'm okay. Thanks."

"So I hope I'm not speaking out of turn," I said, cautiously, "but Brooke said that you had... you had pretty strong feelings for Hal."

Louise laughed.

"Yeah... I guess you could say that. It's, like, the worst kept secret in town."

"And what... for all these years? That's... I couldn't."

"Look, I've tried. Believe me, I have," Louise replied, softly. "Most days, I've just learned to live with it. Just one of those things. And some days, my heart breaks all over again. Today happens to be one of those days."

I looked at her to see tears flowing down her cheeks, yet her voice wasn't even quivering. How must it feel to be so hardened and used to such pain, and yet still so on the balance, constantly on the verge and periphery.

"Surely he knows," I said.

"Yeah," she replied, taking one final draw of her cigarette and slowly exhaling, before flicking the butt onto the grass. "Yeah, he knows. I, erm... on his sixtieth birthday, I told him how I felt. He'd been such a support for me after my husband left us and you know, I fell for him. I lived with it, until I couldn't live with it anymore. I thought I could tell... I could sense there was something between us. But he said it straight up. Betty was gone, but she'd always be there."

"That was it, that was what he said?"

"If only that was it... that was all of it. I was a *nice* woman, he valued my friendship dearly. It was... yeah, not a fun conversation. Not one I wanted to revisit."

"So, what happened after that?"

"I didn't talk to him for a few months. I couldn't face up to it. But then Brooke saw him in the grocery store and asked why we didn't talk to him anymore. She went right up to him and said *hey*. The innocence of kids. And then, I thought, you know... it would be okay. And it has been. Okay. But the feelings never went. You just... I just fell more and more in love with him. Fool that I am. And I know I can't say anything, so, I just... well, you know. I love him, and I'm as close to him as anyone can get. So, there's that."

I didn't know what to say.

"Look, I'm not saying that he doesn't care. Or that he disregards my feelings. I know he cares. I know he appreciates what I do. I just... I can't be her. I'm *not* his beautiful wife. I can't replace her. I just used to pray that one day, maybe I would be good enough. And now..."

As I looked at Louise, my heart ached for her. Compared to her troubles, mine had been trivial. I had to say something.

"I came out here on the back of two bad relationships. Or messed up ones, at least. I felt heartbroken. But, you know, better to have loved and lost, as they say. I don't quite know how that compares to what you're going through, but you're a lot stronger to deal with it."

"Am I?"

Now her voice was cracking a little, her tears a little heavier.

"Well, you're here."

"Yeah," she smiled, and laughed, wiping the tears from the corners of her eyes. "Yeah, that's true. I guess I am."

I kissed her on the cheek and hugged her. She held on tightly to me, crying into my shoulder.

I didn't remember falling asleep on the porch, but I woke with the sunrise and found a blanket placed over me. Earlier, there were so many mornings where I had woken up, not knowing where I was, or taking time to realise. Here, I knew instantly where I was and I could clearly remember the events of the previous evening. And while I felt as though I should have been sad, I wasn't. I just lay there, watching the sun rise, gazing at the miles and miles of emptiness at the back of Hal's property, observing the ebb and flow of the trees in the ever-so-slight breeze.

I felt warm—mostly because of the temperature, but also inside, and for what felt like the first time in weeks, or even months, I really felt as if I was in a good place, personally. Mentally, at least. I didn't know what lay ahead. I considered the thought that soon—possibly even later on in the day—I may well be boarding a plane. But for now, I could savour every moment of the scenery and feel that, for a few moments in my life—be it these literal seconds, or the past few days—I had seen some wonderful things and met some wonderful people. I felt the realisation that things are what you make of them. Solitude could be a time when you descend into your darkest self. Inversely, it could be a time when you are at your most productive. Or it could simply be time taken to relax and enjoy life. Yes, I knew I would have to deal with some tragic news sooner than I would like, but I also knew that, even though I'd be thousands of miles away, I would at least get the opportunity to say goodbye to Hal, a person who had given me so much in such a short space of time.

Louise apeared on the porch.

"Freddie. You're awake," she said, smiling. "Good. I was about to put some breakfast on, if I can find anything in the cupboards, that is."

I went to sit up and discovered that my entire body was aching from the hard bench. It took quite an effort to push myself to sit up. Eventually, I was able to do so, and I walked inside, sitting at the table, where Louise had placed a couple of plates of toast. Soon we were joined by Hal, who seemed surprised that Louise had stayed over.

"Mornin'," he greeted us.

"Morning, Hal," I replied.

"Morning," said Louise, brightly. "So, do you know what today is?"

"Tuesday?" Hal said, somewhat confused.

"Right," she responded. "It's also the second day of the week. Now, we wasted Monday. I'm gonna let that one slide, but, as we all know, things being as they are, time is very precious. And you boys have work to do."

Both Hal and I went to interrupt.

"Now, Louise, I already talked this over with Freddie, and he's happy... you know, we agreed. It just isn't going to work," Hal said, firmly.

I didn't agree, but I wasn't going to argue.

Louise stared at us both.

"Yeah, I knew you were going to say that, Hal. So, I was thinking. You like having Freddie around, right?"

"Well, yeah..." Hal almost spluttered his admission out, bashfully.

"Well, I know you do. I've seen that you do. And Freddie... you've been paid to work, right?"

"Yeah, but..." I tried to protest, not really sure where this was headed, but Louise put up her finger to stop me.

"So... I've got an idea. You gonna hear me out?"

"Sure," Hal agreed, looking somewhat flummoxed, waving his hands and banging them on the table. "Hit me with it."

"Well... one horrible day, we're going to sit around talking about the good old days and telling all the stories you used to tell," she said, holding Hal's hands. "And I got to thinking... there ain't no way I'm gonna remember every piece of shit that comes outta your mouth. Hell, I don't know how much of it is even true. But when you're right there telling the story I feel as if I can recite every word. So, I'm thinking... you've got a writer right here... why not *write* your story. Cos, you know... you got one."

"Oh? Um... you know, I'm not... I'm not that kind of a writer," I insisted. "I don't know..."

"Well that's alright," Louise interrupted, turning to me, now holding my hands with her free left hand, "in that case, it will simply all just go horribly, horribly wrong."

Louise and Hal both burst out laughing.

"Honestly, there's just no way... I don't know what I'm doing," I protested.

"It's okay, Freddie. I have written down a list of stories that Hal has told me in the past. Well, those that I can remember. And I'm sure that he can fill in the blanks."

"That easy, huh?"

"It's a start."

I looked at Hal, expecting him to be unconvinced, but to my horror he appeared to be warming to the idea.

"You know," he said. "*That* sounds like just what I need. And hey, gives you an excuse to stick around."

That much was true. But in all honesty, I wasn't entirely sure that I was *looking* for one. Maybe I had? But the implication I got from Hal's comments was that maybe *he* had been looking for one, and now had one.

In those circumstances, could I really say no? Shouldn't I at least humour him?

"Okay, well... when do you wanna start?"

Hal glanced toward the calendar on the kitchen wall, making a salient point without saying a word.

"I'll wash up, then I'll get out of your hair," Louise said excitedly.

5

"So, truly, I have no idea how this is going to work," I said, as we sat in the basement surrounded by microphones. "Am I supposed to go through Louise's list, or do you just wanna..."

"Well I think the first thing we ought to get you is a dictaphone or something," Hal sighed, "because this just ain't gonna work long term. I ain't gonna be spending the majority of my last days down here, I can tell you that for sure."

"Well, before you do that, I would like to renegotiate my terms. I took your generous cheque and tore it up," I started, and I could sense Hal starting to stir a response. "But, if you're serious, I'm happy to accept slightly reduced terms from our original agreement, considering you're hiring someone who doesn't really know what they're doing."

I passed Hal a sheet of paper that had a fee of half of what he had originally offered. He looked as if he was going to put up a fight, but before he was able to, I spoke up.

"I have free lodgings, I am fed every day, and Louise gives me free beer. I'm well looked after, and I think you'll agree, in the circumstances, that's a very handsome sum of money."

"Well, you know, I think you should just keep that cheque. But, hey, well... it's your life, kid," he said, trailing off, and appearing to make a number of unintelligible grunts.

"Okay, Hal. Well... humour me," I replied. "Consider this part of my payment. If I'm writing your life story, let me ask you about your career in music. We're in a good setting. And, you know, if you still feel up to it, after, play a few songs. Not for anyone else, just, for me. For us. I would love to have you play a few more of my songs."

"Okay... okay kid. Deal," Hal replied. "But can we do the songs first? Get them out of the way."

"Sure, but... you know, you go alone."

I set up the mic and the recorder, and also put my phone on the side to record Hal playing on video, unbeknownst to him. I was emotional and nervous, considering that these could well be his final performances.

Hal's playing was certainly not flawless. He had not played for so long that the callouses on his fingertips had healed and not yet fully reformed, so, at times, the fingering of the strings gave a little rusty sound which, if he knew was being recorded, he would probably have hated. But in my eyes, it merely served to give his performance a greater authenticity.

I genuinely wanted to sit back and fully take in these surreal moments, but found myself in the midst of a creative burst of ideas which I could barely control. Hal was, thankfully, oblivious to modern technology recording him in this setting, and I got to thinking about how much we could capture in that fly in the wall method, with Hal talking so candidly and so naturally. It was an idea to think on, but in order for it to work visually, we would have to visit several different locations to speak about certain topics.

Hal played three of my songs and I could tell he was done after that. He held on to the guitar and seemed to be deliberating with himself, lost in thought.

"You know, I gave you this idea that life with Betty was perfect," he eventually started. "And, for the most part, it was. But that time in Toronto where we agreed to get married... man, I must have asked her a thousand times. But the first time she thought I asked her, I never did. See, I was playing this show up in Denver and you know... I was with a band. And Betty was back home, here in Idaho. And well, the band will be the band. Long story short..."

"'Hal,' I interrupted. "Keep your long stories long."

"No, short for now. For what I'm saying to you," he insisted. "But anyway, the band will be the band, and we were on tour. And one night, our drummer, Pete, he got himself in a bit of a tangle, and he hooked up with this... you know, a lady seeking payment for services, if you know what I mean. And I gotta tell ya..."

Hal broke into a spluttering, laughing fit, and it seemed as if his grasp on the guitar was the only thing keeping him upright or holding him together.

"God, I can remember the conversation that he was having with this girl as clearly as if he were having it now," Hal said, through outbreaks of laughter, shaking his head in remembrance. "He was in the room next to mine and the walls were paper thin. It was like some Woody Allen movie or somethin'. Man, he was going back and forth. Should he do it? It was the wrong thing to do. Would they see each other again? This woman is barking back at him to get the hell on with it, that she ain't looking for no commitment. She doesn't need a daddy for her babies, she already got two. I tell ya, you had to be there. Better than any radio play I ever heard."

"So, did he...?"

"Oh yeah, he's a man. That charade was never gonna last too long, but it sure was fun while it lasted," he laughed. "And I get to thinking, I'm finding all of this funny, but I know Pete, and I know Pete is going ten to the dozen in his head, these are real questions he's asking himself. So I start writing this song from Pete's point of view and I find the whole thing so damn funny that I have to immediately call home and tell Betty."

"Right..."

"So I make the call. It's quite late, and remember, the walls are really thin, so I'm having to speak real low. And I don't know now if I was still laughing or what, but I was finding it hard to keep it together. And I don't know what Betty was thinking on the other end of the phone, but I was speaking real low, quiet, slow. I say *'Betty, I gotta tell ya...'* and no word of a lie, she yells back at me, *'Hal Granger, I ain't having you ask to marry me at one in the morning on no goddamn telephone call from Denver!'* And she slams the phone down on me. One of the funniest nights of my life."

"Yeah it sounds like a bit... it's a good story," I laughed.

"Oh yeah. But wait! So I write this song. I've got Betty's words ringing in my ears, so the song is now interspersed with Pete's worries and then Betty's over-reaction to something I never said..."

Trailing off, Hal starts playing this song. It's beautiful, slow, romantic. Familiar.

Our time is still, I never see you,
and nerves like time, erode,
do you remember scenes
that night we played
with just the things we know...
A lover's scene, a nervous feeling,
but I've never been afraid...
You race ahead, with words I said,
it's what I meant, anyway...
I'm dancing with your shadow,
turning down the lights,
the moon goes down in Denver
and I'm wishing you goodnight.

It really was quite something.

"That is brilliant," I said. "I've heard it before, but like that... it's just perfect."

"But you see, I played that song for the first time up in Toronto a few months later. And that's when she... she knew I would ask if given any encouragement on that day. She was in control of that."

"That's nice."

"But that's the thing. She went... God bless her, she went to her grave thinking that song was about her, and the first thing I had to tell everyone when she had gone, it was just as much about Pete and this hooker! I could never have told her that. I think if I had, we'd never have married!"

Hal was uproarious, and then, once his laughter had subsided, he kept a smile on his face for a long time, looked down at the guitar and sort of stroked the body of it. It was a very poignant moment that grew in significance as he placed the guitar against the wall and said, "More stories later, kid," as he walked up the stairs and into the kitchen.

I stopped recording once I heard the basement door close.

I wondered if, maybe, I had just witnessed the great man's final performance, and that, for the majority of it, he'd played songs I'd written. I felt wowed, humbled, and privileged. I sat in silence, alone, in contemplation. I felt tempted to watch the video recording, but felt that it could wait. It felt so precious. I thought again of how this might be replicated. I would have to talk to Louise, to Brooke even, to see how we might set up situations where we could work together, so that it wouldn't appear to be so contrived; so that Hal's stories could flow naturally, in the form I had just witnessed, in the way I had presumed Louise would want.

Then, I checked myself, wondering if it was too clinical to see things in this way. If, even with the best of intentions, I would still be manipulating situations and recording moments that ought to remain sacred. It was certainly a decision I didn't want to make by myself. The best course of action would be to speak with Louise.

I made my excuses to Hal, telling him I needed to get out for a bit, have a run, do some exercise, and that I'd meet him at Murphy's later. And, though it was an excuse, that's what I did, running along the country road in the opposite direction until I was far enough to feel that turning and running back past Hal's house, to Murphy's, would make for a worthwhile workout. I was burning off energy, getting the adrenalin going with the thought that I might be able to see things more clearly afterwards. As I got far enough to stop and turn around, I took a few seconds to take in the beautiful scenery. Flat, and reaching for miles and miles. It wasn't exactly how I had pictured it in my dreams, but still, it was pretty much my ideal. And yet, strangely, I considered that I could probably find something just as picturesque back home. I was a little curious about my own perception in that regard. I didn't dwell for long, I just enjoyed it, and by the time I reached Murphy's, I was in need of refreshment.

Louise, as ever, was behind the bar. The place was decidedly empty. I suppose Tuesday afternoons wouldn't necessarily be the liveliest. Empty, that was, except for Brooke and an unfamiliar man sat at the bar. It was noticeable because the man was a lot older than Brooke, and not young enough to pass for a son of Louise's. I figured he must have been early forties.

"Hey! Well, speak of the devil! Here he is! Your ears must have been burning," announced Brooke, smiling.

"Sorry?" I said, gasping for air. "And sorry, I'm knackered... tired, I mean. What do you mean?"

"I should think you are sorry," Brooke snapped, playfully. "If you were going to put on a show last night, then why wasn't I told about it?"

"Oh... err... Hal. He put me up to it. It was a spur of the moment thing."

"Well, I've seen it anyway. It was posted online."

"What?!"

"Here. Look..."

Brooke pulled out her phone to show me one of her social media pages and found a video someone had uploaded of me performing the previous evening.

"Oh, well... that's embarrassing," I laughed.

"Why?" Brooke quizzed, "you were awesome."

"You were," insisted Louise, "you got a good reception, sweetheart, you know that."

"Oh... yeah, it was fun," I didn't have the strength nor the inclination to put up a fight. "Could I get a beer?"

"Sure," Louise said.

"So, anyway. Freddie, meet Tyler... Tyler, Freddie," Brooke introduced me to the stranger. "Tyler's a friend. He's a musician too."

The four words that anyone in the business hates to hear. In fact, I'd guess they are the four words anyone in any industry hates to hear, particularly the arts. You can tell from the introduction that the purpose is for this person to possibly get some advice, or some help. I never thought I'd get bored of that, because I never considered myself an expert in the field, and it was always fine to talk to someone, but after a while, it would grate on me at events when a complete stranger would be introduced to me. Yeah, great.

Half the time, these people wouldn't really want to be introduced to me anyway. What an awkward, ridiculous social convention.

My response was tried and tested. I had the patter down, able to deal with the situation on auto-pilot, against anything I was feeling about it internally.

"Oh, cool," I said, enthusiastically.

"He saw the videos. He normally does the open mic night here but missed it last night. Tell him, Tyler..."

"Yeah." Tyler extended his hand for a shake. I accepted. His demeanour was polite and yet apprehensive, presumably due to nerves, even if I couldn't understand why. "I'm a big fan. I was devastated to miss out last night. If only I'd have known. Man, I woulda been here, front row."

This was embarrassing. I was naturally deferential to anyone older than me.

"Thanks, Tyler. It's nothing, really, I'm... well..."

Louise brought my drink over. A welcome break, and an opportunity to change the subject.

"Thanks. Hey, could I talk to you for a minute?"

"Yeah, sure."

Louise looked at me as if to say, "well, go on then." I was hoping that she'd suggest moving somewhere private.

"Well... actually... could we..."

I motioned toward the far side of the bar.

I could feel Brooke's eyes burning in the back of my head.

Louise looked a little concerned.

"Yeah, sure, honey. No problem."

Louise walked away and through a door. I followed her down a corridor that was packed with instruments into a small office, barely large enough to fit a desk.

"So, what is it, Freddie? What's wrong?" she asked, softly and with concern.

"Oh, don't worry, nothing's wrong," I reassured her, only now realising the severity in the implication. "Everything's fine. It's just... yeah, I was thinking about your idea with Hal. And we've kind of started in on it already. But, you know, I don't really know what I'm doing... I recorded some in the basement, and it went really well. We were talking about Hal's career... and I just thought, if you wanted, if you could think of anything, or you know, if Brooke could... I'm thinking, it would be good to try and get him in places which would be comfortable for him. Or places that you most associate him with, and try and get his stories that way, in these different settings."

"You know, that sounds like a great idea," Louise replied, smiling enthusiastically, much to my relief.

"I was really hoping you'd say that. I got a recording of him in the basement and I've watched a bit of it. I know you're working now, but I can show you later."

"Okay hun," Louise said, ushering me out of the office and into the small corridor.

I followed Louise back into the bar where Brooke and Tyler were sitting expectedly. Brooke looked at us both suspiciously.

"What's wrong?" she quizzed.

"Nothing," I said, holding my hands up. "Everything's fine. Honest. Nothing to worry about. I'll let your Mom tell you later."

"Okay... so, before you rudely got up and left, Tyler was telling you he's a big fan of your work."

"Oh, I'm so sorry, Tyler, mate," I said. "Thank you so much. That means a lot. It really does. I'm just not used to hearing compliments. So, you're a musician, then?"

"Yeah," he replied, "but obviously, nothing like at your level."

"Woah," I interrupted, "Yeah you are. I was up on there last night, but you're there almost every night. I was following *you*... so, you know..."

"Well I mean, just, you've won awards," Tyler replied.

"I haven't, actually... just, you know, got close. But not quite." It sounded more of an aggressive reply than I meant it to be. The pursuit of awards hadn't ever mattered to me, even when I'd been nominated. "But, yeah, thanks. Go on... sorry, I'm interrupting."

"Yeah, anyway," Brooke stepped in, with an authority like her mother. "Tyler would like to know if you would listen to some of his songs and tell him what you think."

She pulled out a CD.

"Oh... Sure. Tyler, I'd love to take a listen. But can you email them to me?"

"Yeah, sure. No problem. Thank you, so much," Tyler responded enthusiastically.

"Actually," Louise said. "Why don't you play something now? We've got some guitars in the back."

"Oh... no... I don't... I can't." Tyler seemed cautious. And all of a sudden, I was entertained by that.

"No, come on, that sounds like a great idea," I insisted.

Tyler went quiet.

"I'll go grab a guitar," Louise said.

She returned, guitar in hand, and passed it to Tyler and went back around the bar.

"Um... so did you want me to play you something of mine?" he asked nervously.

"Up to you," I said.

"Sorry... it's just... I'm... I've never played for anyone this important before."

"Are you kidding me?" I said. "All jokes aside, last night was the first time I've performed in front of more than three people for nearly five years. I know Brooke, and if she thinks that I should be listening, then, I'm sure you've got something worth listening to. But you know, if you're nervous, I can take the song files..."

"Come on, Tyler," Brooke said. "You might not get an opportunity like this again."

I scratched my head, thinking how bizarre this whole thing was. I almost felt like looking in the corners for hidden cameras. I didn't feel as if I should be treated with such reverence. But then, it struck me. Maybe it wasn't anything to do with me. Maybe, it was their respect for Hal, and the fact that he had sought me out and brought me over. It had somehow created this illusion that I was, in some way, important. Okay, fair enough, I could live with that.

Tyler appeared to take Brooke's advice on board.

"Okay, sure. Where shall I..."

"Up on stage," I suggested.

"Okay, sounds good."

I could tell now that Tyler was nervous, by his downward gaze and heavy breathing. I, in turn, felt a little of that awkwardness, as if all of this was over the top and unwarranted. I was just about to repeat that I'd simply listen to his MP3s when he began to play.

It was a song about being miles from home. I don't know if it was deliberate, but it certainly caught my attention. I guess that was inevitable. I tended to listen to the lyrics and associate myself with them anyway, but to a certain extent, the song has to meet you halfway—and it was at least doing that.

"Um... shall I play another?" Tyler asked after finishing.

"Yeah, sure. Go for it."

And so he did. His next song didn't connect with me as strongly, but it had a catchy melody and gave cause to think about the potential of its sound with a fuller band.

"That was great," I said, after he'd finished. "I'm not just saying this, but you don't need any help from me."

"Thank you! Wow, I can't... you really like them?"

Tyler appeared almost disbelieving.

"Yeah, really good. Honestly, I can't see how I could help you."

"Well will you have a listen to the other songs, if I email them to you?"

"You know what, I'll take the CD and give it a listen," I promised.

"I would love to work with you... if there was any way of making that happen?"

"Well, I'm a bit busy for now, but you never know."

"See! Told you he was good," Brooke interjected, saving us both from the awkward tail off to our conversation.

"You should hear Freddie's idea," Louise chipped in.

She told Brooke—much to my surprise, as I would have expected some secrecy with regard to Hal's condition, but I guessed they must have been familiar enough with Tyler for it to not really matter—and Brooke's response to the idea was just as enthusiastic. Pretty soon they were coming up with ideas for outings: fishing on Snake River—which didn't sound like much fun to me, but, which, apparently, was one of Hal's favourite pastimes. I don't think they'd thought of the logistics—quite how I was supposed to record him in secret—but the thought was there, at least.

They then began to talk about camping out in the Craters of the Moon national park—but, apparently, that was too close to be considered worthwhile.

"Oh, you know where we should go. Hells Canyon! We should camp out there," Brooke exclaimed.

"Where's that?" I asked. I was clueless.

"It's a bit of a drive. It's near the border of Oregon and Washington."

"You did say you wanted to do some travelling," Louise added.

And so, quickly, the idea of a road trip was being born. It sounded like fun to me, but I wondered how Hal might take the surprise, particularly with his words about not wanting to fly anymore? I wondered how that connected with travel of any sort.

Tyler stuck around for a while but left, just as Hal arrived.

"Right in time for dinner," Louise joked. "Regular as clockwork."

Louise's comment prompted me to check the time, and I noticed it was 5:00 p.m. Only then did the thought occur to me that I hadn't been in touch with Kaia for a while. I decided that I'd better call her.

I went outside and tried to call but got no response. It was midnight back in England. She was probably already asleep. I followed the call up with a text, just to let her know that I had tried to call and to say that I hoped she was alright.

By the time I went back inside, I could tell that Hal had been informed of the plans, and Brooke was already on the phone making a reservation.

It transpired that Hal was, in fact, very keen indeed to go to

Hells Canyon, and Brooke had looked online to find that there were some available cabins. Louise was saying how camping for Hal would be a bad idea in case the weather turned bad. I was concerned that he might feel railroaded into it, but then I figured his concept of time would feel very different to mine. It was a strange contrast. I had always bought into the idea of "act now"— something that had really been brought into my life in a big way by Ailie. Still, as liberating and exhilarating as that had been, there was something even greater in what Hal must have been feeling. In this instance it meant not waiting for anything and just *doing*.

The roadtrip plan was fine by me. My sole reason for being in Idaho was to work with Hal. Louise could find someone to run the bar for a few days. I was still unsure exactly what Brooke did. I gathered that she would occasionally work at the bar, and had been a student, but couldn't say for sure. Whatever she did, she was obviously able to take off on a whim and make those decisions in an evening, too. It didn't matter. The life in Hal's eyes and the enthusiasm he had about going was infectious, and illustrated the value of the tremendous compassion these women showed him; a compassion I couldn't help but feel myself.

It was a little after 4:00 a.m when we set off for Hells Canyon. It was so early that it was still dark outside. In fact, it remained dark for so long that it began to mess with my concept of time. Were we really in a new day?

Brooke and Louise sat in the back, with Hal driving, and me in the passenger seat. We had the radio on low, and it didn't take long for both of the ladies to fall asleep. I couldn't blame them, I was tired myself.

"So," I said, in a low voice, after we'd been driving for some time, "have you ever been there before? Hells Canyon?"

"No, no I haven't. Just one of those things, you know. I've always wanted to, always said I would, but just... and I probably never would, if it wasn't for those two."

"So, does it make you think if there's anywhere else you'd like to go?"

"Yeah. You know, it probably should. There are probably a

thousand places, but I know I'm gonna get out there, enjoy it a bunch, and then, you know, sooner or later I'll be wanting home again. See, I've never really been that much of an explorer. Don't get me wrong, I love seeing new things, new places, but... you know, if you find a good place you find beautiful. No place like home, you understand me?"

I paused, not really knowing how to reply. No, actually, I didn't know. Where, indeed, was home, for me? It was the first time I'd really thought about it, and the fact that I had nowhere when I got back—home.

It was still dark outside when Hal said he was changing direction. Against his protestations and on the wishes of Louise, he'd put the GPS on, but with her asleep, he turned right just outside of Boise.

"We'll go up by Lake Cascade. More scenic. We should get there in time for the sunrise," Hal said, quietly.

It was starting to get light as we approached the town of Cascade. As Hal began to slow down, with the reduced speed limits, Louise began to stir in the back seat.

"Where are we?" she asked, sleepily. "We nearly there?"

Hal remained quiet until the sign for the State Park came into view.

"We're in Cascade?" Louise said, with a hint of annoyance.

"I just... I wanted to show the kid."

Hal turned left before the park and drove down to a small car park that had two piers coming off of it.

Hal exited the car and walked along the one of the piers. I followed.

"You know, when it snows in this area, this whole lake freezes over."

"I thought you said you've never been here."

"I've been here. Just haven't been up to the canyon. We're still a couple of hours from there, son. I was told that this is one place you need to see at sunrise, at least once before you die."

"Yeah, I can imagine how it would look in the snow."

I couldn't, really. I'd seen pictures of lakes frozen over, but never actually seen anything like it. Never been close enough to walk from land over water on ice thick enough to not be concerned about it cracking.

I thought about sitting on the edge of the pier and taking it in, but thought about Hal and how it would be too much of an effort, so we remained standing, waiting patiently for the sun to come up. As it did, it brought a colour and freshness to the landscape, changing the hue of the water to match the backdrop of the sky. Even accounting for the fact that I had never seen a sunrise over a lake before, I imagined this would take some beating.

We were joined out on the pier by Louise and Brooke who commented on how beautiful and quiet it was. Louise must have felt as if Hal was toying with her, because no sooner had they got there, he decided to turn around and walk back to the car. The sun was now full and that had been his cue. We, on the other hand, remained, taking in the sight. I felt torn between staying with Louise and Brooke, and going back to Hal, and I did feel as if Louise stayed there a little while longer than she had intended, just to teach Hal a lesson in return. Hal honked the horn on the car, making us all laugh, but forcing us to return, so we didn't wake up anyone who lived locally.

I gathered that Louise was only jokingly cross with Hal, but she did seem to have a point with her frustration with regards our change in route. Driving through the valleys, we had to go much slower than if we had taken the highway, but, the payoff was some absolutely beautiful scenery. All that really mattered was that Hal was enjoying himself. I checked my phone to see if Kaia had been in touch and noticed that it was out of service. I reasoned to myself, I had tried to call and text. She would see that, so surely she couldn't be too annoyed. Funny how I spent more time worrying about it now I couldn't do anything about it.

On the outskirts of Cascade, we stopped at a diner that was serving breakfast. Hal made a few jokes about how the food would taste better if Louise cooked it, and kept saying she should go back in to the kitchen to show them how it was done. It was good to see him in such great spirits.

After breakfast, we journeyed on, finally arriving at the Hells Canyon Creek Visitor Centre, where we picked up the keys before setting off to find our lodgings, which were still another twenty miles away, past the state border and over into Oregon. I was hoping that Brooke had booked us into an oak lodge, but instead we approached a rustic looking house—the kind of place you'd expect to see in a horror movie.

"Hal, this looks even older than your place!" Brooke exclaimed.

The interior matched our expectations, with that lingering dust in the air to suggest that it had been unoccupied for several weeks.

On trips like this with my family, or with Ailie, we would already have a clear plan of what we were to do, so it would always be the case of putting down our luggage and going out to explore. Normally, I'd be the one leading, but today, I was one of four, and once I put my bag down in the living area, I went out on to the porch and sat on the steps. I wanted to embrace the scenery and let the others make themselves at home. I would just fit in with whatever they were doing.

As I sat there, taking in the stillness and wonderfully cool and fresh air, I considered just how much my life had changed in the space of a week. One week earlier, I was boarding a plane in Manchester, with no expectations and no real plans, other than escape. Here I was, with three people who, days earlier, had been complete strangers to me, but who, now, felt like family. I couldn't say that I'd ever been truly alone in the purest sense of the word, though I had often felt that way. Even in those times when I would travel around the country, I knew I had family. But my wanderlust seemed to be directed more to a place where I felt I belonged in my life, rather than a point on a map. For the longest time, I had that with Ailie. Music had been a big part of my life and yes, perhaps the deepest part of me had always wanted to do something in the industry. So in that regard, Ailie had been so good for me. And yet, putting all the pieces in perspective, had I really been happy at any time in that period? Had I just been coasting along that entire time, merely drifting. Could it be that instead of pulling me into a personal abyss, Eddy's death had somehow jolted me awake, providing me with a subconscious realisation of how truly unhappy I was? These thoughts remained, strong. It wasn't *me* whom Ailie had fallen for. It was a persona that I had created for myself. And given that, had I even accepted her love or given it back in any way that was pure? These moments of introspection were more about me than they were about Ailie. But this was the first time I had accepted that. Wouldn't it just be freeing to be myself, rather than some version of myself that may well have been the truth, but not the whole truth?

I was beginning to consider whether Eddy's death had, in fact, been the catalyst for me to take ownership of my own life and follow through my own vision, rather than continue along on the, admittedly very enjoyable, path I had walked down with Ailie, when I was interrupted in thought by Brooke who had ventured outside.

"Wow. It is so beautiful out here," she beamed.

"I suppose it's a bit further than the falls. You don't come here every day."

"That's for sure."

"By the way, I will give Tyler's stuff a listen. He really is very good."

"I honestly... he's a really big fan of yours. He just wants to work with you."

"That's, just, really kind of surreal."

"Why's that?"

"Because..."

"Hal wanted to work with you. So why is it surreal that someone you never heard of before wants to?"

"Oh, I don't know," I admitted. I seemed to be saying that a lot these days. "I think it's more to do with the fact that he asked me directly. You normally get a letter or an email or something. Easier to digest. It's a friend of a friend. I was introduced to Hal. He didn't seek me out."

"Yeah, I guess that makes sense."

"Anyway, I'm not quite sure how we're going to work out some of this stuff. Recording Hal, I mean."

"I've got an idea," Brooke said. "Trust me."

Hal and Louise came outside.

"I thought we'd go down to the lake and see if we could do some fishing," Hal said, as he went toward the car to get the fishing rods.

"Yay!" Brooke said, excitedly.

"Now, sorry, I only brought two. I didn't think... so, I don't know..."

"That's okay," I replied. "I'm happy to just chill out and watch."

"You know me, Hal. I'm the same," added Louise.

I went back into the house to go through my bag and get my mobile tablet and laptop, so that I could set up filming. I passed the laptop bag to Brooke, and I went to get the two folding chairs out of the car.

We all made our way down the hill, which was at times a little steep, making me wonder how we might make it back up—or, more to the point, how Hal might. Once we had made it past an embankment of trees, we were presented with our utopia: a pier, a small, rickety wooden boat attached to it with a rope, and a small grass embankment which was worn to mud around the edges. We followed the path that others had stamped into the ground before us, and Hal set up the fishing rods.

I set up the chairs and took the laptop bag off of Brooke. There wasn't really anywhere suitable to set up the laptop, so I had to balance it on a few stones, so that I could manoeuvre the screen to frame Hal. All I could do was hope that it would pick up any of the audio from our conversations.

Hal was showing Brooke how to put bait on the rod and explaining how it was beneficial to switch your bait at certain times if you weren't having any luck. Louise walked over to the pier, just too far to have a conversation with, although within shouting distance.

"Sorry to interrupt, guys, but you know, we do have some work to do," I interjected, conscious of the battery life on the laptop.

"Yeah, sure. So... what do you wanna know?" Hal said.

"From the beginning, I guess. Your earliest memories."

"Well, damn, son, now you're reaching," he laughed, as he cast his rod into the lake, and helped Brooke do the same. "Alright. Well... I grew up just outside of Albany, down in Georgia. A real country place. Kind of like this, you know. Lived in a big old house with my Grandma and my Mom and Dad. We had a dog. Mussel. Spelled like the sea thing. One of those, you know, My Own Brucie dogs..."

I had no idea what he was talking about.

"A cocker spaniel. They were all the rage. I can remember when Dad brought him home. I must have been about five. Dad said he felt the dog was strong, that he had muscle. So I began to call to the dog... *here Mussel, here boy*! I guess the name stuck."

"I'd love a dog," said Brooke.

"I loved Mussel. He was so protective of me. I was always falling over or doing somethin' crazy. I was a terror as a kid."

"Why?" I asked. I had figured that asking *why* at various points in conversations about major points in his life would be a good way to get the fuller story.

"Can't really remember, to be honest. I didn't have a bad heart. But I simply had no fear..."

He appeared to be drifting away.

"Do you have any funny stories? About Mussel?"

"None I can recall right now. But I do remember he brought me a lot of joy. I just remember that warm glow, that companionship. My first love, that dog... even... shit, one day, I ran in front of a car when I was six... and, of course, Mussel followed. I can't even remember that now, but everyone told me that's what happened for years after."

"Oh no. And Mussel?"

"No, he didn't die. But I thought he was going to," Hal said, his voice cracking. "But they had to take one of his back legs off. I couldn't go near him. I was so heartbroken. I felt like I may as well have killed him. You know, three days after he had the leg taken off, he came into my room, hobbling, as if to say, *Hey... Harry, it's okay.* I don't remember nothing of what happened before, but I can remember that. It was one of the best moments of my life. I kept him with me all the time after that. I felt like I had to repay him for all of his loyalty. Then, you know... the surfers started making the skateboards. And even us inland kids got into the craze. It literally came out of nowhere and was suddenly everywhere. I got a skateboard and took the crate off the front of it, and I took Mussel around on that thing. I think in every picture I got of me as a kid, there's me and there's Mussel, on his skateboard, just waiting for me to run around with him."

"What doesn't kill you makes you stronger," I offered.

"Then you know... one day, I went to school, and I came home, and they told me he'd gone to Heaven."

"What happened?" asked Brooke.

"He just... I don't know. He just died and went to Heaven. That's all there was to it. No other questions," Hal said, with a heavy sigh.

I felt as though I ought to change the subject, and said, "so ... were you brought up with religion?"

"Well, funny you should bring that up. But, losing Mussel was the first time I really thought about it, you know," Hal replied, carefully. "My Dad, he was God-fearing alright. And that's how we were brought up. My sister and I. But as he grew older and he got more responsibilities... I mean... he fought in a war, so I wouldn't have to. That's what he thought, you know. I know that he changed, but I didn't realize how much. For the better. I think. He became less attached to God and more to the people around him. I think he still believed, and you know, I do too. But his sense of responsibility seemed to change. He became more about protecting us. They wanted me to go to Vietnam, but my father knew a doctor. He sorted it out so it was put on my medical records that I was legally blind. A million people died. I wasn't gonna be one of them, my Daddy told me that."

"Are you?" I asked, naively.

Hal spluttered with hysterical laughter.

"The point is, son, is that... yeah, I do believe in Heaven," Hal said after he'd calmed down. "But my Dad taught me... or, what I should say is, what I learned from him is, ain't no crime to be happy. Do good to others, do good to you, but your duty ain't to nobody but your family."

I felt that I wanted to ask him about family. His sister. The fact he and Betty never had kids. But it didn't seem right to challenge him to talk about family when, technically, as far as I knew, he didn't have any left. At least not now, while the mood was buoyant.

But, then, Brooke intervened, asking about how he had settled in Idaho when he was from Georgia. Hal started talking about how he met Betty. I felt that Brooke could more or less get the theme of the conversation and knew the stories she wanted to capture, so I rose from the side of the bank and went to sit with Louise over on the pier.

"Hey. How's it going?" she asked.

"Okay. I felt... he's talking, you know. But I felt a bit funny, awkward, asking him about family," I confessed.

"He'll keep talking. Just give him time," she said.

"Yeah. I feel... I don't know. I feel like I'm always dwelling on my own problems. And when I consider what other people are going through, it... well, I just feel selfish. Like I've got my priorities wrong."

"Well, you need to stop feeling like that. You've got to know yourself. That's square one."

We both looked over at Hal and Brooke. Brooke was taking in everything Hal was saying, occasionally, apparently, cracking a joke, which would make them both laugh.

"You could easily mistake them for father and daughter, or, grandfather and granddaughter," I said.

"Yeah, they're really close. I worry, you know," Louise admitted.

"About Hal?"

"About Brooke. She's never really known proper loss before. Well, her asshole Dad, but... she... I think I did a good job at protecting her from that. I hope I did at least."

"I think you did. From what little I know, obviously."

"That's my world over there. It's difficult to see, you know, that world's gonna become a lot smaller... I just wish I could see that forever..."

She pulled her hands up, and positioned her fingers as if to frame what she could see, Hal and Brooke, sitting there, chatting away. Hal must have thought that she was waving as he raised his hand to wave back, causing Brooke to turn around and wave too. Louise turned her frame into a returned wave.

"I've never been like this before. I just feel as if I wanna spend every second with him. I'm worried, I mean... this is Hal, who we see. I know soon, it won't be him. But then, is that a healthy way of looking at it?"

It was the first time I'd really considered that she'd asked such a question. Something she couldn't answer, or deal with. I wondered what she meant by *healthy*.

"Do you think it would be easier if you told him exactly how you feel?" I asked.

"No. He knows. He knows. It would just be a burden now. Plus, I don't wanna be hurtin' any more than I am."

"I'm sorry, Louise."

"Don't be sorry. I appreciate that you're so concerned. But you know, once you reach a peace in knowing that something isn't meant to be, you don't want to make yourself a slave to that all over again. Well, I don't."

"How can you ever be at peace with something like that?"

"You learn to live with it. And sometimes you can just..."

She didn't know how to complete the sentence. She didn't really need to.

"You know, I think Brooke will be okay. She seems to have all the answers. And why wouldn't she? She's your daughter, after all," I joked.

"She's very sensitive, you know. A lot of that is a front."

I thought about saying something about how Brooke might surprise her, but I didn't feel it was my place to question how well Louise knew her own daughter. And, after all, what did I know? I'd only known Louise, Brooke, and Hal for a matter of days. Sudden realisations, like that moment of over-familiarity, jolted me back into some sort of wider perspective, where I felt the need to be a little more respectful of the fact that I was a guest, witnessing this relationship between the three of them that had lasted for well over the fifteen years I initially assumed it might have been.

"You know, I really can't thank you enough for your hospitality, and how generous you've all been since I've been here," I said. "I've seen some amazing things. I mean this view is just... something else. Memories I'll cherish forever."

"Well, that's our pleasure, y'know," Louise replied, placing her hands on mine. "I honestly believe that you coming along was... serendipity. For Hal."

"It's been good for me, too."

"Brooke was telling me about your girl troubles."

"She was?" I laughed. "She was quite helpful, actually."

"Well, that's good."

We must have sat there on the pier for about an hour, just talking about nothing in particular, Louise, wondering if everything was fine back at the bar, and me, wondering if there was any wifi back in the lodge, although, in truth, I was not necessarily bothered either way.

We heard an excited shriek. It looked as though Brooke had caught something. She ended up being disappointed, but then, almost immediately, Hal got a bite, and shouted for us to come and help. They managed to reel the fish in before we got there, and we had barely joined back up with them when Hal had thrown it back into the water.

"Hey," said Louise. "That was our dinner!"

"That thing couldn't have even filled up Brooke," Hal protested. "You want dinner? Come on kid."

Hal tapped me on the arm, and picked up his fishing rod and bait tin. I guessed it was a signal to follow him and had a bad feeling that he was heading over toward the pier to get into the small boat, a feeling that was confirmed as he told me to pull the boat closer to the shallower water so that he could get in it without too much physical effort. He sat down and looked at me as if I were wasting time. I thought, *surely he doesn't want me to get in there with him*, but that is exactly what he meant. After all, I couldn't let him go out on to the water by himself.

"But we don't have any life jackets." I tried to reason with him.

"Come on, kid. Stop fussin'."

I did as told, and Hal pushed the rope off of the boat, and proceeded to row us out into an area that was roughly central in the lake.

He didn't say a word until we reached the middle. Once there, I was convinced that he was about to say something profound.

"Brooke's the sweetest kid. Love her like my own. But God damn, I needed a break."

"Yeah, she talks!" I had to laugh.

"I'd never stop it. But sometimes, you just gotta pull yourself away. You know. Recharge. I got another day of that coming."

I didn't know how to respond. I began to think about how fishing was essentially the pursuit of silence and contemplation, and so I figured I'd respond only when spoken to. Turned out that Hal wasn't so much tired of conversation as he was of having his ear chewed off by Brooke.

"So, what's on your mind, kid? You're being very quiet."

"Nothing, really. I'm fine. It's really nice out here."

"Yeah, it's really something, ain't it?"

"Hal, I have to say, honestly, I'm not a big fan of fish, so, you know, whatever you catch... all the more for you guys."

"Oh, I'm just out here until I see fit to go back over to the house and climb up that hill, that's all. Besides. It's relaxing."

"Yeah, that's certainly true."

"And besides... I think you and I ought to talk."

"About what?"

"About anything. You keep asking me all these questions. Well, you know me pretty well. I think it's about time I got to know you. So, what do you say?"

I smiled, and with the stretch of my lips pulling my cheeks, I felt the tiniest drop of water well up into my left tear duct. It wasn't enough to make me anywhere near close to crying, really, but it was enough to cause me to be surprised at how sentimental Hal's comment had made me feel.

"Well, what would you like to know?" I asked.

That would buy me some time before I had to speak again, or so I thought. I could compose myself a little better.

"I had a friend. An old friend. He had to... go away for a while. You know," Hal said.

"I think so."

"Anyway. He came back. He got cancer, and he beat it. At the time I remember thinking he was real strong. Then he got set up for this crime which he swore he didn't do. A robbery. All the pieces fit, so it didn't really matter if he was innocent or not. He knew they were coming and I thought he'd be... you know, he'd been there before. That he'd be okay."

Hal looked out onto the lake.

"Well, he, um... he shot himself before the cops came to get him. Reckon he was just about strong enough to make it through the first time. But he couldn't go through that again. So, you know... you said whatever doesn't kill makes you stronger. Just because someone once said it, and someone repeated it, that don't necessarily make it true."

"No. I guess not."

"I don't mean to be all negative. That was just something on my mind, you know. When you said that. Always makes me think of Billy."

There was nothing I could say in response. Not really.

"But enough about that. I wanna know more about you. Come on, talk to me, kid."

I considered just how much it meant to me that not only had he forced us into seclusion from anyone else so he could talk to me about me, but also, that here was a dying man with weeks, or days, left to live, and he was sincerely wishing to spend time learning more about me. It was all I could do to stop myself from welling up or reaching out across and hugging him tightly.

"What's up?" Hal noticed my silence.

"Oh, nothing, it's just... it sounds trivial after what you just said."

"No, it's okay. Go on."

"Well... what you said, in the car, earlier. I actually... I don't understand. I wish I did. I don't know if *home* is a place, or a person? I don't have either."

"You have your parents. You got parents, don't you kid?"

"Oh yeah, I mean... I'm an adult now, that's all. Yeah, I guess I could go there, but when I think of *home*, I no longer think of where I grew up. I think of the place where I live, the person I'm with. I mean, right now, if you ask me where home is, home is a house that's being sold and a person I'm not with anymore. I never thought about it so plainly before."

"You can stay with me for as long as you need," Hal said. I could feel the sincerity in his voice. "I mean, even after... you don't worry about that."

"I'm not worried... it's, you know, it's not money."

"I know what you mean. But you just need to know, and once you know... then, well..."

"Then I'll know!" I laughed.

"Did you ever read the Wizard of Oz?" Hal asked.

"I've seen the movie."

"Yeah, but did you ever read the book?"

"No. Why?"

"There's a line... something said in the book. It's not in the movie—*Toto didn't really care whether he was in Kansas or in Oz, as long as Dorothy was with him.* It's something like that."

I think I understood what he meant.

"So, what will you do about the girl?" he said, after I didn't reply.

"Just move on, I guess. I know it's over. And, you know, I'm alright with that, most of the time."

"And the other one?"

"Well, that, I *don't* know. I was hoping that once I had clarity in one regard, it would provide it in the other."

"How do you mean?"

"Well, once I knew how... once I'd processed everything with Ailie, I thought everything else would make sense. And I'd know how I really feel about the other girl... Kaia."

"Right... and I'm guessing you don't?"

"Not really. I'm sort of... Maybe the reason I never asked Ailie to marry me was more to do with my own reasons of rejecting that idea than what I thought hers would be. I'm coming around to the idea of being with Kaia. I had this fear of being by myself and this fear of losing her again and I didn't want to make those kinds of decisions while I wasn't entirely clear in my own mind."

"You're coming around?"

"Well, yeah... Look, I could do worse."

"So this girl was your first love, right?"

"Yeah."

"And do you still feel that way about her. That first love way?"

"I can't tell. I don't know if I'm the same person anymore."

"It's pretty simple, kid. Yes. Or no. If you can't answer yes, then everything else is no. I mean, not everything is like that. But this is. I think your saying you don't know is just trying to figure out *why* the answer is no. Don't lie to yourself, kiddo. I told you that."

Seems like Hal could read me like a book and make more sense out of it than I had with hours and hours of introspection.

I didn't speak for a while.

"Did you always want to be a songwriter, a musician?" he restarted the conversation. It was a welcome redirection.

"Yeah, I think so. Pretty much. Well, that was something, anyway. I had that thought in mind from the age of fourteen or fifteen. I really enjoyed it, playing piano, playing guitar, then, you know, I got my heart broke, thought of myself as Lennon, or something."

I stopped, thinking I was going on too much.

"Well, go on," Hal encouraged me.

"I got a weird complex... So I wrote these songs, about my

ex-girlfriend, but everyone I knew would know they were about her, so I started travelling around, wherever I could really, to play shows at these pubs... bars, I mean."

"I know what a pub is!"

"Alright," I laughed. "But yeah, anyway, I got drunk a lot. Before I'd play. And then that would affect my performance. I was pretty terrible."

"Yeah, I've been there."

"You're better on your worst day than I am on my best, believe me," I insisted. "So, yeah, my confidence really took a hit. Until I met Ailie."

Hal looked pensive.

"So, what you gonna do, kid? When you get home?"

I shrugged.

"I meant what I said. There's always a place for you here," he said, and then, he looked right at me and took hold of my forearm. "Always."

"Thank you, Hal. But you know, I think I'm in a pretty good place."

"You're not gonna... that Kaia girl, you know."

"No. I think you're right. I'm probably just hiding from the truth. But it's that thing, that... I'm scared of being alone. Or making that decision, because, I'm in a good place, and if I convince myself of that, I don't know if I'll welcome being in a relationship again."

"Yeah, you will," Hal laughed. "You can't help that."

"No, I'm serious," I insisted. "That's the one thing I keep coming back to, that if I am making the break with Kaia, then, I think I would just prefer to... I don't know, you've been..."

I paused, regretting the path I was taking.

"Well, go on," Hal said.

"Nothing."

"No. Go on. Say what you were gonna say."

"I just meant... I don't mean this the way it sounds, but, you've been on your own, and you're a happy guy. You can deal with it.

There's a happiness and a fulfilment to be had in that."

Hal sat in silence for a long time, for so long, in fact, that I thought he was really pissed off with me.

Finally, he spoke.

"What do you see as the worst that's going to happen if you go from this Kaia girl and then fall in love again?" he eventually said, with no anger, or notable annoyance, much to my relief.

"It's just... there will be sadness... there will be conflicts."

"Why?"

"Because... I don't know, there's always conflict. That's just life."

"Is it?"

"Well, everyone disagrees from time to time, don't they?"

"Then you have a conversation. Talk it out."

"Well, it's not as easy as that."

"Look, I'm not saying life's a fairytale," Hal said. "Or that there aren't hard times. But conflict, well... you know, it depends on your definition of that, but if you can't get over something with conversation then..."

"Well, then, it's probably not worth being in that relationship, right?" I said, proving my point.

"Right, I guess," conceded Hal. "But what do you do, you stop trying? Because we're not talking about flings, are we? We're talking about commitment. And if you're entering into commitment with someone you don't know well enough to say you can't predict if conflict will happen, well, I don't know, you're doing it wrong."

"But, you know, there are plenty of people who are in relationships who don't always agree on everything, and they're happy. They get by. That's just not for me," I said.

"Well, I don't pretend to know everything," said Hal, pulling in his reel and casting it again in a different area of the lake. "But what I do know is that I didn't *choose* to be alone."

I understood Hal's point, but as I looked at him, gazing across the lake, looking for a bite from the fish, I wondered if he was deliberately trying to get a rise from me, to say something about Louise. How could he sit there and tell me he didn't choose to be alone? Even if he believed that, how could he preach to me about lying to myself?

"You know what I think?" he said.

"What?"

"I think Brooke's sweet on ya."

"What!? What makes you say that?"

I was a little taken aback.

"Just... you know, little things."

I felt a compulsion to look back to the shore, where Brooke and Louise were sat, talking to each other.

"Little things like what?"

"The way she looks at you. Talks about you."

"What did she say?"

I couldn't tell if he was joking, or simply trying to deflect the conversation.

"She didn't *say* anything. But I can tell. Intuition, you know. And for what it's worth... I think there's a good match there. I know you don't talk a lot, but you're always thinkin'. You're logical. I like that. And Brooke, well... she's one of a kind. She goes her own way."

"Well, I have to say I think you're off. I would've thought she was interested in that guy from the bar. Tyler?"

"I don't pretend to know everything," Hal repeated.

He had to have been messing with my head. I fell back into silence, observing and appreciating the stillness of the lake. *Just say nothing*, I thought. I couldn't consider a motive for his comments. Was he trying to make me feel better, give me a place where I felt I belonged?

Hal continued. "So, that friend I was telling you about. Billy. That must have been about ten years ago now. I mean, he was ripe for dyin'. I don't mind admitting that I was angry at him. But I got it, eventually. He wanted it on his own terms. I knew Billy for over thirty years, and I honestly thought he was eighty when I first met him. Never did find out how old he was. He was from the south, you know, and he moved around. In some ways we've moved on as a people and in others... well, you wonder how much we've learned. He was the sweetest man, you know, he would never steal anything from anyone."

Hal paused, clearly choked. "What I mean is, I moved here, and I see all the people I played with maybe once every five years. Some I ain't seen for twenty. Billy's been gone for so long, and, well, there are some people you think have gone through just about enough and you wanna do what you can to spare them more, you know. So what I'm trying to say—and pardon an old fool for stumbling on to it—but *my* time is coming and I was wondering if you would mind saying a few words, when that time does come."

"What do you mean?" I asked cautiously.

"At my funeral."

"Oh, Hal. Wow. I'm... I'm not sure... What about...?"

I thought of saying Louise, and then it dawned on me what he was actually saying. "Like you just said, you don't even know me that well."

"I reckon I know you," Hal replied, almost dismissively. He was looking out over the lake as if he was asking me the most straightforward thing in the world. I took a deep breath, and although my gut reaction was to refuse out of respect, there was another part of me, equally respectful, that made me think that his request was just as much to do with the people he *didn't* want to have to ask, probably more so, than any revelation about our friendship.

"You want me to tell you I'm fond of ya?" he said.

"No."

"I coulda kicked you out, you know. I coulda said anything and you could be back home. And, you know, you don't have to be here doing what you're doing. It means a lot to me."

"I'm not doing anything," I said.

"Yeah, you are."

I couldn't understand what he meant. But I thought of the sincerity in his voice when he asked to know more about me, and I didn't really feel as if I had much of a choice in the matter.

"Of course I will, Hal. It'd be an honour," I replied.

We sat in silence for what must have been a full five minutes. Louise and Brooke were sitting on the grass verge, throwing stones into the lake. In the silence I was able to digest just how deeply Hal's conversation and concern had moved me.

"You know, I've always been a terrible fisherman," Hal eventually admitted. "I think, including today, I've caught barely a handful of fish in my entire life. I just... It's always been a good excuse to just do *nothing*. Because, sometimes, well... it's nice to just do nothing."

"Yeah, I guess so."

"But you know, I think I done enough of nothing for this lifetime."

With that, he reeled in his line, and began to row us back to the pier. When he realised it would prove too much of a struggle to climb out of the boat on to the pier, he steered us to the shore on the embankment, and when it was shallow enough, I helped him get out.

"What? *Nothing!*?" Louise laughed when she came over.

"I think there was a problem with our bait," Hal said.

"Yeah, sure."

"You're just gonna have to invent something up," he ribbed her.

"Don't I always? Hal, have you ever caught a damn thing in your life?"

"Well, yes I have, and you know I have."

I stood on the shoreline and watched Louise help Hal up the hill and out of earshot. I was enjoying their pantomime act.

"Hey!" I heard Brooke say, from just behind them, "you gonna stay down there all night?"

I had no idea how long we had been out there but the sun was showing no signs of setting just yet, so it must have been only a couple of hours. Still, I felt like hanging back. As much as it was heartwarming to hear Hal and Louise bickering, it was also bittersweet, and I felt that I needed to give them some time alone. I realised, however, that wasn't solely my decision to make, and as Brooke walked back to me, I begun to question that choice.

"Hey, what's wrong?" she asked.

"Nothing, honestly," I replied. On the one hand, I meant it, but on the other, as I recalled what Hal had said about Brooke, I felt a powerful wave of awkwardness wash over me. I found that I could barely even look at her.

"Is Hal okay?"

"Yeah, he's fine, I just... you know, thought they could do with some time alone."

"Yeah, that's a good idea."

Brooke walked down to the pier and sat down at the edge of the lake, taking off her shoes and dangling her feet, so that she could skim the top of the water. Having created this scenario, I could hardly leave her alone without raising more questions, so I followed and sat beside her.

My awkwardness quickly faded as I realised that Brooke was, of course, oblivious to the comments Hal had made. More than that, I was comfortable in her company, so as she started talking about what she was going to do when we got back, it was easy conversation.

"What did you do, when you were my age?" Brooke asked.

"Well, when I was your age, I... I wouldn't look to what I did for advice, or guidance."

"Why?"

"Because I've always... it's hard to explain. I've always looked for reasons *not* to do things."

"You gotta be kidding me. With all that you've done."

"Well, that's all a matter of perception."

"It's really not," Brooke insisted. "If you can't see that just with how Tyler acted when he was around you, then I don't know what else will show you."

"Okay, well, imagine this. Where we are right now, you and me, sat on this rickety pier."

"Yeah."

"I've worked all of my life, and this is where I am. This is where I've got to. I worked to get here. And you're here, you're in exactly the same place, and you've got years on me," I explained.

"That doesn't make sense. I don't understand what you mean."

"That it's just... choices. The choices that we make from this moment define what will be in the future just as much as the choices we made in the past define who we are today."

Brooke thought about it for a while. I wasn't sure how much sense it made myself, although it seemed to make sense when I said it.

"Yeah, but the difference is, you have more options, tomorrow, because of everything you've already done," she said.

"I was in no better place than you when I was your age. Sometimes I think I'm in no better place now. In myself, I mean. There are still as many questions."

"Maybe there always will be? And maybe it's better to simply stop worrying about the possible answers."

"Yeah, maybe," I replied. "You should try listening to your own advice."

"Maybe. But that's your advice too. From that new song you played the other night. *Take the time to think it over, don't take time to over think it.*"

I felt somewhat self-conscious about having song lyrics I'd written quoted back at me, but in context I guess it made sense. I had to laugh. I was also touched by the thought that Brooke appeared to have really paid attention.

"Yeah, well, who knew? I'm a freakin' genius."

"Tell me about that song. I love it. Was it about Ailie? Because it sounds like you asking her to come out here."

"I don't know, to be honest. Maybe, on a subconscious level. Probably about both Ailie and Kaia, really. And also the fact that I never did ask."

"Would you have liked her to? Ailie?"

"If you'd have asked me when I was literally on the train to the airport I would have said yeah, for sure. But, now... I think I needed to do this alone."

"Well, there's no shame in admitting that."

"No, I know. I just... it sometimes feels weird, you know. When you're conscious and aware of stuff, but, it really does sometimes need time and space to give a greater perspective. I'm glad you like the song, anyway. Thank you!"

"No problem. Thanks for writing it. And for playing it."

We remained on the pier for a while. I asked Brooke what she had studied, and she talked about how she had wanted to study philosophy, but found herself too distracted. Then, she wanted to study art, but grew frustrated with it, because she felt she was naturally inclined to be an artist and couldn't comprehend instruction in creative pursuit. And now, she just didn't know, and that's where she was, apart from working the odd shift at Murphy's.

On the one hand, she was grateful to Louise for always being there for her and making sure she never wanted for anything, but on the other, she was crying out for independence. It was that indecision which seemed to be holding her back, but as much as she was reaching out for guidance, I considered that she must know that she had to figure it out for herself. It felt odd to me that the more I grew to know Hal, Louise, and Brooke, the more I became in tune with the thought that all four of us were in some sort of transition.

We talked for so long that the sun began to set.

"I was saying to Hal this morning, that I'd never seen the sun rise over a lake before. And I've never seen it setting over one either. Quite a day, all in all."

"Yeah, it's been fun," Brooke agreed. "I think, I'm getting hungry though, now. Should we go back?"

Approaching and entering the cabin felt like returning home, even I had only ever been inside it twice. The door was open and as we reached closer, I could hear Hal talking and Louise laughing.

That was the way it remained for the rest of the evening. An evening which mostly consisted of Hal trying to get the television to work, and growing frustrated when it wouldn't. The kind of everyday normalcy you take for granted, which is only really put into perspective in situations such as this.

As we all said our goodnights, I lay on the sofa, where I was going to sleep, filled with thoughts. There was an open fire which had warmed the room up nicely, its embers now glowing in the dark. It felt, to me, as if there was an air of restlessness throughout the house. That, I am certain, was due more to the amount of stories we had all exchanged, as opposed to any words being left unsaid. Certainly, as far as I was concerned, I felt that I had absorbed an incredible amount of information, and I was struggling to wind down.

I checked my phone and saw that there was no reception. With no internet connection, either, I made my way outside into the dead of night, as quietly as I could, to see if being out in the air, I might locate a signal. I couldn't.

6

three months earlier

It was a typically overcast afternoon in Manchester when I received the phone call from Eddy's manager to inform me of his passing.

At first, I felt nothing. I told Ailie I was going shopping.

At the supermarket, I could feel it approaching. A black cloud of grief beginning to envelop me. I tried to shake it off, but to no avail. You know when you see a shopping cart left full of groceries in the middle of the store, but no customer, and you wonder what happened? Well, that was my cart that day. As the grief cloud took hold, I simply turned and exited the supermarket. At that moment, nothing seemed to matter. I arrived home and when Ailie asked about the groceries, I looked at her and grunted some kind of unintelligible response. And so it began. My gradual withdrawal, from grunted responses into almost complete non-communication, as the cloud covered me and refused to loosen its grip.

It was several weeks later when I finally admitted to Ailie that I was struggling. She already knew, of course.

I felt stuck. Frozen in grief and incapable of breaking the moment and summoning the strength to continue. There remained, for me, an inherent and impolite implication that life was simply going to continue. That the grieving was finished, and, although we would accept its role, it would now become merely a part of what we did instead of all of it.

For some time, I felt as if every action I made, every word I said from that point on needed, somehow, to be profound. That it should be significant, it should mean something. No moment should be wasted. I considered what I could do with everything at my disposal. And I felt so useless, so insignificant. I knew that I wasn't. I knew that I could achieve. I could do something. I had, already. Some days, I felt as if nothing could stop me. Sometimes, I even felt as if I was on the verge of becoming the person I'd always wanted to be.

I would love to say that I took on board these things that I felt were true and instantly approached life in a vigorous and empowered way, but the truth is I wallowed for quite some time. I was grieving, yet the *guilt* was even worse. I felt guilty for having such ownership over my grief, as if *I* mattered. I felt as if I were caught in the midst of what must be my existential crisis, and yet felt as if the issue that prompted it—an everyday issue, the only certainty we face, death—was not significant enough to warrant such introspection.

The morning after Eddy's funeral, I opened my email and saw a message entitled "Collaboration?" It was from a Harry Granger. The name sounded familiar. I wracked my brain as to whom it could be, but with my mind drawing a blank, I clicked inside to read.

"Dear Freddie, it was a pleasure to meet you last Tuesday."

In my haze, I had momentarily forgotten that the day after Eddy had passed away, we had been obliged to attend a record release party for a new band, Von Erich. I was determined not to go, until Ailie—right as always—suggested that we should. It would be a welcome distraction, and who knew, she suggested, something may come out of the networking opportunity.

And so it was. We were way more popular than usual, with people flocking around us to pass on their condolences, asking us to pass on their best wishes to Eddy's family. I had hoped to be a wallflower, as was normally the case at such events, before those introductions which would generally elicit responses such as *oh, you did that?* but now I found myself being introduced as a "somebody."

And now that I had been reminded, I could quite clearly re-member being introduced to Hal Granger. I had been surprised that he knew of my work with Eddy.

"I've thought about doing something similar."

That's a business opportunity. Regardless of the grief.

"Sounds interesting. I'd love to hear more. Here's my card. Please get in touch."

It was an impulse reaction, one so time-worn, I barely even recognised that I did it these days.

I continued to read the email. "I wanted to give you some time before contacting you. I would be very interested in working with you, if you were serious, that is. Please get in touch if you would like to talk further. You can call me or email. PS. I don't work with agents."

The name Hal Granger seemed vaguely familiar, but I couldn't place him. I had to take to look him up online to discover that he was an American singer who had enjoyed prominence in the 1960s and 70s with songs such as "The Road" and "Rolling." I was pretty sure that a couple of his songs were featured on some of my parents' numerous "Hits of the 70s" compilation albums.

It was interesting to me, on a purely human level. But with my lethargy beginning to dominate me, I closed the email and decided to impolitely decline to even reply. Sure, it could well be an interesting experience. But my grief was too raw to contemplate exploring all of the crevices of this open wound again. I know that for some, they would have perceived it as getting right back on the horse, and I could hear those words being said by Ailie, even though she wasn't in the house. But I couldn't do it.

Of course, I didn't admit that to myself. I was too smart for that. Instead of admitting to myself I was too scared, instead of embracing that emotion and challenging the natural energy it presented, I decided to concoct what I felt was a practical excuse. It wouldn't make financial sense. The guy lived in America. My new solution was that I should earn as much money as possible, to be able to afford the time to procrastinate over such trivial matters. We were hardly struggling, but the fact of the matter is we were living something of the lifestyle of people we hobnobbed with; a financial consequence of the decisions we had taken was that we didn't benefit from appearance or interview fees of the acts we had written for.

I didn't procrastinate over Hal Granger. I simply forgot all about him. And I didn't make good on my solution. I continued to pontificate over my own purpose, neglecting Ailie, who tried in her way to bring me out of the shell I was burrowing myself into. I was conscious and aware of what I was doing, but felt that deep unhappiness and sadness, which became an unhappiness with everything within my life, because I allowed it to.

Ailie tried so hard to get in, but I had frozen. I had become so obsessed with the concept of owning my sadness and hating myself for it that I resented anything I now associated with what I had considered successful achievements in my life. I could reasonably associate that with grief and so I could acknowledge that it may be an irrational resentment. And yet it existed, larger than life, all the same. Before Eddy's death, I was going along for the ride and I felt like I was a part of it. I felt worthy of inclusion in conversations about our work together. But ever since he passed, it seemed as if I were watching my own life through a thick pane of glass, able to witness events, even able to participate in them, but the ability to *feel* anything had disappeared so suddenly it made me question how much of it was ever real at all.

I felt I was at rock bottom, but worse was to come.

Some months after Eddy had died, I summoned up what I described to myself as courage to go into town and run some errands. These were normally left to Ailie, who would never give way to that feeling of wasting time, but one evening I had suddenly felt the urge to do something helpful, as my way of acknowledging my appreciation for her support during a time I was far from myself. My real self.

So, the following day, I went out, and it was refreshing. To be out and about, among people again. It was so easy. I couldn't say that I had exactly been *afraid* to go out by myself, but my lethargy dictated that as soon as any hint of indecision had presented itself, I had backed away completely. Making a choice, or decision, about *anything* was something I hadn't embraced. But now, here I was, shopping for odds and ends. As if it were some big occasion, I decided that I would get myself a new notepad. I felt like this could be the beginning of a new me, so, I wanted to make what I felt were bold statements.

A fresh notebook. Fresh pages. Fresh possibilities.

"Freddie?"

As I was browsing in the stationary store, I could hear my name being called by a familiar voice.

"Yeah?" I impulsively responded before looking up and seeing who it was.

I was surprised to see Kaia, my ex-girlfriend.

We had dated in our teens, and had that carefree and reckless attraction, an intense and intimate connection, and then almost immediate dissolution. We spoke of how our love would never die, and when we spoke those words, they felt so true. Kaia was my first love. My first heartbreak. And in subsequent years, relationships would fail horrendously, because of the comparison I insisted I wasn't making, but really was.

When I met Ailie, I felt like I finally realised what love was, and the difference between *thinking* you have it and actually having it. Over time, I had lost sight of that and taken it for granted. Although I knew that Ailie was facing a testing time in our relationship, despite my attitude, she was demonstrating real love. Yet, I felt oblivious to it. I mean, I was well aware of it, but, in the clutches of self-pity, I had convinced myself that I didn't deserve it.

Seeing Kaia at that moment instantly transported me back to a time where I felt fearless. A time where I was full of the bravado of love and the belief that it conquered all.

"I don't know if you remember me..." she started.

For about a month I found myself meeting up with Kaia, reminiscing about old times and just generally chatting about how things were going. The distraction was continuously welcome, yet it increasingly felt as though it was heading towards somewhere it shouldn't.

I think, really, we both knew from that first exchange of phone numbers that it would head into territory that was probably not the best choice. For me, anyway. Kaia had made several references to her ex-boyfriend wanting her back, but said how she wasn't interested. That's how the conversations would mostly start. Her asking how I was, how Ailie was. I had always been extremely complimentary about my better half but this particularly early afternoon I found myself frustrated. Ailie was working especially hard to keep the money coming in. As far as she was concerned, I was still coming to terms with what had happened; Ailie was facilitating this concept of my struggling for grief coming up to half a year after Eddy had passed, and shamefully, I was accepting that indulgence. I wouldn't go as far as to say I was putting on an act, but my efforts at acquiring new work weren't as intensive as they might have been. I wasn't writing much. I was less responsive to requests, even knowing full well that opportunity wouldn't knock for too long. The effort always felt too much.

And still, the way I made it sound to Kaia, the next time we met, it was as if Ailie didn't care or understand. I enjoyed the freshness of the distraction. Kaia was not associated with my grief. Kaia was sympathetic. Pandering to me. Time got away from us and before we knew it we'd spent hours just talking.

"So... you know when we met the other week. You said that you loved me," I said.

"Yeah... I did."

"I always felt like you... you said it but didn't feel it."

"Are you kidding? Of course I did. I can't believe that you're saying that!"

I had manipulated the conversation to that point, but there was a truth in what I was saying. And now I felt like I was getting somewhere towards achieving the closure I had wanted when I was younger. How much of what she was saying was honest? How much of what I was saying was? I could sense that Kaia still had feelings for me.

When we broke up, it had been unpleasant. Now I felt as if some moment between us was inevitable, but there was something of a power within that. I had never felt that I had achieved closure from our relationship and that had dogged me for years;

wondering if true love was that bolt of lightning people spoke of, if it only occurred once.

There was an innocence and naivety in that, sure; I knew you could love more than once. You could recover. I also knew that feelings change and the way you love feels different. I had experienced that. But now I didn't know who I was tricking. Kaia? Myself? If I wanted, I could probably coax as much of a statement of closure as I had wanted in those years I'd pined for it. Why, if you loved me, did it end?

But now, would it even be the truth? The modern version of events in her eyes would have to be more sympathetic to me to bring us back around to this point. It wouldn't have been the brutal truth which tore us apart back when it did. How much of that was an over reaction from my point of view? How much of it was simply part of growing up?

"I did love you, Freddie," she said. "You were the sweetest. I probably loved you more than anyone I've ever known. It hurt me that I hurt you."

"So, why did you?"

"Honestly, I don't know. The number of times I've thought about that..."

I could almost feel her squirm. What could be the right thing to say? Part of me felt like I wanted to stop, but the other part of me felt like I wanted it to continue, that I needed it to.

"Sat here now, I can't think why. Because everything... feels like it used to, you know?"

Yeah, I knew.

"I know I wasn't the easiest to get along with," I admitted.

"No, you were fine. It was me. I was a bitch," she said.

"Nah, you weren't." And with that, I found myself realising, again, she really wasn't. And in this period of reaquaintance, maybe she had come to her own realisations.

"We were good friends. Just probably not good partners," I continued. Things were hitting a little too close to home and I was beginning to question the wisdom of my actions.

I didn't want to betray Ailie; talking to Kaia had been an escape from something else. And now I felt as if I was really leading Kaia a merry dance when I should really have been handling it in a more mature way.

However, my little plan had worked out too well, and I was putting myself in a very awkward situation—I had these thoughts of clarity and compared them against these unresolved problems and emotions I had revisited. Sometimes, things are just better left. But now, I couldn't avoid it, and I knew I would have to face up to some big truths in my own life. Before that, I had to be brutally honest with Kaia. I knew that she had once held strong feelings for me, and it was only now, sat talking to her so bluntly about it, that I could really see that. Why couldn't I back then? Did I need unrequited love? Did I crave it? Was that an experience I felt I had to go through? I remember how I pushed her away unnecessarily, taking my hurt out on the person who deserved it least. I had been quite horrible. Not unforgivable, but, horrible enough to justify walking away from. Who needs that negativity in their life?

We left the restaurant and Kaia led the walk, away from the centre of the town and down toward the canal, where we found a bench and sat. I remembered that we had once spent many afternoons along there one summer. Some of the landscape had changed, but the memories hung vividly in the air to make it feel as if nothing had changed.

The conversation turned to matters more trivial. About the time, while we were still together, I'd taken a temporary job at the office of the newspaper where she worked. The fun that we'd had that summer before I quit. And then our relationship quickly fell apart. We didn't bring that up.

"Sometimes I feel as if I've not changed at all," I said. "I know I have. I know that if I could revisit how I felt about everything all those years ago, I would probably cringe, but at the time, I felt like I knew everything."

"Yeah, I know what you mean."

"Of course, I still feel as if I know everything," I laughed. "But I think now I know, really, that I don't. Ailie taught me that. I've learned a lot about myself."

"Like what?"

"Well, today, I've learned that I'm a pretty shitty person," I said.

"What? No you're not. Why do you say that?"

"Look at us. You're a really amazing girl. I was so lucky. What we had was special and I made it *not*, special. I know that you loved me, and I know that you put up with a lot. I was going through my own... well, I suppose I was growing up."

"We both were. You're amazing too."

Of course she would say that. I was being the nice guy now. Not the person she had grown used to. I was realising that our break up had very little to do with her being capable of hurt, but more a situation that was a making of my own, much like this one. Oh God, what a thing to realise at this of all times.

But no matter what I said, this searing honesty seemed to draw Kaia closer in.

"What we had was special," she said. "That's not something you imagined. It was the same for me. It was intense. We were just young."

She was speaking to me, but I was hearing Ailie. I was doing the same thing to her. But the vulnerability being shown by Kaia was also alluring in a way that I knew was going to prove impossible to resist. I could tell in advance, with full control of my actions, I was going to make a bad mistake.

"I'm sorry... it was a long time ago. I just wanted to say, you know... you weren't the bad guy," I was using all of the willpower I had. "Anyway, I'd really better get going."

I stood, instantly and impulsively, and I could tell that Kaia was surprised.

"Oh. Okay."

She leaned in to say goodbye and we embraced. I couldn't resist, even though I wanted to. And as our heads touched, and then pulled apart, we looked at each other, a glance to ask the question without uttering a word. Everything was so familiar and yet new. It was Kaia who moved, kissing me on the cheek, and then, moving her lips on to mine when I offered no resistance.

They remained there too long for it to be simply a gesture between friends. We both pulled away and it seemed for a second that we would kiss again, but we stopped ourselves.

"I have to go," I said.

I turned, almost like a coward, ashamed of the situation I'd created, and moved briskly away, not thinking to turn around.

Ailie returned from work in London the following day. I had planned to talk to her and tell her everything. About how I'd encountered Kaia. I'd invent some falsified and contrived story about us bumping into each other once or twice and then how she kissed me in a moment of impulsion. That was close enough to the truth.

And yet when I went to tell her, over dinner, the guilt-fuelled words which came out of my mouth were that I'd consider moving to London.

"You're constantly down there. Let's move back and make a fresh start. It makes the most sense."

Ailie's response was less than enthusiastic. The doubt in her voice, tangible.

"Really?"

"Yeah."

She looked at me. It was a different look. As if she were trying to determine who it was she was talking to. She took some time before replying.

"No. It's not going to work. I'm sorry, Freddie, but it's over," she said.

"Wait! What? What is?"

"I'm going to move to London... and I think we should sell the house."

She had tears in her eyes.

"We've not been right for a while. You know that. And I've tried..."

"It's me, I know... hold on. I know I've not been dealing with things right."

"There's a huge gulf between us, Freddie. You can't see that?"

She composed herself, and now, there was a steely coldness in her gaze. She was serious.

"What? So, I want to move to London, and you think suddenly we don't have a future?"

"Freddie. You've barely acknowledged me for weeks."

I felt like using Eddy's death. No, I couldn't do that.

"Are you seeing someone else, in London?" I asked.

I didn't even realise that I could say something so uncaring, until the words had already left my lips.

Ailie didn't respond.

"I just don't understand. Why?" I continued.

The reality of what was happening started to hit me.

"You know. You do."

"No, I don't. Give me a clue? Please, Ailie."

Was I really challenging the person I loved to show me that she had figured out my deception? How low I had sunk.

She didn't give me the clue I'd asked for. There was no screaming or shouting. I stayed on the sofa that night. Ailie slept upstairs, in our bed. But I could hear she was as restless as me. She had tried her best to be cold but her eyes betrayed the real emotion she was feeling. I knew she was hurt, and I knew I was at fault. How far would this go before I admitted it to myself? Neither of us got any sleep.

At around 4:00 am, I decided to go upstairs and see if we might sort it out.

"Ail," I said, pushing the door open. "You awake?"

"Yeah."

I had dwelled upon our future all through the dead of night, the immediate future, and now I was fully embracing the weight of what was about to happen. I was powerless to stop the tears rolling down my cheeks. I composed myself between crying to push out the sentences.

"I don't know what you think I have done wrong. I don't know what I've done wrong. Please tell me."

Sat in the dark I could still make out the expression on her face. Sympathetic yet stoic. She had obviously already spent countless hours dealing with these emotions, steeling herself in advance for this showdown. And she could probably read me pretty easily too. She could tell that I was lying, but I was acting like the damaged party. The truth remained hidden but evident.

She wouldn't tell me, but she held me as I cried. I stopped, trying to figure out if I had really hit rock bottom. Was this it? Had I willed this upon myself? How much of a coward was I being by not admitting what I'd done?

The following morning, I walked her to the train station. We were both exhausted, mentally and physically. I had resigned myself to her leaving but, as the train to London approached, I found myself panicking, begging almost, for her not to get on it.

"Please, Ailie. Don't go."

Ailie's eyes fixed on me, this time almost pitying me. I barely recognised her.

"I'm sorry, Freddie. Goodbye," she said, holding me close and then releasing me. She boarded the train without looking back. I tried to find her, hoping that she would regret her decision. I waited for her to get off the train, even as the doors closed. And then the train pulled away. And just like that, my life was completely changed.

I couldn't bring myself to talk to anyone that day. Kaia texted me a few times and I deleted her texts without reading them, feeling the guilt of betrayal heavy on my conscience. I hoped for something from Ailie; it wasn't forthcoming. I started writing long emails and text messages and deleted them, thinking, no, I should wait for her response.

The first thing I did the next day was check my phone. No message. I walked downstairs and into the kitchen. I picked up the juice carton and held it, before putting it back down, and running my fingers across the top of the vodka bottle.

I checked the time. 7:47 a.m.

I poured myself a juice, all the while eyeing the vodka.

No-one would know. Nobody would care.

I thought of what I wanted to do.

What would I do if I started drinking? I'd lose the day. What would I do if I lost my inhibitions and accountability? I'd write to Ailie. With a clear mind I could see what a mistake that would be.

So I stayed sober. And it was tough. But mid-afternoon, I found myself writing to Ailie anyway. I didn't know if I was going to send it, but I thought it would be cathartic to at least write everything down. It was. I was in a place of clarity, and reading it all back, it didn't seem so bad. I wasn't the ogre I'd felt I was becoming. I had been struggling. That's all. Problems caused by Eddy's death, pushing Ailie away, and then being distracted by Kaia. Sure, it would be tough for Ailie to read about Kaia, but surely she would be sympathetic? A mere distraction was all it was. She would understand. I went out and posted the letter to the hotel where I knew Ailie was staying.

That evening, Ailie texted me.

"How are you?"

"I'm okay... you? You want me to call?"

"I'm tired. Been a long day. Can we talk tomorrow?"

"Okay... I sent you a letter."

"Why?"

"Just to explain some stuff."

It was painful. Our relationship was reduced to this.

The next morning, Ailie texted. *"Got your letter."*

I waited for her follow up. It never arrived.

I thought she might email, so I checked all of my accounts. I even checked my work account, which I'd neglected for weeks. I just hadn't been interested. There was nothing from Ailie, but, I did notice an email from Hal Granger.

"Hi Freddie, should I presume from your failure to respond that you are not interested in working with me? Please let me know. Best regards, Hal."

I felt bad about my lack of response. I wasn't normally so poor with that. I sent Hal a brief reply.

"Dear Hal, so very sorry about my delay. I'm of course interested, and also interested in how it would work. When are you back in England? Freddie."

The rest of the day went by as I intermittently checked my emails. Kaia tried to call a couple of times. I couldn't bring myself to respond to her texts or call her. The next time I checked my email, I had two replies waiting for me. A reply from Hal Granger—suggesting that I go out to Idaho to work with him, all expenses paid—and also one from Ailie entitled "Letter."

"Freddie, I have to admit that I was surprised by your email. Do you have any idea how difficult it has been to stand by you for weeks on end as you grew increasingly distant? How hard it has been to try to stay positive and support you? It has been so hard to watch you become this different person. I thought that maybe it was something that I was doing wrong. You weren't talking to me. And now I know why. You were seeing your ex. If you honestly think telling me this is the way to get me to come back, you're wrong. I'm sorry, Freddie, but we're over."

I responded immediately.

"Ailie. Nothing happened with Kaia. Please believe me."

Ailie replied by text about half an hour later.

"Freddie, it doesn't matter if it did or didn't. I'm over it. But you went away from me in the first place and that's what really hurts. It just proves to me that I'm right, that this is the right thing to do."

I thought about responding, but couldn't. I couldn't argue with her. I had tried to reasonably explain that I had not been unfaithful, but how could I argue with Ailie's own conclusions? How would I have felt? It was still a betrayal, even if only emotional. I was stuck. There was literally nothing I could do to recover the situation, and all I could see was Ailie's cold stare in the seconds before she turned to board the train.

I ventured to the bottle of vodka that I'd somehow resisted for around thirteen hours. After a couple of shots to fuel my adrenalin and impulsive decisions, I wrote back to Hal and said I would love to go out and work with him. An escape seemed like a good idea.

I drank until I drifted off to sleep.

My headache the following morning felt like a worthy souvenir from one of the worst days of my life.

7

"Sorry, Freddie!" I heard Hal's voice before I realised that I had been disturbed. I adjusted my eyes and realised it was still dark. I looked at the clock, the face reflective in the shadow of the moonlight. Five after two. I must have been asleep for at least an hour, yet it felt like I'd only blinked.

"Couldn't sleep," Hal said, in a hushed tone, as he sat in the armchair next to me. I felt it was an invitation to sit up. "Normally I'd say, you know, go on back to sleep, but the truth is, I could do with a little company."

"You okay?" I inquired.

"Funny thing about sleeping," Hal said, in that way which suggested he just wanted to get something off his chest, "when Betty was ill, she slept an awful lot. I mean, when she was really ill. She once said that she felt guilty for sleeping. You know, I told her she was crazy. But I reckon there's this... see, with Betty, she never knew. I know that I have a few sleeps in me."

"Way more than a few," I said, trying to sound optimistic, without wanting to sound too flippant.

"Yeah, well... I just gotta say that I really enjoyed today. I loved spending all this time with Brooke, and Lou, and yeah, even you. Out here. Away from everything. And even reflecting. I was worried that reflecting might be too much like admitting... well, you know. But it felt good."

"Yeah."

"Do you mind if I'm honest with you?" he said.

"Of course not."

At that moment, Hal got up from his chair and walked toward the kitchen area. He returned with two whiskies and sat back down.

"I don't want you to say anything or offer any advice or anything like that. I just gotta say some stuff to get it out there. I don't know. Some of this stuff you might find useful and some of it, I'm just... I'm saying it for me. And the girls... I know they understand, but sometimes I think... the reality might be a bit much for them. Now, this one *is* for you. You can't erase and you can't delete. You only get one life and it's way too short to spend holding onto the hurt. The hurt that is caused by life... the hurt people inflict on you, and the hurt you inflict on others. I'm not saying not to feel *bad*, but if you do wrong, make amends, and if you can't make amends, you can live with knowing you tried." He sighed a deep breath, took a drink and continued. "Life is too short to hold on to grudges. Because you lose. Even when you win, you lose... Listen to me. I'm an old fool.'

"No, you're not."

"Who am I to be giving out advice? I'm the guy who is too afraid to go to sleep and I'm talking to you like... I ain't trying to be your father or anything. You already got one of those. Who am I to be listened to?"

"Listen, Hal. You are one of the most insightful people I've ever met," I said, honestly. "It doesn't matter if you've had kids or haven't... I mean, sorry, I don't know if..."

"No, I haven't. Well..." he said, pausing again. "Betty and I looked after a couple of boys. Took care of 'em for a while. But then, Betty died, and I was no good. Their real mother showed up and I was... I spent so long grieving that I wasn't living. Those twins will be out there somewhere, and they probably don't even know who I am... probably don't even remember. I think about them every now and then. I thought about looking 'em up, once I was back on track. But their mom... she had a lot of issues. When she took 'em, she said if I dared to put up a fight, she would say some things, I don't know, like we'd kidnapped 'em, or somethin'. We didn't. But I was fighting enough at the time. And you know, I figured if they were ever curious, those boys would come knocking one day and I would always have an open door. But that day never came."

"How old were they?" I asked. "I mean, if you don't mind me asking."

"Five or six. Yeah, Betty loved those boys like they were hers. It was difficult for me. It was like a constant reminder. Maybe I'm saying too much, so stop me if you're uncomfortable. We weren't blessed. In fact, she was at the doctors because she thought she was pregnant, when she was diagnosed. You think life can't be any crueller than that. But it can," he said, pausing as he had a lump in his throat which broke his voice a little. He coughed, quietly, and strengthened his own resolve. "It really, really can. And the only thing that ever kept me going was the idea that no matter how cruel life was to take her away from me, I was still..." Hal sighed and waved his arms to his chest, as if to accentuate the point he was about to make. "I was still incredibly blessed to have experienced those times and to have these memories of being with her. You think of what you might have done differently, but none of that really matters. You have to let go of that. For a while, after she passed, her doctor would come around and talk to me. I couldn't get over that idea that I could lose someone like that. I think they were worried that I might... you know, that I might do something stupid. But I never could. It's not that I'm scared of dying. I'm more scared that I won't *feel* this love or *remember* the love. I'm scared that sometime soon that time is gonna come. I'll be gone, and I won't be able to feel that love anymore. I don't know if that's right or wrong... maybe it ain't healthy... but, anyway, you do what you do. I always thought of life like it was two parallel lines, like those running machines. One of them is life and one of them is you... the life line is always moving, and so is yours, even if you don't always feel like it is... and I mean, you can jump on, jump off... none of it really matters. I'm sorry, kid. I don't know if any of that makes any sense," he gulped.

"It does," I said. I thought about what Brooke had told me about Louise and thought it wasn't my place to say anything. Hal was certainly wrestling with his conscience on that score.

"Anyway," Hal said after a brief silence, "I think it's about time that I told you something. I always thought I was a pretty decent songwriter, you know."

"You are," I replied.

"Just shut up a minute and let me speak," he laughed. "A pretty decent songwriter. Like, I could make things that sound good. But I was never... I never thought I was *great*. I never wrote anything that made me go, *wow*... and now that I have you here, I just want to say... well, you know, there are some amazing moments in musical history... Elvis, The Beatles, Johnny Cash, the list goes on... but, quite honestly, I think there are only a couple of times that I can recall saying *wow* out loud. The first was when I heard *Pet Sounds* for the first time. You know on *Wouldn't It Be Nice* when Brian Wilson sings, 'It seems the more we talk about it, it only makes it worse to live without it'? We were just starting out right then. And I was simultaneously inspired to create and devastated that I could never write anything as damn near perfect as that."

"Yeah, that's a great line."

"And the other time," Hal continued, "was when I heard one of your songs. And you know, initially I thought it was that band... The Cause... but when I asked them to track down the guy who wrote it, it was you."

I felt my heart swell with pride and my cheeks redden with embarrassment.

"Really? That's amazing. Thank you, Hal."

"Would you like to know which song it was? Which line?"

"No, that's okay."

I shrugged it off, although the egotist in me screamed *yes!* I was embarrassed I found myself trying to change the subject.

"But on that topic, you know, I felt like that the first time I..." and I laughed, feeling young, inexperienced, and self-conscious, "well... I don't know if you heard of them, but there was this band called the New Radicals. There was this line, 'I can't help failing to remember to forget you.' At the time I was getting over my first broken heart and I think those are the kind of lines that stay with you. I was just starting out writing and I was like, yeah, that's the kind of thing I want."

"Gregg Alexander," Hal said. I was stunned he would know someone I was sure was relatively obscure. "He was the guy I tried to get before I turned to you," Hal laughed.

It took me a second to realize that he was joking. "He's brilliant. I'm more surprised, actually, that *you* know. That stuff made it to the U.K.?"

We talked about music a while longer before Hal decided he should call it a night. At that point we were both falling in and out of sleep anyway.

Before I knew it, it was early morning, and I was awake. I was again disturbed by Louise, who was as apologetic as Hal had been, but because she had to cross through the living room area to get to the bathroom, it was unavoidable. On this occasion, I didn't mind, as it gave me more time to enjoy the scenery.

Louise and I went outside to sit on the porch and watch the sun rise through the trees.

"So... you talked with Brooke yesterday," she said.

"Yeah, we talked for quite a while."

"Is she... does she have any idea of what she wants to do? Did you talk about that at all? Because she doesn't talk to me and I'm her mother."

"Yeah, funnily enough, that was pretty much all we talked about. So I don't think you have to worry. She's just trying to figure it all out."

"Okay. Well, you know, at least she's thinking about it. So that's something. She's turning twenty-one on Sunday. I just... well, every parent wants better for their kids than they had for themselves, you know?"

"Yeah, I get that. But she's smart, and ambitious. She just needs to figure out her direction."

"Yeah, I guess so. Hal always says she's digging to Australia with a pebble."

I laughed. It pretty much sounded like Brooke. Or what I knew of her.

Louise had asked Hal if he wanted to go fishing again, but he said he'd had enough, and wanted to head home. I wasn't surprised that he wasn't keen to fish again, but it did come as something of a surprise that he would want to leave so soon. We went back to the Visitor's Centre and stayed there for a while, watching the Snake River twist and turn. Brooke and Louise walked toward the edge, so they could feel the spray of the water as it raced against the rocks.

"The state line is down the river," Hal said to me, performing a divisive gesture with his hand. I thought it was a strange thing to say until he continued a few moments later. "Don't you think we spend a hell of a lot of time worrying about, and thinking about, what other people tell us, instead of what we can see for ourselves? I reckon we give way too much weight to the opinion of other people."

"You mean, like, a free world?" I asked, trying to understand.

"Yeah... I guess that's something like what I mean. None of this free world shit they tell us, though. I mean, really free."

"But, you *are* free," I countered.

"Yeah, but only 'cos I got money. I'm as free as I can be... but I mean free of the baggage of that perception... free from the influence of social convention. Or always behaving in the manner that we're told we should."

"I think I get you... but that's kind of how we evolved, isn't it."

"Yeah. But it's also... not."

It felt as if he had something else on his mind. As if he were articulating a thought to see if it made sense, but, still, I think he wasn't quite sure where he was going with it himself.

As we returned to the car, Hal asked Brooke if she would drive. He was beginning to find the driving a bit tiring and he wanted a chance to take in the view. I offered Hal the front seat, hoping that I could film some conversation from the back, but he insisted I remain in the front—maybe, to avoid having the camera on him.

We took the highway home, partly because it was quicker, and partly because it presented different scenery, if only from the car window.

Hal may have seemed reluctant to be recorded in the car, but as soon as we got home he became dedicated to finishing that project. It was something he felt he *had* to do, and *wanted* to do, but also, something that I began to feel was an obstruction from allowing him to enjoy his life rather than an indulgence to celebrate all he had achieved. Maybe arriving back to the house had literally brought home the concept of time and how limited it was becoming for him. I couldn't say that he was looking any less well, but perhaps it accounted for his desire to wrap up the recordings swiftly.

And so, accordingly, we spent most of Thursday evening, and almost all of Friday and Saturday, talking tirelessly about Hal's life: his experiences of working with various people, and his reluctance to continue to be involved in the music industry, due to the recent changes. On anecdotes alone, Hal's stories could have filled a book, but it was more in the tender moments, the way he spoke about Betty, Louise, and Brooke, that really got me. Occasionally, he would impart advice about dealing with people in the business—advice that would usually end with him saying that I should just ignore him, since he knew so very little these days.

Appreciating that we would be busy working, Louise came over to Hal's to cook, and Brooke came over to help on the Friday after she had finished her shift at the bar. This was much appreciated, as she was able to ask Hal questions about local people they had known, and stories from years gone by.

By late Saturday afternoon, we had reached a point where Hal considered that we had finished, and he thought we ought to toast to the completion of a successful project at Murphy's. He insisted that he didn't want to have any further part in whatever we did with the recordings, and the reality of that decision meant that it would be some time before they were ever revisited, allowing for the time to pass with Hal's own eventuality and enough time for those left behind to grieve.

Of course, to go to Murphy's to celebrate was as much an excuse to simply get something to eat with Louise on duty that night and unavailable to get cover. I had tried to protest, saying that I still felt that there were several key parts missing, but Hal's words were "there will always be something left unsaid. And that's the way it should be."

He had a point, and what was I if not his employee, after all? Having said that, even though it appeared that my official duties were over, I felt somewhat of an obligation to stick around. I had, for a moment, thought of flying home, and then back again for the funeral, although, in reality, I knew that I was going to, and wanted to, stay.

As we arrived at Murphy's, I noticed Louise and Brooke engaged in conversation with a man, a woman, and two boys, who I took to be their sons. There was, as always, an open bar stool for Hal, and one for me beside him. These people were familiar to Hal too, and as I sat on the outside of this group, I couldn't help but *feel* outside of it, too. It wasn't anything that anybody did to make me feel unwelcome—Louise was as welcoming and friendly as she always was, and I was included in conversations, but these appeared to be friends who only caught up once in a while, and who had made a special effort to be there for Hal. The longer the conversation wore on, it became evident that they'd come in from out of town and used to live locally.

I couldn't really engage fully in the conversation, and caught myself staring into space, lost in thought, and then, so as to not appear rude, trying to laugh at the appropriate times, even if I didn't get the jokes.

On one occasion when the father was in the middle of regaling the group with a long story, I looked across the bar and noticed Brooke staring at me, only for her to divert her glance quickly. I kept my eye on her, and eventually, she looked again, sheepishly. I couldn't believe it. Hal appeared to be right. I had no idea what I was supposed to do about it, nor how I was going to bring it up.

I had become almost completely disconnected from the conversation, lost in thought, when I was jolted back into focus by a comment from the mother of the visiting family.

"We always thought Brooke and Josh would end up together."

"Mom, please, shut up!" said one of the young boys—apparently, Josh—who appeared to be slightly younger than Brooke. So this was the last guy Brooke had dated.

"Well y'all sure did make a cute couple back in high school," the mother protested. Brooke glanced over at me again, and then looked down. "Oh, I dunno about that, we were young," she said.

"Yeah, but you only split up because Josh went to college. You should take Brooke out for her birthday. Didn't y'all always go to that Italian place?"

"Valentino's!" everyone called out together.

"Well, we don't leave town until Monday," said Josh. "You know, if you wanted..."

At that very moment, my phone rang. It was Kaia. It must have been 4:00 a.m. back home.

"Sorry, um... I'll have to take this," I said. I answered the phone quietly. "Hello?"

"Hey, Freddie," Kaia said.

"What's up? Is everything alright?"

"Yeah... more than alright, actually. I bet you're wondering why I'm ringing so early?"

"Yeah."

"Well... I'm coming out there to see you! My flight's in three hours, I'm just on my way to the airport."

"You're coming... here?" I said, signalling my apologies to the group as I wandered outside.

"Yeah! I was gonna come out sooner, but some of us have responsibilities... jobs... couldn't just up and leave... but I got some time off. I should be there Monday afternoon if there are no delays."

"So where are you now?"

"I'm in the taxi, we're almost at the airport."

"Oh... right."

I felt stuck. I didn't know what to say, but my immediate internal reaction, was "no, no, no!"

"Kaia?"

"What? Is something wrong?"

"I just... I don't know if it's a good idea."

"Well don't tell me that now!" she laughed.

When I didn't respond, she began to sound more serious.

"Are you joking, Freddie? Wait, one minute... just have to... we're just pulling up."

I heard her tell the taxi driver to wait a second while she got out.

"What do you mean, it's not a good idea, Freddie?"

"You know, things aren't great here. And I really don't know how long I'm going to be sticking around."

"That's okay. I'm only going to be there for a week. And then I'll come home."

Come on, now. The truth.

"You aren't going to like what I'm going to say."

"Then don't say anything, then," she said quietly.

"Kaia, you know I have to."

"Why are you doing this now?"

"Because you're literally about to get on a plane and come all this way. And I've been trying to convince myself... and... Kaia, I shouldn't be trying."

"I don't mind waiting. If that's what it takes."

"I *want* to tell you that I love you," I said, "and I think, you know, a part of me is always going to be that person who did. But that's not you, and it's not me."

"Wait. So are you saying that you're going back to Ailie?"

"What? No! It's..."

"Are you mad at me? Are you mad at yourself because we met up and you're punishing yourself because Ailie left?"

"No. No. This is about us. You and me. It doesn't work. It's not the same."

"Yes it is. Well, actually, it's even better."

"You think that way, because I was putting myself into it. I don't know what I'm going to say here that doesn't make me sound like a dick, because I am, but I just... if I'm being honest, completely, totally honest with both of us, then I *used* you, and I feel really shitty about that."

"What do you mean?"

154 : WAYNE BARTON

"Well... I can tell you now that I didn't mean to do it. That I was hurt and that you helped me at a time I needed it."

"Well, doesn't that tell you something?" she interrupted.

"Yeah. It does. But not what you think it does. It just tells me that I'm a bad person who should have got my own shit together. I shouldn't have dragged you into it, because I hurt Ailie and I'll end up hurting you."

"Look, Freddie. Let me come out and we can talk about it, okay?"

"Kaia, it's better this way. You're going to come out, I'll say all the same things, because it's how I feel. It is really, really bad that we met when we did because I... I can't tell you how special you are to me, your place in my life, but... that *was* our time and place. It's been. We can't just go back and be those people again."

"I know, but it can be better."

I could tell now that she was getting upset.

"Look, I can't pretend. It's not fair on you."

"Just tell me, are you not in love with me, do you not feel the same?"

"I can't tell you Kaia. I can't tell you these things because I'm just not sure how I feel. But we can't build a relationship on being unsure, not while I'm trying to figure myself out."

"But... I can wait. I'll wait. I'll still be with you while we get there."

"What I'm telling you is... what I'm feeling is not what I think I'm supposed to feel. Don't come out, please. Look, I'll pay for your flight."

Kaia did not respond.

"Kaia?"

"Yeah?"

"Please. It's for the best. I can... I'll talk to you when I get home, okay?"

"Okay," she barely whispered, before hanging up.

I took a moment to compose myself—sighing—and was surprised that it was a sigh of relief. I had been as honest as I could, and yes, it had been difficult, but I felt that I had said exactly what needed to be said. I felt guilty and terrible for Kaia, but I knew that I had made the right decision.

I couldn't tell Kaia that I didn't love her. I would do that later, hopefully after I had figured out what it was that I had felt. Lust? A temporary attraction? Or perhaps more appropriate to how it was at the time—an escape. Kaia had been such a help to me in one regard, more than she could have known, even if there was a little confusion, due to the timing of our reintroduction. I was starting to feel as though Kaia was once more part of my past, even though I understood I owed her a proper explanation. I owed her that, at least.

My relief was quickly outweighed by the guilt that she had gone to so much trouble to organise a flight and come out to surprise me; but, not the guilt one feels when someone has let down a partner, or even a loved one, just, the guilt that is felt when you have done something that you know is bound to have hurt. If there was anything I could take from all of that, selfishly, it was that I was at least free, now, to make the right choices. I could remember how bad it felt to hurt someone. Now, I could try to ensure that I never did that to anyone else again.

As I went back in to Murphy's, I noticed that the mother had now switched places with Josh, so that he was sitting next to Brooke. I sat back next to Hal.

"Really sorry about that," I said to Louise, and then to everyone else when there was a break in conversation.

"Was that Kaia?" Brooke asked.

"Yeah."

Thankfully, before she asked any further questions, Hal interrupted.

"Freddie, I ordered food and got you a burger. Hope that's okay," he said.

"Yeah, cheers. That sounds good."

The others were talking about what the youngest son, Alex, was going to do at college. I took a swig of beer and could feel Brooke's eyes burning on me. This is silly, I thought, avoiding her looks. This was all based on Hal's hunch and he had admitted that he was often wrong, even if he knew Brooke well.

I met Brooke's stare as if I had only just noticed she was looking at me.

"So, is she coming over?" she asked, casually.

"Let the man drink his beer in peace," Hal said.

"That's okay, thanks, Hal. No. No, she's not. Well, she was going to, but not now."

Brooke took a sip from her drink and looked down at it.

I didn't know what I was supposed to make of all of that, but I knew I was looking at her in a different way now.

Louise brought out the food for Hal and I. The family who had been sitting with us chose that time to get up and leave. Josh said he would pick Brooke up at six the following evening, and Brooke sheepishly nodded to confirm their prior agreement. I looked at her as he spoke to her and she seemed conscious that I was looking her way. There was surely no mistaking Hal's theory, but if so, why had she agreed to go out with this guy?

The rest of the evening felt awkward, with conversation drifting between what we had planned for the week ahead—nothing—and Brooke's twenty-first birthday.

In the car with Hal on the way back to his house, I felt like I had to say something.

"So... I think you're right about Brooke maybe liking me."

"Yep."

"But I don't know what I'm supposed to do about it."

"Ask her out to dinner," Hal replied, as if it were the most obvious answer in the world.

"I can't do that! We're friends. We live in... you know. Besides, she's going out with that guy."

"Josh. You can't even say his name," Hal laughed.

"Yeah, I just forgot it."

"You got a thing for her?"

"No, it's you. You're messing with me."

"How'd you mean?"

"I'm just out of a relationship. Two, in fact. I don't need any more drama."

"Just as well she's going on a date, then, right?"

In bed that evening, I thought of texting Kaia. I even thought of sending a message to Brooke, although we hadn't messaged each other, and it felt awkward, and very, very weird. Brooke was the kind of person who seemed like she would just address that kind of thing head on, so I decided that I'd wait for her. And, given our recent conversation, it was probably not the best time to be sending a message to Kaia. That didn't stop me thinking about both of them until I eventually fell asleep.

I had expected to wake up to a hub of noise downstairs, with Louise and Brooke already being over, or the sounds of Hal pottering around downstairs, but even though it was already 9:00 a.m., it was silent. Eerily so.

I got up and went to the bathroom, noticing that Hal's bedroom door was closed. I went downstairs and poured a glass of juice, before heading out to the back porch. As I opened the screen door, I was struck by the biting cold; not quite the winter's frost I was used to in England, but a chill that suggested I was a fool to still be in bedclothes. Nonetheless, the air retained its freshness, and I was too tired at that point to go back up and change. The cool in the air caused me to huddle for warmth and seemed to have magically improved or altered my visual capabilities, looking out at the grass to see thousands of individual tiny dew drops. The cloudy sky hid the sun. I was struck by how radically the change in temperature could influence my perception of this little utopia. It was still beautiful, but different, and my mind drifted to the realisation that one day, probably a day very much like today, we would wake up and Hal wouldn't. And then I worried. *What if that one day was today?* It didn't bear thinking about, yet I couldn't shake the thought. I sat on the porch for another ten minutes, hesitant to go back inside. I thought of doing something else to distract myself, but every two or three seconds my attention went back to Hal and this horrible sense of dread overcame me.

Don't be silly, I told myself. *He looked fine yesterday... yeah, but people die in their sleep all the time.*

I finally summoned up the courage to go back inside. It was cold and I wanted to get changed anyway. And just as I went in, Hal was walking through the inside kitchen door.

"Mornin'!" he said, cheerfully. He had no idea how relieved I was to see him.

"Hi, Hal," I replied, casually. "I'm just off to get showered and dressed."

"Okay, see you in a few."

As I stood in the wonderfully warm shower, I was trying to prepare myself, between those unexpectedly strong shots of relief: there would be time enough to worry, time enough to be sad. There was no need to let these feelings overwhelm me before it was necessary. I didn't think that I was crying although my eyes felt fit to burst. In the shower, it didn't matter.

I felt slightly anxious, and almost sheepish when I went back downstairs, as if Hal would know my innermost thoughts merely from the way I was acting.

Hal was out on the porch.

"So, you know, she was just testing ya, right?" he said as I joined him.

I sat on the steps.

"Yeah, I think you're right. But I don't really know what to do about that."

"Just play the game and have fun with it."

"Shouldn't you be threatening me to keep away? She's more or less your granddaughter?"

Hal straightened himself on the bench, going from a comfortable relaxed pose to a much stiffer and stern one.

"I was thinking more like my daughter," he replied, annoyed.

"Even worse, then," I smiled.

I could tell that he dispensed with whatever response he had ready once he noticed that I was joking.

"I'm just enjoying where I am at the minute. Without all that extra... you know. It feels like the first time in forever that I'm not in a relationship, and not troubled by feelings that I have for someone. I'm not in love. And that feels good," I insisted.

Saying it out loud felt right.

"Yeah... okay. I get it," replied Hal.

We sat in silence for a while—a comfortable silence—with the sun suddenly making an appearance and providing warmth and visual beauty to the landscape.

"So... have you given thought to what you're gonna say... you know, at the funeral?" Hal asked.

"Well, given that it won't be for quite some time yet, no, I haven't," I responded, bullishly.

"Can you say a couple of things for me?"

"I thought it was supposed to be my words?"

"I'd just... I would like you to say that I lived a *truthful* life."

Our eyes met. I could tell how important this was to him.

"How do you know I wasn't going to say that?" I asked.

"Because you haven't thought about it yet." Hal smiled. "Here. Come see this."

I followed him into the kitchen where a box was placed by the chair he normally sat on. I hadn't noticed it when I was in there earlier.

"I've decided to open some of these letters from Betty," he said. "Only, you know... up until the one I should read. I'll have two left. But I thought, you know... the next one I haven't read is the one for my seventieth birthday. And because today's somethin' of a landmark for Brooke, I thought it might be fittin' if I read this one and shared it with someone."

He looked at me again, a fixed stare, a kindly glance that unsettled me emotionally. I put the back of my hand to my mouth and just nodded.

"H, you made it. The big 7-0," he began to read, slowly, as if reading to a child. *"In these letters I have often wondered how you will look now. And as I write this note, it's the first time I consider how you will look different to how you do now. Your hair will be white—or, sorry, gone—and your kind eyes will bear*

the sign of the worry and concern that you have for others. I hope that your smile remains to show your kind face and isn't pulled by the gravity of sadness that inflicts others. You're an old man now, my love. I know you tell me today, and you'll tell me again, that you'll never change. But I hope you do. I hope you embrace it. Embrace the change in the world around you. In yourself. And in the people you know. Not everyone is going mad. And I know you'll tell me today that you will love me forever. I cherish those words, H. But love again. Love as much as you can. Because I'll still be here waiting for you when it's time. All my love, B."

Hal's lips tightened and he simply nodded. His eyes were downcast, and filled to the brim with tears.

"That was longer than the last few," he said sighing, after a short pause. "She must have saved her energy for the occasion."

"That's really nice," I offered.

"No."

Hal stood up and walked outside again.

I didn't know whether to follow or leave him. But, he had included me in this, so I felt an obligation to stick with him, and went back outside with him, sitting on the steps once more.

"Betty wrote that thinking I'd read it on my seventieth birthday," he said, eventually. "To think she was, you know... she sat with that in mind and saved the energy particularly for that. And me? I just let seventy come and go."

His voice broke, the tears on his face betraying his hardened expression.

I couldn't empathise. I had nothing I could compare it to. I couldn't imagine the hurt, the feeling that he had let something so meaningful go to waste. His tears grew stronger and his shoulders began to shake. I could feel his heart breaking, and had to sit beside him, holding him. I loosened my hug after only a few seconds, allowing him to compose himself.

After we'd sat there for a while, Hal continued, "I think I'll read the others alone, if you don't mind."

Maybe it was the externalisation of the words, bringing them off of the page and giving them life, which had provoked such resonance. But I could also understand Hal's determination to carry on, and read the others, such was the guilt he was feeling, however misplaced I may have thought it to be. It was rational, logical, that he would feel that way.

Hal went back inside but the thought stayed with me; the way that universal emotions can be so arbitrary. That Betty, God bless her, wherever she was, was not here to tell Hal he shouldn't feel so heavy with that sadness and guilt over merely leaving the letters unread. So, there was nobody who could reasonably tell him that he needn't feel such strain.

It was so personal to him, to his way, his own personality, that it had taken on its own perception of what was wrong and what was right. What I sympathised with and could understand was something he had perceived as a lack of respect to someone he had loved for longer after her passing than the time she had been alive. Only, to Hal, he hadn't made the distinction. It was one and the same. Those were his choices (even if he hadn't seen them as such at the time), and the choices he made were not *wrong*; they were simply decisions that he made to help him cope, which grew into things which *became* him over time.

He should forgive himself, I felt.

We didn't speak again until we heard the door go in the early afternoon, the unmistakeable noise of Louise and Brooke filling the house within seconds of their arrival. I had picked up my guitar and was playing on the porch, with the sun now fully out and warming the landscape, betraying that morning chill. It would be the ideal late spring weather back in England, unseasonably warm for mid-autumn. Perfect. I was a little lost in thought, wondering how I might remember this moment in time in months or years to come. Earlier that morning, the cold had made me think of Hal not waking, and now, within but a few hours, everything was as good as it ever had been. Not even the reality that this was only temporary was enough to sadden me. I had a fleeting thought that I was being anti-social, though I gathered that they would understand I was simply relaxing with the intermittent sound of the guitar.

"Hey! There you are," Louise said, joining me after a while, and sitting beside me on the bench.

"Hey," I said.

"It was weird sitting in there, with just the three of us."

"Sorry... just, enjoying the nice weather."

"So, how's Hal doin'?"

"He's good. How are you guys?"

"Good. We're thinking of heading out for lunch."

"Yeah?"

"Yeah. You should come along."

I considered the invitation, which I felt was kind and offered in sincerity, but then thought of how she had effectively said we were like a foursome. If I was really invited, surely, it would be implied without being stated. I didn't feel put out by that, or excluded, but I did take from Louise's comment that I should perhaps politely decline the invitation.

"Oh... erm, thanks," I said, "but, I think I might give that guy Tyler a call and set up a meeting."

"Oh yeah? As long as you're sure."

"Yeah, he's really good you know, so if we can work something out, that'd be cool."

Louise put her hand, and then her head on my shoulder. I felt a feeling of gratitude, and then I started to think that maybe it was simply that she wanted them to spend this special day in the way they had intended to as recently as two weeks ago. The way that it used to be.

We were interrupted by a squeal, and Brooke running out to tell Louise that Hal had promised to double whatever she had saved for her own car as a birthday present.

Louise rolled her eyes, with the impression that it had been done against her wishes, but Hal just couldn't help himself. Hal joined us on the porch and asked if we were going to dinner. As the girls agreed, and walked through the kitchen, Hal remained at the screen door and looked at me.

"You not comin', son?"

"No, I've... I'm going to call Tyler."

"Right," he looked curious. "Well, okay. I'll see you later."

"Have a good time."

"We will!" he called from the kitchen.

Having made my excuse, I felt it would be odd if I didn't contact Tyler, so I sent him an email asking if he was around, we could meet at Murphy's. He replied within the hour, saying he'd love to. I set off to walk there and on the way, I heard the patter of running footsteps behind me.

"Hey! Freddie!" It was Tyler. "I shoulda said that I could have come to Hal's. I have to pass there anyway."

"Hey," I replied, "don't worry. We're on our way now."

As we reached town, we passed a supermarket, and I thought it was probably a good idea to get Brooke something for her birthday. There wasn't much to choose from inside, and I didn't really want to give alcohol to the daughter of a bar owner. I went down the children's aisle to see if there was anything silly that I could find. And there it was. A Magic 8-Ball. Perfect.

By the time we got to Murphy's, Tyler and I had talked a fair bit more about the songs of mine that he liked and those of his that I had enjoyed. Tyler suggested that he could play some more for me now. I was happy with that and with the bar relatively empty inside, the bartender on duty didn't mind us borrowing a guitar for practice.

The other songs of his which he played for me were good, and I found myself enjoying his take on mine, too. After he'd played about six songs, we called it a day. I said we should have a drink and talk more.

It was clear that Tyler's intention was to record something, and I was happy to provide him with material or work with him to make new music. I thought about suggesting working at Hal's, but with things as they were, I instead said that I would love to work with him, but we should put any plans on temporary hiatus for now. As we talked more, we discovered that we shared many of the same interests in music, film, and comedy—and the rest of that afternoon was spent with Tyler showing me video clips on his mobile phone, of a stand-up comedian he liked.

We lost track of time, and Tyler eventually said that he had to leave due to a prior engagement. I promised to keep in touch and contact him once my schedule opened up.

Not long after Tyler left, I was about to leave myself, when Hal and Louise walked in.

"Hey, hey! There's my boy!"

Hal greeted me, obviously merry, already.

"Take him outside, please!" Louise said to me, laughing.

I took two chairs outside, and Hal came out to sit with me. Louise brought out a coffee for Hal, a beer for me, and promised sandwiches were on the way.

"A bit too much to drink, then?" I laughed.

"Too much on an empty stomach. I had a little something to eat but the girls didn't want dessert because Brooke is going out with Josh. So..." he said, "I'm under strict orders to have coffee and a sandwich before I'm allowed any more beer."

"You don't look drunk."

"I'm not. She's just fussing."

"So, you had a nice time?"

"Yeah, it was... really nice. You know, I was about to say that I was going to miss it. But I won't, will I," he said, matter of fact.

"They will, though."

"Yeah."

"They won't be the only ones. A lot of people around here will miss you. I will."

"Thank you," Hal said, touching my arm, to make me look at him as if to rubber stamp how much he meant it.

"You're welcome."

"I don't mean for that. I mean, for talking to me and *not* pretending that I'm not dying, y'know."

I laughed, uncomfortably.

"You're very welcome, Hal."

"I've never been a fan of that," he said. "Avoiding the subject.

The elephant in the room. People pussy footin' around and acting like what's happenin' just ain't. My brain's just as fast as it was. I'm no fool. Just my legs are slow and my bones creak. You gotta remember something. People are born, they live, then they die. I'm seventy-two years old. I could die in my sleep and nobody would even... what I mean is, I got the best thing anybody could get—a reminder, and a chance to really not waste time. So even those minutes I'm sat out there on the porch, I'm loving it. Every second. I'm not robbed of anything. Now, I know, you guys might see that different. And I know that with death comes a lot of sadness. But, please, don't cry for me."

"I get what you mean. But I don't think you can ask people to not cry for you, though," I confessed.

"I mean... okay. Did I ever tell you about my friend, George?"

"No."

"I say, friend, by which I mean that our parents knew each other. But they weren't... his parents weren't as smart as mine. Or something. Anyway, he went into the army, and he never came home."

"Right."

"So, you see?"

"See what?"

"That's what you cry for. *A life not lived.* I cried tears for Betty and... you know, that was justified. I don't think I... well, what I mean is, I *lived* my life. Don't be crying for anything lost, because I'm as content as content can be."

"Aren't you worried, at all?"

"Nah. If I worried, I'd be wastin'... wastin' my time away. And I ain't gonna be wastin' my time with that."

I had been caught offguard by Hal's frankness and so I had been carried along with it, but the brutal honesty in the conversation was something I wasn't really used to. I did, however, see it as an opportunity to ask Hal something.

"How are you feeling?"

"Like I said, I'm really good."

"No, I mean... are you in any pain?"

Hal stiffened his lip, as if *that* was too far.

"Yeah," he said, softly. "Yeah, it hurts."

"I'm sorry, Hal."

Hal shook his head, as if to dismiss my apology, yet to indicate that he appreciated that I had asked, he reached across to tap my hand.

Out of nowhere, one of the very first conversations I'd had with Ailie came to mind, about the propensity of man to consider that only one emotion generally be dealt with, or felt, at one time, and now, here I was feeling happy, and sad, and I guessed that Hal was too. I almost felt like sharing that with him, as if it were some revelatory kernel of knowledge that he would never have been aware of, but as the words were on the tip of my tongue, I felt foolish, almost like a kid, and remained quiet.

"What's changed in you?" Hal asked, catching me off guard.

"What do you mean?"

"You don't give me much, but I got when you came here you were reserved. Shy. Real polite like," he explained. "And I know you were looking for answers. You got some. But there's something going on there."

"I'm fine," I insisted. "I just... you know, you might be ready to say goodbye, but, I'm not. And I know I'm not the only one."

"I'm not saying it's *easy*. But if you made the choice, if you waited until you were ready, then you'd never say when," he said, softly. "But... some people, they're just kinda dying from the minute they're born. You know?"

I nodded.

"Don't be one of those people. You're better than that," he said. I could feel him looking at me, but I couldn't look back.

"Yeah, but you had done more before you were my age than I'll ever do," I said, with a sudden flash of self-awareness, remembering something remarkably similar Brooke had said to me a few days prior.

"And I've done nothing since," Hal stopped me. "Look...

you've got your whole life ahead of you, kid. You can do whatever you want if you want to change that, but *just don't be wasting time*," he said, stressing those last few words. "I don't want to be wherever I am going, thinking of you and hearing you say *if for this* and *but for that*. And you know, I get that Eddy dying affected you deeply... but it would really, *really* fucking upset me if you used me going to my better place as an excuse to start dying yourself. You have to promise me you won't."

"I promise, Hal," I said.

"Well, okay then, that's that!"

We were quiet for a while.

"Oh yeah, one other thing," he said.

"What's that?"

"You need to keep an eye on those two. I mean, they will look after you far more, but you know... they're my family. Like you."

The last remark provoked tears I could not stop. But I couldn't let Hal see just how deeply I was affected. I looked down toward the table and remained silent for a few seconds, before coughing and waving my bottle to show I was going to the bar. In my peripheral vision, I saw him nod, so I stood and went inside.

"I was just about to..." Louise started, before looking at me. "You okay, Freddie?"

I nodded and shook the bottle, standing at the bar to compose myself.

Louise came around the bar and gave me a hug.

I remained inside while Louise got me another drink. Part of me felt too embarrassed to go back out and face Hal. If he was trying to make me feel like a son, then it was working. And if he wasn't, then, in my eyes at least, I felt that our relationship had naturally evolved to that stage anyway. I thought about how people speak of how they fall in love at first sight, and how quickly that had happened with Ailie. Now, these nine or ten days in Hal's company had led me to believe that lifelong connections really could be created and built in such a short space of time, beyond, really, our understanding. I couldn't tell Hal. He would scold me for the saccharine, but I was struggling with the weight of the words he was saying to me, and what they all meant.

As I drank from that next bottle of beer, I found myself nervously and anxiously praying that I had grown as a person in these few months, grown enough to tolerate the inevitable pain of Hal's death and what would follow.

Suck it up Freddie, I told myself.

I would have to.

Louise came out with the sandwiches and directed me outside with her eyes. She could sense that I was having a difficult moment, but she also knew that Hal would know it too. There was no sense in spending these moments apart.

"I'm going to have a bit of a tab when I eventually get out of here," I joked as we went outside.

"Yeah, well, I stopped counting Hal's a long time ago," Louise said, handing him his food.

Hal had a mischievous and contented smile on his face in response to that comment.

"Small place for you to have got lost," he said to me.

"Just, getting another beer, and I had to go to the bathroom," I half lied.

As we ate, we didn't talk. There was no communication aside from a couple of contented grunts from Hal to confirm the deliciousness of the sandwich.

"I wanted to tell you, Freddie, just so you're not offended or left wondering. I really did wanna work with you," Hal said, after we'd eaten. "If I'm being completely honest, that was the reason for my trip to London in the first place... to meet this guy who had done such great work with Eddy... to put a face to the name, you know? But then, they said I was ill, and... well... I had all that stuff going on in my head and I just wanted to let go of it all."

"It's okay. I wasn't offended. I know."

"Because you are good, you know. You have so much talent. I only wish that you'd have been around when I was hitting that peak because... well, that would have been pretty damn special."

"Do you think... believe that things happen for a reason?"

"Yeah. Sure. Why?"

"Oh, I don't know," I said. "Just thought, you know... wishing for things to be different. It conflicts with the idea of letting things go."

"Yeah. Yeah, it does," Hal admitted. "But life ain't so simple as to say that we all follow one pattern. We're all hypocrites, we all contradict ourselves, and each other. I've tried to be the best I can, you know... the way I wanna live my life. The way I hoped I lived it."

"Nothing's over yet," I said, insistently.

Hal looked at me, then gave me this beaming smile, wider than any I'd ever seen, as if he were really connecting with that thought. Whether it was the content of the statement, or the implied hope within it, I couldn't tell, but I too had to smile in response.

We both sat there, smiling like a pair of fools.

"You know what I see when I look at you?" he asked.

"What?"

"I don't see somebody who is lost. I see somebody who is *free*. The only difference is state of mind. But... I think you're there."

I thought about that, as Hal continued.

"Your freedom. Man, nobody can put a price on that. A value. You spend your childhood developing yourself with no influences other than those around you. You're encouraged to try new things. To embrace difference. Then, when you're a teenager you're pressured to conform to the standards of society. Pressured by peers and pressured by those who are supposed to be guiding you. How many voices are lost? Man is suppressing the voice of his child."

He paused.

"... but you still have your voice."

Hal had said so many things that were wise and profound. He had said so much that I'd tried to keep on board, so that at some point in the future, if I couldn't apply it to my past, then I could at least use that wisdom when those feelings resurfaced, or situations came around again. But these words of freedom and liberation spoke loudly and clearly to me right there and then. It seemed like he was finally articulating the thought he'd had as we were preparing to return from Hells Canyon.

"Do you mean, like, hedonism?" I asked. I felt like I had a stronger grasp on what he meant, even though I struggled with a definite term. I wasn't even sure if there was one.

"Well, I never understood the problem with hedonism," he replied, after another pause. "You know, as long as what you're doing to be good to you ain't bad for others... but that's only a part of it. I just mean, as I see you. You seem free. You're not the product of anything you've been through."

"I would say that I'm the product of *everything* I've been through."

"Everything and nothing."

I talked to Hal about Tyler, how I enjoyed meeting him, and how we'd planned to work together, and that I was sure I'd be back around. I didn't say when. I didn't think either of us felt I needed to.

At times, we talked like old friends, me playfully laughing at his failure to catch fish out on the lake and feeling comfortable enough to joke about his repetitive use of the story about his dad not wanting to send him to Vietnam, and him calling me "hound dog," to mark his perception that I'd been moping around for the first few days.

At other times, we conversed like the new acquaintances we were. Hal asked with genuine interest—and, it seemed, envy, as if he really did see me as *free*—about my own travels around the U.K., back when I was just one guy, a guitar, and a CD of karaoke tunes. I still felt like I was that person, yet in Hal's company, I felt like I was so much more. He loved that idea of being on the periphery of stardom, able to enjoy many of the benefits without— as he called them—the pitfalls, the intrusion, for one, which he had happily lived without for many years. I could tell from Hal's words why he loved it here. He was just about the right level of star for someone of his ego, someone who would lap up always being the centre of attention, but never too prominent that there would be intrusion or controversy.

And, for the rest of the evening after I'd gone back outside, the spectre of Hal's illness vanished from my consciousness and disappeared from our collective thoughts. As we laughed uproariously at each other's stories, a few of the regulars came outside to talk to Hal, almost as if he were present at his own wake, but in that sense where people refuse to accept sadness, even in its bittersweet form.

I was enjoying myself more than I had for a long time, when Louise came outside with another beer for Hal and asked if she could speak to me inside.

"Have you had much to drink?" she asked.

"About four or five," I said. "Why?"

"Brooke just texted me and asked if I'd pick her up. But I can't... you know, I don't wanna leave Hal," she said.

"Oh... I don't... I've never driven out here. I don't even have my license with me. I left it back in the U.K.. I didn't thank... " I said.

"If I pay for the cab, can you go and get her and take her home? I'll get the cab to take you to Hal's after, or back here if you want?"

I felt hesitant. "Can't she just get a cab herself?" I asked.

"Well, my friend, Nancy, happened to be having dinner at the same restaurant and just sent me a message to say that Brooke seemed pretty drunk," Louise replied. "I'd feel much better knowing that she's with someone I trust. Please, Freddie. You'd be doing me a huge favour."

"What about Josh?" I asked.

"Let's just say that didn't go too well," Louise replied.

I couldn't really say no, so I gave a small nod.

"Thank you, Freddie! You're a godsend!" Louise said, giving me a hug and a kiss. "She's here," she added, writing down the address on a piece of paper, before adding, "but don't worry. I'll tell the cab driver where to take you."

I took the note and nodded, then Louise added, "I know you'll look after her."

I went back out and told Hal that I needed to do a quick errand and asked if I could take the keys. Hal refused to give them to me at first until I told him where I was going and that he'd have to talk to Louise to find out why. Fortunately, the cab pulled up just as he started asking me why. The driver took me to a part of town I didn't recognise, pulling up outside Valentino's. I recognised the name from the previous evening's conversation.

Brooke was waiting outside the restaurant and looked somewhat confused when she saw me. She was dressed to the nines and appeared almost unrecognisable. She also seemed flustered, and almost annoyed, to see me.

With no Josh in sight, I could feel my pulse begin to quicken.

"Hey, you. Happy birthday!" I said to her, casually. "Your mom sent me to get you. You okay?"

"Yeah, I just... yeah, I'm fine."

We got into the cab, and as we drove around town, we sat in complete silence. Brooke seemed preoccupied and didn't appear in the mood to talk. We can't have been driving more than five or ten minutes when we pulled up in front of a modest bungalow.

"Have a good night, Brooke. Happy birthday," said the driver.

"Oh, hey! Vinny!" she responded, reaching for her purse to tip him. "I'm so sorry. I didn't realise it was you."

"Don't worry, this is on me," he stopped her. Then he looked at me. "You good?"

"How far is Hal's from here?" I asked Brooke.

"You can walk," she said. "Or you can ride. Whatever you want."

"No, I'll walk."

We both got out.

I could feel an awkward tension as the cab drove away.

"So, where's... Josh?" I asked, knowing I was deliberately pretending to not remember his name for that split second.

"He's not here," Brooke replied, flippantly.

"Yeah, I get that."

"I think he expected something to happen that wasn't ever

going to." She appeared agitated and refused to look at me.

"I'm sorry. You okay? That's not a good way to end your birthday."

"Well thankfully, it hasn't ended yet. Why didn't we go to Mom?"

"Hal's... you know, he's being Hal. He's fine, but she's just looking after him."

"I wanna go there."

"Well, that's up to you. You could've said that in the cab."

"I thought you weren't talking to me," she said.

"Wait. What? Why would you think that?"

"I don't know."

I took "I don't know" to mean, she presumed that I'd be jealous that she'd gone out with Josh. *Unreal.* Although, she was right.

"Ugh," she continued. "I've had too much. I feel dizzy."

"You okay?"

"Yeah... I'll... I'll be okay."

She walked up the garden path and sat on the front porch steps. I stood by the wooden beam supporting the porch roof.

"You sure?"

"Yeah, I'm sure. So, how come your girlfriend didn't come out?"

"Because... you know. She's not my girlfriend. And I'll be going home soon, anyway."

"You'll be going home soon?" she repeated, slowly.

"Yeah. You know."

"Yeah... I know."

She looked at me, sorrowfully.

"I'll miss you," she said.

"I'll be around," I said. "I'm going to be working with Tyler."

Her eyebrows raised, almost hopefully. "Yeah?"

"Yeah. He's got a lot of talent."

Brooke appeared distracted, tapping her purse, and looking

away from me, into the distance.

"Hey, what's wrong?" I asked.

"I'm just... I'm trying not to think about Hal. But I can't do that when you're here."

"I'm sorry," I said, without really knowing what I was apologising for. I sat down beside her and put my arm around her shoulder, pulling her in, before releasing my hold.

"No, sorry, I don't mean that... I mean it in a nice way. So, anyway, why didn't she come out?"

"I told her not to," I admitted. "It's not the right thing. We're done, we're through. I don't know if she got that message but, that was the one I was trying to send."

Brooke was fumbling with her hands. I could sense she was trying to think of something else to say, to move the conversation along.

I could feel it too, the anticipation, that sense of being where we were, but trying to speed the words and dialogue up to justify that position. It felt right. It felt unsteady. I watched her click and flick her fingers together, and then, I looked at her as she turned to face me. Her eyes were hopeful, keen even. There was a deliberate pause between us, a drawing together, and then a stop. And in that moment, I remembered Louise's words: "*I know you'll look after her.*"

"You should go inside."

Brooke looked hurt, disappointed.

"You said, you've had a bit too much to drink. And I need to walk back to Hal's to make sure I'm there for him."

"Sure," she said. I could sense the sarcasm in her voice.

And yet, I didn't make a move. I was fixated on the moment and could feel the tension, her eyes fixed on mine.

"You know... those girls were really dumb to let you go. I'd love a guy like you... you're *perfect*," she said.

"No. No, I'm not. You really must be drunk," I laughed, awkwardly, although, of course, it was exactly what I wanted to hear.

"I'm serious. Country girls like me don't get to be with big stars."

We were so close that I could feel her breath on my cheek. I saw her eyes glance between mine and then to my lips. She was telling me, without words, that she was going to kiss me, and she bit her lips before opening them slightly, in anticipation. For my part, I sat there, waiting, a willing participant. I had forgotten about doing the right thing in that moment, with the thought that everything but the kiss would be safe.

It wasn't.

Brooke kissed me. Softly. Perfectly. Our lips came together almost with a sense of curious urgency, after all of the words, all of our procrastinations, all of the things left unsaid, and all of the feelings that were so new. With an aching, and a longing, so powerful that I was a stranger to its strength.

Then, her lips pulled away, and our eyes opened, hers fixed on mine, as if to clarify that what we had done just felt right. I couldn't tell what she affirmed from my own look but as she drew in for a second kiss, I once again remembered Louise's words.

"Um... I have to go. And you need to sleep," I said, repeating, nervously, "yeah, I have to go."

"Okay." Brooke looked confused.

I stood and walked toward the gate, before turning around to ask where I should go. Without a word, Brooke pointed to her left.

"You okay?" I asked.

"Yeah," she replied, in that curt way which really means *no*.

"Okay... well, see you soon." I turned to walk away.

The adrenalin in my body was pumping so hard that I felt I could walk to Hal's and back three times. I was sorely tempted to turn around and go back to Brooke, but it had been so difficult to pull myself away the first time I knew that I wouldn't have the willpower a second, and, further, I did not wish to have that kind of complicated conversation with a disappointed Louise.

Our kiss had released an avalanche of emotion, all positive, and extremely overwhelming. It was real. It was *everything*. And it was the only thing on my mind.

There were only two reasons, to my mind, why we couldn't be together; one, my word to Louise, was only temporary, although it may well be the case that she would disapprove for her own reasons. The other, the distance between us in normal terms, might make things difficult, though the world was a small place. Yes, it was soon after Ailie, and Kaia for that matter too, but I was in a true place of clarity, one where I knew, without a doubt, how I felt.

But then, what about Brooke? She was drunk, after all. Even if the alcohol had provided her with the courage to act on what she was feeling, how real was that? I thought about the emotional problems that she was going through. Was I merely a crutch, a distraction, a reaction? I replayed our conversation leading up to the kiss. The way she looked at me was the same way she had looked at me in the bar the day before. There was definitely something real between us, but I couldn't help but feel that I was taking advantage of her vulnerable position.

I was back at Hal's before I knew it, although I remained awake for hours, replaying events over and over in my mind.

Capo 2   The Avenue

The two of us are staring at the shore
   sharing things we've never shared before
of coorse- here I am, the Soul that no one sees
the Voice that no one hears, the person I can't be
I'm a long, long way from home
    a long, long way from home.

you say my name and I go out of style
On the Avenue you always change your mind
   where's the time? where am I?
here I am the one that no one sees, the voice
that no one hears, the person I can't be.
  I can't find my feet, but I will not let that
beat me, I'm a long long way from home
a long long way from home.
    a long way from home.

8

For the first time since arriving in Idaho, I woke with no real plans or ideas as to what the day would bring. I woke early, and after making some toast, I again started to worry about Hal, who was late to rise. I couldn't lecture him about drinking, but given his words about time, and not wasting it, I did feel as if I should say something. That said, maybe he just needed the sleep.

It was a dull day, with the rain on and off, and, in all fairness, it felt like a Sunday, or at least, the kind of weather you hope for on a Sunday, so you can be rained in and watch TV. I thought I'd do just that, and was watching some television when I heard Hal's footsteps, out of his bedroom, and then down the stairs and into the living room. He looked worse for wear.

"Morning, Hal. Sorry, did I disturb you with the TV?"

"Morning," he replied, sounding rough. "No, I just don't feel too good. Bad headache. I was gonna get some aspirin, but I'm not sure if I can with all of these drugs they've got me on. I think I'm just gonna sleep it off"

"Okay. You need anything? I can go to the store if you want?"

"Yeah... maybe some orange juice. Something fresh, you know? Fruit or something. But take your time."

"Are you alright?" I asked.

"Yeah, yeah, I'm fine." He dismissed me with his hand, an acknowledgement that my question extended far beyond his current headache.

"Okay, I'll go in a bit."

"Thanks. Well, it's back to bed for me," Hal said.

I heard him fumble around in the kitchen, then shuffle back

upstairs. There were bound to be bad days. Slow days. And there was no hiding from his sickness, and the change within him. He didn't talk about it, or complain, but he couldn't hide it. He was getting slower. His time spent in bed was increasing.

It would be wrong—guilty as I felt to admit—to say that I was consumed with concern for Hal because, I found my thoughts constantly drifting back to Brooke. There was a real anticipation within me, in the truest sense, of seeing her again, and how it would be. And I was completely buoyed by Hal's words about what he saw in me. I felt confident about myself and my decisions— and, also, *free*. I could perceive free as something I could now *feel* rather than just be, and knowing that I had control over that, and that others saw it in me. I don't think it would be overstating it to say that I felt a sense of empowerment over myself that I really hadn't ever felt before.

I decided that I would go to the store for some groceries and also stop for lunch at Murphy's. After shopping, I went to the bar and was happy to see that Louise, unsurprisingly, was working.

"Hey," I said.

"Hey you!" she smiled.

Oh, *thank God*, I thought—no drama, no annoyance. I don't know why I had felt apprehension. I hadn't done anything wrong by Brooke, but, if she had been upset at all, I thought maybe she might have said something to Louise, like I'd been mean to her, or something. It was so irrational that, pieced together logically in the wake of Louise's friendly greeting, it was frankly ridiculous.

"Thanks so much for looking after Brooke last night," she said, as if to confirm my thoughts.

"My pleasure, honestly."

"So, what can I do, a beer, food?"

"I'll have a short beer and the Philly, please."

"Sure thing," she said, sweetly. She took my groceries and put them in the fridge to keep them fresh.

When she brought my beer back, she asked how Hal was. I told her that he had a sore head. Louise said that Brooke was the same.

I couldn't shake that Sunday feeling. In fact, it felt as if every day here was a Sunday. I had to commend Louise for getting work done at all and showing the commitment to do it. The glue, as Hal had said. In more ways than one.

It was quiet in the bar, as it would be on a Monday afternoon, and so Louise spent most of her time talking to me. I thought we'd navigated past the tricky subject of Brooke, but later on she was brought up again.

"So, yeah, Brooke's date didn't go too well."

"Yeah, she said... that was a shame."

"Yeah, a real shame. On her twenty-first as well. You would want her to have something to remember it by."

I shifted nervously in my seat, as if she knew everything that had happened. It wouldn't have surprised me if she had cameras on that place, or an extra pair of eyes. Louise, after all, did seem omnipresent.

"I'm sure she did... I mean... she had that meal with you and Hal."

"Yeah," she smiled. "That's true. Still, it would have been nice... but, you know, I don't think that Josh is right for her. He's a nice boy, but... to me, they just didn't fit right, y'know?"

Louise turned and walked away, picking up glasses to clean that I was certain had already been cleaned. It made me think that she had left that comment hanging deliberately, as if to make a point. Was she saying *I* fit right? Was it her way of granting me permission to see Brooke, to say she thought I was a good guy?

As I finished my sandwich and drink, I asked Louise if I could have the groceries, as I was about to get on my way.

"Oh, but you'll miss Brooke. She's on her way over!" Louise insisted.

"I really ought to..."

"Well, speak of the devil!" Louise said, cheerily. I turned to see Brooke.

"Hey," she said to her mom, and then me, a little more sheepishly.

"Do you want a water, or a juice?" Louise asked.

"Water sounds good, please," replied Brooke.

"Sore head?" I asked.

"Yeah, something like that."

As Louise went off to get Brooke a glass of water, we sat there, with an ominous silence between us. I was wondering how much, if anything, she remembered of the previous night, but her awkwardness suggested she had a pretty good idea. Breaking the ice on a subject that both of us were hesitant to broach, however, was another matter.

Louise returned, to what I felt was collective relief between Brooke and myself, and after some small talk about Brooke having done nothing that morning, I made my excuses about having to go and see to Hal.

"Oh, okay," Louise said reluctantly, fetching me the bag of groceries.

"Sorry, it's just that, I said I wouldn't be too long and I've been out a while now."

I said my goodbyes, and couldn't quite make out the tone of Brooke's response. In that moment, I was sure it was relief, and so as I left the bar and stood outside, I, too, felt relieved. It was another of those occasions where the smallest amount could be said and yet a million different thoughts are created. Had it simply been a drunken mistake that she was keen to forget? At least, if so, we had gotten over that first hurdle. My train of thought was interrupted.

"Freddie!"

Brooke.

"Yeah?" I tried to act cool with it.

"Thanks. You know, for, looking after me last night."

"That's fine."

As we both stood there, it seemed like there was so much more to say. But, in my stubbornness, and under the thought that Brooke must have something more to say, or she wouldn't have come out, I bit my tongue.

"And, um... I'm sorry... for kissing you," she said, staring down at the ground. Her apology was genuine, as if she honestly felt that she had made a mistake.

"That's okay. You were pretty drunk, you know, you were saying and doing some crazy stuff."

"Right," she replied.

"Okay, well, I..." I raised the shopping bag, as if to say I really needed to get back, and turned to walk away.

"No. Wait!" she said.

I turned back toward her. She ran her fingers through her hair, nervously.

"I mean... I meant what I said. You're a great guy. And I, you know, um... meant the kiss. I just mean sorry for putting you in that position."

I was lost for words. She was pretty brave. I couldn't be that forward. Apparently sensing that, she gave me a free pass.

"But, yeah... you need to get back to Hal. So, I guess I'll see you later?"

"Yeah, sure."

The walk back was a curious one. Now that I had allowed myself to see her that way, I couldn't believe someone as beautiful as Brooke was being so blunt with her emotions and so forward. Well, I could believe that about Brooke, but just, not toward me. It felt like luck I didn't deserve. Yet as good as her words had made me feel—and they made me feel like the luckiest man alive—I had handled it wrong. I froze when I should have spoken up. Perhaps I wasn't used to this amount of conscious control over my own feelings.

And now, what must Brooke be thinking? I had essentially accepted her apology for kissing me—as if I didn't want it.

It wasn't my finest hour.

It was early evening by the time I arrived back at the house. I half expected Hal to still be in bed, but when I went inside and walked into the kitchen, I saw him sat out on the porch. I went to join him and noticed that he had a whisky.

"You sure that's a good idea?" I said, half-joking.

"Oh, hey, Freddie!" Hal said with a smile, in a croaky voice. "Good old hair of the dog. Why don't you join me?"

"Yeah. Okay, sure."

I went inside and poured a small whisky, and then sat down on the porch steps as Hal relaxed on the bench.

"Sure is a miserable day," Hal said.

"I don't know. It's been quite nice," I replied, perhaps with a hint of deliberate fishing for Hal to notice.

"Oh yeah?" He looked at me.

"So... last night. I had to go and take Brooke home. And, erm, well... she kissed me."

"Is that so?"

"Yeah. I don't know if I did the right thing, though. I sort of walked away."

"Don't worry, kiddo. It'll work itself out."

We sat there for a little while, in a silence that was becoming increasingly comfortable, before Hal eventually called it a night.

I thought of doing the same, but I had a little too much adrenalin at that point. I also considered giving Brooke a call, or texting her. She had been so brave in putting her thoughts and feelings out there, the least I could do was send a message. But, even with that in mind, I harboured the procrastination, that nervousness. In a masochistic way, I think I enjoyed it, and felt that the uncertainty was somewhat good for the heart, good for the soul, and good for creativity.

So, I decided to simply get my guitar and just relax until it was time to go to sleep.

For a moment, I thought it was an alarm on my phone that I'd forgotten to turn off. The persistent tone told me otherwise. I ignored it the first time, and then it came again. I looked and saw it was Kaia. *Ignore it*, I told myself. Go back to sleep. And then the phone bleeped with a text message. Against my better judgment, I checked it.

"I'm here!" it read.

What?

Before I'd had an opportunity to even gather my thoughts, much less respond, another message came through.

"Didn't want to have to tell you over text, but you didn't answer my call."

"Where are you?" I wrote. I already knew.

"Idaho."

I was writing *where* when my phone rang.

Kaia was calling.

"Hey," I answered.

"Hey, Freddie! So, yeah. I'm in Idaho. Boise."

"What are you doing there?"

"Where are you?"

"Miles away from Boise."

"Oh."

"And I thought I said not to come."

"Oh."

A very awkward silence followed.

"But I'm here now," she eventually said, as if that somehow negated every point I'd previously made.

I knew that I couldn't leave her there. She had travelled all that way, and I couldn't just leave her there, on her own.

"Have long have... when did you get in?" I said.

"Yesterday. But I was nervous to call in case you were mad at me."

"I'm not *mad*, Kaia. I'm just... I don't know. Well, I suppose I'm going to have to come and get you."

She told me where she was staying, and that she'd text me the address.

I went downstairs. Hal was already awake and watching television. He didn't look so well.

"Hey. Still feeling rough?" I asked.

"Yeah, not the best."

"Do you think we should call the doctor?"

"Maybe. I'll see."

I got the impression he just wanted some time to himself, so I went out on the back porch.

There was no way I could ask Hal to drive me. This left me with few options. A cab or a bus, which would have been expensive. I wasn't even sure if there was a bus. I couldn't call Louise, since that would create a very awkward scenario. This left me with only one viable alternative, though for every other reason, reaching out to Brooke was an impractical-as-any-other method.

I hadn't even called Brooke yet, and the prospect of that first time being one to ask for a ride to visit my ex-girlfriend, who I felt sure Brooke doubted was my ex—and, maybe Kaia even doubted that too—was so anchored by certain awkwardness that it wasn't a thought I really wished to entertain. Yet, I knew I must.

I checked bus times on my phone, looking for any way out, but nothing looked viable. I didn't know what I was really looking for.

And so, with much reluctance, I found Brooke's contact in my phone and pressed her name.

"Hey!" she said, clearly not expecting my call.

"Hi. How are you?" I asked, trying to sound as natural as possible.

"I'm good. How are you?"

"I'm okay, thanks."

"So, what's going on?" Brooke inquired.

"Well, I hate to ask, but I've... err... got a bit of a situation. And I really need your help. I understand if..."

"Sure, no problem, Freddie. I'll be happy to help," she interrupted, eagerly. "What's the deal?"

"Thanks, although you might not be so keen when you... I got a text from Kaia. She's in Boise."

"Oh. I thought you said..."

"Yeah, I did. But..."

"Right. So..."

"I feel terrible asking you this, but I really need a ride to go and see her. She... I can't ask Hal. He's not feeling that great," I said.

"What? Is he okay?"

"I don't know."

"And you're going to leave him?"

"No, he's not bad like that. He's just... under the weather. I wouldn't leave him, you know I wouldn't... it's just, I can't... she's flown all this way."

"So, you want me to drive you to see your girlfriend. And then what?"

She didn't sound happy, to put it mildly.

"I don't know. Stay in Boise. I know it's far. I'll pay for a hotel room for you."

"Wow. I don't know if this is a joke."

"'No, no it's not. Look, I know how bad it sounds. I wouldn't ask if I wasn't... if I had another choice."

"I'm working this morning."

"Oh, right. Sorry."

"In fact. I'd better go get ready now."

"Okay. I'm sorry Brooke."

"Bye." She hung up.

I had barely had a chance to think about what I was going to do when I got a text message.

It was Brooke.

"I'm off at 3:00 p.m. I'll pick you up."

"Thank you so much. I really, really appreciate it."

It was the most appropriate thing I could think of saying.

"K." she replied, curt as you like.

I sent Kaia a text message to let her know we'd probably be arriving between 6:00 p.m. and 7:00 p.m. The guitar was still out on the porch, so I played for a while before I decided it was best to go get ready and pack a bag.

You say my name and I go out of style
on the avenue, you always change your mind
where am I... here I am,
the soul that no-one sees,
the voice that no-one hears,
the love that I can't be,
I can't find my feet,
but I will not let it beat me,
I'm a long, long way from home,
I'm a long, long way from home.

I was interrupted by Brooke's cough, as she stood in the doorway of the kitchen. I stopped instinctively, almost a little bit embarrassed, as that was one of my own songs.

"Hey," she said, without emotion.

"Hey, Brooke. Did you see Hal?" I asked, in an attempt to deflect the issue at hand.

"Yeah," she sighed. "So... you ready to go?"

Our conversation felt every bit as awkward as I had anticipated. But there was nothing I could do to change the situation. Of course, Brooke was her usual self with Hal, fussing after him and insisting he ought to go to the doctor—and yet she was as cold as ice with me. Hal, now fully aware of the situation, found it all very amusing, giving me one or two knowing looks, as if to say, *rather you than me, buddy.*

For the first part of our journey, Brooke flipped from station to station on the radio. I concluded that she probably didn't want to speak to me, but after a while, she turned off the radio, and then I wondered if she was revelling in the tension in the air. I noticed that Brooke's journal was no longer in the car. No chance of using that for easy, warm, conversation.

"I'm sorry, Brooke," I said. "I know this is putting you out quite a bit." I had considered saying something completely innocuous, to try and get the conversation started, but small talk would have seemed rude, like I was being evasive.

"It's fine. I mean, you can't let her down," she replied, in that way that seemed to imply I would prefer to let Brooke down instead.

Having been put in my place, I remained quiet, thinking it would probably not be the wisest decision to speak again. Brooke was bound to have a smart response for everything, and, truth be told, I really was in no position to challenge it. I knew that I had few other options, but I still regretted having asked Brooke.

I felt as if Brooke was purposefully avoiding looking at me. In the bar that night, with Josh, Brooke had been watching me in a way that suggested she liked me. And she had been braver than I ever had in any relationship by effectively confirming her feelings when she had followed me out from the bar. Now, I could feel a coldness, a distance, and an annoyance that I undoubtedly deserved.

Even though the current situation was not really anything I had planned—Idaho, Kaia, Brooke—it did feel as if my chickens were coming home to roost, and that I needed to deal with the consequences of my actions. My immediate concern was Brooke. But I hadn't been fair to Kaia either. I deserved Brooke's coldness. Not to be a martyr, but, I could accept her frustration. I resigned myself to the likelihood that it would be difficult to return myself into any sort of favourable light in Brooke's eyes after making such a terrible impression.

As we pulled into the parking lot of the Riverside Hotel in Boise, Brooke appeared even more annoyed. It was a fancy hotel in a picturesque location, and I got the impression that Brooke thought I had somehow contrived this scenario, or that I had intended to spend time with Kaia here.

"Nice place," she said, in that sarcastic manner which said a thousand words. "Kaia's obviously got good taste," she continued, saying a thousand more.

"Yeah," I agreed, as if to say I was as clueless as she was, but realising, as I did, that it sounded like I was simply agreeing. "She must have just thought *go to the capital*, as if I'd be here. I don't think she's ever been to America. I mean, that shows how little I've talked to her about it."

"So, what happens now? Do you go in and leave me here, or... do you introduce me to your girlfriend? And do I have to apologise for kissing you?"

"What? No!" I said. "She's not my girlfriend. I just... you can't stay here. You should come in."

"Okay."

We walked into the lobby, and just as I was about to approach the reception desk, I heard my name being called out. "Freddie!" Kaia—who had obviously been sitting, waiting for me—jumped up to greet me. She hugged me with a broad smile and held on to me, as if nothing was out of the ordinary. I tried to pull away a little, conscious of Brooke, and as I did, I looked over at her. She was not impressed.

"Hey, Kaia. Erm... this is Brooke," I introduced them. "Brooke, Kaia."

"Hey," said Kaia, who suddenly looked confused. I knew I ought to elaborate, but how could I describe either of them when I had no idea how to?

"Brooke's, erm... I guess the best way to describe Brooke is, that she's like the daughter of the guy I'm working with."

"Yep. That's me," Brooke said, pointedly, as if I'd given her some drastically irrelevant introduction. She went to shake Kaia's hand, and Kaia went for the hug instead.

"And you're Freddie's girlfriend, right?" Brooke said.

Kaia smiled, and then smiled broadly at me, as if I had been the one to pass on that information.

"Yeah, I guess you could say that," Kaia said.

"He's told me a lot about you. He didn't say how beautiful you are, though," Brooke said, twisting the knife.

"I... err, better go and book our rooms," I said, turning toward the reception desk.

"Have you guys eaten?" Kaia interjected. "I was waiting for you. I booked a table in the restaurant. For two. But I'm sure we can add one more."

"Sure, sounds good," Brooke said.

"Two rooms please," I said to the receptionist.

"Let me see," the receptionist replied. "Oh, I'm very sorry, sir, but it looks like we only have one more room available for this evening."

"You're joking," I replied. Now I was really starting to panic.

"That's okay. I'll take the room and you can stay with Kaia. That's why we're here," Brooke suggested.

"So... you'll take the room?" the receptionist asked.

"Yeah, we'll take it," Brooke confirmed.

After booking the room, Brooke went to get her things, saying she'd leave me and Kaia to it.

"So... girlfriend?" Kaia said, smiling.

"I just... Brooke's got a weird sense of humour. But she knows about... you know, what happened... with Ailie and with you."

"She does?" Kaia stated, with a twinge of jealousy. I wasn't cut out for these conversations.

"Well, yeah. I've made a few friends since I've been here. And Brooke's really nice."

"Yeah, she seems it. So, are you happy to see me?"

"Yeah. Of course," I said, trying my best to sound enthusiastic.

Kaia gave me another hug, right as Brooke returned, with my bags as well as her own.

"Here," she said, nudging me with my bag to interrupt. "I'm off to my room to freshen up."

"Cool," Kaia said. "We can take your bag up to my room."

Kaia was oblivious to the funny look that Brooke gave me. It was a look that said *you created this—if you don't like it, it's up to you to find a way out*. My immediate problem was that as much as finding a way out seemed ideal, I simply couldn't run away from the situation and leave Kaia high and dry.

I followed Kaia up to her room, making small talk along the way. In her room, I kept hold of my bag, consciously not wanting to put it down and give the wrong message. I was well aware, however, that the longer I made a point of holding it, I was also sending out a message. When I eventually did put it down, I noted a change in Kaia's demeanour, more positive, more certain.

"So, Brooke seems really nice," she repeated, as if to verify what I'd said earlier.

"Yeah, she really is. I mean, in the town where she lives, everyone's so friendly and welcoming."

"So... we need to talk," Kaia started.

"We'd better go down," I replied, hurriedly, "I'm hungry and it's not polite to keep Brooke waiting."

"Oh. Okay. But can we talk later?"

"Yeah. Sure. We've got lots of time."

On the way back down to the reception area, we didn't talk at all, until we were back in the lobby and met up with Brooke.

"Hey," said Kaia, taking the lead. "The rooms are really nice, aren't they?"

"Yeah, they're amazing," Brooke agreed.

I was strangely relieved that the only awkwardness appeared to be felt by me. Brooke was trying her best.

Kaia said she'd check to see if our table was ready. Brooke and I stood in silence. It seemed as if she was about to say something when Kaia returned.

During the meal, we'd discussed that it would be best to go back to Hal's the next morning and try to figure out what arrangements we could make for accommodation for Kaia. Kaia offered to get a hotel room, but Brooke kept saying that she was sure Hal would let her stay at his. That wasn't a conversation I was particularly looking forward to. I wasn't particularly enjoying this one. Brooke was asking questions that seemed straightforward and reasonable; what did Kaia do for a living, where did she live and so on, and then when Kaia answered, Brooke's responses were always gushing with praise. It was uncomfortable for both Brooke and I as Kaia went into the history books to recall the media course we were both on at college, and how she had gone on to study journalism and continue on into a career. "So you're smart *and* beautiful," Brooke said, which I felt was more for me than for Kaia.

After we had eaten, Brooke decided to make a quick getaway.

"So, I'd better leave you guys to it. I'm gonna need a decent night's sleep before the drive back tomorrow," she said, standing up and yawning as she talked. "So nice to meet you," she said, reaching down to hug Kaia.

She just turned to me and smiled smartly.

"See you tomorrow, Freddie."

"Goodnight. And... thanks," I replied.

"Hey, no problem. You are so very welcome."

As she spoke, and smiled, I saw a glassy glaze come over her eyes, as if she were trying to stop herself from crying, a feeling that was seemingly confirmed as she tightened her lips.

"Well, g'night, *you two*," she said, with an emphasis on the last two words.

As Brooke walked away, my attention was diverted back to Kaia, who smiled and suggested we go back to the room.

Once there, it was time to talk. There was no way of avoiding it now. We both sat on the bed.

"I, um... so, yeah, are you pleased to see me?" she asked, as if my earlier affirmation didn't suffice—as if that was her lead-in comment to the conversation that she wanted to have.

"Yeah, of course. I told you I was. I am."

"Only, it's just that... it seemed as if you didn't want me to come out."

I sighed.

"What? What is it?"

"Well, I... this will sound like I'm being horrible. But you're asking me a question now when I told you on the phone... and you're acting like I didn't say it. Or you ignored me. It's not a case of asking until you get the answer you want to hear."

"So what you're saying is you didn't want me to come?"

"Now you're putting words into my mouth. I did tell you not to. But, you know... well, you're here now."

"I'm sorry. I didn't know what else to do. I just thought... I could come out, and we could talk about it."

"Yeah, well. I've got a lot going on here."

"I'm sorry, Freddie."

"You don't have to be sorry, Kaia. I just..."

And in the realisation that she was here for answers, I was able to know for myself what the answer was.

I felt bad for Kaia, sorry for her. But I felt way worse about the situation with Brooke. Every passing second of Kaia being here was potentially damaging my relationship with Brooke.

I knew that I didn't feel for Kaia the way I thought I should, or had, and I was able to come right out and say it when she interrupted me. "I love you. You know. I'm in love with you, I really am. I know that. And I know you've had a tough year, but I'm here now, and there is something really good that has come out of it. Like you said, you always come back to me. That's a sign."

"It's... Kaia."

"What?"

"You *can't* be in love with me."

"I am. Why can't I be?"

"To be in love, you need two people feeling that way."

She looked me square in the eyes. I couldn't tell if she was angry or upset. Or both.

"So, you're saying that you don't love me?"

"I'm not *in* love with you. Sorry. And you can't..."

"Don't tell me what I do and don't feel," she snapped.

"You can't be in love with me, because I haven't been myself. You don't *know* me. You know this messed up version of me that was trying to be with you, for... I don't know what reason. And I'm really sorry for that, and I'm sorry that you've come all this way to be told that. But I did say..."

"Okay," she gulped. I could tell she was getting upset. "But like I said, I can wait. You admitted yourself, you're confused..."

"I'm not, though."

"You said you needed time."

"No. Not anymore."

"So what's changed in two days?"

"It's not two days. Nothing's changed, I just... it wasn't what you thought it was. It was *never* the way I made you think it was."

"It's fine, you know. I've waited years, and I can wait longer," she said. And with that, she drew closer, and tried to kiss me. I had to pull away.

"Kaia, come on," I said, and stood up, walking toward the window.

"What?"

"You weren't waiting years for me."

"I already told you, you don't know how I feel."

"But I wasn't hiding for years and years, Kaia. You knew where to find me."

"Why are you being like this? You're being cruel to be kind, is that it?"

"No. Don't be stupid."

"So now I'm stupid?"

"No, you're *being* stupid. I'm trying to be honest and up front with you."

"Well thank you very much."

"I don't expect you to thank me, but I'm being as honest as I can, like I was on the phone. And yet, you came out here, anyway. What do you want? You want me to feel guilty? Well, congratulations, of course I fucking do. I hate myself for doing this, but you chose to come out here. I can't feel guilty for you coming all this way to hear something you already knew, something I told you, you wouldn't like. You can't put that on me. That's not fair."

"You're talking to me about *fair*?"

"Well, why are you angry?"

"I'm not, my heart is just fucking breaking, so pardon me for not reacting rationally."

Her hardened glance broke, and she didn't hide her pain any longer. And I was reminded of how I'd felt on the day we reconnected with each other. That I saw her as a person, not just a girl who was capable of inflicting pain. I was doing the same to her, and not even an explanation which appeared perfectly logical to me was one that could appease her. But now, I was certain that she must have seen me as someone completely uncaring. Since when did logic have anything to do with love?

"I don't know what else to say or do," I admitted.

"This is messing with my head. You don't get to be the good guy out of this."

"I'm trying to make the best out of a bad situation."

"You tell me how you're going to make it better. I'm thousands of miles away from home and all alone."

"Okay. That's fair. Let's just keep using that to beat me with. I'll own all the shit things I do. I'll take responsibility for this entire mess. But you're here now. And you know... you don't want to hear this. But I *do* care about you.'

"Yeah, sure," she replied, sarcastically.

"Of course I do. But this is the situation I wanted to avoid. I'm not saying that to deflect any blame or responsibility."

"You mean you're lumbered with me now?"

"No, but... you know. We're lumbered with each other, aren't we? I know this isn't fun for you."

"I'm right aren't I? I'm a burden. Did I get in the way of you and Brooke? You move fast, don't you?"

"No, you're not a burden at all," I tried to reassure her. "But we do have to get through this time together. I can't simply leave you here on your own."

"Forget it. I'll just get the first plane back."

"No, you're here now. You shouldn't be doing long journeys like that, particularly not while you're so upset."

"So, what? I get to play gooseberry?"

"What?"

"You and Brooke, like I said."

What was the point in lying?

"Look..." I started.

"I knew it!" she interrupted.

"There's... I can't say there's nothing. But I like her, yeah. I admit that."

"See! I *am* a gooseberry. How fucking tragic. This is so embarrassing."

"Don't... no, it's not like that. She doesn't even know."

"Oh, I see. It's *complicated*," she sneered. "Get over yourself, Freddie. You try and be so different, but you're a walking fucking cliché."

Ouch. Okay, so she could be hurtful.

"Well, no. I just thought... I've told you about Hal. And I didn't think it was right, the timing's not..."

"Sorry."

I could tell that she meant it.

"It's okay. I deserve it," I admitted. "What can I do?"

"Nothing, I don't think. I just need time to... to get this all right in my head.'

I watched as she lay on the bed and curled into a ball. I went and sat on the chair. She was checking her phone.

"I can't afford to go back. I booked a return ticket. I have around $200 in cash, so now I don't know what to do."

I thought about offering to pay for a return ticket, but in the circumstances, I decided that it would only make her feel worse.

"Remember when we bumped into each other and we went out for a drink?" I said.

"Yeah, of course. It wasn't that long ago."

She turned around to face me. Her eyes were red, but her expression had softened.

"Well, I was with Ailie, and... I felt guilty, because I knew what we were doing. Almost from the first second. But even so, I had that... you know. I was still mad at you. Because... you know. I was heartbroken when you left."

Suddenly, she didn't seem so friendly.

"So, what's this then? Payback?"

"No, no!" I insisted. "No, I mean something different. I just meant that... within about five seconds, I mean, that's all it took me, about five seconds to realise that you were... I know that you weren't bad. You didn't mean to hurt me."

She wasn't impressed.

"I think I want to be alone. You should go to Brooke."

"But..."

"Please, Freddie. I want to be alone. I don't want to talk. I just want to sleep."

I rose and left the room, momentarily pausing and wondering if I should repeat that I was sorry. However, at that moment, I was sure anything I said, however well-intentioned it may have been, would probably cause more harm than good.

Not knowing Brooke's room number, I felt I had little choice but to go down to the lobby. I planned to ask reception if they would mind me sitting or sleeping on a seat in the lobby, or, I may just sit there anyway and drift off and wait to be questioned on it. But as I got there, I looked through to the hotel bar and saw that Brooke was sitting at the bar with a beer.

She didn't notice me.

"Do you have a place to crash?" I said, to get her attention.

"I thought you had one," she replied, deadpan, barely even bothered that I was there.

"You okay?" she said.

"You really wanna know?"

She didn't reply.

"So, are you having a good time?" she said, raising her eyes from the bottle to look at me.

"Do I look I'm having a good time? What part of you thinks this is a situation I would like?"

"I dunno. You were up there a while. And didn't you say that you couldn't live with losing her again?"

"Well, if it helps, I was just called a *walking fucking cliché*, so there was that. I guess if you call that enjoyment, then, yeah, sure."

Brooke smiled.

"And you know, you haven't exactly been very helpful."

"You're only getting what you deserve."

I sighed. She was right.

"I can see why you like her. She's gorgeous."

"What am I supposed to say to that?" I said, in a tone that

immediately felt harsher than I'd intended. "That's just your assumption."

"OK. Whatever you said. Well, *you got me*. So I should just keep my opinion to myself?"

"No, sorry. I didn't mean *that*. I just meant assumptions. They don't help."

Predictably, I'd said the wrong thing, and Brooke didn't reply for a while.

"I get there's some stuff going on," I said. "And I know that's it's probably just as awkward for you as it is for me, but, you know, it's... what is it, midnight?"

"Yeah, I should probably get some sleep."

"Yeah."

"What are you gonna do?" Brooke asked.

I didn't say anything. I didn't have a solution.

"I've got a sofa in my room. You may as well sleep on that. At least your back won't hurt. As much."

"Yeah. Thanks. I left my stuff in Kaia's room and... well, I don't think I'd be welcome back there."

"I'll go if you want?" she offered.

"No, probably for the best if she just sleeps."

We grabbed a couple of beers and headed up to Brooke's room. I sat down, and Brooke got ready for bed; coming out of the bathroom in her underwear and a t-shirt.

"I, um... I thought I'd be alone," she said.

Though she had said she was tired, she clearly had some energy left, turning on the television and then sitting beside me on the sofa. I was going to lay down, but then she sat across the sofa with her back against the arm rest and her arms wrapped around her legs. As much as I tried to avoid it, my eyes were drawn toward her bare legs. Her feet were almost resting against my legs. Briefly, they'd touch them, and the physical connection sent shockwaves through my body. I knew that I couldn't act on my impulses, as it would make things much more complicated. But she looked irresistible.

"I don't know how relevant this is. But just so you know, Kaia kissed me... or at least, she tried to," I confessed.

"Right," Brooke replied, as if she didn't care.

"I didn't kiss her back. I pulled away. It wasn't even really a kiss."

"Okay," she said, looking at me and not the television.

"I really am sorry about asking you. But I... I didn't know what else to do. I didn't really consider how much of an annoyance it would be to you."

"Why should it bother me?" Brooke replied.

"You're right. It shouldn't, sorry."

She smiled at me, and I couldn't really tell if she was being genuine, or if she was messing with me.

"So you travel half the world and you still manage to bring all your baggage with you. You really are a walking cliché," she laughed.

"A walking, *fucking*, cliché, I think you'll find."

"I stand corrected."

"You're right though. But I didn't... I wasn't coming out here to escape. That was just... it was something that came up. But even if I was, or wasn't, it doesn't matter. It's here."

"It?"

"I mean the mess."

"Oh."

"I wouldn't talk about her like that. Or anyone. I don't think. It's just... you know. I feel so guilty."

Brooke turned back to watch the television, and I looked at her as she did. I could tell that she had almost half an eye on whether I would look at her. Her feet brushed against my leg again. It felt intentional this time.

"Are you okay?" I asked.

She turned back to me.

"Yeah. Just... worried... about Hal. And Mom."

"Have you talked to them?"

"I sent a text earlier. He's okay," she said. "You know what you were saying about escaping. I used to want to escape. I used to imagine that my Mom wasn't my Mom. You know. I'd look at her hair. Her eyes. And I'd think, you can't be my Mom. And some nights I'd pray real hard for my real Mom and Dad to come back. And they'd be rich. Rich enough so they didn't have to work and they could spend all their time with me. I dreamed like that for nearly a year and then I gave up. It wasn't until a couple of years later, I was like, twelve or something. Mom got ill... not real bad, but she had to go in hospital. And I had to stay with Hal for a couple of days and he made me do chores. Mom never made me do that. And, he tried... I mean, he's like a Dad. But... you know that way that your Mom is always looking after you? And you always take that for granted. And then I didn't. And I felt so guilty after that. You know? I've felt guilty ever since."

"You were just a kid."

"I know. There's no real logic to any of it. But it doesn't stop. You know. She's done so much to give me everything she could. And I feel guilty that I didn't appreciate what she has done for me. But, yeah."

"You know what?" I asked.

"'What?'"

"Sometimes I think there are things... you know, these little reminders that we are given by certain situations in life, that let us know how to feel. A lot of people take what could be relatively minor pieces of information, or guilt, and shape their entire lives around them. What I mean is, you *could* take that guilt about your mom and make it your life's purpose to make sure she knows you appreciate it. You could do that, or, you could just be at peace with the fact that you've been reminded. I mean, you're not wishing to run away or escape anymore, are you?"

She was quiet for a while.

"Sometimes. But for different reasons these days."

"That's natural, though. Don't beat yourself up. It's all part of finding out who you are. Look at me."

"Yeah, that doesn't exactly fill me with inspiration," she joked.

"Twenty-one feels *old*. I don't know. Like before, I felt like I should decide what I want to do... but not like I had to. And now I feel like I should. And I just don't know if what I'm looking for is where I live."

"There's no real time limit."

"No, but I don't want to waste my life."

"No."

"I kinda wanna travel. Like you."

"No, when I travelled, that *was* to escape. I was always travelling *away* from somewhere. It was never about the destination."

"Oh, right."

"I'm talking about a long time ago. Before I even met Ailie."

"Yeah."

"This is a great place. This is a place I wouldn't mind travelling *to*. If this was my destination."

"You have to be kidding?"

"Why?"

"Oh... I don't know," Brooke replied, before changing topic. "You know, Mom wanted to hold another open mic night tonight. Last night there were a lot of people asking for you. We expected you to come."

"Oh, right. Sorry."

"No problem. It certainly couldn't be helped."

The conversation was drifting, but in a good way. We were both keen to keep talking, but were also fighting tiredness. I imagine there must have been a few more attempts at meaningful interaction, but I couldn't remember any. The next thing I could really remember is that I was laying on the sofa with a blanket draped over me. Brooke was on the bed. She seemed to be still awake, or watching me, but I was drifting in and out of sleep, and although I tried to smile, I'm not sure if I did.

When I woke up properly, it was morning, and I got the impression that it must have been a noise that woke me, because Brooke apologised for disturbing me. She had already showered and was looking for a hairdryer. It must have been a knock from one of the drawers that stirred me.

"Morning," I said. She looked at me and smiled.

For a few moments, I thought only of Brooke, and how comfortable we were getting with each other.

And then I remembered Kaia.

"I hate to bring this up," I said, "but you know I can't just send Kaia back, right? Not just yet. So she's going to have to come with us."

"Yeah, I know," Brooke replied, nonplussed.

"You okay?" I asked, to confirm.

"Yeah. You?"

"Yeah."

"Mom asked if we were coming back today. And if you'd do a set at the bar."

"What did you say?"

"I said I'd ask you."

I couldn't really turn Louise down.

"Yeah. I'd better."

Brooke smiled, as if I'd just agreed to do her a big favour.

"That's cool. I get to see you play. I'm working tonight. I owe Mom after yesterday."

"What was yesterday?"

"Well I should really have worked all day. But... you know."

I couldn't really say anything to that, but I suddenly appreciated the lengths that Brooke had gone to a lot more. She could easily have given me a convenient excuse. Honestly, as awkward as this trip-within-a-trip had started off, I was now feeling strangely happy that it had. I might not have had the opportunity to have spent such a close evening with Brooke, and though the circumstances were not exactly ideal, I wouldn't have changed it.

I showered and dressed, and when I was out of the bathroom, Brooke told me that my phone had just beeped.

I checked, and it was a text message. Kaia. *"Morning. Where are U? I'm in lobby x."*

"Was it Kaia?" she asked.

"Yeah, she's in the lobby already. I don't know what I'm going to say to her about where I slept."

"Just tell her the truth."

"Yeah. Why not?"

"You know... and I'm sorry, I'm just asking. You said that you didn't know if you wanted to be with Kaia," said Brooke. "Do you know, now?"

"Yeah. No, I don't."

"You don't know?"

"Yeah, I do know. And I don't want to be with her."

"Okay."

There was a calm quiet between us before we left the room. I guessed that Brooke was searching for some reassurance—that she had gone out on such a limb and was now looking for some confirmation that it hadn't been for nothing. And, I admit, her doing that provided reassurance for me, that the feelings I was beginning to develop were not unrequited.

Yet I did still feel awkward as soon as we approached Kaia in the lobby. There was no avoiding her realisation that we had been together, and no appropriate way to say that nothing had happened. I wondered how such a conversation could be struck and handled in a manner which wouldn't end with both Brooke and Kaia being upset, so I decided I'd just wait and ride it out and see if either of them would bring it up.

If I'd thought that the time spent with Brooke would be enough to appease that situation and dampen any prospect of her trying to make things difficult, I was sadly mistaken. In fact, I was a little put out by her suggestion that we take the long way home if Kaia wanted to see the Shoshone Falls. I felt a little put out, as if it was reductive of Brooke's part; a harsh reminder that Kaia and I were both tourists, considering that's just where she had taken me. I spent most of the journey looking out at the sparse countryside and considered the irony of all I considered freedom

204 : WAYNE BARTON

as opposed to being trapped in this difficult situation.

As we passed the sign for Bliss, Kaia—sitting in the back seat—tapped me on the shoulder.

"Were they sure?"

"What do you mean?"

"Calling this place Bliss," she said. "All that's missing are tumbleweeds."

Entering the town from this side, rather than the side where Hal lived, one could effectively see what this area of Idaho had to offer, with its dusty roads and sparse properties.

"It's really nice," I protested.

"We're staying here?"

"Yeah. Well, not too far. Gooding, it's the next town."

"Oh..."

I could sense her searching for an apology, but she remained silent.

"Don't worry," Brooke saved her. "Tumbleweeds would make front page news." We all laughed, though I was sure that Brooke wasn't so very disdainful about her home town. I couldn't tell if she was being sarcastic about it just to keep up appearances or if she was making a mental note about Kaia's comment, getting things off on the wrong foot. We passed the town sign for Gooding, which bore the motto, "Gateway to a Good Life."

"Well, I like it," I said.

"You would," Kaia said sarcastically, apparently buoyed by Brooke's support. I squirmed a little in my seat.

"So, you know, Freddie's playing at an open mic night at my Mom's bar later," Brooke told Kaia. "So you'll get to see him perform."

"Really?" said Kaia. "That's great, I've never seen you play."

"No, me neither," said Brooke. "But he played the other night when I wasn't working and apparently everybody loved it."

"Well, not exactly," I interjected.

"And there's already someone who said they want him to help them write songs," Brooke continued, with an intonation that suggested this backwater place was good for something. A bit of local pride, and a bit of inflation of my ego to boost.

"That doesn't surprise me. Freddie's really talented," Kaia agreed, and then, instead of feeling flattered, I just felt really uneasy. Instead of bashfully shrugging off the compliment, I remained silent, hoping that the conversation would move swiftly on.

It didn't, and I kept thinking that Brooke was either waiting for me to say something, or Kaia felt that after speaking last, she couldn't be the next to speak.

We pulled into Hal's, but he wasn't home. There was a note on the table to say he had gone to Murphy's. Brooke called Louise to say that we'd be over soon. I put my bag in my room and took Kaia to one of the other bedrooms, saying that if Hal was okay with it, she could stay there. While she freshened up, I went to quickly change, and then I went down into the living room.

"Will you play some of Hal's songs tonight?" Brooke asked. It was unexpected.

"Yeah, sure. Although after hearing the master first, and then hearing some dodgy British tribute act, I think it'll be a massive let down."

"Hal would like it. And I would too."

"Yeah, okay. Sure. So... yeah... thanks so much for taking me to Boise and sorting it out. And thanks for not... well, you know. It could have been worse."

Brooke laughed. "I thought I was a pain."

"Well, you are, but... you know."

She smiled, and brushed her hair behind her ear, flirting. Or so I thought, anyway.

The moment was interrupted by the sound of footsteps on the stairs and into the living room. In walked Kaia, looking glamorous, dressed up far too elaborately for Murphy's, though I could barely say anything. The transformation in such a short space of time was incredible.

"Wow, you look stunning," said Brooke. "That dress is beautiful."

"Oh, thank you," replied Kaia, who then looked at me hopefully.

"Yeah, you look really nice," I added, awkwardly. "But I should say, you know... it might be a bit much. It's just a pub."

"Oh," Kaia responded, disappointedly. "Should I change?"

"No, no, of course not," snapped Brooke. "You can add some glamour to the place." Brooke punched me on my leg. "But, if you don't mind, I need to get changed, too, so we'll need to go to my home first, before we head out."

We did, and as Kaia and I sat outside on the porch waiting for Brooke to get ready, I wondered what to expect. Brooke was impossibly beautiful, and I knew that she could look good in anything, as I'd seen her the other night for her birthday. But I was a little anxious about seeing her dressed up like that again, because I knew that my natural reaction to seeing her would be a dead giveaway, and probably even more awkward than having to give her a compliment.

But as she came outside, I was surprised to see that she was dressed in jeans and a Murphy's t-shirt.

"I thought we were all dressing up," I said, before I'd had time to think.

On second glance, I saw that Brooke had really made an effort with her hair and makeup; a contrast to her clothing. Kaia didn't seem to notice—of course, she barely knew Brooke to know the difference, and I can't say that I knew with certainty to be able to distinguish, but I did have the distinct impression that she was trying to compete. Or at least, make some sort of an effort. And now I'd spoken and made an idiot of myself. Hopefully she wouldn't have noticed or taken it the wrong way.

"Thanks. Some of us have to work, though," she said in a dismissive tone that I knew was anything but dismissive.

We arrived at Murphy's and, as anticipated, Kaia was overdressed. I wondered if she would feel self-conscious, but she didn't appear to be. Heads certainly turned, and I guessed that she probably enjoyed the attention.

Hal was on a stool at the bar and Louise was with him. We'd

barely had an opportunity to greet each other before Louise was telling me to go on to stage to warm up. It was barely 6:00 p.m. and there weren't many patrons, but I felt that I ought to do as she said.

I took a guitar from the side of stage, and as I looked out at the audience, I pondered whether I would feel right playing songs that I'd written about Kaia in front of Brooke. In front of Kaia, even. In front of Kaia in front of Brooke. Although I'd envisioned, hoped, even, that there would be a bigger crowd for Brooke's idea of a performance of Hal's songs, I figured it would probably be better to start off in front of a smaller crowd in case they bombed.

"This is a song by someone way more talented than me," I started, while still trying to decide on the song that I'd probably murder. I decided on "Divide," one of Hal's more recent songs. It was a completely spur of the moment decision to try and illustrate a point that I enjoyed his later songs.

It received a smattering of applause from those in the bar. I decided then to go a bit bolder and try one of the songs that Hal and I had worked on together. I had already accepted that he didn't want to continue working with me in that vein, but there was some bravado in me at this point, some confidence in my performance, so much so I wanted to prove a point; that these songs would have been liked.

As I started playing "More Than You Know," I looked across at Hal, and he eventually realised what I was doing. If there was a look of realisation, then that was all; he seemed neither annoyed nor impressed. The reaction of the rest of those in the bar was appreciative, although the keenest applause came from Kaia and Brooke.

I thought two songs was a strong enough warm up, and so rose from the stage afterwards. As I left the small stage, Hal and Louise walked over to one of the booths with Kaia. Brooke was behind the bar and so I thought I should go to Hal.

"Nice work, kid," he said.

"Well all the good in that came from you," I insisted.

"I thought I recognised one of those songs," Louise said.

"Yeah... the second one was one that Hal and I were working on. I like it, I think it might sound better with a band or some more instruments."

"That was what you were working on?" Brooke, who had walked over to bring me a beer, interjected. "That was really good. Hal, you should keep working."

"Ah, so *that* was your plan?" Hal looked at me, laughing.

"No, not at all. I just think it's a really good song."

"Right."

"Honestly!"

"Well, I loved it. And I loved what you did with Hal's song as well," Brooke continued.

"Yeah, it was brilliant. I can't believe how good you sound," Kaia added.

"You've really never seen him play before?" Brooke asked.

"No, never. He would send me songs that... well, he *used* to send me songs, once upon a time. But he never played them live."

"Well, those songs were pretty bad."

"No, they weren't," Brooke replied. "Aren't they the songs that got you your fame and fortune?"

"Apart from neither, yeah, I guess. But, yeah, not quite as good as these I've been working on with Hal."

"Don't be ridiculous," Hal said.

"Why not just admit that you're both outrageously talented?" Kaia said.

"Yeah, okay," I replied.

"Anyway, what would you guys like to eat?" Brooke interjected, as if to remind us that she was working.

"I'll have whatever Hal recommends. That's how it usually works."

"Just a cheeseburger for me, please," Hal said, and then he looked at me.

"Yeah, sure. I'll have that."

"Me too," said Louise.

"Do you have anything like pasta, or salad?" Kaia asked.

"Sure, I'll fix something," Brooke replied.

I felt somewhat uncomfortable as we all sat together, particularly with Brooke waiting on us.

"I was gonna have to say something if you didn't go for the salad," Louise told Kaia. "Brooke... let's just say she's in remedial as far as being a chef goes. But we'll get her there. At least we know she can't burn a burger."

"They're great. The salads," Hal confirmed, before turning to Kaia himself and extending his hand over the table formally. "Young lady, it's a pleasure to meet you, seeing as this guy isn't going to introduce us. I'm Hal... and this is my good friend, Louise."

"Kaia. So pleased to meet you," Kaia responded.

"Hey, sorry, I would have, but I was forced on there," I complained, thumbing toward the stage.

"So, where you gonna stay? Because you're more than welcome to stay at mine."

"Well, I think that... we already went there?" Kaia looked at me.

"Yeah, we dropped Kaia's bags there, but you know... I would... if you think we should stay somewhere else?"

"No, not at all! You're prefectly welcome to stay with me."

"Well, I wouldn't want to put you out," Kaia said. "And, you know... if there's a hotel, maybe, it's more... I don't mean to sound rude, but..."

"Yeah, a girl needs her privacy, her own space," Louise said. "There's a place about fifteen minutes away. 1000 Springs. It's beautiful. It's where Tyler works. His sister owns the resort."

"Why haven't you mentioned it before?" I said.

"One day at a time!" Hal said.

Louise continued. "Well, I think if you're going to see any sights around here, I'd go to Shoshone, but if you're going to be sticking around for a while..."

"I think I'll only be here a couple of days," Kaia interrupted, coyly.

"Okay, but even so. If you're staying somewhere around here,

I would recommend down there, because it's beautiful. You have the springs coming out over the lava cliffs. Really is a wonderful sight."

"Great. Thanks. Do you think they'll have a room?"

"Honey, this time of year, I'm sure you'll be able to take your pick. We can have Brooke take you down later after she's finished work."

"That would be great. Thank you."

If that solved one problem—that Kaia wouldn't be staying at Hal's, thus removing that constant awkwardness—it created another, as now I would have to decide on the right thing to do. Surely, knowing that I was staying at Hal's, Kaia wouldn't expect me to go and stay at this place with her.

When Brooke brought out our food, I noticed that she seemed to observe how closely Kaia and I were sitting together; not that we were, at all, but it seemed to be of some importance to her in the way she looked at me.

As we ate, our conversation drifted between Hal's stardom, the retelling of stories I was now familiar with, but still fond of hearing, and how long Louise had owned the bar.

By the time it came around to performing again, Murphy's was much fuller, so Louise had gone behind the bar to help out. Kaia, Hal, and I had been sat together at the bar, and with a couple more beers in me, I went up on stage, following a generous introduction by Brooke, stating that I was one of the U.K.'s best songwriters.

"Well, no pressure there," I said into the mic, to some laughter.

Motivated by Brooke's and Kaia's encouragement earlier I decided to run through the repertoire of songs Hal and I had worked on together, giving a warning before starting that these were new songs I was trying out.

I hadn't really realised how much I had enjoyed the previous two times performing here until I was in the middle of the first song. No pressure, and in fact, a mostly receptive—if, admittedly, expectant—crowd. There was at least some sort of attention, some relevance for my being there, not like the dives that I'd made my way around in the U.K. all those years ago.

It barely mattered that Brooke and Kaia—and probably Louise and Hal, to the locals—had made such a fuss over me. I didn't feel any pressure, or any undue weight of expectancy. After four or five songs, I decided to play a couple of my own, only realising that I had played one that was written about Kaia, and released with The Cause, after I'd done it. I winced internally as I thought about what Kaia might think once I went back to join them. And so I decided on one of the non-person specific songs I'd written with Ailie which also went on that record, one I was sure that some of the audience might recognise, and I was able to close my set to a very generous applause.

As I returned to the bar, Louise said that she would bet Tyler would be bummed to have missed out. I was flattered by her kind words, but a little embarrassed as they continued with Kaia telling me how wonderful I was, how I should release a record of my own, and how you hear about "overnight success" stories all the time. She even suggested I should go on to one of the television talent shows I detested. I knew she meant well, but it was these little pockets of conversation which were revealing just how little she knew me these days.

I hadn't really realised it at the time, but arriving in Idaho, I had not only left a place, or situation, behind but "then." Or "now." I'd left *now* behind, and *now*—in the form of Kaia—had come back to me, before I was ready for it. I found it absurd to think I could have changed so much that I now had such strong, negative feelings about the past, and there was an absolute multitude of emotions attached to this that they were simply too overwhelming to begin to confront.

As the others talked, I let these thoughts weigh on my mind until I was introduced into conversation. I wasn't the most sociable or gregarious of people, but being here with Hal, Louise, and Brooke, had brought out a side of me I barely recognised, though I enjoyed it more than anything I'd known of myself in my entire life. That scared me. That it had taken just two weeks in nearly fifteen hundred of my existence—I counted them—to arrive at this conclusion. Had it required distance from everything else to provide the perspective that I had been lacking? If so, was it only the distance and the perspective at that moment in time? Could I have done this before I met Ailie, and reached some conclusions about myself that were completely different? Possibly. But how far back could I go? And where would it end if I did? I could pontificate about all the wrong turns I made in life, and wonder if they even were wrong turns, ignoring the fact that I was now in a place I had always pretty much wanted to be.

If that were my cross to bear, I wondered, what were the conditions of paradise?

I wondered whether I was only feeling like this because I had been confronted with my past and that it had reminded me that soon enough it would be my present again? So, was it Kaia that didn't belong in my present, as my discomfort had tried to suggest, or was it in fact me?

As Kaia began to talk about of how she had judged Gooding before entering but commented how she was enjoying it now and couldn't wait to see what her hotel would be like, I didn't know if I resented or appreciated and empathised with her turnaround of emotions that may have seemed gradual but were—in human terms—fairly rapid. And with such an emergence in the transience, I too couldn't trust in the stability of my feet or my mind.

That withdrawal from any meaningful dialogue almost caused me to neglect the performers who followed me onto the stage, bar the customary applause, which in turn made me wonder how much of that I had received had been genuine and fair. And, guilty that which I had given hadn't been, in case that which I had received had.

I went to the bathroom, with the hope that some momentary space in that instance would give me a restored clarity. I stood, staring into the mirror, when Hal came in.

"You okay, son? Noticed you were kinda quiet out there."

"Yeah. Just... it's a bit weird, you know. With Kaia being here."

"Man, she's really something. At least I can tell why your head was turned. If you don't mind me saying."

I laughed.

"But I can see how things are difficult. I wouldn't wanna be you."

"No."

"Yeah, must really suck, having two beautiful girls wanting to spend their time with you, and having youth on your side."

Put against the perspective of Hal's situation, how could I complain?

"I hope it doesn't seem like I'm being over the top about trivial things." I said.

"No. You're only human. But you know... days like these weren't made to be spent in no bathroom."

And with that, he put his hand on my shoulder and we headed back into the bar. I realised that the sole purpose of him coming to the bathroom was to check on me, and I felt a wave of guilt come over me.

"Are you okay?" I asked Hal.

"I'm fine, now, come on, son," he said.

Our return to the girls provoked a change in the direction of conversation. It seemed as if they had been plotting in our absence, and were saying how much of a shame it was that we weren't working together. I had to go to that bit of an extra effort to convince Hal that if this had been some set up, I was as much a victim as he was. Louise and Brooke were almost insistent, particularly Louise. Hal looked perplexed, although I couldn't tell if he was genuinely upset or actually enjoyed the henpecking. I was beginning to think it was the latter. I wondered if it was a conversation just like this which provoked him to email me that day, and, knowing Hal as I did now, I found it odd that he would use a computer at all.

That back and forth went on for a while, before Kaia started to get restless and said that she thought she had better go to her hotel if she wanted to get a room. She called, and they had some availability.

Louise let Brooke off her shift early, and I of course was duty bound to go with Brooke and Kaia, first to Hal's, and then to the 1000 Springs resort.

Even long after sunset, it was easy to see how beautiful this place was, and I imagined that on a sunrise or sunset it would be even more outstanding, considering how incredible the drenching gold of the autumn sun had looked on the landscape. I loved the way that there seemed to be these small areas in and around Bliss that were eponymous and although they were all part of the same landscape in some form or another, they all seemed like individual landmarks, standing on their own as natural beauty spots, which should be admired on their own merits. I hadn't heard of any of the places I had visited prior to this trip. It made me think about how people say the world is such a small place nowadays. As much as I considered that to be true, I also felt tremendously small, although that thought was comforting rather than overwhelming.

We all got out of the car and I helped Kaia carry her luggage into the lobby. There were a couple of young children running around and a familiar looking woman serving as the receptionist—a woman I took to be the mother of these youngsters as she told them to calm down, though she could have easily passed for an older sister. As Kaia confirmed the booking, I looked at the receptionist's name tag, which read 'Misti: Manager,' and thought of the tremendous responsibility that she must have. She had a kind face, but tired eyes; she had something of a lead cheerleader look about her, and I found myself wondering about her own story.

Kaia had rented a cabin and to get there we had to walk past an RV camp and a small campsite area where a couple of families had fires burning. As I helped Kaia with her cases, I noticed more than a few heads turn as we walked toward her accommodation.

"Wow, you weren't kidding," she said. "I really am overdressed!"

"Well, you know, you've definitely made an impression," I tried to reassure her. "Something to live up to. I hope you've got more dresses like that. Anyway, erm... I suppose I'll be seeing you tomorrow. Text me in the morning."

"Yeah, sure," she replied, with a hint of *aren't you staying* in there.

"Brooke's waiting," I said, in answer to a question that hadn't been raised.

As I walked back to the car, I felt a tinge of excitement about spending some time alone with Brooke. It would only be ten minutes or so, but that would be reward enough for a long day. I even looked forward to some wisecrack about what I'd been doing with Kaia in her room and was trying to think of how I could respond in this imaginary conversation, thinking that if I said some witty remark, it would make it seem as if I thought of it off the cuff.

Brooke, however, was subdued and barely engaging in conversation, let alone initiating one.

"Hey, you okay?" I said, after a couple of attempts at small talk hadn't been successful, and we were pulling into Hal's.

"Yeah, fine."

"You sure? You seem quiet."

"I'm just tired."

"Oh, okay."

"I'm guessing you'll need me to take you to Kaia in the morning as well."

I felt tremendously awkward. Of course, I would need her to, unless Hal was feeling good enough to drive.

"Well, I'll see about Hal first of all," I suggested.

"I'm not working in the morning. I can, it's no problem," she replied.

"Only if you're sure."

"Uh-huh."

It was time to get out of the car. I felt as though I had to say something.

"You know, I was being honest earlier. I don't want to be with Kaia."

"Yeah, I get that," Booke responded, coolly. I'd hoped for a smile; some kind of receptive response. She just smiled tightly.

"Okay then. Well, I'd... I suppose I'd better go to bed."

"Okay. Text me tomorrow, yeah?" she said.

I stood outside as she turned the car around and waved at me. She was friendly enough. But there was something wrong, something missing. I tried to figure out if I'd done or said something wrong or out of turn. Had I really not appreciated what a huge effort it had been for Brooke to help me out? I thought we had shared some kind of connection again in the hotel room, but maybe it was just complete naivety on my part. The anti-climactic end to the evening brought back all of those disconnections I'd been feeling earlier, and I went to bed under a cloud of melancholy and doubt.

Kaia sent me a text message at 8:00 a.m. to tell me she was awake and asking if I could come over. I didn't quite know what to do in regard to messaging Brooke, so I went downstairs and thought I would ask Hal, but he wasn't yet awake. 8:30 a.m. struck me as a time that I felt was not too early, so I messaged Brooke to tell her that Kaia had been in touch.

"Okay, will be over soon," she texted back.

It was about 10:00 a.m. when Brooke arrived at Hal's, sending me a text to let me know she was there.

"U not coming in?" I texted back. I had showered and dressed and now Hal was awake, having breakfast.

Brooke didn't reply, and so I went out to the car.

She still didn't get out on seeing me and so I got into the passenger side, and instantly, I realised exactly why she hadn't come into the house. It was the smell of perfume that hit me first, but as I looked across at Brooke it was almost as if it were a different girl sat in the driver's seat.

"Morning," I said.

"Hey," she replied. "You good to go?"

We set off. Brooke was wearing a tight dress, and behind her sunglasses I could see that she had gone heavy on the eyeshadow and mascara.

It was enough of a distraction to throw me off my game totally in terms of conversation, because all things being normal, there was no way I shouldn't have started with a compliment or remark about how she looked, and how different she looked. And it seemed wrong to do so, or, even, too early.

"It's a nice clear day, so Kaia should get some great views of the springs if she's staying around the resort," Brooke said.

The weather: that most wonderful of conversation starters.

"Yeah, I'm looking forward to it."

"How's Hal doing?"

"He's okay. Having breakfast. You should have come in."

"I'll see him later," she replied. I guessed that she wouldn't have wanted him to see her like that; he'd certainly have had something to say. As we arrived at the 1000 Springs resort, Kaia texted me to say she was going for a swim.

"We're here, so we'll be down by the lake," I texted back as we got out to walk toward the tables and chairs that were down by the water. I got out first and waited for Brooke. As she exited the car and closed the door, only then could I truly appreciate the effort she had gone to. A figure hugging and very revealing dress, her chest threatening to burst out. Her mouth seemed almost in a permanent pout to accentuate the plumpness of her lips. I couldn't tell if she had gone to such an effort to bring her 'A' game and blow Kaia out of the water or making herself as close to naked as she could to prove another point. We walked to the water and I noticed she was taller, too; walking in heels, as glamorous and womanly as she could possibly be.

She sat on the seat of the table and I sat across from her, unable to avoid the obvious.

"Wow! You look... different," I said.

"Do I?"

I didn't know what to say next. Of course she looked different, we both knew that. I either had to ask the reason why or compliment her on how incredible she looked.

"You look nice. Really nice," I decided on, finally.

"So, I don't normally?" she tested me.

"Yes, of course. You always do. But... come on, help me out here."

She simply smiled back. I was unable to tell what her eyes were saying, and I wondered if the sunglasses were being worn for purpose or as some kind of last layer of protection in this kind of situation.

"This is a really nice place," I said, thinking that Brooke's intention was for her appearance to speak where words weren't necessary.

"Yeah, nicer in the spring. Or at least when it's warmer," she said.

"You say that about everywhere round here."

"Because it's true."

I found this "new" Brooke difficult to talk to. Because, as much as I wanted to, she just didn't look like herself, and so those conversations like we had had in recent days, however heavy, however light, seemed to belong to a different couple of people. She'd raised the stakes so much that I found myself effectively speechless. I felt like if I had to say something, it should be bold, game-changing, but it was too early in the day for that, and completely the wrong setting.

Lost in these thoughts, I didn't realise that I was staring at her until she stopped me.

"What?" she said, scrunching her lip, self-consciously, and pulling down her glasses so that our eyes connected for once.

"Sorry. Nothing. You just... you look really nice."

Was it for my benefit? Kaia's? Her own?

Perhaps Brooke was doing it to see what I would do, to find out for certain how I felt, even though I was sure I had dropped more than enough hints. What sort of reaction I could offer, however, was questionable, even with the best of intentions—we were there to see Kaia and Kaia knew for certain how I felt about Brooke, because I'd told her straight up. I guessed that Brooke liked me too; she'd basically said as much, and kissed me, and we'd had these moments, but Kaia's presence had thrown everything so much up in the air that I wasn't sure my own perception of what people were trying to tell me was entirely accurate.

These long silences—long and mostly uncomfortable—were thankfully broken by Kaia who came out to see us after we'd been sitting there for nearly forty minutes. Maybe Kaia had seen Brooke and didn't wish to be upstaged because she too was dressed too extravagantly, as if she was going out for the evening. Maybe she thought that was how things were done here, although surely, she had seen enough the previous evening to have felt like she was sticking out like a sore thumb. Clearly not. But I didn't have her down as someone so lacking in self-awareness, so I wondered what the motivation was for both of them.

There was nothing to say that either of them didn't dress like that normally to the casual observer. Nothing that made them look particularly out of place in isolation or indeed to any of the campers or resort guests. It was simply my own experience of both of them which told me that they were not dressed in their normal attire. To me, they seemed at least nine hours early for a dinner party, but to others I suppose they could have passed for two young ladies who simply went to a considerable effort.

There wasn't much I could offer in the way of conversation and so the small talk that floated between them was occasionally interrupted by the rolling of a soccer ball from a father and his two sons playing nearby. I found myself willing the ball to come over more and more often so that the conversation could become a group one.

My wish was answered by an unlikely source.

"Hey!" It was Tyler, carrying two heavy looking bags.

"Hey," said Brooke. "Tyler, come meet Kaia. She's over from England... a friend of Freddie's."

"Hey, pleased to meet you," he said. "I'd shake your hand, but..."

"How you doing?" I said.

"I'm good, thanks. My sister has me doing all sorts this morning."

So *that's* why the receptionist looked familiar.

"You missed Freddie at the open mic night again last night," Brooke said.

"Oh, man, *what*? I thought that was Mondays?"

He seemed genuinely annoyed.

"We had an extra one, just for Freddie. Guest of honour."

Tyler sighed. "Okay. That sucks. Hey, you guys sticking

around? I've got to run the charter in a little while but if you're going to be around, I could probably get you on there, if you'd like?"

"Yeah, thanks. That'd be great," Brooke said, and as Tyler went to carry the bags to their destination, she explained that each day, boats would sail over the lake to the various springs.

Brooke, Kaia, and I continued to converse; small talk, to simply pass the time. I didn't want to make Kaia feel unwelcome, but all I could think about was how long would she be staying?

Tyler returned and was directing us over toward the small dock to board the boat when Brooke's phone rang.

"Hey," she answered, cheerfully. But then her mood changed immediately to panic. "What? When? I'll be there as soon as I can."

"Mom's taken Hal to hospital. I'm gonna have to go," she said when she hung up.

"I'm coming with you," I insisted.

I turned to Kaia. "I've got to," I said. "You'll be okay here, right? I'll come back later. I just... you know."

"Yes. Of course. I'll be fine. Hope everything's alright."

I asked Brooke what was wrong, but she said all she knew was that Hal was feeling very weak and that Louise felt sufficiently worried to have taken him in.

As we reached the hospital and were directed to a waiting room next to one of the wards, I saw how upset Brooke had become. Her eyes were red and try as she might to have hidden the fact she'd been crying, the running mascara told the truth. It was Brooke, as real as I'd seen her that day.

"Hey, he'll be okay," I tried to reassure her, speaking the words loudly as if to convince myself at the same time. She put her head into my shoulder to stop others from being able to see her upset, though she didn't care about anyone seeing when Louise came into the waiting area. She looked surprised by what Brooke was wearing but shrugged it off quickly.

"Hey guys," she said, before looking at me.

"Hey hun, do you mind if I have a quick word with Brooke alone?"

I feared the worst.

"Of course."

"You can go through and see him, though. He's in room two."

Okay—so, not the worst. But I didn't know what to expect when I went through. I certainly didn't expect to see Hal sitting up and joking with the patient in the bed next to him, as if nothing was wrong at all. He looked pleased to see me.

"Hey, what's wrong?"

"Hey, kiddo! Oh, nothing."

"Louise is talking to Brooke in private. I got the feeling..."

"Oh, you know doctors. And Lou. She's always worrying."

"So why are you here?"

"Beats me. I don't wanna be."

"Seriously, Hal, come on."

"I don't know what the medical term is for bad news. Seems like the doctors have a different idea as to how long I'm going to live than I do."

Suddenly, asking *when* seemed like a very stupid question. I felt my cheeks suck in and my eyes almost descend into sadness; my mouth, into an involuntary frown. As you grow into adulthood and deal with the entire palette of emotions, it is not always the case that things that make you happy make you smile. Nor is it always true that things that make you sad have a visible impact on your exterior, but now, it was as if I had been caught with my guard down.

"So, when are you coming home, then?"

I tried to make light of the situation.

"Oh, they won't be keeping me here long. But you know, Louise... she's not having it. Apparently, she thinks I deserve to die in some sterile hospital room surrounded by strangers and the last of my dignity stripped away from me. So much for love, huh?"

"Hal, you know she loves you."

He nodded. He just needed to let that out.

"Maybe, you've just been overdoing it. You probably just need to take it easy," I suggested, grasping at straws.

"Yeah. Maybe."

Brooke and Louise came in to the room. Brooke clung to Hal so tightly, I feared she might break him. As she let go, he gave her the most curious of looks.

"Thank you, young lady. Now, has anyone seen Brooke?"

I couldn't stop myself from laughing, and nor could Louise, though I worried that we might offend Brooke.

"So what's all this for?" he asked her as she sat beside him.

"Oh, no reason. I just wanted to look nice today," she said with an innocence that really spoke to me.

"You're the most beautiful girl in the world," he said to her, with a sparkle in his eye.

I couldn't see her face, but I noticed her shoulders shake as she began to sob.

"Yeah, maybe now, because I'm all dressed up," she tried to joke between tears.

"No. Always... always," he said. "Now come on, don't be like that. Remember what I've told you. It's your job to happy the sad." Hal's voice sounded too strong for him to be in a room like this.

"Why is he here?" I asked Louise, not caring that Hal could hear me. He knew where I needed to go to get the straight answer.

"Well he wasn't looking this good when I went around to see him..."

"Sorry," I interrupted. "I feel really bad. I left him at breakfast and I didn't..."

"Hey," Hal snapped, as if I were speaking in ignorance of his presence.

"It's okay," Louise reassured me. "They told me that they want to keep him in for observation. They've got a couple of scans to do."

"I wanna go home," Hal said with an insistent stubbornness. "And you can take me, or I can get a cab."

"You have to have the tests, Hal. It's important."

"And I will. I just wanna sleep in my own bed. This ain't my deathbed."

"Well... I'll go ask the doctor, okay?" Louise said.

She went to find one, and Brooke went with her.

"I don't know what the fuss is about," I said, trying to put on a brave face. "You look great."

"Right, son. I don't need to be wasting no more time in here, that's for damn sure."

And then, a solemn silence fell over us, an uneasy acceptance to fill the void where neither of us could find the words.

"So, Brooke, huh?" he laughed.

"Yeah... I mean, she looks amazing. Just, different. Not like her."

"Yeah."

Hal paused for a while. I could tell that he was thinking of the right way to articulate a point he wanted to make.

"You know, son... I've been giving you all this advice as if it were worth anything, at these times I thought it was, you know... relevant, or something," he said. "Like I lived my life with these things that were worth passing on. But every path is different. Yours is different to mine."

"Trust me, more than you know, I appreciate what you've said, Hal, I really do," I told him.

"I guess what I'm trying to say is... just so, you know... you got a good one with Brooke. If you choose to go down that path. But please don't hurt her. I can't do anything but ask you to give me your word. Don't go into it if you think you're gonna hurt her."

"I wouldn't. But, you know... even with the best of intentions, I always do something to screw it up. I think... if I make that decision, I have to make a few more."

It was true. If I wanted to be with Brooke, then, I would have to move. Put into context, moving was the easy part.

"Yeah. Well, something tells me you've made a few of those choices already. In here," he said, pointing to his head.

"I'm just... I think I'm attracted, and scared, you know, in equal measure. Everything's a blank page."

"Yeah. But you won't get too many more of those."

Hal was right again. Everything attached to my past now had some form of baggage and I was at the age where I couldn't expect new relationships to seem as perfect as the opportunity I had with Brooke.

"And anyway. Ain't a blank page exactly what you've been chasin' this entire time?"

"Yeah, I guess so."

Brooke and Louise returned. The doctor had agreed that Hal could go home after they had done the scans. I didn't know what the scans were for, nor was I certain of what had been said earlier. I figured that if it was important for me to know, I would be told, though I gathered from the half-stated comments and the sad atmosphere that the outlook wasn't good. The ominous reference to a deathbed—even though Hal appeared to be as healthy as he had looked since I'd met him two weeks ago—made me wonder if we were dealing in days and hours, as opposed to weeks or months.

We sat with Hal for a while longer until the nurses came to wheel him in for his scans. Not knowing how long they would take, Louise told us that we should go home and she'd keep us apprised of any updates.

Driving back, Brooke was more talkative.

"Sorry, I must look a mess."

"No, not at all. You look fine."

"My mascara has run everywhere. I look like a panda."

"For what it's worth, I agree with Hal."

"About what?"

I had fallen into this trap too many times before to go in blindly now. Even in trying to compliment, I knew that it could be taken as a preference, to infer that she didn't look as nice on other occasions.

"That you *always* look nice," I said.

A safe answer, I thought.

"I know what you're thinking. And it's okay. I don't know if I can compete with Kaia. She's *so* beautiful."

"Who said anything about competing?"

"Oh, I didn't mean..." she said, as if realising that she had unwittingly given the game away.

"You're not competing with her."

"You don't get it. *This* is me. Well, not this, but this is all I am. I don't go to fancy places and have everyone turn their heads to look at me. Kaia is the kinda girl who would go out with celebrities."

By celebrities, I knew she meant me, and even though she had the wrong end of the stick as far as that was concerned, I quite liked being held in that sort of esteem. I held Brooke in similar esteem; the unspoken truth was that I also agreed with Hal that she was the most beautiful girl in the world. On her more natural days, those days where she hadn't felt the need to make such an effort, she grabbed my curiosity so much with that girl-next-door appeal that I felt she was in complete control over it. And even on days like today—she may have dressed up out of character, but she was every bit as beautiful as she'd ever been, and every bit as alluring as she'd intended to be.

"Trust me, heads would move. But you're in a place where everybody knows you. So I guess there's the familiarity thing."

"No, I don't think I could ever be like her."

"That's a good thing. You are you."

Brooke seemed a little uncomfortable with the nature of the conversation, even though she had brought it up.

"So... yeah, you were really great last night," she said, changing the topic.

"Thanks."

"Did you think that maybe... I know that Hal doesn't want to record any songs. But maybe, if they're all that good, maybe you should work on some for you?"

"What do you mean?"

"You could do a record."

"No, no... no, I couldn't."

"Sure you could."

"No, but... I like the idea. I'll ask him. If he's up to it."

"You don't have to make it a thing. Just, get your guitar, and what... do you have a notebook, a pen and paper?"

"Or a computer these days."

"Probably best to use a pen and paper. Hal can barely use a computer. Mom had to show him how to email you, and even then he couldn't do it. Besides... a computer looks more formal, doesn't it?"

"Yeah, I guess."

"So... what are we doing? Did you wanna go to Kaia or to Hal's? The turning's coming up."

"Just go to Hal's for a bit? Could use some unwinding and you know, no awkwardness for a while."

"Sorry if I made you feel awkward."

"You didn't."

The truth was that now, with things between Brooke and I in a better place again, I was hoping that we could spend some time alone.

As we pulled up to Hal's, there was a surreal atmosphere. There was nothing particularly unusual about the house, but as we walked inside to the absolute quiet, I think we both had a sense of realisation that one day soon, the quiet would be all there was.

I walked through on to the porch, that small place being somewhere that I could associate other memories and not just Hal, somewhere where a smile could be felt without feeling bad about it.

Brooke followed me and sat beside me on the porch steps. I couldn't tell, but it was very much like when we had sat together on the front porch at her home on the evening of her birthday just a few days ago. Was that her way of telling me, inviting me, even?

This was all I wanted and yet as I savoured the moment, Hal's words rang in my head: *don't hurt her*. Don't do this if I wasn't sure. And it wasn't that I wasn't sure. I just wasn't completely sure it was the right time.

"Um... do you want a drink?" I asked.

"Yeah, a beer, please."

"I'll see if he's got some. I was going to have something stronger. But I guess you shouldn't."

I went back in and found a beer for Brooke. I poured a large whisky for myself. When I returned to the porch, Brooke was stood resting against the beam. I stood against the other.

"Thanks," she said, taking the bottle. "I'd better only have a couple of drinks of this."

"Lucky me," I said, waving my small tumbler.

I tried to make it look like I was looking out over the fields, but I couldn't help but continue to stare admiringly at Brooke. She leaned down to place her bottle on the ground, and, without a word, moved towards me.

I put my arms firmly on her waist, the sense of anticipation almost overwhelming. She pulled her head back up and then—an unusual sound. My phone, vibrating in my pocket. We both looked down towards it, and then back up at each other. I waited for it to stop, but it didn't, and as I pulled the phone out of my pocket, Brooke stood away to give me some space.

It was Kaia.

Of course.

"Hello?" I answered.

"Hi, Freddie. Is everything okay? How's Hal?"

"Yeah. Everything's fine. Thanks. Don't worry."

It was my default response, and one that I said without even thinking that everything was, in reality, far from fine.

"So, um... are you still at the hospital?"

"No, I'm at Hal's now."

"Oh, are you going to come over? It's just... I don't want to be funny or anything, but obviously, I can't get anywhere."

I looked up at Brooke, and I didn't really need to ask, she just nodded.

"Yeah, sure. We'll come over now."

We decided to spend some time at the resort with Kaia and after I explained what had happened with Hal, she was apologetic and started making plans to go home. I told her that it was unnecessary, but she insisted. She tried to book a flight for the next day, Friday, but there was nothing available until Sunday.

Kaia had become friendly with the other families on site and so we had dinner in a group around one of the open fires, with a makeshift barbecue. Tyler was playing some songs.

There was a moment before we got out of the car to join them where I felt an indulgent moment of pure magic. There was a real sense of anticipation with Brooke and yet the idea that we had all the time in the world: the landscape in front of us was postcard perfect, with the orange setting sun in the distance, the burning fire and the group of people sat around Tyler, whose makeshift stage consisted solely of the table he was sitting on. It was an ideal moment in time, the kind I instantly knew would become a fond memory. I wanted to soak it in.

We only needed to get within fifty yards of the group for them to cheer at our return, and Tyler looked around with a smile. Tyler was playing one of Hal's songs, "The End Of Time," which was one I loved.

So go, call on what you know,
call on what you feel to be true,
a second set of eyes will see this differently, you say
I'm sorry that I said, I'm sorry that I stayed
This is the end of time,
and since the end of time, I've been fine.

We had barely arrived before Tyler was offering me—with some insistence—the guitar. I don't know why I found it so easy, but I took it without any protestation, and settled right into the same position he'd adopted on the top of the bench. As I tuned the guitar, Tyler brought me a beer and only then I looked up to see a fairly expectant group of around twenty people. Walking up to them, I hadn't taken any notice of the numbers. Not that any of it mattered. I could only see Brooke. I smiled as I started playing, instinctively going into one of my own songs; not one of Hal's, nor one I'd written or released for or with anyone else, simply one of my own.

The sky's on fire,
burning all the desperate things
we've done, just for fun
we were young,
we were running wild and free
you and me.

It was a relatively short song that I had written some time back, between relationships, not about a love interest in particular, but about the idea of one. It just seemed to fit. The warm applause I received cemented what I knew would be a vivid memory that would stay with me for some time. After I had played four songs, Brooke and I walked away from the party, down to the water's edge.

"So, what was that first song about?" she asked. "It was really good."

"Really, the best thing about it is that it was about nothing and nobody," I admitted. "Just an abstract idea, a feeling."

"Do you have it on mp3 or something? Can I listen to it?" she asked.

"Sure, no problem." I smiled.

"So why is being about nothing the best thing about it?"

"I don't know. I guess it just feels like it was from a better place."

"Aren't songs supposed to be better if they're about broken hearts?"

"You tell me."

"Well, that's what they say."

"I haven't written anything new, by myself, for... well, not for quite some time, anyway."

"How come?"

"Well... I was gonna say no particular reason, but that's not true. I think it's maybe because, you know, being here, this is the first time I've actually thought of myself as a songwriter rather than just someone who writes songs. I don't know if that makes sense."

"Yeah, I guess it kinda does."

"So I'm like, I'm a songwriter, the next time I write something, it's going to be this professional effort... I don't know. It's weird."

"What's the difference?"

"What do you mean?"

"Between when you did it before and what you want to do?"

"I don't know... I guess, I wrote because I wanted to say something, and now, maybe there's this expectation. I never wanted to be Bono, or... I don't want to feel like every word makes a difference, but I do want it to matter. You know, now it stands as something of a representation of who I am."

"Yeah. I suppose that's an odd kind of thing to deal with."

"Yeah. It's a good odd, though."

"So, how's the heart?"

"It's mending. You know, a little help," I smiled, and then, frowned, hesitating.

"What?" Brooke asked.

I found myself feeling impulsively candid, and also conscious of Kaia's presence. "I should say, that we... I did all of the damage myself, so you shouldn't think of me as someone who was wronged and trampled on. I know I give that impression."

"You don't need to explain yourself."

"Well... either way, we'd better go back up," I said.

And though we did spend the next couple of days with Kaia at the resort—wanting to give Hal and Louise plenty of time, as Louise had taken some time away from work to be with Hal—the lingering tension between the three of us never fully dissapated, despite our best efforts to not make Kaia feel like the odd one out. Interaction between Brooke and I was non-existent to the point of making it obvious—such was our determination to *not* make everything so obvious.

On the Saturday night, as we left the car to go into Hal's for dinner, Brooke looked as if she was going to trip up as she walked in front of me. I grabbed her—it was the first physical interaction we'd had since we'd almost kissed on the porch. Even just touching the softness of her hand threw a shiver down my spine and I was certain that she felt it too. In that moment, we could wait no longer. My hands moved from hers to her waist, and Brooke wrapped her arms around my neck, pressing her lips softly and gently against mine.

We heard Louise call to Hal that she'd heard the car pull up and had to break away to go inside. Brooke looked at me and smiled.

The following morning, Brooke offered to drive Kaia to the airport. Our ride to Boise, was nowhere near as uncomfortable as it had been when we were first all together, and I could feel that there was almost a sense of relief that this small period of our lives had come to an end.

Brooke stayed in the car as I helped Kaia with her luggage. There was a very real sense of this conversation being a meaningful one in our shared history.

"You've changed," she said.

"Yeah, but it's been almost ten years."

"I'm just saying, you were right. That you had. I still feel like I'm the same girl. But, you know, there's still some of you in there," she said. Her statement was delivered in such a way as to imply that if I changed back, to the *good* me, she would always be there.

"What's change?" I said. "I'm still me. I've evolved."

"What's that supposed to mean? That I haven't?"

"No. Just that I have, and because I have, it doesn't mean that it's change for the worse. I'm happier with who I am now than who I was back then. And... come on. Whether or not you were happy with yourself, you weren't happy with me."

"What I hear is, *I like Brooke now, and I'm so glad you're going home.*"

"No... but, I... you know. Come on, Kaia. Now's not the time or place for this conversation."

"No," she sighed. "You're right. Look, I'm really sorry about Hal. And I should have listened. I shouldn't have come out."

"No need to worry about that now. Hopefully you managed to have somewhat of a good time."

"Yeah…" she sighed. "Well… I'd better get going."

"Keep in touch, okay?" I said. But Kaia did not respond. We hugged. There was no real sadness, no real emotion. It just was what it was.

Capo 3 — am - dm - E - E7#1

Young

Dry your eyes
  it don't matter where you are
  so far
you fall behind
  you know you're just a day away
  from yesterday

the sky's on fire.
  Burning all the desperate things we've done
    Just for fun

we were young, we were running wild & free
  you and me

9

I knew that Louise was extremely concerned about Hal, but in the brief moments that Hal and I had been alone in the house together, prior to Kaia's departure, he appeared as well as he had been before he was taken into hospital. I began to accept that my perception of Hal being well may not have matched up with Louise's—that my perception of Hal being well may not have matched up with reality.

Nonetheless, I saw it as something of an obligation to treat Hal as I always had in the short time that I'd known him, not least because I guessed he would be upset with me if I behaved differently.

So it came to be that I was fairly insistent that he help me write some songs out on the porch, and we spent most of Sunday evening and all day Monday out there, working.Brooke was working, so we made plans to do something together on Tuesday.

Hal would put words together and suggest chord changes, and I would do the writing and playing, suggesting my own ideas and presenting basic structures of songs I'd previously worked on. Hal insisted once or twice that he wanted to play, but I had such a strong last memory of him playing that I would keep saying, *one more minute*, until he got tired of asking. I could tell that he was struggling with his movement and he'd complain of aches and pains, but he was determined to keep active.

Late on the Monday, we had a sudden burst of creativity, coming up with three really good ideas for songs, but no strong formation for full songs after one or two verses. We decided to call it a day at that point—with something to look forward to the next day.

"So," Hal said, as he returned out on to the porch with two whiskies, "you care to tell me how you got this bee in your bonnet?"

"What, you mean? Writing?"

"Yeah. No, don't tell me, let me guess, it's about yay high and blonde," he said, putting his hand to his chest, indicating Brooke's height, "or maybe yay high and a brunette."

I raised my eyebrows as if to say *yes*, and went to take a drink. Hal put his finger up to stop me.

"Here's to Murphy's girls," he said with a smile, holding his glass in salute. We toasted.

After I finished my drink I got up to get another and went to take Hal's glass from him.

"Nah, not for me, thanks. I'm still not feeling right. I think I'm going to go back to bed."

"Are you sure?"

Hal thought about it for a while, a little while longer than you would assume it normally takes someone to make such a decision.

"Ah go on then. One more," he said. "Ain't it crazy? The inordinate amount of bullshit we tell ourselves just to say we're okay."

As we sat watching the sun go down, Hal seemed lost in thought.

"What are you sure of?" he asked, out of the blue.

I thought about what he was asking. What he meant. I contemplated the various strands, the implication. For someone who would usually be verbose in his delivery, I considered that this more succinctly delivered question carried many more words of dialogue.

"Myself, I think. Now."

"Well, hold on to that. Hold on to that."

With that, he finished his drink, and rose.

"Do you need any help?"

"No, I'm good, son. Thanks. Goodnight."

"Night, Hal."

I thought it an odd yet strangely appropriate thing to ask. I hadn't given the matter any thought at all for a while but, yes, sure enough, I was certain in my own logic, my own decision making. I made sense to myself again, thanks to a little, or lot, of help from many different people, and also myself. I had regained a pure equilibrium.

Yes, that was a good place to be.

Having fleetingly considered going out again, I found myself yawning widely. Perhaps, for the first time, I was acknowledging not just the exhaustion of the day, but that of the entire trip. I had packed a lot into it and it felt like there was a lot more left to come.

The following morning was just like the previous day; cloudy and overcast. I went out on to the porch and opened my phone to read the news from back home.

I was waiting for Hal to get up, thinking of suggesting to him that we should go to get groceries, so he could be a bit more active than the previous day. But when 10:00 a.m. came and passed, I was suitably concerned, so went upstairs and knocked on Hal's bedroom door.

"Hal? You okay? Can I come in?"

I heard a murmur inside the room, but it wasn't an angry grunt, something that would tell me to go away. I opened the door and saw Hal. His eyes were struggling.

"Hal, are you okay? Hal?"

I went over to him and leaned in close.

"Hal, come on. Are you okay?"

I held his hand, and was encouraged and relieved to feel it warm, and pressing back, albeit very weakly.

"Hal, come on."

"Lou," he whispered.

"Yeah, okay."

I sent Brooke a text message. *"Can you and Lou come over. Urgent."*

Hal was struggling for breath and I kept telling him I would call the doctor, at which point, he would just squeeze my hand as strongly as he could, and wheeze.

"Save your energy, Hal. Save your words," I said.

I remained with him in silence; just the two of us, looking at each other. He barely resembled the man I'd spent most of the last few weeks with, not even the man who yesterday had shared a drink with me out on the porch. Yes, his features were the same. You could barely tell he was ill to look at him. Just old. But his eyes, trying as they may have been, were dulling, losing the fight.

"Hal, come on. Come on now."

I heard the front door go. Louise and Brooke had made it over in less than fifteen minutes. The fast, rhythmic patter of two pairs of footsteps up the stairs carried an urgency, one that didn't really have any place in this room.

And, the slow opening of the door, with those on the other side not sure what it would reveal, illustrated the ultimate cautiousness and fear in their approach.

"Freddie?" I heard Louise say quietly.

"Yeah. In here."

I heard the door creak open.

"Hal. Oh, Hal," Louise said, already in tears, as she sat on the other side of the bed.

This was a moment he should spend with his family, I thought. His girls. I stood, and as I was about to let go of his hand, he squeezed it. I looked at him and for a fleeting second, saw the old man I knew, so very briefly. I smiled at him, and though his face was too tired to do the same, I saw it too in his look.

With a heavy sigh, I turned around and gave Brooke a hug, before stepping out of the way so she could sit with Hal too.

Not really knowing the protocol, yet fearing the worst, I called Hal's doctor's office from my mobile phone—thankfully, the number was on a post-it note on the fridge, in Louise's handwriting—and informed them of the situation. Then, not wishing to intrude on these private moments, I went out to sit out on the porch.

Sometime later, I heard a knock on the front door.

I was too numb to get up, but thankfully, either Louise or Brooke let them in.

I gather I'd been sat out on the back porch for two, maybe three hours, lost in a daze, when Louise came out. Somewhere along the way, the continued silence out here had made the events inside the house obvious.

"That man," she said with a firmness, lighting a cigarette. "Sorry."

She walked down the steps and on to the back yard, seemingly with plenty of adrenalin to burn.

A couple of minutes later, Brooke came out.

I looked up at her, and she just nodded, as if to confirm what I already knew to be true.

She sat beside me.

"She seems angry," I said, nodding toward Louise.

"Yeah, well," Brooke paused. "He didn't say much. He, um... he had just about enough strength to tell Mom to get a letter from the side. And then he pulled her close to him and told her that he was sorry."

Her voice broke, quivering.

"... and that he loved her. And me too."

She passed me a piece of paper, and began to sob.

Dear Lou,

It turns out I may have been a fool. I know that now. I want to thank you for all that you have done for me over the years, these wonderful years. And in case you didn't know, but I hope you do, I love you. I have loved you in the way that I know you always hoped, and the way that you deserved. I am so sorry that I have been unable to share this with you before now, but I think you know why. I thought I understood a lot of things. I thought I understood the power of love, but I can't know much at all because I can't begin to comprehend what you have been through. But you put up with me. You had faith in me. I don't know if these words will bring you comfort or if they will make you angry. I've been reliving my life these past days and the message I keep telling folk is not to lie to yourself. Not to waste time. Don't live your life with regret. But me? I've been lying to myself. Regretting. These last few days, the thing that has hurt me the most hasn't been the illness. It hasn't even been the thought of dying. It has been the crippling pain of regret, every time I looked in to your beautiful eyes and wondered. How much more happy you could have made this old fool if only I'd had the good sense to allow you to love me completely. Because I love you. If I could do it all again, I wouldn't hesitate. I consider that you were my wife. Brooke was my daughter. I'm so sorry. I'm sorry I didn't share that with you, more sorry than I can ever explain.

Hal.

"Wow." It was the only word I could muster.

Brooke and Louise didn't stay very long after the undertaker had been. Brooke was concerned about Louise's state of mind and wanted her to get some rest at home. It was clear to see Louise was not herself. Louise finished her cigarette and came over to us. For once, she was at a loss for words. I could appreciate that. They made the decision to go back home and asked if I wanted to join them, but I thought I ought to stick around.

I should have gone.

I was left with silence.

I knew it would be difficult, but at that same time I thought I was well equipped to deal with it. It may hurt just as much, it may hurt more, but I had the tools—the awareness, the experience—to know that the way I dealt with things after Eddy wasn't the best way.

I hoped this moment, this feeling, was fleeting, because it was all too familiar. The suffocation. And now, something new. Fear. That thought that someone would say *live each day as if it's your last*, an adage meant to provoke some kind of impulsive behaviour, or a *carpe diem* mentality. But I felt incapable. The overriding feeling was one of helplessness, of the unknown, that today might be the last. I was desperately trying to retain hope in Hal's words, that his time was here, there was no need to be so down about all of this, but even with all of that logic, it still felt like it was too soon. We had weeks, and although we hadn't said it, we hoped for months. Days, well, that was cruel. No matter how Hal had protested he was at peace, it was too soon.

I didn't like feeling like this, but I couldn't shake it. It was more than a sense of loss of direction, a greater pain, it was as if I was pressing the stop button, feeling incapable of moving forward. The grief in these seconds, these minutes, was acute. It wasn't so much a lack of direction, but more a lack of *anything*. I was willing my mind to reach out for positivity and couldn't. All I knew is that I did not want to embrace the grief in the same way as I had before, but I felt powerless to let it do anything other than consume me.

I went inside to pour a drink and couldn't. I felt as though I shouldn't touch anything, that I shouldn't move anything, consume anything, that I should leave it all as it was.

I went back out on to the porch and laid on the bench. I felt an unspoken obligation to stick around, but really would rather have been anywhere else.

I was a slave to my indecision. Far from free.

Thankfully, before the sun set, Brooke returned. She had figured I would still be out on the porch and came around the side without going in the house.

"Hey," she said. "So what you wanna do?"

Amid all of this returned uncertainty, there was one thing I knew; that I definitely did not want to stay there that evening. With no willpower, I was just relieved that someone was here to take charge.

"Have you eaten?" asked Brooke as we walked away from the house.

"No," I admitted.

"Come on."

I had anticipated we would walk to their house, but Brooke took my hand, and lead the way. A day before, our holding hands would have come complete with the most tangible of tension, but today, it presented, simply, comfort. That familiar walk to Murphy's had a feeling of newness about it, owing to the fact that for the first time, there was no telling what might come afterwards.

Arriving at the bar, I was a little surprised to see Louise working. "Brooke insisted," she said when I asked. Her movements were almost robotic. It was clear to see that she was on auto-pilot.

And while nobody could argue that there was a sombre air—a seat at the bar for Hal left empty, never quite felt right—Brooke did her best to lift the spirits of those of us who had ventured to Murphy's, those who had known Hal and had now heard the news. I guessed that Brooke was trying her utmost to make this into a wake but the problem with that was that wakes come after funerals, when people have had time to digest the news and started to come to terms with the loss.

That said, as fruitless as Brooke's endeavour initially appeared to be, her sheer doggedness in seeing it through was inspiring enough to drag me out of my own stupor and I eventually was cajoled into livelier conversation; laughter, even. And then so was Louise. I'm not quite sure whether it translated to the others in the bar but by closing time the mood was far more positive between the three of us.

Louise must have read my mind, because as she locked up and we stood outside, she said, "You should stay with us tonight, Freddie."

It was such a relief. As late as it was when we got there, Louise headed straight to bed. Brooke went to get changed for bed and came back out into the kitchen, where I was having a drink of water.

Wearing just a t-shirt and underwear, she caused me to be immediately distracted, though I don't think that was her intention at all. In fact, Brooke was all I could even think about. It wasn't appropriate to be thinking like that, but I did wonder if she was feeling the same energy as me as we shared a moment of silence.

In the dead of night, as close as we were, and despite all that had been, it felt as if tension was all there was.

"Quite a day," she sighed.

"Yeah. For sure. I think you did great. For your Mom."

"Thank you."

She looked at me and we stood in silence. There was almost an affirmation of that connection between us, and yet, an acceptance that remained unsaid that nothing needed to happen that evening.

"Well, night..." she said, leaving that last word trailing, as if I could suggest something else. And that if I did, she could be agreeable.

I was tempted, again. So, so tempted. But I felt it would be disrespectful to Hal, disrespectful to Louise.

"Night."

Only on my saying that, did she turn around and walk to her room.

On the drive home, Louise mentioned that Hal's solicitor—a mutual friend, which, for a small town, didn't surprise me—had been in touch shortly after hearing of Hal's passing to say that he'd be over the next day to go through the will.

I didn't feel as though I ought to be there when that happened, and so after I woke, earlier than the others, I quietly left the house and decided that I'd face up to going back to Hal's and getting my belongings. I felt I could go in to the house, I just couldn't face staying there.

These were the things I had conditioned myself to think, to feel, but I still had no way of knowing how I would be when I turned to walk down Hal's driveway and saw the house. I thought about Brooke coming back the previous day and how she had come around the side of the house, through the porch, and somehow that seemed fitting to me. Approaching the front of the house, I couldn't shake off a feeling that I had, a feeling I'm unable to describe as anything other than strange. I wasn't numb or overcome with grief. But it felt like I was approaching Hal and Betty's house, rather than just Hal's. As if, magically, through the night, it had settled back into what it once was. It wasn't a bad, negative feeling, nor was it comforting to any real extent, rather, it just *was*. But it did leave me feeling relieved that I hadn't stayed there the previous evening.

I was a tad slow with my movements, taking my time packing, putting my guitar and laptop away, and making sure there was nothing left in the bedroom before I left. Before walking down the stairs, I looked over at Hal's room and noticed the door was ajar. I don't know what compelled me, but I walked over and pushed the door open. Hal's bed was made, and although I couldn't be sure—maybe my mind was playing tricks—it seemed as though the bedsheets had been changed. Louise must have done it before she'd left. It was difficult to describe how I felt in that moment. I ran my hand up and down the door frame and thought of Louise and her strength and love to do something so heartbreaking in the moment. That she might have had to do it in order to spare herself further pain in the future. And now, it seemed as if the house was waiting for Hal to return home.

As I took my belongings downstairs and put them in the hallway, I went down to the basement to take one last look around. It still seemed strange to have all of the new equipment down there as opposed to the old decor of the house above it. But, that was Hal—doing his own thing, going his own way, not bound by convention.

In the basement I admit I was looking for some solace, hoping for one profound thing I could remember Hal saying to me, that would mark this personal goodbye I was making, but as is the case in such times, my mind drew a blank. There was no point fabricating something, or contriving a situation. I should just leave well enough alone.

I went into the kitchen and looked out onto the porch. Where yesterday, I had felt an oddness, out of place, now, I felt a comfort and a greater sense of belonging. Of being welcome.

I thought I'd sit on the porch one final time before leaving, as if sharing a last moment with Hal. That much was true, it didn't need to be contrived for the purpose of a memory or the convention of simply doing something because it *seemed* like the right thing to do. For the first time in days, the sky was clear; a perfect blue. There was a serenity which applied itself to this setting. Not that I was one to believe in spirits, and I hadn't really considered much about what happens to the soul once it has passed, but still, the sense of peace in the air seemed perfectly apt.

A Moment

Capo 2

V.1

G
I'd like to say - It wasn't easy

D
I'd like to tell you - I can't recall

Cadd9
There's only vague and fleeting memories of it all

I'd like to say - I can't remember
That it was easy to forget
All of the guilty conversations I regret

Chorus: Cadd9   G   Dsus4
There was a time, there was a moment in my life
There was a light, there was a goodness, there were smiles
All my mistakes, locked up and lost forever
There was a moment in my life

V.2 I'm on my knees as if I'm sorry
as if it's easy to repent
for all the days, and months, and years, we never spent
I'm only sorry for myself
that I was someone else
And you were blooming into this flower that I met

Chorus 2:
There was a time a moment in our lives
There was a light, no need to keep it locked inside
All our mistakes, locked up and lost forever
There was a moment in our lives

Em7   Dsus4
Now take a walk into the tunnels of your mind
This echo chamber of shadows you left behind

Cadd9   Dsus4   G   Cadd9   Dsus4   (Rpt Chorus 2)
No one was there - No one could hear -   No one

10

I had gathered my suitcase, laptop, and guitar case, just about able to walk with them all, and made my way back out to the porch. I felt it best to leave the way I came in.

As I stood on the back porch, I heard a noise coming from inside the house. I put down my belongings and went back inside.

"Hello?"

"Hey, only me," Brooke replied from the hallway. "I figured you'd be here," she said, as she entered the kitchen.

"Yeah... I was just getting my stuff. I was going to ask Louise if it would be okay to stay with you until after the funeral. I... you know, if not, I can stay at a hotel in town. I haven't decided."

"It's cool if you want to. Stay with us, I mean. We figured you would."

I went back out on to the porch and stood by my stuff, hoping that Brooke would help me, and we'd get going. Instead, she sat down on the bench.

"So... Hal left everything to Mom," she said. "Well, to us."

"Yeah. That doesn't surprise me."

"I don't know what she's gonna do. It's hit her so hard. She already said she doesn't want the house. She can't live here, can't sell it. But I can't... you know. He left me money. I'm already thinking of giving that to Mom and you know, saying I'll have the house. I get why it's too hard for her. I spent a lot of time so frustrated with Hal. And Mom. But, I don't know, yesterday... Hal saying what he did. And the letter. It makes me believe, you know? Believe in love."

She smiled at me.

"Yeah, I get that," I said.

"So, I'm thinking... it kinda makes everything I thought was fake, real, you know? It's weird. Because people normally have that the other way, don't they? They grow up and think their Mom and Dad love each other, but then find out they don't, or they find out some horrible family secret. And... I know it wasn't the best thing for Mom to hear. Or easy. But it was for me. It's not about the money. I just... this feels like my home as much as Mom's house. It should be ours."

"Give it time."

Brooke stood up, taking my laptop bag, making it easier for me to wheel my suitcase and carry the guitar bag.

"So, tell me about England," she said, as we walked along the dusty country road.

"Well... it's small. Compared to here. That's the first thing," I laughed. "And not as laid back. But I think that's probably just here... sure there are cities here that are a bit more... I don't know if *energetic* is the right word?"

"I know what you mean."

"I don't think you'd like it," I added.

"I love English stuff!" she protested.

"Oh yeah, like what?"

She paused for thought.

"See!" I laughed.

"You put me on the spot. England has some amazing architecture. Europe has. I like that most. I'd love to see it."

I felt bad for questioning her naivety. I guess there was a lot I didn't know.

"So, when are you going back?" she segued.

"When's the funeral?" I asked.

"Friday, I think. Mom is sorting that now."

"Wow, that's... soon."

"Yeah. I guess."

"So, maybe I'll check on flights for Saturday or Sunday. Have to get back and sort a lot of stuff out. Ailie is selling the house. I haven't heard anything though. I suppose it all takes time to sell. I don't really wanna go back, to be honest."

"Yeah."

"Feels like another life."

"You've got two lives, I'm struggling just to get one together," Brooke said. "I have my dreams, you know. But I can't leave here. Not now. I wish I could be like you, just go, anywhere in the world. But I can't leave Mom."

"Well, what do you wanna do?"

"I don't know. I still don't know."

"Where do you wanna go?"

"Everywhere. Anywhere."

"What's wrong with here?"

"It doesn't have what I want."

"What do you want?"

A car horn sounded. It was Louise.

"Hey! I'm just on my way to work. You guys wanna come?"

Though I was always made to feel welcome, it still felt at times as if I was imposing. Yes, things were going nicely with Brooke, but I didn't really fancy a repeat of the previous evening's awkwardness and temptation, and the frustration that accompanied it. Being that close to Brooke was something I could hardly deny myself, but the respect I had for Louise provided a huge barrier, significant enough to make me feel uncomfortable, and so by the time we'd reached the bar, I had decided that it would be best for me to stay at a hotel.

As we entered the bar, I told Brooke that I'd like to sit at a table, since being at the bar would feel weird. I made an excuse to go to the bathroom, hoping that when I returned, Louise would be behind the bar and Brooke would be sitting down.

Thankfully it worked out that way, and I went to Louise at the bar to order drinks.

"Hey," I said.

"Hey" Louise replied, curiously.

"I, um... I just wanted to say something."

"Yeah?"

"About Brooke…"

"You mean that you like Brooke, and she likes you?" Louise smiled, giving me a side-eye as she was pouring a beer.

"Yeah, something like that," I replied. I could feel myself beginning to blush, embarassed by my childish reaction.

"It's okay. I think it's pretty obvious. I don't think Brooke was making it a secret with what she was wearing the other day."

"Well, I was going to… I wanted to say two things. First, you know… I wanted to say, Brooke said I could stay at yours until I leave. And I do appreciate that. I really do. But I think I'm… I can't really stay at Hal's, so I'm gonna find a hotel for a few days before I fly back."

Louise looked at me, unconvinced. I half expected her to just say yes. She raised her eyebrows as if to say *continue.*

"… and I was going to ask, if it was okay, if I could take Brooke out. On a date. Only if she says yes, of course."

"Freddie," Louise replied, noting my nerves. "Take a deep breath. It's fine. I know it's not an ideal situation. And I know how Brooke feels about you. Or is starting to. A mother knows these things. And I know you're a good guy. Hal was very fond of you… we all are. Hal was a good judge of character. And you, asking, doing this… just shows. Of course, if you want my permission, then *yes*… but I want you to know that you are more than welcome to stay in our home until you leave."

"Thanks. I appreciate it. But, you know, I think I'd just, rather… I would feel more comfortable if I found a hotel."

"Well, I'm not going to argue. But just know that you're welcome, okay? Now, go on… I'll bring your drinks over."

I went over to the table and sat with Brooke, fidgeting nervously.

"What were you talking to Mom about?"

"Oh, nothing. Just ordering a drink."

"That long to order a beer, huh?" she said, unconvinced.

"Well, no… but, you know, I said it was probably a good idea if I didn't stay with you guys."

"Oh, yeah?" She sounded disappointed. "How come?"

"Well, I'm Hal's friend, I came here to work with him. I really appreciate the gesture, but... you know."

"No. I don't."

"Okay."

"Okay what?"

"You're not making this easy for me, Brooke."

"I don't know what you mean."

I couldn't tell if she was being playful, or if she was genuinely confused. This was my moment to meet her halfway. At least as much as I could.

"Well, I just thought, we... there is something... unless I've got it completely wrong..."

At that moment, Louise came over with our drinks.

"Oops, sorry," she laughed. "Did I interrupt?"

"Thanks," I said.

"Well... carry on," Brooke said, clearly amused, and taking a sip from her straw as I pondered my response.

"Well," I said, more quietly, "I just thought that... we... well... I like you."

"You *thought*, or you *know*?" Brooke replied, with a smile.

I leaned back.

"Look, if you're going to make this difficult, then I'll just not say anything at all."

"Would you like to take me out on a date?" she asked.

I laughed awkwardly.

"Freddie. Would you go on a date with me?" she rephrased.

I would like to say I was speechless; but I wasn't. I just spent way too long searching for the perfect response.

"You're not making this easy for me," she joked.

"Obviously."

She laughed, nervously, and toyed with her hair.

"Well, where are you gonna take me?" she said.

"Your choice... your town."

"So, no road trip then?"

"Your choice. I mean, provided we can get there and back in a day. And you'll have to drive."

"Can I think about it?"

"The date or the destination?" I asked. "I thought you asked me!"

"The destination."

"Yeah, sure."

There followed a comfortable silence.

"So, what is this?" she eventually said.

"Well... I guess you could call it a date, technically. But you know. Maybe I should find a hotel room first, then maybe we can go on a date?"

"Okay. If you're sure?"

I asked Louise where the nearest hotel was, and it turned out that there were a couple right down the street. I gathered my belongings and walked until I found the first one, an older 50s-style motel. I thought it'd be fitting to stay in such a place, with its small-town vibe. As I turned to enter the reception area, my breath was taken away by the incredible view of the hills and valleys behind it.

They had plenty of rooms available.

"Name?" the receptionist asked.

"Freddie. Freddie Ward," I replied.

"Oh, you're from England," she said, excitedly. She could tell from my accent, or so I thought, until she followed that up with, "so *you're* the guy who was in town to work with Hal Granger, right? Such terrible news."

"Yeah, that's me."

"So, how long are you staying for?"

"Oh, I'm not sure. Can you put me down until Sunday?"

"Sunday? Sunday's fine. So that'll be $270. You'll be in room five which is to your right."

Check in time was 4:00 p.m. It wasn't even 1:00 p.m.

"I'm a bit early. Is it...?"

"Yeah, you're all set," the receptionist said, handing me the key.

"Thank you," I said, taking it and walking away.

"Oh, and I love The Cause!" she said excitedly.

"Thank you," I repeated, turning around and adding, "hey... you should check out Tyler Wilson."

"Oh, yeah, I know Tyler. Are you working with him?"

"Yeah."

"That's amazing. So cool."

I got the impression we could have continued this fragmented conversation for quite some time, so I made a nebulous excuse. "Sorry, I really have to get this to my room."

Once there, having just said that I would be leaving on Sunday, it did seem as if Sunday felt like the right day—enough time after the funeral to not make it look like I was upping and leaving, and not enough time that I was outstaying my welcome. I booked a flight to London from my laptop and then looked for the best train fare. However, they were all so expensive I decided to hold off until I had arrived in England.

Hesitating and then, finally, pressing the "confirm" button on the computer left me with a feeling of deep sadness. There was now a definite end to my trip—but I knew that it had to be. There was never any intention for me to stay for the full ninety days as permitted on my work visa, and I didn't really want to start pushing the boundaries, considering I hoped be back out to work again. And, with the way I was starting to feel about Brooke, the quicker I could pull myself away, the sooner I would be able to return to Idaho.

I walked back to Murphy's and I guess I must have been a good hour or hour and half getting into my room and settled, and then back to the bar. I remembered to bring the Magic 8-Ball as I had not given it to Brooke on her birthday.

When I walked back in, Brooke was sitting at the bar talking with Louise. She turned around and gave me a smile.

"Hey! Sorry I was so long. I'm staying at the Amber Inn," I said. "Oh, and I forgot to give this to you on your birthday," I said, passing the 8-Ball to Brooke. "It's just a small gift, but I thought, you know... it's kind of fitting."

"I love it," she said, after opening it. "I can definitely use it to provide me with answers when you're not around."

"Yeah, well... speaking of that. I'm going on Sunday."

"Oh. Right," she said, with surprise, and then, with disappointment, "oh."

"Did you want to get out of here? I mean, I love your mom and everything, but it feels kind of awkward, like we're going to be... under her watchful eye."

"Can we do that tomorrow? I'd just... I like being close to mom at the moment."

"Yeah, of course," I said. I felt a bit awkward then, as if my eagerness had come across the wrong way. Too keen, too soon.

"Thank you," she said, in a sweetly polite way. "So, I've been looking online, about good conversation starters."

"You don't have any trouble starting a conversation."

"Well, you were gone a while," she replied. "So, where do you see yourself in ten years?"

"You really have!" I laughed. "So what's the next gem?"

"Hey!" Brooke exclaimed, laughing.

"Go on... is it what's my biggest weakness? My biggest fear?"

"Well this isn't going very well. You made a good first impression Mr. Ward, but you clearly don't know much about the etiquette of dating."

"I don't know if this is a date, actually. If it is, then we've already had a few. I don't know if I can class it as a date when we're being waited on by your Mom," I smiled.

"Well, fine. But you can consider this a warning that I expect better," she said.

"So, yeah, your mom told me that you like me. She said a mother knows," I smiled, teasingly.

Brooke blushed.

"Yeah, I do. So you gonna stop bringing that up?"

"No, not any time soon. It's a pretty good thing for me to

mention. It's good ammunition."

"It might be. But a girl's gotta prepare herself. And from what I know, you have a bit of a reputation for awful relationships."

"Ouch!" I laughed. "But, yeah… you know enough about mine. All I know about you is that you're just having fun. You'll be the last girl standing, or something?"

"Oh, ouch," Brooke laughed back. "This *is* fun, right?"

"Let's just use every word we ever said against the other."

"Sounds like a plan."

For a few moments, it didn't matter that we were in Murphy's, with Louise. We might as well have been alone or in a secluded restaurant where nobody knew us. We shared a smile that was too long to be considered normal and almost so long that it could be perceived as ridiculous. Brooke ran her fingers through her platinum hair, putting it behind her ear, and tipping her head to her left-hand side, looking away shyly.

All I could see was Brooke. All I could think was how astoundingly beautiful she was, here, casual, barely trying.

I felt more alive than I had in years. I was aware of every emotion, in a truly positive way. I guessed I would have probably appeared hesitant or reluctant to Brooke, but I was so keen to absorb every moment of this feeling, to remember it and carry it with me, that I wished I could press the pause button on my life and bottle it all. That, of course, was not only unrealistic but impossible. Yet, I could still take the time to appreciate it, appreciate these good times, enjoy that electricity, as Hal had told me to.

We would never be as young as we were at that moment, free enough to carelessly explore these emotions, as if all other responsibilities we had were meaningless, inconsequential thoughts or processes we could fit into whatever the future held for us as a pair. I wondered how long we would be able to hold on to that fresh and exciting energy.

"You know, it's a shame you're going so soon," Brooke said. "It was Hal's wish for us to scatter his ashes down in a garden of remembrance. Where his parents are. So after the funeral Mom and me are driving down to Georgia. Would have been nice if you could have come."

"Well, if I'd known!" I said. "They give you the ashes that soon?"

"Yeah. He had it all planned out."

"Well... I could possibly cancel. Or rearrange my flight."

"I didn't think you'd want to get out of here so soon."

"You know it wasn't that," I insisted. "But Hal said a lot of stuff that made sense to me. One of the things, most of all, was about living... and dying. I'm... this is really good, out here. But I do feel like I'm on holiday. On pause. And I need to start living again."

"Yeah. I think I get what you mean. As long as *living* means living here," Brooke replied.

I heard myself saying those words and realising that my future had to include Brooke. How long that would take, I didn't know. Nor did I really consider how it would logically work, but other elements of Hal's advice, such as not wasting time, were words I was very conscious of. Time, our friend, our enemy, that inanimate and inevitable force, that most precious commodity. I supposed I ought to seize some control over proceedings and regain true ownership of my decisions, my life, although, I was attracted to simply letting things go, letting them happen as they naturally ought to. I was adjusting to what freedom actually meant to me.

Our conversation flowed happily; I explained that I still needed some time to get Hal's eulogy right, and so, Brooke and I arranged to go back out to the fields with the dried lava and the singular tree—a place that offered an opportunity to think. We also arranged that afterwards, we'd go on an "official date," to a drive-in theater, as I'd never been to one.

With the evening winding to a close, I was about to head off to the motel, when I received an email on my phone. At first, I wasn't going to open it and instantly wished I hadn't. It was a lengthy message from Kaia, and I felt like it was the kind of thing I ought to dedicate some time to reading properly, but I knew Brooke was wondering who it was, so I took a quick glance and then shut my phone off.

"Everything okay?"

"Yeah. It was Kaia."

"Oh?"

She didn't seem surprised.

"I can't... I didn't read it properly. Or I would tell you what it says."

"You can read it. I'll go get us some more drinks."

Yeah, that was a good idea. I'd probably need the extra Dutch courage to really explain it, warts and all, to Brooke.

Kaia's email was expressing regret at the way things had turned out. Apologising for anything she had done or said; saying that she hoped I didn't hate her. And hoping one day we could really sort out what had happened between us. She then closed with a goodbye—which I took to be permanent.

When Brooke returned, I told her everything. I admitted that it may make me sound like a bad person, but I'd moved on from that. I wasn't bound by that weight anymore and, since Kaia had returned home, to me she seemed, and felt, like part of my past. I found myself trying to explain it in such a way as to reassure Brooke that she had nothing to worry about or be jealous over, in that way that I was over-compensating, downplaying the significance of my relationship with Kaia altogether. Now that Brooke had witnessed everything first hand, I felt that she completely understood in the proper manner. No half-truths, no white lies.

I could recognise the truth of it all as I made my way back to the motel that evening. There was a candid honesty in how I was expressing it to Brooke, as callously as that may actually have dismissed my time, or times, with Kaia. I knew I could keep a part of that with me, the good parts, the parts I had learned. I contemplated whether it was cruel or selfish. Was it? As I had begun to reevaluate the inherent meaning of freedom as Hal had meant it, I had also considered the weight of emotions. To Kaia, it would barely matter how I perceived the value of our relationship in my own life, moving forward. Unless I told her. And there would be no point in that. So, how could it be cruel? No, it wasn't. It was guilt, manifesting itself in a fashion that could remind me that I wasn't all bad.

I remembered how I had just recently debated with Hal the point of being a product of our environment. The older me—the me I was growing less and less familiar with—would have carried this confusion over whether I was cruel or feeling guilty and I would have procrastinated over it so much that it would have held me back. But I had been honest when it mattered, how it mattered, now—delivering the truth to Brooke without contemplation. I recalled how, unbeknownst to Brooke, I had sat on the porch after Hal had passed, lost, momentarily caught in the trap. Regressing into familiarity. She couldn't have known it, but she freed me, by returning and being herself. It was the tonic I needed. It was a lesson learned, to be honest, but in the heat of the moment, I had done just that. And so, maybe for the first time, my conscience felt clear.

The lava fields appeared even more desolate. Maybe it was from the tree shedding more of its leaves? But that subtle change was enough to have a profound effect on the way I now perceived it, and that hope that I'd once harboured had apparently dissolved with it. I shared my theories with Brooke and she contested that there *was* hope, and where there was hope, there was regeneration. Something new was to follow in the spring. I liked that.

"Just before I started first grade, I had an accident in the summer," Brooke said. "We were messing around in the woods and I fell from this swing... well, it was more of a rope. I broke my arm and I had this..." She stopped to pull the side of her shirt up, but shook her head and pulled it back down. "Well, I used to have this scar. The cut was quite deep, and I had to have stitches. I was in agony, laying there, waiting for my friends to get help. Hal came with Mom, and drove me to the hospital. I thought the cut was so deep that my insides were gonna fall out, and I was worried about getting stitches. I didn't want to go to school and was begging Mom to keep me off. I was at that tender age, you know... I guess I still am in some ways. But Hal was trying to calm me down. He did that thing where he talks about something else and you think that he's... well, you don't realise he is talking about the same thing. I can't remember exactly what it was. He said something like—she held up her two index fingers and started to mimick Hal's voice, with deep, slow pauses—"*There are two lines in life, you can imagine them as conveyer belts that are always moving... one is life, and one is you. Life is always moving. And so are you. Even when you don't know it, or you don't feel it. That is progress. And sometimes you worry, and you panic, and you just wanna go away. And you know what? Sometimes you can. But you stay with your back to the world for too long and you have to catch up.*" I don't know. It was something like that. But I dunno, it was like he was saying, it's okay, that this is normal, that it's part of what you have to go through, in our best life we will all experience pain."

"Yeah," I said, familiar with Hal's turn of phrase.

"And anyway, where I had my stitches... it's all gone now," she laughed. "All faded. But I mean... what you say about it being dead out here. I kinda like this... this idea that it isn't. It seems the same, but it must always change. The wind must change something. There must be millions of tiny little microscopic bugs out here. Everything is always changing all the time because that's simply what progress is."

I realised I felt more relaxed here than previously. For so long these flat, vast landscapes had seemed like my idea of utopia, but I hadn't felt like that at first. There had been some disconnect, probably due to my unfamiliarity with the places and the people. In many ways, I had felt insignificant; particularly in addition to all I felt I was going through. Now that I felt more balanced, it was probably no surprise that I felt more relaxed. There was nothing more beautiful.

I had my own issues to think about, and noticed that Brooke seemed to be distracted too. We had grown so comfortable around each other that I felt as if I could at least now tell when she wasn't being herself. We assumed similar positions to the last time we were out here, Brooke resting upright against the tree trunk with her journal, and me over on the embankment, trying to make notes with a paper and a pen.

We were there for a couple of hours and it got to the stage where I was simply sitting and watching Brooke, wondering if she was okay, but not really wishing to invade her privacy. She waved at me, as if it was okay for me to go over, or indeed that she wanted me to.

"You okay? Good to go?" I said when I reached her.

"Yeah."

"You okay to go out later?"

"Yeah. For sure," she said, and I didn't know if she was trying to convince herself, or me. I knew she obviously had a lot going on and that she would probably tell me what she was thinking in her own time. I had thought her own time would be sooner, perhaps on the drive back to the hotel where I would get changed for the night. But it wasn't, though that is not to say she was lacking in conversation. It was almost a diversionary tactic, asking me more things about myself: if I enjoyed travelling, if I liked being the passenger or the driver—mundane conversational topics that I really had no right to question, though I was aware that we both knew that there was something not being said. Brooke's journal of foreign words sat on the dashboard like a loaded gun. I could barely say that I knew her inside and out but in our short time knowing each other, we had created a fond memory of that time, at least in my mind. It felt wrong to pick it up and continue with those emotions. But closed and unexplored, it felt like a metaphor for the weight of things unsaid.

It remained that way until later on. Brooke arrived at the motel in Louise's car and texted me to let me know she was there. It felt a bit odd, not exactly how I'd envisioned our first official date, and she appeared to be in the same kind of absent minded mood even though she had clearly gone to an effort with her wardrobe, wearing a navy polka dot skirt and delicate white blouse, with a slight curl in her hair and deep red lipstick. Now I knew that she had gone to the effort for me, I felt as if I could say something to her.

"You look really great," I said.

"Well, thank you. You look good too," she replied.

"... even if I would have liked you to have at least gotten out of the car," I joked.

"Well, we can't be talking about a traditional routine, can we. I asked you out. And I'm driving you around!"

"Yeah, fair enough. But you do, you look... really amazing."

"Thank you, again," she smiled.

The movie was pretty unmemorable; it wasn't a case of picking something to watch, as there was only one movie showing, and really, it was more about the experience. Midway through it, Brooke made a huge sigh.

"Wow," I said, "Well, that's not a good sign."

"It's not that..."

She trailed off. I waited for her to finish her sentence, but she didn't.

"What's wrong?" I asked.

"Nothing... well," she replied. "I was trying to write a poem. For you to read at the funeral. But everything just sucks. So I was just thinking that maybe I could send you one of my favourites. It was our thing, really. Mine and Hal's."

"Sure. Of course. Thank you."

Brooke continued. "So, I talked to Mom about the house," she said, with a sense of apprehension.

"I take it that it didn't go well."

"Well, you know, Hal left us everything."

"Yeah."

"Well, as it turns out, everything was quite a lot."

"Well, yeah, you would... I'm sure he made a lot of money... So, Louise doesn't want you to have the house?"

"No, she's happy with that. She doesn't care, she thought it was a good idea. But it was... so, Hal had this house in Georgia. His family home. And, well, he left that to me."

"Wow! That's... yeah."

"Yeah."

"Well... I still have to sort things out with the plane ticket. But

I can come to Georgia. If you want. I'm guessing we'll fly there, right?" I said, filling in the gap of what I felt Brooke was really suggesting.

"Or we could drive? Road trip. I looked it up. It would take us about three days to get there. I love the idea of that kind of an adventure."

The idea certainly seemed appealing. I'd always wanted to travel Route 66 and this was close enough. But I was conscious of my hormones, the way I was feeling about Brooke, and being cooped up with her and Louise for that length of time would be tantamount to masochism on a level I was not willing to put myself through.

"Yeah... sounds like a great idea. But I think... you know, I'll be flying as it is. That's a lot of travel, and I'm not sure if adding three days would be good for my body."

"Yeah... I guess we could always drive back. Me and Mom, I mean."

"So, what is it then. I mean, I get that it's a big deal. But why have you been so quiet?"

"It's just so much to wrap my head around," Brooke admitted. "You know, when people do something nice, or make a nice gesture... I'm not saying that I'm an angel, or anything like that, but you normally politely decline. Well, I do, anyway. But you can't decline something like this, and I can't thank Hal because he's not here. And you know... well, I've been kinda wondering what I'm gonna do with my life. And then Hal goes and does something like this. See, I wanna thank him. But then I also wanna scream and shout at him."

"Why?"

"Because... well," she sighed, exasperated, as if it was a struggle to articulate what she was feeling, "he knew. He knew me, he knew me like a father, and he's even said that's how he saw me... as his daughter. I'm not saying that I wanted or expected anything, because I didn't... I don't. But he had this capability to change my life the entire time. And now, I know, I can live comfortably. He has given me things. But I wanted to grow, so I could... I don't know. Does any of this make any sense?"

"I'm not quite sure I follow," I admitted.

"It's just that, I'm so appreciative. For all that he did. But it makes me angry and annoyed that he's gone and done this..." she paused, as a lone teardrop fell, dragging a dark line of mascara down her cheek. "He went and did this right when I'm in the middle of trying to figure myself out. So how can I give myself the motivation to do that when he's just given me all of the excuses I need?"

"Well... first of all, he didn't *choose* to die when he did. He just... you know. And you can't be angry with him. You said it yourself. If you're angry with him for giving you an excuse, then what you're really saying is, you're angry with yourself for *taking* an excuse that was given. Why not see it positively—that you've been given an opportunity?"

"Yeah, I guess." She was really hurting with this conflict, more than I had known. "But, then I feel so guilty, y'know. Because I really wanna say thank you. And I can't deal with the guilt of the anger because it's so, fucking... what I would really say, if I saw him, is just that I *miss* him. I miss him so much, Freddie, I can't stand it. It hurts so much." She sniffed and composed herself. "But," she continued with a shaky voice, and drying her eyes, "you're right. You know. This *is* an opportunity. And I do agree, with what you say. It's time I stopped hiding behind excuses."

"You're also allowed to give yourself a break, you know."

"Yeah, I know. It's just... Mom, you know? She's a tough act to follow. I know she thinks she hasn't done anything with her life, but she has. People here... they see her like they saw Hal. He always used to say that. That *she* was the star, whenever she would talk about his fame. 'Better to be loved by those who know you than those who don't,' he'd say. And he was right. Everyone knows her. And everyone speaks so highly of her, too."

"Well, you know... it's not a bad thing that you've got time. You obviously need it at the moment. You'll be alright."

We continued to watch the movie, but by that point, neither of us had any interest in it. Brooke reached out to hold my hand.

Her palm was warm and clammy, but, just sitting there with that minimal amount of physical interaction seemed to change the mood. A tension grew in that silence, at least within myself. My lack of interest in the movie had manifested itself in a restlessness and that thought of the bigger picture. The social convention of dating and spending this time together with the underlying thought of what we were doing. I knew that Brooke was catching my occasional glances at her and as bashful, as I tried to cover it up, I couldn't help myself from admiring just how attractive she was. There were moments where I was sure she intentionally remained quiet, trying to catch me looking. She was clearly enjoying yet another frustrating encounter. On the other hand, it was beginning to feel like almost one too many for me.

It seemed like even in doing nothing, we were flirting with each other. Even when she took out some chewing gum and offered me some, it seemed like it was an opportunity for some physical contact. I declined and felt like an idiot. Now she'd moved her hands away from mine, and I didn't know if that was intentional.

Hating that I'd missed my chance, I thought of any excuse that might initiate some kind of physical interaction.

"Do you have a drink?" I asked.

"No."

Oh, great, I thought.

I tried to concentrate, but then I could smell her perfume. I was so nervous.

"So... you all set for tomorrow?" she asked.

I looked at her, and even her chewing the gum seemed seductive.

"Yeah, just about. I just have to scrub up a bit."

"What do you mean?"

"I need to have a shave. Haven't shaved since before I got here. You know, appearances, et cetera."

"Right. Well, do you wanna go do that now? This movie is pretty lame."

"Yeah, sure. Well, at least I can say I did it. The whole drive-in experience."

The drive back felt tense, and we were mostly silent. There was an awkwardness in our expectancies. An acceptance that *something* would happen. *What*, however, was uncertain. I could feel the shared anxiety from Brooke as she messed around with the radio station, eventually deciding to just turn it off as we were pulling in to the motel parking lot.

"This looks nice," she said, entering my room. I had gotten out first and she had followed me. Upon hearing her talk properly for the first time since we'd left the drive in, I turned to face her, as she leaned against the pale orange motel room wall. She was breathtaking. I could barely maintain my composure. It was a ridiculous feeling to have with someone I had spent such a long time with. We had shared so many words, and I now felt incapable of breathing. She was familiar and yet completely different. As she had on that day where she had dressed up so much that it seemed inappropriate; it was now completely appropriate. She hadn't reapplied her make up from when she had cried; where she had pulled off that glamour-puss image, there was now more of the real Brooke I knew again, the vulnerability, the country girl. Irresistible.

"Um... yeah, it's a pretty decent room," I said meekly, moving towards the bathroom door.

"Do you want me to help you shave?"

"Sure," I laughed.

But as she moved towards me, I remained in the doorway of the bathroom, compelled to keep still, and somewhat frozen by anticipation.

Brooke walked towards me, probably thinking that I would move into the bathroom. I couldn't. She reached me, and instead of walking past me, she drew closer, pushing her body towards mine, her breasts pushing against my chest. She was so close that I could feel her breath on my neck and I thought she may back off from the beating of my pulse.

"I like your beard," she said, stroking at my stubble with her fingertips.

And then, her eyes came up to mine. It was a familiar look, yet different. The first time she had kissed me, on the porch, she had looked at me with something of a determination. Now, perhaps a little unsure, she seemed to be waiting for permission, or, at least, some resistance to tell her to stop. That was the only remaining obstacle between us. And I couldn't tell her to stop. She closed her eyes and pressed her lips against mine, providing a reminder of that perfect kiss.

This time there was no resistance; no caution. We wrestled and tugged at each other's clothes with an urgency and we made love, almost with anxiety, that mixture of keenness and relief, the kind of exhausted relief that comes with giving in to the tension, the urges. It was overwhelming.

As we lay together, trying to get our breath back, all I could consider was how right it felt. The arrival at this moment revealed an altogether new feeling. I felt, simultaneously, like my heart was going to explode out of my chest, and also like it was already out of my body, weightlessly floating above me. There was a newness to this. A freshness. So much of my recent past had been defined by a lack of clarity, though I knew that there would still be troubles and there would still be grief, to feel as strongly and clearly as I did was a bizarre sensation. As Brooke's fingers ran slowly across my chest with her head resting on my shoulder, we remained in a comfortable and relaxing silence.

Eventually, I decided to pull myself out of bed and have that shave. When I went back into the bedroom, Brooke was sitting up with the quilt wrapped around her. Earlier in the day, I had picked up a suit for the funeral and she was sitting tying the tie around her neck.

"I can do that myself," I laughed.

"Sorry," she smiled. "Just trying to help."

"Thanks." I sat beside her.

"So are you gonna come to Georgia with us?"

"Yes. Of course."

I cancelled my flight, and booked tickets for all three of us to fly to Atlanta the morning after the funeral.

Our conversation was easy, if a little awkward, shifting into this new situation, our newly discovered dynamic. I got the feeling that Brooke would have liked to have stayed with me all night, but considering the situation, really couldn't. We didn't speak of what had happened between us, but words were unnecessary. There was a closeness, a tactility that now existed, with Brooke keen to touch me and hold me, and for my part, I was more than happy to have her soft hands and lips on me. After a time that seemed like it was so long and yet gone so soon, Brooke got dressed.

The next day was going to be difficult.

11

"How he would say it is, *Hal Granger lived... and then he died.* But those of us here know that there was an awful lot that went in between."

I was standing nervously at the altar in front of a crowded church. "Some of you may have been fortunate enough to have seen Hal at the height of his fame. Others got to know him as the person he was. I stand here, having only known Hal for a few weeks, and now having the honour of speaking to you all about his life. Now what that means to me is that if I knew him as well as I feel I did, then he meant at least the same and likely more to each and every other person in this room."

I looked out over the faces, some of which were familiar from Murphy's, a few very familiar, and some I did not recognise.

"Hal had a tendency to say things that carried weight. When he spoke, you naturally presumed each word would be important. Because that's how it was. He had a tendency to repeat certain phrases. These were usually really good pieces of advice—whether he had thought of it himself or picked it up from somewhere else. I would guess that many, if not all of us, have at one point benefitted from that advice. I can't say I knew Hal as well as some of you, or as well as I'd have liked. But I was given this honour to speak of him, and for him. I think one good thing about knowing your time is coming is that you are able to prepare accordingly. Hal asked me to say something. Just one thing. He asked me to say that he lived a *truthful* life... and I think we can all agree that he did just that."

I paused, almost unsure of myself.

"But truthfulness and honesty can sometimes be different

things. Hal knew that difference, and as I stand here speaking to you, I have the impression that he departed from us thinking that he was one and not the other. There are things that I don't need to say here. Hal was honest *and* truthful. So much so, that I think it set him free, and helped more than he would know. I cannot pretend that I am able—as much as I would like—to go into anecdotal references about the time he did this, or the time he said that. But Hal Granger did a lot for me and while we mourn his loss, we ought to celebrate his life. Not in the way that people rebel against the inevitability of death to suppress the real grief, but in the truest form—the fact that he had a life well lived, and the fact that he was able to embrace this in his last days. I wanted to close by quoting part of Percy Shelley's poem *Ode To The West Wind*, as chosen by Brooke."

> *Make me thy lyre, ev'n as the forest is:*
> *What if my leaves are falling like its own!*
> *The tumult of thy mighty harmonies*
>
> *Will take from both a deep, autumnal tone,*
> *Sweet though in sadness. Be thou, Spirit fierce,*
> *My spirit! Be thou me, impetuous one!*
>
> *Drive my dead thoughts over the universe*
> *Like wither'd leaves, to quicken a new birth!*
> *And, by the incantation of this verse,*
>
> *Scatter, as from an unextinguish'd hearth*
> *Ashes and sparks, my words among mankind!*
> *Be through my lips to unawaken'd earth*
>
> *The trumpet of a prophecy! O Wind,*
> *If Winter comes, can Spring be far behind?*

"Thank you Hal."

There was a silence among the assembled crowd. Brooke and Louise gave kind smiles.

"Oh, and there was something else. I wasn't sure if I should do this, but I also kind of think it's relevant. And Hal would have liked me to. I'm sure he told some of you this, but, before his wife Betty died, he asked her to write him forty letters. He would open one for every birthday. Anyway, the point to this is, he stopped reading them because he thought there would be a rainy day where he could read them all. And then, he got ill, and it made him upset to think that she had spent all that time to provide comfort on his birthdays, and he had wasted that. But, he read most of them, save for the two letters remaining for birthdays he hadn't yet enjoyed. We had this idea that his family—Louise and Brooke—decided was fitting... so. Going with Hal is the thirty-ninth letter. It will remain part of their ongoing conversation and should remain private. But what I have here," I said, pulling out the unopened envelope, "is the fortieth."

As I read the words, and before I had read them out loud, I could feel my hands begin to shake. In this moment I was privy to a conversation that was started long before I was born. A conversation, and a life of love, concluded by my speaking these few words.

> *Dear Hal,*
> *Love.*
> *Be free.*
> *Betty*

I have to admit that the silence and rustling of paper among the congregation as I returned to sit beside Brooke and Louise was a little unsettling.

"Thank you," whispered Brooke, tugging on my arm.

We arrived in Atlanta via a stopover in Denver. I couldn't help but smile, remembering Hal's song, *Denver*. On the flight to Atlanta, which was just over four hours, Brooke made a few jokes about how she would much prefer to have driven, and that she'd never forgive me. I did wonder if Brooke had told Louise about everything that had happened between us, but I gathered Louise would be drawing her own conclusions with Brooke's familiarity with me. It wasn't over the top; nonetheless, it was notable. I suppose it may have made Brooke think she was doing something wrong with my uptight response to her touch, but I couldn't help it with Louise around.

The journey between our first and final airport took around five and half hours. By the time we reached Atlanta it was late in the afternoon and we were all tired. We hired a car and Louise drove. We decided to stop off in Calhoun and find a motel to stay the night. As far as I could tell, we weren't too far from the garden of remembrance, and Brooke was keen to see the house she had inherited, but after the long trip we all agreed it was probably for the best that we got some good rest for the following day.

Since I would be heading back to England from Georgia, I had all my belongings with me, and was playing guitar when Brooke came to my motel door. She said she and Louise were going to get some food and asked if I wanted anything, so I asked for something easy like a burger and fries or the like. When they returned I had already taken my chair and put it outside the room. The weather was a little warmer than it had been in Idaho and it was welcome in the evening.

I heard Brooke and Louise talking before they arrived with the food and when they saw that I was sitting outside, they went and got two chairs from the poolside and sat with me. Brooke finished eating and said she would go and get changed, leaving Louise and I to talk.

"Freddie, I just want to say that your words at the funeral were really nice. And the poem at the end, it was really fitting."

"It was an honour, Louise. I can't take the credit for that, though, that was all Brooke," I replied.

"It was really nice."

"You know it was only a few months ago that... well, I've had an unlucky year."

"Yes, oOf course... Eddy Crowe, too."

"Yeah. But I reacted badly to Eddy's passing. Now... I'm not saying it's a good thing, but... well, Brooke has been so good."

"For me too," Louise said.

I wondered if I'd said too much, so, bit my tongue for a few moments.

"So, when you were speaking about honesty and truthfulness... you think Hal wasn't?" she asked, "because that's what he said. In his letter."

"No, I think he was, but... it's not my place to say, because I don't really know you guys anywhere near as well as you knew each other."

"Sure you do, go on."

"Okay, well. I just think that there's a whole... a whole range of truth. It's not as simple as a black and white divide between the truth and a lie. And for a very long time I thought it was. But I see now that we all live with our truths and sometimes it takes some... I don't quite know how to put it... clinical honesty? To change our lives."

"I don't think I follow," Louise replied.

"It's just... take Hal... he loved Betty. Nobody could deny that. And you know... the integrity he showed and value on his marriage is just... I know it wasn't something you wanted to hear at the time but it was *his* truth, and *his* way of living his life. But, he wouldn't have written you that letter if he didn't mean it. He was reading those letters that Betty sent him... And I think what got to him most was, that she wrote a long one for his seventieth birthday. It's only what I think, but I think that opened his eyes to regret, as if he had somehow let her down. And he had been so scared of admitting that he loved you that entire time that... you know, he was scared of doing that for letting her down. But when he felt like he had anyway, that's why... I think that's why he wrote you."

"Do you really believe that?"

"Yeah. I do."

"That's nice." Louise reached out and held my hands. "Thank you. Freddie. I so wanted to believe in the things he said. But I thought... these are the words of a man trying to make someone feel better. Like it wasn't all for nothing."

"It wasn't."

"No," she said softly. "Hey, so... that last letter from Betty.

272 : WAYNE BARTON

Really something."

"Maybe if he'd had read that first? Or if she'd written it first?"

"Maybe she did."

"Yeah, maybe," I agreed. "You okay?"

"I'm getting there. It's just weird, you know. I don't know who I'm grieving for. My best friend, my life partner, my soulmate."

"Yeah."

"But, like you said, Brooke's been such a great help."

"Just don't do what Hal did," I said. "That's all I'll say."

"Yeah, I know. I sometimes think there's no point wishing for things to work out in a certain way. You just... you gotta deal with the truth," she said, wistfully.

"Sometimes it's good to wish. And hope."

"Hey!" Louise said, noticing Brooke. "We were just speaking of you."

"Oh, yeah? Should I be worried?"

"No, but, you know... you two. If you wanna, I don't know, hold hands. I ain't gonna say nothing."

I almost felt like cringing.

"Mom!"

Clearly Brooke did too.

"I'm just saying, we're all adults here. If you wanna stay with Freddie then..."

"Okay, okay, enough!" I laughed.

Brooke did come to my room and it felt as if she were making some overtures to stay. We lay side by side on the bed and talked more about the day to come. About seeing the house, and scattering Hal's ashes. Then, inevitably, about my leaving.

"I really don't want to," I admitted, "but, you know... probably the day after tomorrow."

"I wish you didn't have to."

"But I can come back. I just... you have to do these things properly."

"Can I come with you?" she asked, though I don't even think

she expected me to say yes.

"You have to stay with your mom. She's relying on you."

"Yeah, I know," she swallowed, with tears in her eyes. "I'm just really gonna miss you."

She held me close and kissed me hard. I could feel her tears rolling onto my cheeks.

"I'll be back, you know that. Anyway, you have to go back, you know, your mom will be wondering. And I can do without that awkward conversation," I laughed. Even though Louise had given her blessing, her awareness of it still made me uncomfortable.

"Okay," Brooke replied, smiling through her tears. "See you in the morning."

She kissed me, and then deliberately didn't move, to see what my reaction would be.

"Can you pass me the crisps? On the side?" I asked. There was a tube of Lay's on the bedside cabinet.

"You mean the chips?"

"Yeah," I replied with a rueful smile, "the chips."

Brooke passed them to me and I took one, putting the container on the bedside cabinet at my side of the bed. After taking a bite, I coughed with the strong taste.

"What is it?" Brooke laughed.

"I think it's the spicy flavouring," I laughed.

"Flavouring? You mean powder?" she replied, confused.

"What... yeah, the thing. You know!"

"Wow."

"What?!"

"Is that a British thing?"

"No idea. I don't think so," I smiled.

"I just realised."

"What did you just realise?"

"If this is a thing. Us. Like a long-term, forever thing, well, there's *so* much stuff we need to figure out."

I laughed. "What's that supposed to mean?"

"Well you know, you have one word for something, I have another. We'll need some kind of defined mutual vocabulary. It will save a lot of time. And petty arguments. I suggest we go with mine, I'll never get on board with flavouring."

I looked at her, humoured, but didn't respond.

"What, you don't get what I mean? You know, all those idiosyncrasies."

"Yeah, all those things that make me *me*. Maybe we need a new book, just for us."

"No, don't be silly," she laughed. "But you know how it goes. That's evolution."

"Sounds like regression."

"Not at all," she smiled mischievously. "After all, I *am* the best, right?"

She kissed me again and held me close, before letting go, wiping her cheek and standing up. After she left the room, I lay there for a few minutes, enjoying a contentment that I hadn't felt in quite some time.

I had a repeat of the same feeling I'd felt on the morning of Brooke's twenty-first.

As if I were on the outside.

That wasn't necessarily a bad thing, just odd. And, further, oddly apt.

After all, I felt close to Hal. I had an acceptance with that and I knew in all that he didn't say, simply through his actions, that for some reason I had grown to mean something to him. And I knew, with Hal, that for him, actions spoke louder than words. That's what he thought, anyway. When he finally did speak, it always meant a lot, and when he had spoken his truth to Louise, it really had set her free. She was stood at the open door, waiting to walk through it.

At least that's the way I perceived the situation as I stood some yards away, watching Louise and Brooke scatter what remained of Hal's ashes over the headstones bearing the names of his parents and his sister. Back in Idaho they'd scattered most of his ashes in the back yard of his house, where, apparently, Hal had done the same with Betty's all those years earlier. Hal would have no blood to follow. No more ashes would be scattered on this patch of ground. It was sad, very sad, but still peaceful. I had looked at the gravestones in the accompanying cemetery, of others who had died; some ten years ago, others, fifty, even one hundred, years prior. Their stories now consigned to the few lines that were inscribed, somehow completely contrasting the pride in the size and grandness of the stone which marked the spot where they were laid to rest.

How long before Hal was forgotten?

Would anyone even be here to see his name added to the stones of his parents? I made a mental note to make a point of coming back out here at some time in the future. I gathered that this moment represented a significance to Brooke and Louise, not only in the scattering of the ashes, but in the way that it was a final goodbye, of sorts. A time to move forward. I knew that Brooke would be okay, but I worried for Louise. Easier said than done, as I knew myself, but I hoped that she would take the messages that Hal was sending in his last few days. They had their own private moments, their own conversations, and I felt that any message he was trying to convey to me was probably intensified to her. *Thank you, but don't waste your life now. You're free.* Just as Betty had told him. If only he'd known. Like Louise said; maybe he did. But witnessing his regret should have taught her not to make the same mistake. Easier said than done.

I was almost relieved, but in any case, so very heartened to see them both with smiles on their faces as they walked back toward me.

"We were just saying that we really should come back here when they put his name on the stone," Brooke said.

"Yeah. That's a great idea," I replied.

We used directions printed out from the motel lobby that morning to find the house. They indicated that it was around nine miles away from the cemetery.

I don't know what Louise and Brooke expected to find, but I really felt it would be run down and modest. My mouth nearly dropped open in disbelief when we pulled up to this home which looked modern, and most confusingly of all, recently lived in. It was huge, and stood proudly and dominating in its plot. Well kept, maintained, more so than Hal's own home. Brooke and Louise must have been equally shocked because they didn't say anything right up until the point that we walked up the driveway and knocked on the door.

"There must be some mistake," Louise said. "Try the key."

Brooke put the key in the door and it did seem as if she didn't expect it to open. When it did, it revealed a modern and well-lit hallway with a spiral staircase in the middle.

"Hello?" Brooke called out, apparently feeling like we were intruders.

But there was nothing, aside from papers on the island unit in the kitchen which looked as if they were legal documents. Louise was going through them, as Brooke explored the house, coming to terms with its grandness, running to the staircase and going up it. "Oh my God, oh my God!" we heard her squealing upstairs.

I walked to the back of the house and saw a modest sized pool out there.

The house could have been built this month. I didn't get it.

"I don't believe it," I heard Louise say.

"What is it?"

"Take a look at this," she said.

I walked over and looked at a set of pictures, showing a house—this house. The interior, old, as we would probably have expected it to look, had we expected this house at all. And, atop them, a note.

"Sometimes you have to tear it apart and rebuild from within. All my love. Hal."

I tried to make sense of it. But it was difficult with Brooke floating around like a butterfly; she distracted and attracted my attention at the best of times but especially now, when she was excited and lively.

The morning was filled with squeals of excitement with unexpected discoveries; the rooms all furnished to a high standard, every appliance provided, the house was essentially ready to move into. Brooke near enough went crazy when she went into the garage and discovered a brand-new Jeep. She came out sobbing as if she had just had all of her birthdays. It was an extremely touching and sentimental moment to see Louise holding her as they both struggled to come to terms with this.

I considered that even if Brooke didn't want to stay in this house—and I could see why she wouldn't, since it was so far away from Louise—if she sold it all with the contents, she would easily be an instant millionaire.

They took some time—and photos—going around the house, getting used to it. As time wore on to the mid-afternoon, the absence of Brooke's comments as to the future of the house was conspicuous. I began to feel that she didn't want to hurt Louise's feelings, but that she had been drawn to this place.

Brooke insisted on driving her new Jeep, and so I went with Louise back to the motel. The idea was that Louise would drop the rental car off and they would have the Jeep to drive back to Idaho, and even take me to the airport, which I really appreciated.

It reminded me that I really needed to book the plane tickets, and so when we got back to the motel I did that right away, using the hotel lobby to print out my information and taking it back to my room. I thought just doing it without thinking would lessen the emotion I knew that I would feel. Pressing the "reserve" button evoked a deep intake of breath, so involuntary it almost caught me by surprise. A foreboding sense of it being the wrong thing to do, even if it was necessary.

As I showered, I heard my door open, and Brooke call out. I grabbed a towel, answered and got back in the shower; Brooke was sitting on the bed holding the papers in her hand when I got out.

"Why so soon?" she asked.

"The sooner I go, the sooner I can sort out coming back. It's like a plaster. You have to rip it fast to get the sting."

She looked at me, puzzled.

"Oh," I laughed. "I mean Band-Aid. Maybe we really do need a book?"

"I'm not ready for you to go. Can you come with us back home? You can help me. I don't know what to do."

"I can't, really. I've got to be careful about my visa, you know."

"Yeah. But, it sucks."

"So, tonight's our last night."

"For now."

She hugged me, tightly, not caring that I was still dripping wet from the shower. She began to kiss my neck and then my face, hurriedly.

"No, we can't," I said.

"Why not? We can... we can," she insisted, kissing me again.

"Because Louise... your mom," I said, temporarily giving in, then restraining myself, "we can't make it too obvious to your Mom. She'll be waiting for us."

We went out for dinner at a local bistro. To me, it very much had the air of that meal on the last evening of a vacation, with us reminiscing about how we had first met and their first impressions of me—to Louise, I was a shy kid, and to Brooke, I was a star who she couldn't believe was there. We talked of Hal, and Louise stressed the point that she was sure I had become very dear to him. To them all. I said the feeling was more than mutual. And it was.

At that moment, I got a little upset, overwhelmed with the feeling that I had felt lost, arriving in Idaho, not knowing where I belonged. Longing for a sense of home, as if home were a place, but now it seemed that that wasn't the case at all. *Home*, at least for me, was people, people you belonged to, and with, and I had found that. And now I had found it, I had to leave. It was sentimental, bittersweet. And overwhelming.

Brooke held my hand and as they saw I was upset, Louise got up from her seat and came around to hold me. All of the emotions came flooding out. So much had happened in such a short period of time. New friends, joy, loss, grief and sorrow... new love. A new future. Pressing "reserve" on the flight tickets really had made me aware of these emotions which were very much present, and speaking openly about them was all too much.

"Hey, hey, it's okay," Louise said.

"Sorry... I feel like an idiot," I said, composing myself. Brooke had her head on my shoulder and was running her fingers through my hair. I could tell that she was upset too, and lost in the moment, as my defences had unexpectedly fallen. It mattered not to her that Louise was there. It was as primal a reaction as could be. Natural.

We had all maintained such a strong positivity that it felt piercing it may provoke the breaking of a dam; the avalanche of emotion would prove too strong. It weighed heavy in the air the next morning as Louise and Brooke drove me to the airport. We didn't speak much on the way there, but Brooke sat in the back with me, holding my hand, squeezing it tightly, resting her head on my shoulder.

It felt *wrong*, but inevitable, as we pulled up to the terminal. The air was cold, bitter, foreboding, as if to match the atmosphere that had lingered in the car.

"Ooh, are you warm enough?" Brooke asked as we got out.

"Yeah, it'll be fine inside."

"It'll be colder when you get back to England though."

"Yeah. I'll be fine."

Such small talk after the way we had conversed over these last weeks. I could barely believe the connection that had been built between us. Pulling myself away felt as great as any grief I had felt, as strong as any hurt I had felt in my life. Brooke held on to me and didn't want to let go. I didn't want her to.

"Hey, give me a go," Louise said, providing the break. "You're a good kid. We're really gonna miss you, you know."

I nodded into her hair, fighting the tears in my eyes.

"And you're a good girl."

She laughed and pulled away.

I composed myself, stretched my shoulders.

"Right."

Brooke took advantage of the opportunity and jumped in where Louise had left me to hug me again. Her eyes were red, and her breath was shaky as she fumbled, pushing a piece of paper into my shirt pocket.

"What's this?"

"For later," she said, kissing my cheek, and then my lips, "come back. Soon! You hear?"

"I will. Soon as I can."

"Okay, come on Brooke. He'll miss his plane," Louise said.

"Good," Brooke replied, eventually pulling away.

"Come back," she repeated.

Louise led Brooke back to the car. I stood outside the terminal and waved as they drove away.

In the departures lounge, I went to the bar to get a beer and rest my feet. And head. It had been a draining and fulfilling time and I thought I ought to get ready to relax on the flight. As I went to pay for the beer, I pulled out the paper that Brooke had pushed into my shirt pocket.

I opened it with interest; the opening folds of the paper revealed nothing but a crudely drawn heart in thick red pen. If it was her way of telling me how she felt, as it seemed to be, then I admitted to myself that I felt the same way. I noticed some writing on the back, and turned the paper over. On it Brooke had written, "This was the poem I wrote for Hal," and below it read:

Every now and then

I think about you

As here

The power and the simplicity of the very short prose caught me off guard and choked me up. Aside from her talent, which had been completely unrevealed until this point, it seemed almost the perfect summary of the emotional rollercoaster I'd been on. A succinct memento of this change in myself.

It wasn't so long ago, five or six years ago, that I'd seen time away from home as an opportunity to be a different person. That much was true this time, too, only the person I'd become was, for once, the person I truly was. Who I'd always wanted to be.

On the plane back to England, I thought about the house that Brooke had inherited, and the note Hal had written her. I guess Hal intended a lot of things with what he had written, though I guess it was easy to get carried away with reading too much into the words someone wrote after they passed. Still, those thoughts kept returning and recurring as they tend to do on an eight-hour flight. I know that Louise wasn't exactly at total peace with the letter Hal had written to her, but hopefully she would find some with this. I took it to mean that thanks to Louise, he had rebuilt himself.

That, and his regret, was his way of telling her.

Perhaps he knew that she wouldn't take the house in Idaho. Perhaps that was his plan all along? She was a proud woman, but I got the impression she never stood in the way of anything Hal did for Brooke. The house in Georgia, to me, represented something of a metaphor for Hal's own soul and I took some comfort in that. Whether she would, too, I could only hope.

I opened the complimentary newspaper to catch up on news from England and was scanning through, not really reading, until I saw a picture in the celebrity gossip column which caught my eye.

Ailie. And James, one of the guitarists from The Cause.

Underneath was the caption: "Stepping out—James Delaney and Ailie McIntyre celebrate their engagement."

Wow! What?

I read the article.

James Delaney of The Cause looks the worse for wear after celebrating his engagement with songwriter Ailie McIntyre. The pair were at the Ivy until 1:00 am drinking and partying with friends. McIntyre has previously been linked to music industry professional Freddie Ward.

I reread it and was surprised to discover I felt no real emotion. If anything, it was the humorous thought of the way I was described. It was the first time I had been mentioned in a newspaper. It barely registered to me that Ailie had moved on, that it had been so quick, that there must have been some overlap with our relationship. Unless she had been impulsive; she was, of course, like that.

But still, I felt nothing. It was fine.

12

The plane arrived in London early the following morning, and though I was going to go to the train station, a recurring thought I'd had towards the end of the flight compelled me to go to the U.S. Embassy in Westminster and enquire about applying for a work visa, just in case I wanted to dedicate more time to working with Tyler. I thought, as an excuse, it would be pretty good. I got the train and tube from Heathrow to Westminster; only upon leaving the station in central London did I have any service on my mobile phone, where I discovered I had three text messages from Brooke.

The first, *"Thank you xxx"*; then, *"Hope you've landed safely xx"*; and finally, *"Text me when you get this xx."*

I texted back to let her know that I had landed, and I would text when I was on the train back to my parents' house.

If Tyler was a convenient excuse and an opportunity, then Brooke was obviously the real reason that I wanted to return. I had been honest when explaining how I'd felt as if I were on holiday, or in limbo, at certain points towards the end of my time in Idaho. That was far outweighed by the contentment I'd felt there, but I had headed to America in a state of uncertainty and had returned to the U.K. with a purpose, to get back to Brooke as soon as possible. I had a desire, and a place to be. It had been a long time since I had felt so alive. And so, amid the grey of the city and in place of the desolation one normally feels when returning from a particularly pleasant holiday, I had a real spring in my step.

I could return to Idaho and while Brooke was considering what to do next, I could work with Tyler, possibly on some of the songs that Hal and I had been working on together.

Brooke had suggested that as a project for the both of us—Hal and myself—but I wanted to share it. I had no dreams of being a performer myself, even if I had enjoyed those moments where everyone made me feel like I was such a big deal. What I had felt was a stronger connection to my initial reasons for working in music in the first place, which I felt had become lost after Ailie and I had split. It had been a joint endeavour; or that was how I had perceived it, and it was easy to disassociate myself with it completely. Of course, in those early weeks after Eddy had died, I had lost the motivation to do anything. But Tyler was really talented. I looked forward to working with him.

The U.S. Embassy was helpful, but could only give me forms. I explained my situation and my credentials, and the receptionist said that if what I was saying was true, then it may be the case that I would be able to apply for a special visa as "an alien with extraordinary ability." I found the description comical and definitely an overstatement, but it appeared to be my best shot. I would have to provide evidence of my achievements and testimonials if I wanted to satisfy the criteria. I hadn't won any awards, but had been nominated for several, and I thought that album sleeves with the credits would be proof enough, along with possible letters of commendation from labels.

I left with a bunch of papers, and my luggage, and a real sense of optimism as I headed to Kings Cross to catch the train back north.

By the time I boarded my train it was already past noon, and given the time difference in Georgia, I felt it was okay to text Brooke again.

"Hey. Just on the train now. Miss you x."

Within thirty seconds, my phone rang.

It was so comforting to hear Brooke's voice. We spoke for almost my entire train journey. She told me how she was thinking of staying in Georgia, and how she could see herself settling there. But she didn't know how she was going to bring it up to Louise.

"You've got time," I insisted. "Time to make the right choices."

I thought about Brooke's concerns. About how she felt guilty about her mom; feeling guilty that she hadn't fully appreciated the sacrifices Louise had made as a single mom, and how much she had taken for granted. I wondered then if—although it wasn't done for this purpose at all—Louise's "reward" for all she had put into the love she had for Hal, the love she had felt was unrequited for so long, was the financial security for Brooke. She was set for life, and not because of the sacrifices Louise had made in the hours she had toiled at the bar, but more, the hours she had toiled with Hal. Neither Louise nor Hal could have known that, but as far as I was concerned, I felt that was some way of the universe repaying karma in the way it is supposed to.

The next few days were an impatient blur. I felt exactly as I had for a little while in the U.S. On pause. Concerned. In limbo. I knew now where I needed to be. With Brooke. It didn't matter where she was. Idaho. Georgia. I was so restless after having this realisation, as obvious as it was.

Home, now, was my parents' house in Prestwich, North Manchester. No longer mine. It was a place I had visited, but barely ever stayed at for years, even prior to meeting Ailie.

Curious, I did take some time to walk around the neighbourhood, as if I were seeing it for the first time, and in some respects, I was. Old family businesses had closed, houses knocked down and communities rebuilt, providing a backdrop of unfamiliarity and disorientation amidst those small areas more recognisable to me. It made me feel small even in this place. Change, change, change, all around me. I knew that I could bump into someone I once knew, any old acquaintance, who might well presume that I'd done nothing but roam these streets for the last ten years. My mind was quite frequently catapulted back to Scotland and Ailie on the pebble beach, and how she talked about her destination. How she had all but lamented about the prospect of a journey if that was where she ended up. And although she perhaps didn't quite mean it like this, and I certainly didn't appreciate the bigger picture at the time, I now understood it in a completely different context. But it wasn't until maybe the second or third day of being back there that the frustration that accompanies restlessness begun to eat away at me, making me feel as if I was doing nothing. The visa application was a little over my head, so I contacted a solicitor friend of my parents who assured me it would be a straightforward process. I shouldn't have to wait too long. He spoke so assuredly, that he suggested I might tell my parents that I was planning to move.

And so, that's what I did. I made a bit of a fuss about it and took them out to dinner at a local restaurant where I knew they would probably be a little apprehensive about the cost.

It dawned on me that throughout all of these periods of introspection, and even in the tough moments of the last year, I hadn't confided in nor sought solace from my parents. I wondered if they saw that as a sign of distance between us or a sign that I was well rounded enough that I didn't need to; though I knew, of course, that the latter was untrue.

At dinner, I opened up about everything. I told them how I had become very low after Eddy had died and how I had pushed Ailie away, and that it was my fault that we had split up. That, plus the fact that I had essentially cheated, though why I felt the need to defend myself and add what I felt was an important fact when it barely mattered either way, I don't know. Perhaps pride, perhaps, that sense of letting them down. So I insisted that they shouldn't feel angry or upset if they saw pictures of Ailie with her new partner.

"So, you'll be with us for Christmas, then?" Mum asked, hopefully.

"Well..." I started, tentatively.

"He'll be moving out, see," Dad interjected, as if he could predict my every movement.

"Actually, I did want to talk to you about my time in America."

"You can tell us about your holiday after we've had our tea," Mum said.

"Well, that's just it," I replied. "It's not... it wasn't really a holiday."

"Well, I would hardly call it work."

"No, no, I'm not... but, look, just listen," I insisted.

Mum's face stiffened a little, perhaps in surprise at my stern tone.

"So..."

"You met a girl on holiday?" Dad interrupted again.

"Well..."

"I knew it!" he said, with all the euphoria and self-satisfaction of winning the lottery.

"Just listen, will you! It's more than that. Yes, I have met someone and... well, I'm thinking of going back out there."

"Oh, right," Mum replied. I could tell immediately from the tone in her voice that she knew what was coming next. Mothers all have that sixth sense.

"I'm thinking that this could be long term." I said. "I've already asked Gordon about sorting out a visa for work."

"How are you going to do that?"

"There's this singer. Tyler. He's undiscovered, but really talented, and I'm going to work with him on a record."

"But how?" Mum repeated. "Don't you have to have... I don't know?"

"I think I may be able to qualify through some kind of special talent visa, as an alien of extraordinary ability. Gordon thinks I have a shot, anyway."

Dad looked at me dubiously.

"I'm not saying I will for sure," I shrunk into myself. "But I think I might be able to meet the criteria."

"Who's the girl?" Mum asked.

"She's called Brooke. She's absolutely..." I said, and then realised I could just show her a picture on my phone. "Here."

"Oh, Freddie! She's gorgeous. Look," she said, passing the phone to Dad. "And are things serious?"

"They can't be, you were only out there for a couple of weeks," Dad snapped, harshly.

"Well, it was closer to a month, actually, but I know her well enough to know I really like her. I'm not saying..." I found myself drifting, defending myself, embarrassed, barely the confident person I'd been just a few days ago. "Actually, yeah, I love her, I think. I was starting to feel like that before Hal died. She's like his daughter."

"Don't you think you should try and work things through with Ailie?" Dad asked.

I looked at him, unable to think of how to respond.

"Don't confuse your grief for love, I mean that, you know for both of you, it might not be real. It might simply be an escape," Mum tried to advise.

"Maybe, but... oh, I don't know," I said, hoping that relenting a little might make them understand, or help them to. "I don't think so. But anyway, going back out there would at least give me the chance to really know."

"So, if this lad's undiscovered, then who's going to be paying you?" Mum asked.

"It's not about the money."

"Yeah, because *she's* the one with all the money," Dad proclaimed, another conclusion he was proud to have correctly jumped to.

"Well, yeah, she does, but I won't be relying on that."

"So, how, then?" Mum asked again.

"I'm not broke. I've got the house money coming in, too."

"You're not spending all that on a holiday," Dad insisted, as if I planned to fritter everything away.

"So what if I did? That's money I've made over the last few years. Easy come, easy go."

"You're not thinking right," Mum said, with that undertone of concern that mothers carry in their voice.

"I am, actually, it's... this is the most logical and well thought out decision I've made in years."

Mum remained silent, leaving the words etched on her face instead.

"You know, I think he could be on to something," Dad repled, surprisingly. "A pretty young rich girl. So, how much are we talking?"

"Yeah, like I'm bringing nothing to the relationship."

"He doesn't mean that, love," Mum said.

"That's exactly what he means! It's not even about her, or anyone else, it's... I can't explain it, but even being back here for these last few days... you know, I was happy out there... you know when something just feels right?"

Mum appeared sympathetic, but Dad was as volatile and unpredictable as ever.

"So what you're saying is that you're above living around here, then?"

"No, not at all... just that, it doesn't feel like home to me any more."

"Well don't forget, lad, that these streets made you who you are. They made me who I am and I'm not ashamed of that."

"I'm not saying that you should be. But you had something to do with that too, to me, to yourself. You're not only a product of your environment... well, you can be. But it's a big world. Don't you just want me to be happy?"

"We do. He does," said Mum trying, as ever, to defuse the situation. "We're just worried. It's a long way if anything were to go wrong. It's a long way away to be alone."

"I've felt more alone here," I admitted. "I'm happier. I'm just happy. And I know this feels right."

They could see I was sincere. And they seemed to change their tone, realising I was serious. I was able to then talk more comfortably about Brooke, and then about Hal and Louise, explaining how my time out there had affected and changed me, and how much I felt like I belonged there. They had always known of my hopes to one day move to the U.S., but I think they had dismissed it as a pipe dream. I think their resistance was more to do with their own shock of hearing the news, and having to process it as a reality. But once they had come to terms with that, they appeared more accepting.

With one potentially troublesome hurdle overcome, I awaited news of the visa. I didn't have to wait too long; the next morning, I received a phone call from Gordon, the solicitor.

290 : WAYNE BARTON

"Are you sitting down?"

"Yes. Why, what's wrong?"

"Well, your former partner, Ms. McIntyre, is refusing to write a statement to the effect that you worked together."

"What? Why? I don't understand."

"Well, she's contesting your version of events. She's basically saying that you didn't do any of the work you are claiming that you did."

"But... well, she can't do that."

"I'm afraid I've been through the documents and your name isn't on them."

"No, it definitely is. Stuart. Stuart is my pseudonym."

"Well, Ms. McIntyre is claiming that Stuart is another party, one of the members of The Cause. A certain James Delaney."

"You've got to be kidding! That's ridiculous. So, what can we do?" I replied, exasperated.

"Well, we challenge it. Obviously this is a very different procedure to your visa application. As we will have to have meetings, and probably a court hearing, I'd advise that you put any plans to leave the country on hold."

"And then what?"

"Well, assuming that we can prove that you did the work you claim..." Gordon said.

"I can!" I interrupted. "Of course I can! Most of them are *my* songs. I've got copies of them, saved online with data inscriptions, or whatever, with the date on. There must be loads of people I can ask too."

"Well, that's good, assuming she hasn't got to them first. Gather as much of that evidence as you can. And, if the court believes you, then we can restart the visa process."

"Can't we just go ahead with it anyway, and then, when the time comes, add in what we need?"

"I don't think that would be advisable. It could harm your application and be a waste of time and money."

It was a nightmare.

How could Ailie do this? And why?

When I called to tell Brooke, she was as upset, if not more, than me. I attempted to calm her down by trying to make it sound as if the situation wasn't as serious as it appeared. That must have worked, because she then appeared a little more upbeat. She told me how Louise had been much brighter in the last couple of days; thinking of how Hal had shunned a life in the beautiful house in Georgia for the small-town modesty of the life he had in Idaho. It had made her realize and accept a lot of things, most pertinently, the love that Hal had professed for her.

Brooke later sent me a text to say she had been looking into it and she would sell the house in Georgia; that it would be enough to effectively pay for a green card. As I read her message I felt sorely tempted to accept, but knew that I couldn't. I even tried to rationalise it with myself, that Hal had provided that money and the houses for Brooke's future, for her happiness. If she saw happiness as being with me, that was justification, surely. But then the doubt in myself crept in. I shouldn't feel or behave so selfishly. I shouldn't take advantage. What if Brooke later felt she'd made a big mistake because I let her down? No, I couldn't do that. She loved that house and had talked so excitedly about living there. I'd have loved to have said it was integrity, but it was the thought of the guilt I knew I couldn't live with, guilt I knew would eventually kill a relationship regardless of how strong it was. I had to be there on my own merit, for my own reasons, not tied to Brooke, so no pressure would be put on her.

Gordon suggested that I try to contact Ailie directly. I did, but received no response. I wrote letters pleading to her better judgement, or to the girl I had once known. I received no reply. Then, I sent straightforward letters, with an affronted tone; how dare she take credit for my work. We both knew it was my work. And so on. Warnings that if it went to court, it would eventually all come out. I didn't mention Brooke, or the purpose for my wanting a visa, though I gathered that her resistance to agreeing that I had done at least as much of, if not most of, the work, was in response to that phone call I had made from Idaho.

At that point, I knew it was in vain; if she hadn't replied earlier,

292 : WAYNE BARTON

she wouldn't now. It was almost for my own sense of sanity, to get all of these words out. Now, all I could think of was the icy, unforgiving stare at the train station, that apparent inability to forgive. Her tone on the telephone to me. In some respects, I could understand her coldness, but in others, I thought, how harsh could one person be? How could she do something like this without any explanation? These problems that had arisen served as an uncomfortable reminder that I couldn't just simply assume that my past was something under which I could draw a line. The fresh start I was hoping for, the fresh start that Idaho represented, was far from a reality.

I even contacted Simon, the lead singer of The Cause, and met up with him for a coffee, asking if he would mind going on record and settling the matter. It was difficult, of course; his bandmates were also his friends, and the conversation was filled with awkward moments where he would appear unwilling to confirm even to me that I was in the right. As if he thought I was recording the conversation. He agreed that the conflict needed to be sorted, but kept saying that he hated being stuck in the middle and would prefer to keep out of it. It was fruitless, and I felt stuck.

I wondered for some time if it would be worth trying to get my name out there; to "accidentally" get word spread that I had written the songs, and "accidentally" get confirmation from someone else, so that this would be a non-issue. A deliberate leak, so that it would be seen as a matter of fact in terms of public record. Straightforward. But I ended up doing nothing. As anxious as I was about having to resort to legal action to get a matter sorted, even though I hadn't done anything wrong, the potential extra stress of creating a situation that may complicate matters even further was not welcome.

I should have used my energy for better purpose, and worked on the songs I intended to record with Tyler, but I didn't. Instead, I did nothing. I could sense myself reverting toward being the ambitionless and directionless young man I had once been. I felt powerless to stop it. And the thought of returning to that past was not a pleasurable journey.

I could sense my parents' concern for my well-being, and they tried to encourage me with conversation.

Dad suggested that we go the local pub for a drink. This was not something we normally did. Dad had his own friends, but I think he had noted my disconnection from my home area and wished to at least get something of that back. Not that it was an attempt to get me to change my mind; it may well have been nothing more than him being at a loose end and being nagged to do so by Mum.

Our local, The Plough, was busy. A pool tournament involving another local pub team was happening. There were many familiar faces, now ten years older, and much like those soulless shells I'd witnessed at The Anchor up in Scotland, men drinking to while away the hours until they were back at work, where they would undoubtedly count the minutes to be here. It made me look at my father differently, as if he was one of these men that I so pitied, and that too made me feel guilty. I think that, in some respect, I was simply looking for further excuses to wallow.

I had made arrangements with Brooke to video call her while I was there. She was keen to see what my local pub was like compared to Murphy's. I did make the call, but I felt self-conscious talking to her, like it was a conversation completely out of place, or she didn't belong in a dive like this. It made me think about whether I really did think I was above it all, even if Brooke was amused, insisting it was no worse than Murphy's. I guess, in direct comparison, she had a point. Perhaps it was more pertinent a point that I was a little reticent to introduce Brooke, my present and, hopefully my future, into my past. I was beginning to see the old me as someone spoiled, and someone I could leave behind, and it would serve no positive purpose giving Brooke an insight into what I perceived as the old me. I would have to come to terms with that as if things were to develop with her, she would undoubtedly want to know. And as serious as I may have been about moving to Idaho, if I made such a move and things worked out the way I hoped, I couldn't reasonably think we'd never end up here together at some point, even if it was another ten or twenty years from now.

I felt relieved when the short video call was over. I could feel the prying eyes and hear the whispering voices—"sounds like an

American girl"—and so on, from people familiar enough to nod in acknowledgement of knowing you, but not so much that they could have a conversation.

I couldn't say I was alone, but even with my father present, I felt it. Out of place. Out of place at "home" is a weird feeling. Being a tourist where you grew up. But, now reintroduced to this watering hole, I found myself drawn there on a more regular basis over the coming days, even without Dad, and some days I would go in pretty early, remembering those lunch times I'd spent at Murphy's. It was clear to see that prior to dinnertime, the pub would be filled with the unemployed and the unemployable and those who considered themselves to be a class apart from those categories; the amateur wordsmiths and psychologists, keen to tell everyone who will listen about the problems of the world and how they have all the solutions. Nobody challenged them. Nobody asked why they were throwing these words into this black hole instead of shouting them where it really mattered. I wondered if anybody really cared enough to ever have challenged them. I also wondered if this would be my destiny. It worried me that I could see it.

I began to wonder how long it would take for a genuinely depressing situation to transform itself into full-blown depression. I was still conscious enough of Hal's words to not waste time, and so I stopped wasting it in the bar and set up a poor replica of his makeshift recording studio in my parents' garage, among all of the boxes of my possessions. There I had a space where I could become a tortured artist, drinking more by myself and creating less than I should. However, I felt as though I was still wasting time, waiting on the phone to ring with an update from Gordon. I'd call him from time to time, but there would be no update.

I had been back in the U.K. for four long weeks before Gordon told me that he had managed to organise an arbitration session in London. I'd been back in England for longer than I had been out in Idaho; long enough for me to fall in love with Brooke. Long enough for her to have forgotten me? Not in person; we talked every day, enthusiastically of how much we felt for each other, though with a growing acceptance that we were running out of options in the short term. I worried that she would forget the feeling of us being together. I hadn't, or at least, I hoped I hadn't. I was concerned for myself that maybe I was romanticising it, as people tend to do. Keeping Brooke at arm's length from my true emotional state was the opposite of what I really wanted to do, and at odds with what Brooke was trying to do. I felt like I was able to convince her that this was merely a hiccup because she spoke with speed and rhythm and ease about our relationship, and what we would do when I went back out there. And when Gordon called with an actual update, I, for once, allowed myself to indulge in some of that optimism.

On the day of the arbitration meeting, Gordon and I arrived early. I was hoping that if I could see Ailie beforehand, I might be able to speak to her informally and appeal to her better nature.

However, Ailie wasn't present when our names were called. We entered the small meeting room. Gordon and I sat on one side of a table opposite another man who appeared to be a solicitor.

"Ms. McIntyre is running a couple of minutes late," he informed us.

The mediator said he would give Ailie five more minutes and then we would begin in her absence. After four minutes had passed, Ailie arrived. Dressed in a business suit, with her hair up and wearing glasses, I barely recognised her.

She only looked at me after greeting her solicitor and the mediator and even then, it felt like it was only that she had to.

What transpired was a bizarre conversation with these people who were effectively strangers—and I include Ailie in that statement—debating my right to assert ownership over my own work. I was being presented as someone who had made minimal contributions, pretty much a studio engineer who butted in occasionally. And it was said that they were being generous to credit me as *that* involved. I was incredulous but felt it better to keep my mouth closed rather than argue for the sake of doing it.

I did say, though, that Ailie herself had written an agreement that clearly illustrated the work I had done, justifying my argument and correlating with the credits given for the various songs. However, I didn't have a copy of the agreement, and Ailie's solicitor denied all knowledge of it.

When we provided screenshots that indicated that many of the songs were dated from prior to the release, and prior to my relationship with Ailie, I felt that would be enough to really trump everything, undermining their entire argument. But the mediator called for a break in the proceedings to investigate whether he could treat the screenshots with any legitimacy.

I'm sure she would have preferred to avoid it, but Ailie came out of the toilets at the same time as me. There was nowhere for either of us to go, leaving little alternative but to sit down next to each other in the empty waiting room.

"Why are you doing this?" I asked, after a brief silence.

"Doing what?" Ailie kept up the pretence.

"Okay... look, it doesn't matter. I just don't understand what you are getting out of it. Not really. You're hurting me, and for no reason. Do you want to know why I'm doing this? It's not for credit. It's so that I can move out to America. I'm happy to be co-songwriter. I don't want all of the credit, I just want acknowledgement for the work I've done, so that I can apply for a work visa."

Ailie turned and looked at me, and for the first time I saw a glimpse of sympathy in her eyes.

"Look... my publicist says it's a bad idea to give away any acknowledgement. I'm just starting to build a name for myself now and it will be detrimental to my career if I say you wrote some of those songs."

"But I did! Most of them are one hundred percent mine. You can't let James get the credit for the work I've done."

"You can start again."

"That would take me ages."

"Look, I shouldn't say this," Ailie said, as if she was doing me a favour. "But if you carry on with this and it goes to court, my... there are people who will work against you. Say that you're just trying to get a name for yourself from my success."

"That's ridiculous."

"I know that there's a story in place to say that you went out to the U.S. to work with Hal Granger and that you did it fraudulently. They're going to threaten you with that to make you drop everything, so that it doesn't reflect badly on you in the future. You know, it might hurt your chances of going back there."

"I've got the screenshots though. Digital proof that the songs are mine."

"The documents might have existed since then, but you could have easily updated the files."

"What? Of course I haven't."

"Well, it's hardly a conclusive argument."

I could barely believe what Ailie was saying.

"So, you're doing this just so you can be famous? Is that it?"

"I'm not doing anything, I'm just defending myself in a legal situation, as I've a right to do. Like I said, you can start again, if you drop all of this."

"I can't start again! It was hard enough the first time. I have to use my experience to open doors. You know that."

"You can go back out to America the same way you did last time."

"But that was on a visitor's visa."

"I'm sure you'll find a way."

"But that could take years."

"Well, I'm sorry, Freddie, but that's not my problem."

"Yeah, actually, it is. That's why we're here."

"No, it'll be your problem. The band all agree that I wrote those songs. And the label will back me up."

What a mess. I didn't know what to do.

I sat in silence until we reconvened, and said nothing as the mediator said that he felt that the screenshots presented sufficient evidence to suggest I had a strong claim. He suggested we come to a compromise, and I guess I should have been jumping for joy, but I knew of the threat which existed if I dared to push it further, and so I asked if I could speak with my solicitor in private.

I explained to Gordon what Ailie had told me. He reassured

me that I had a strong case and that I should expect threats. I explained I wasn't sure, because I didn't want anything to jeopardise my chances of obtaining a work visa. Part of me just wanted to simply give in and start all over again. I explained how I hoped that Tyler's work would be good enough, and how I could maybe build strong enough reputation on my own merit. Though the idea of that amount of work over again and the speculative nature of it didn't exactly appeal, it seemed the only way, short of something drastic, like taking Brooke's money. I was certain that, knowing of this scenario, she would probably insist.

Gordon calmly advised me to think about it, and not to make any snap decisions, and that in moving forward with a court date, there may well be an offer of compromise. I didn't hold out much hope for that, but I did at least feel that taking time was probably the right thing to do. After all, these were huge decisions that would influence my entire future.

I think that Ailie and her solicitor were a little surprised when we returned to the meeting room and insisted we would be happy with a court date to be set up. The mediator told us that we could expect to receive documentation in the mail.

A few days later, I received confirmation of a court date in the first week of December.

Brooke did repeat her offer of the money. She also insisted on coming out to see me, although I told her that the timing wasn't right. I was so preoccupied with everything going on that I couldn't really concentrate. I didn't want her to come all that way only for me to not have the time to dedicate solely to her, particularly with everything the way it was.

I was so used to the facade I was putting on for Brooke that I was able to continue to work through it in much the same way as I had before, but as soon as we had finished talking or closed our video chats, that external shield was removed and the increasing probability of how things would turn out would begin to gnaw away at me again.

And now, with the arbitration meeting weighing heavy on my mind, I saw it as a convenient excuse to wallow in self-pity again and head back to The Plough. Those familiar nods and greetings evolved into conversations with people I barely knew. As the topic of those conversations turned to what I did for a living, I spoke of my experiences as if they were lived by a different person, and it started to feel that way. I could never tell if the response was friendly, jealous, or sneering; generally, as more people would join the conversation, my new acquaintances would tell these newer ones about what I claimed had been my exploits. As I listened to their doubts, I began to doubt myself, and realise that if I couldn't even convince these people, how was I supposed to win a legal case? The actual truth barely mattered.

In my frustration, I was almost tempted to pull out my phone and show them the pictures of me with Eddy, with The Cause, with Hal; with Ailie, even. But they could probably think of a reason as to why I got those pictures. Everyone gets pictures with celebrities. And then I thought of the pictures as personal memories. It wasn't worth devaluing them in order to achieve approval that didn't really matter to me.

On evenings where they would hold karaoke, those who were aware of my work—or, to them, what I had claimed was my work—would cajole me and tell me to get up and perform, joking that I would get royalties if I performed one of "my" songs; that I never did, again, seeing it as demeaning myself, was deemed as further proof for them that my tales were fanciful.

On one such evening I had decided that even if propping up bars was to be my fate, I'd at least try and resign myself to a classier place to drink and started motivating myself to go into the town centre. In fact, I made that decision for a number of reasons. Another pretty major one being that any day, a story would hit the press that would reinforce the opinion of my fellow drinkers; that I was simply a nobody trying to achieve credit for someone else's work. I was anxious almost every day, expecting something in the news either locally or nationally, or some rumour online to begin to circulate. I warned Brooke, too, that things could get messy, and she insisted she didn't care. She would stand by me and wait. I admired that determination and it did help me through some tough times, though I didn't feel as if I ought to let on how hard I was really taking it.

Brooke was now talking about doing something productive, starting with using the new studio in Hal's basement to rent out to local musicians. Tyler was keen to use it, but was waiting for me to come back out. She also talked of making that road trip to Georgia, too. The more we talked, the more she seemed set on it; at times, she would hold back, downplaying it all, insisting she was happy to stay in Idaho with Louise and live her life there. But it was those unspoken words and hesitant moments which spoke far louder than anything she did say. It came to pass in conversations that she would start to avoid talk of Georgia; avoiding all thoughts of a positive conclusion. I tried to encourage it. It sounded promising, for Brooke and Louise, but I was still stuck. And I started to wonder just how much of a front Brooke was putting on too.

Waiting was all I could do. I thought of reaching out to Ailie. She had at least talked to me, so that might be a start. But I couldn't shake off the concern I had, the desperate concern, that something would come up in the newspapers, allegations that would make it difficult for me to return to the U.S. I didn't know enough about the legality of what she was saying to reassure myself or even get reassurance from my solicitor. I knew that Brooke and I couldn't survive such a story breaking, and the potential subsequent result of my being marooned here. I couldn't ask her to come to the U.K., particularly not with Louise and all of her responsibilities.

And still, as a full week passed after the arbitration meeting, I began to consider that maybe nothing would be said. No controversy. Once I had almost embraced the nothingness. Now, sometimes I found myself still influenced by or feeling that persistence of Ailie to work hard, seize opportunity, be aggressive about it. That had once helped, even in Idaho where such an outlook convinced me I should email Tyler, but it still didn't feel right. Ailie had a drive to be successful and her success seemed to be measured in size and progress, which I could understand. My perception of success depended strongly on personal contentment, something I was learning now. And now, conscious of it being a trait Ailie encouraged, I resisted it out of sheer stubbornness, using it as an excuse to do nothing. I couldn't reconcile the concept of creating some form of art for the credit which followed with creating it for the love of simply creating; and it was starting to cause some resentment within myself about the way I perceived everything I thought I had achieved. In these low moments, I desperately remembered those last days with Hal and those treasured, precious memories I now had of creating some great music with him. That was all thanks to Brooke's idea. And I felt happy, and sad and wistful, all at the same time. I could hear Hal's words. *Don't waste time.* But I felt as if I had no other choice.

Then, two days went by where Brooke and I missed speaking. She was working, and I was having a morning shower when I missed a late call from her. When I saw I'd missed the call, it had been twenty minutes since she rang, and I thought it would be too late then, at around 2:00 a.m. there, to call back. I was feeling very miserable about everything, so I went out in to the town centre— and my new haunt—for a drink.

Stood in the bar with crowds of people who knew each other, I was the wallflower. I sat at a table nursing a beer and considering wasted time, again. Hal's words had been clear, and I had taken them with what I felt was a strong purpose but now, with nothing in front of me, it seemed that I was even less than the sum of my body parts.

And, as I dwelled over this, I could sense someone approaching. It was the smell of her perfume that struck me first. Kaia.

"Freddie? Hey! I can't believe it. When did you get back?" she exclaimed, as she sat down across from me.

I didn't respond. I felt as if my lips were stuck. Kaia's unexpected prescence had caught me out and my brain hadn't caught up to tell my mouth it was time to speak.

"You okay?" she asked.

"Yeah... yeah, fine, thanks... sorry" I eventually managed.

"You never replied to my email."

She was right.

"... but I got used to you not replying."

"I'm sorry."

"That's okay."

She smiled, a kind smile.

"I really am sorry, Kaia. I should have replied."

"It's okay. I kinda... well, you said what you needed to say in Idaho."

It was only in her saying that, that I realised in some ways, I hadn't. I'd had a great time in America. Even with Hal's passing, I did not equate my time in Idaho with any true sense of sadness. I had grown immediately nostalgic and pined for those days. I felt like I had been the *real* version of me out there. And now, here, back "home" in the U.K., I didn't. In this instant, faced with Kaia's sympathy, I felt unworthy of it, and yet here she was, being nice to me, reaching out.

"That doesn't excuse what I did. Or, rather, didn't do. I am sorry, Kaia."

"Freddie, stop apologising."

"Can I be honest with you?" I asked, after a brief silence.

"Sure, please do."

"I'm going to say sorry again," I said, persisting even when she rolled her eyes, "because I am. I kinda... I wish I'd done things differently. You know, I used to spend a lot of time wondering whether you ever thought of me, and, if you did, *how* you might think of me. I know that's... us meeting again was by chance. But we should have stayed friends."

"Oh. You regret..."

"No. No, I don't. The only thing I regret doing is hurting you. I want to thank you, but I can't explain why. I don't even know if I know myself."

As Kaia looked at me, I couldn't interpret her expression. It wasn't familiar. Confusion, perhaps. I clearly hadn't ever worked out how to articulate these things in a way that others would.

"In some ways I wish I could rewrite everything in my life."

"Yeah, don't we all?" she replied.

I felt a little anxious. Unable to express what I meant properly, yet keen to do so.

"I did, you know. Think of you. Of course I did. You don't need to say sorry. Or thank you."

"Yes, I do... because I think it needed you to come back into my life to show how unhappy I was. What I was... what I thought was confusing me at the time was that I was blaming my actions on my grief. And I didn't know if what I felt was real."

"And?"

"I would have come back to you. But I still... I don't think I would have been... it's not to say I wouldn't have been happy. Or that I couldn't have been. But I wouldn't have been me. And that wouldn't have been fair on either of us."

I couldn't say that the conversation was easy, but we were able to speak fondly of our memories of Idaho, and with that, a small grain of comfort and, bizarrely, hope, was restored within my spirit.

I temporarily felt a strange satisfaction as I laid in bed that night. One of closure, that Kaia and I had managed to resolve things amicably. That I hadn't done what I tended to do in those situations in days gone by and sought physical comfort, creating a far greater mess than necessary.

But closure just reminded me of the emptiness in my life. I wondered if closure is just something we are conditioned to believe is a necessary part of emotional fulfilment, that we need that finality in order to move on. In order to be stable. These are the words we are told, and these are the thoughts we tell ourselves in order to cope. But that wasn't real. I knew at some point I would have to deal with everything with Brooke in this same manner; I knew that it would be much more difficult than simply concluding I ought to do it.

I remembered that even Brooke had said something which suggested the same thing, the very first time we'd met. Some relationships are meant to be and then people move on. Really, in absolute terms, had any relationship I'd ever been in really had that closure? What *was* closure? A thing that happened, or a state of mind? Kaia had emailed me after she had left Idaho and I had assumed that to be our final goodbye, and yet, as life would have it, I had since bumped into her again. Nothing is so final, aside from death, that means the past can't be revisited. And even in death, for that matter, aren't we always wishing for one more moment? One more conversation?

I remembered the countless one-night stands and my own acceptance that they would go nowhere even before they happened. When Kaia and I had first bumped into each other after all those years, she had said herself that sometimes things just end. Sometimes they are just left unresolved. She wasn't the only girl I'd dated in college; and even beyond that, I could remember friendships that might have developed into more. Something where it felt like all that needed was something to be said, someone to be honest. Connections that were never fully made, opportunities and relationships that would forever remain unexplored. There are things I hadn't said to Kaia, the things that I didn't need to say, things would've hurt unnecessarily. The shades of white in a lie that don't have a strong enough relationship with the truth to make it worthwhile to say out loud. A good intentioned mistruth where the only price was the occasional memory of it to remind me of the importance of never letting another relationship get to that point.

Two weeks went by, and still nothing occurred that would provide me with any certainty. Nothing except a phone message from Ailie's solicitor which temporarily made me anxious. All it was was a message to say I should go to the house to see if there was anything left that I needed to pick up as it had been sold. At least that was something.

Ailie had put all my belongings into storage and my parents had already transferred them to their garage. I'd been through them and it seemed as if everything was there. Nonetheless, I decided to go to the house anyway, to see if Ailie would be there, and to see if I might be able to talk reasonably with her.

She wasn't.

It felt a world away from the house we once shared. It was devoid of the personality that once had filled it, devoid of any character, and instead, in its place, hovered an ill feeling, tainting the warm memories of the past. How had it come to this?

I received a call at the start of the third week from Gordon, who asked me to meet him at his office.

"Well, I have some news for you."

"Good or bad?"

"Well, I guess it depends on what you call good. Ms. McIntyre's solicitors have indicated that they are willing to discuss an out of court settlement."

"What does that mean? They've agreed that I will be given the credit?"

"No, well, not exactly. What they're suggesting is a compensation package. And it's attractive, if I might say."

He pushed a letter across the table to me that had a bunch of jargon on it I couldn't understand but a figure that I clearly could; £80,000.

"What's that for?"

"It's a without prejudice offer, made on the proviso that we drop all claims on ownership to the songs."

"Yeah, but, that means that I've still lost."

"Well, I wouldn't say that figure is losing, Freddie."

"Yeah, but that's not the point. I don't want money, I've had that. I've been paid royalties. I can provide the receipts."

"Yes, I'm sure that will all be helpful if you decide to proceed. But, I think this is a good deal, all things considered."

"No, the point is to be in a position where I can apply for a work visa."

"Well, you know..." he said, almost reluctantly, "I don't think that, you know... it's not cut and dry. It's 50/50 if this goes to court."

"But we've got data trails to back up our claim."

"I'm sure they have, too. They're entertainment lawyers. They'll be fully used to cases like this. We waited, and instead of printing rumours about you, they've offered you a good cash amount. I would take that and start again, you know, like you were saying."

"I don't know. I'm just not sure if that's the best solution for me."

"Really?"

"Yeah. Well, it's not really a solution at all," I continued, with an annoyance which even surprised myself. "I'm not sure you're hearing me right."

"I am. I understand you perfectly. I know what you want. I just... I think you're unlikely to get a better result than this."

Exasperated, I sat back.

"So, what if I say no? Because I assume that agreeing will cut me out of all future royalty earnings?"

"Well... then, we go to court next week. But you know, those threats remain. And there's no guarantee, like I said. You said yourself that you've been feeling anxious. We can stop all that now."

"Can I have some time to think about it?"

"Yes. They've given us until the end of the week."

"Okay. Thanks."

I left Gordon's office dejected and defeated.

There was little else I felt I could do other than start again, with the risk of all that came with it, the probability that people would likely have already begun to hear within the industry that I hadn't actually done the work that I had.

Strangely, nothing about that bothered me at all. No struggle to retain my artistic rights. Nothing about the impact it might have on my career. It was all about the visa, that barrier which prevented me from being with Brooke.

I felt barely able to tell Brooke about the meeting. I couldn't bring myself to tell her I'd had one, that it had gone badly. Even in saying 'meeting,' she may get her hopes up fleetingly, and I couldn't do that to her. I felt as if I would be resigned to taking the £80,000, and just trusting in my own capability. I could flit between here and the States, exhausting the ninety days on the visa before returning. But the more I thought about it, the less of a viable option it seemed. The possibility that it could go on for years without resolution and progress. I could be asking for Brooke to wait around for just ninety days at a time and I couldn't do that to her.

I was coming to terms with ending the action against Ailie. That fire was dulling, with lessening enthusiasm for it, no need for justice in many regards, and the promise of conflict should the matter go to court did not appeal to me in the slightest. If my own solicitor didn't trust in me, how could I expect to be confident of winning the case?

Brooke did call, as she always did, and we talked at length about how we were. I avoided telling her about the meeting with Gordon, though I guessed she could hear a sadness in my voice. I deflected it, saying everything was getting on top of me. It was, of course. To counter my maudlin mood, Brooke spoke with excitement, openly, for once, about moving to Georgia.

"I'm just worried about Mom," she admitted.

"She only wants what's best for you. I think you've done your duty. You've been strong for her and given her the support she needs. She expects you to make the most out of life. I'm sure of that."

"Thanks to you."

"What's thanks to me?"

"Can you remember the first time we went out onto the lava fields?" she asked.

"Yeah, that was nice," I recalled.

"Well, you told me that I should be myself. To not let Hal being ill change me."

"Yeah."

There had been times where I had worried about a disconnect between us. Something not right, the first sign of a fracture caused by this distance. But I was so heartened to hear her saying this.

"And anyway, in your absence, I used the Magic 8-Ball to ask for advice about whether I should go to Georgia."

"What did it say?"

"It is unclear," she laughed.

As much as it was refreshing to hear the enthusiasm in Brooke's voice, and as temporarily as it replenished my spirit in the moment, the emotional tumble which followed our phone call was hard to handle.

I knew now that I loved Brooke. *Completely.* I had known it. I had felt it, and I had said it, and embraced it. But there are different stages of feeling in love; a realisation, then, that need to tell everyone, and each other, and then, later, that sudden rush, that reminder to yourself, that love isn't just a word that you tell people in order to justify a connection; it's a bond that describes *the* pure connection. Love wasn't just the word to describe the positive feelings, it also explained the aching emptiness in my stomach. A physical manifestation.

But I also knew that it would be tough, difficult, almost impossible, to consider a short-term solution. I could accept the settlement and begin to spend it, go out there, and exhaust the rest of my visitor visa—and then what? It would be twice as hard to let go the next time. And that was just for me.

That evening, I thought for a long time and considered that it had to be for the best to let Brooke down gently; to prepare her for a future where she could have certainty and look after herself. Look forward, not backwards, hoping. And now she had plans, *real* plans about moving forward, I didn't want her to use me as an excuse to hold herself back. I knew all about that. I couldn't erase my mistakes, but I could stop myself from repeating them. I couldn't allow my mere existence to bring an unhappiness to someone else, particularly when I could not foresee any plausible positive outcome to my ongoing legal dispute.

I tried to call Louise to talk it over and see if she could help, but I had no response. I thought about texting her, but thought it was a conversation best had by phone.

I spent a good deal of time trying to write down the right things to say, but it was pointless. I wasn't ready. I couldn't say goodbye. I was trying to do the right thing. Like they say, if you love someone, set them free. Only, I loved Brooke too much, so much that the concept of walking away was impossible.

I tried again, a little later. I picked up the pen but couldn't even write "Dear Brooke." There was a strong feeling within me, telling me that this was the wrong thing to do, that I was making a mistake.

Like the rest of my life, I decided to push it into limbo and out of my mind. Some of the words Louise had recently said rang like a bell in my head and I considered that even if I had gotten through to her, she would have said the same.

Don't wish for things to turn out a certain way.

Deal with the truth.

I had no other choice. The best thing I could do was to relax as much as possible. Try to calm myself, get in the best state of mind to try and make the right decision.

It was an exercise in futility.

It was all I could think about.

I spent most of the evening in the bedroom I'd grown up in as a young boy and teenager. I would turn on some music, only to have to turn it off again because of the thoughts in my mind. I went downstairs with my parents to watch television, but I couldn't concentrate.

I decided to call it an evening and wentto bed, anticipating many sleepless hours before I would finally be able to drift off.

I'm not sure how long I had been in bed, but I hadn't grown any more tired than I had been when I got in when my phone began to ring.

Ailie.

I ignored it. The phone beeped a few minutes later, telling me I had a voicemail. I thought about ignoring that, too, but couldn't. I checked the time. It was almost midnight.

"Hey," she'd said, somewhat downbeat, "just me, Ailie. Can you can give me a call when you get this? If you get it tonight, that is. If not, don't worry."

Oh, shit, I thought.

Tomorrow's the day. The day the accusations go in the newspaper, the day when any attempt to get back to see Brooke will be made that much more difficult.

It was tough to compose and regulate my breathing as I scrolled on to my last calls and pressed Ailie's name.

After a few rings, I was about to hang up, but she answered.

"Hey."

"Hey. Sorry. I missed your call. But got your message."

"Have you seen the news?"

"No."

Wow, that was fast, I thought. My stomach dropped. I felt numb. I prepared for the worst.

"Okay."

"So, you've done what you said they were going to do then."

"No. Actually, Freddie... me and James. We're over."

"Oh. Right." I felt a strange calm.

"He cheated on me."

"Okay... and I need to know this, why?"

"I've decided that I'm not going to claim that he wrote your songs, that he's Stuart."

A wave of panic and relief simultaneously washed over me.

"Wait! What?"

"... and just so you know, my solicitor has already received notice of my intention. I think they may still try and claim that I wrote the songs, that I'm Stuart... but, you know."

"No, not really."

"I'm saying that if you drop the case, then I'm happy to write a letter to say you're Stuart."

"Is this a joke?"

I felt a wave of nausea wash over me.

"No... I mean. That should help, right? What you want?"

"Yeah," I said, barely believing her.

"So I'll send you a text now too, saying that, just in case you don't believe me. You know, so you have proof. I just... I'd prefer not to go to court. But if there was any way there could be an agreement, that... I mean, if we can sort out something that would publicly give me credit but legally says you did the work..."

My head was throbbing with a million thoughts.

"Yeah, sure... and, for what it's worth, I'm sorry, about James."

"Okay. Well, thanks... and yeah, bye, I guess."

Ailie hung up. I got up and sat on the edge of the bed, trying to compute what she'd just said.

And then the phone beeped.

A text message, from Ailie.

"Like I said on the phone, I'm happy to say you're Stuart, that you wrote all the songs. Let me know if you need anything more. Tc. Ailie."

Without a moment's thought, I jumped out of bed, and made my way downstairs carefully and quietly.

I thought about the right thing to do, about going through the visa procedure now that I was able to, but that could wait. I had all I needed to apply, and hopefully, the procedure could be started in my absence. If not, then I'd just come back. The only thing I knew for sure was that I had been away from Brooke for far too long. The split second where I had feared the absolute worst had made me decide: *I need to leave. I need to go now. I need to take control.*

I opened the laptop and checked for the next available flight to Boise, Idaho. 6:40 a.m. It was too early to get a train to Manchester Airport, so I called a cab.

I left a note for my parents apologising for leaving without saying goodbye, but that I would be in touch, and explaining that everything had worked out with the courts. I spent my time in the cab writing an email to Gordon, explaining what had happened, sending a screenshot of Ailie's message and asking him to initiate visa proceedings as I'd explained originally.

My adrenalin was still pumping as I sat in the departure lounge. I hadn't called Brooke through the night as I knew she would think I was sleeping. It would be a surprise.

As I was sitting, watching the planes take off—ready for boarding any second—my phone went.

It was Louise.

"Hey," she said.

"Hey."

"I missed your call. I hope it's not too early over there."

"No. Actually, believe it or not, I'm at the airport."

"Oh my God! Really? Are you coming out here or are you just passing through?"

"Well... actually," I replied, "I think I might stick around."